The Moon King's Bounty

LAURIE SANFORD

RIVER LEAF PRESS

The Moon King's Bounty

Published by River Leaf Press

The Moon King's Bounty is a work of fiction. All incidents, dialogue, and characters are products of the author's imagination and are not to be construed as real. Any resemblance to actual persons, living or dead, events, or locales is entirely coincidental.

For more information, visit:

www.lauriesanfordbooks.com

www.facebook.com/lauriesanfordbooks

To my Julianne. Each day with you is like living in sunshine. Your spunky, beautiful spirit has captured my heart, and I am ever amazed by you. I love you more than you can imagine, sweet girl.

One

"Get to cleaning the floor, girl. It should have been mopped an hour past." Georgette thrust a bucket into Madeleine's hands, whirling back to resume kneading the dough she'd plopped onto the sturdy kitchen table. "And don't dawdle," she said, leaning her broad form into her creation. "We're half a week behind in chores, and I will not see this home fall apart due to you slothful girls."

Watching the tireless housekeeper from inside a ray of morning light, Madeleine felt her mouth pinch upward. "Yes, ma'am," she said, strangely glad to be home again. The normalcy of work, and the security it rained over her, surpassed her days since waking on Traitor Isle in a manner she hadn't expected. The endless hours of chores, once a burden, brought peace whenever she remembered the perilous world the Guardians had catapulted her into.

"You don't have to mind her, you know," hissed a voice from beside the hearth. Madeleine pivoted to Cecile's lithe form, bent over the fire and stoking the flames. "She should be ironing your stockings by now."

Madeleine wagged her head. "Alas, I am still merely a servant girl," she said, lifting her empty bucket.

"A servant girl the baron can't take his eyes off." Cecile tossed her long braid over one shoulder, her rust-colored hair gleaming bronze in the firelight. "It's only a matter of days before he works up the nerve to propose to you, and then she'll wish she treated you better. Throw her out on her backside, that's what I say."

"Madeleine!" the elderly maid in question snapped. "What did I say about dilly-dallying?"

"*Je suis désolé,* Georgette," Madeleine called, glaring playfully at Cecile. "And in the meantime," she whispered, "you're going to get me in trouble. Now off I go before she starts chasing me with her rolling pin." Madeleine giggled as her friend stuck out her tongue at the old woman who now hammered her aggression into the bread dough.

Winter air penetrated Madeleine's skin as she clicked the front door closed and wandered across the frosty drawbridge. Drawing her woolen shawl higher on her shoulders, she made a careful path to the barren chestnut trees that encircled the well. The frigid season would soon give way to spring, thawing the frozen ground and sprouting a colorful array of flora. For now, the hills dusted in a light snow swept to a gray, cloudless sky. The geese and swans she loved to watch dive and swim around the moat slumbered in the bushes with wings outstretched to shield themselves. The icy winds carried not the scent of wild earth, but a gentle tinge of pine.

Older than the house itself, the Clements' stone well sat lonely before a scattering of thickets. Madeleine retrieved the rope and secured it to the handle of her bucket, softly lowering the vessel into the well's watery depths. Her mind roamed to the days that had brought her here, the handful of moments she could yet remember.

On that fateful night that nearly rent them apart, Baron Clement had hoisted her injured body into his arms and carried her up the grand stairs. Throwing tradition to the wind, he'd eased her into his own bed and ordered the household staff to care for her until her wounds had mended. He'd sat with her, day and night, sleeping in a chair he'd dragged to her bedside, clutching her hand in flashes of pain. He promised the world to her. They'd endured so much together, he would say. The future could only hold blessings.

Joy swelled over Madeleine's face as she heaved her bucket upward, hand over hand on the taut rope. After a lifetime of sorrows, could true happiness really lay at her feet? She could feel it, taste it. Decades of seamless pleasure danced before her imagination, luring her with strands of angelic melodies. She would live out her life with the man she loved. A good man. A man who would never again let her fall back into the dark abyss from which she'd climbed. Madeleine tried in vain to slow her rushing heart at the thought. It all seemed too good for reality.

She turned from the well with her hefty bucket in hand, eager to climb the icy slope back to the house and find him. Two months had meandered past since her upended life had settled, and still the fingers of her left hand lay barren. Sighing, she tried not to think of the wondrous diamond and topaz ring Gabriel had once offered her. As Cecile had stated, he could ask any day.

"Madeleine!" A sudden whisper blasted from the bushes, pulling her from her musings. "Psst, Madeleine!" The dense veil of trees beyond the well parted to reveal a dirty, bearded face with two eyes poking out like polished stones.

Eyebrows cinching, Madeleine plunked her bucket down and shook off the cold water that had splashed her forearm when the man had jolted her. Cautiously, she approached the moving branches, details of his visage emerging before her. Disheveled salt-and-pepper hair stuck out in all directions from beneath a crooked felt hat. Under his bristled chin, he'd knotted a filthy cravat that did nothing to adorn his rumpled clothes. The stench of sweat and cheap tobacco emanated off him before she'd even come within a meter of him.

Familiar dread pierced Madeleine's chest. She'd hoped her maturing memory would prevent her from having to rely on deceptions again, but this sordid-looking character had no place in her recollections. "What is it?" she asked, the calm of her voice betraying the instinct within to run.

"I have a message for ya," he said, shoving a rolled-up piece of parchment at her. "Here. Been trying to get it ya since Christmas, I have. You ain't been at your regular routine."

Madeleine willed her fingers to stiffen as she received his offering. How could this man know her regular schedule? Had he been watching her? Holding the bundled message to her chest, she swallowed back her trepidation. "Who is it from?"

The man released a guttural laugh that could almost have been a belch. "Aw, come on, Madeleine." His tongue clicked. "He just wants to know why you haven't been by in so long. You're making the man nervous, is all."

The man? *What man?* Her thoughts sprinted on without her, grasping for somewhere to land. Madeleine looked up in time to see the bush's branches folding in again. "Wait!" she said, halting the messenger. "Been by where? Where does he want me to go?"

Cocking his ragged head, he spit into the dirt as he eyed her warily. "Have you gone daft, Madeleine?" His narrowed eyes descended and climbed her form, the lips over his browning teeth contorting. "The Black Lion, of course. Where else?" Glancing at the château, he lifted one shaggy brow. "Just come before he bursts a vessel worryin' about ya, would ya? I can't stay." With that, her mysterious courier ducked back into the foliage like a scurrying rabbit, leaving Madeleine befuddled.

Curious, she pulled at the red yarn tied around the letter. She'd have to take it to Cecile, of course. She could trust Cecile. Who on earth would write her? Madeleine's heart fluttered. She knew she couldn't read, and yet the words paraded before her, beautifully scrolled and perfectly comprehensible. *How?*

Letting her legs go limp, she dropped to the well and straightened out the curled edges. *Cara Madeleine.* Yes, she could understand every word. Her native language looked like a bunch of scribbles to her, but this was different. "Italian," she barely heard her own voice hum, her eyes filling. How had this come to be?

Dear Madeleine,

I have been unsuccessful thus far in obtaining any more informa-tion that will be useful to us. Everyone who has met the nameless man refuses to talk. They claim to know nothing, but the letter is out there. I know it is.

I write today in hopes that you've had better luck with Clement. Has he shown you the key yet, Madeleine? Given any clues as to where the map might be located? Rumor would tell that treasure hunters are already scouring the Atlantic, but they're all a bunch of fools here. Nobody really knows. Gabriel Clement is our only real hope.

Weeks have passed since your last correspondence, and I admit to fearing for you often. I should never have sent you into the lion's den, but I have such faith in you, Madeleine. I know you can accomplish what I never could alone. When the money is ours, we may do whatever we'd like. And you'll finally be free to do what you've always wanted—kill Gabriel Clement.

Don't lose sight of that day. It will come, I promise. Please come and see me, for your brother cares for you more than you'll ever know.

Auguste

The parchment slipped through her quivering fingers, fluttering to the snowy earth. Madeleine sheltered her tear-drenched lips in one hand, disbelief plaguing her. The words pealed through her brain over and again. *Your brother cares for you. When the money is ours. Kill Gabriel Clement.* None of it made any sense, and yet she'd ingested it all through a language she hadn't known she could decipher.

Madeleine's gaze rose to the Château des Rêves—a blurry, crys-tallized vision through her fiery tears. High up in the stony walls, she could barely see his bedroom, the even set of windows from which he stared out to the world every morning.

The breath caught in her throat. Her brother was alive, and she was nothing but a conniving, money-hungry opportunist, trying to get her claws on the Clement fortune. And somewhere, deep in a heart that she'd thought free from encumbrance, she'd harbored hate for a man she would die for now.

Kill Gabriel Clement. The words impaled her. So much more of herself lay beneath what she knew, and she'd have to dig through the rot to find it.

Two

Madeleine trudged through the melting snow with shoulders wilted and back aching. Her water bucket felt as if it weighed twice as much, stinging the weary muscles of her forearm. Rather than the haven she'd come to love, the Château des Rêves looked like a prison against the bleak sky, its inhospitable walls glowering down at her as they challenged the whistling winds. She didn't belong here—not even as a servant, much less a mistress.

The heavy front door swung shut behind her with a crash as Madeleine crossed the vestibule and set her bucket on the checkered floors beneath the château's imposing staircase. Georgette was right; several trails of muddy footprints wound this way and that over the black and white marble. Had she always neglected her work in such a flagrant fashion, or had she put on a ruse long enough to lure her unsuspecting prey into her cage?

Biting back her painful self-censures, Madeleine retrieved the mop she'd left leaned against the wall and dunked it into the well water. The sopping head sloshed back and forth with her working arms over the stained floor, wiping it clean of its blemishes. If only she could cleanse her soul so easily.

Careful not to step on the damp floor, she kept on until every inch of it gleamed. She stood back, wishing she could admire her efforts, knowing they'd never suffice. Gabriel had welcomed her into his home and his heart. She wouldn't stop serving him until her every last sin was paid, however many she uncovered.

Just then, two arms encircled her from behind. Madeleine let out a shriek, her mop handle clattering to the floor. "I didn't scare you, did I?" Baron Clement's amused voice touched her ear, prompting her to spin and push him away.

"You most certainly did, you rogue." She tried without success to squelch the smile creeping across her lips. "How am I supposed to get any work done with you roaming around the halls, waiting to pounce from the corner at any moment?"

"Save the work for the others." He reached for her again. Madeleine didn't resist when he pulled her to him, hands planted at her waist. "I just hired another girl, you know."

She glanced away, unable to meet the crystal-blue eyes looking through her. "Yes, I know." Brigitte had arrived for duty that very morning. What it meant, Madeleine couldn't ask. Did he really intend to replace her, to elevate her so high above her station? Her heart thumped at the idea, even as she tried with all her strength to quiet it.

A soft thumb brushed her cheek, his fingers propelling her chin up until their eyes met. "Surely you know you don't have to work now. No matter what Georgette tells you," he added with a grin.

"Surely I know nothing of the sort." Madeleine exhaled at the perplexed look on his face. "The fact is, I am still only a maid here. I kept up my duties while loving you for quite some time before all this happened, and I'd like to be of good use here. What else am I going to do with my days? Sit around and try not to annoy all the others who are actually pulling their weight?"

Gabriel tipped his head, his smirk turning mischievous. "I could think of a few things to occupy your time." Shifting closer, he planted a balmy kiss on her neck, behind her ear, working his way to her face. Madeleine giggled at the tickle of his curly hair on her skin. His musky scent thrilled her. As his lips overtook hers, she allowed herself to thaw against him. In a time she couldn't remember, she'd somehow wished death upon this marvelous creature, but now she *loved* him more than she'd thought possible.

From down the hall, she glimpsed Cecile scurrying Brigitte away, the women sharing a giggle at their expense. Before he could assail her again, Madeleine flattened a hand on his solid chest. "Not now, my love. The household is watching, and there is so much we have to discuss."

His eyebrows tweaked. "What is there to discuss?"

Madeleine inhaled, shaking off the rapture he'd catapulted her into. "The Planters' Ball, of course." She pivoted herself toward the gallery. Better to lead him toward the others, away from the quiet places he could ensnare her. At least until she had time to think about what she'd do with her newfound knowledge.

Digging his hands into his pockets, Gabriel jogged to keep up with her. "The Planters' Ball? Really?" His nose crinkled at the suggestion. "It's all a lot of tedious drivel. Désirée does the planning for me. She loves that sort of thing."

Madeleine shot him a sideways grin as she stepped beneath the sparkling chandeliers of the gallery. "Yes, well I thought it might be something enjoyable we could do together," she said as she passed the oil portraits of Gabriel's maternal lineage facing the windows. "Your farmers are the backbone of your estate, are they not? You want them to feel appreciated."

"Well, of course I'm cordial." Gabriel looked past his cravat and tweed waistcoat to the boots now traversing the rugs of his grand salon. "It's just that Désirée is so much better at that kind of thing. I'm sure to muck it up, you see." His mouth curled thoughtfully. "I hope it doesn't disappoint you to discover that I'm not the most social of God's creatures."

Footsteps slowing, Madeleine allowed her gaze to wander over the open study they'd reached. "Oh, really?" She took in row after row of leather-bound books, his scribbled notes scattered around his desk, and ink-stained quills discarded on the floor. "I hadn't noticed, *Baron Clement*." Indeed, the man would never venture outside his tiny cocoon of solitude if given the chance.

Stepping closer, Madeleine let her hand fall to Gabriel's wrist. "It isn't all bad, you know," she said softly. "The outside world might surprise you if you let it."

Gabriel turned his hand over and let his fingers cup her forearm, studying his gentle movements a moment before meeting her gaze. "Forgive me for having my qualms after my last venture out." He swallowed. "I see I have much growth to accomplish before I am the man who deserves you."

A pensive moment drifted over them, fear and yearning contending on the robust plains of his face. Until recently, Madeleine had assumed her employer a recluse by choice. The more he permitted her inside the secretive chambers of his life, the better she understood the distress that society riddled him with. Withdrawing from it meant his survival.

"Another day, my love." Pulling away, Madeleine turned and skipped into his study. Her thick woolen skirts bounced as she pranced before the fire crackling within his black marble hearth. "We don't have to solve the whole of our problems today. I'll settle for one."

Gabriel trailed her in, eyes pinned to the stack of letters Georgette had deposited on his desk. "The Planters' Ball?" He reached for the uppermost dispatch. "I hate to be a nuisance, but that matter is going to take quite a bit more time than an afternoon."

"Actually, I had something else in mind." Cautiously unwinding her words, Madeleine tiptoed across the floor and glided into a blue brocade slipper chair stationed before a round mahogany table. She licked her lips, her next sentence sounding silly, even to her. "Tell me a little more about this treasure, would you?"

Still busy examining the outer scribblings and seal of the letter in his hand, Gabriel shook his head once. "Oh, you're very funny," he muttered, distracted.

Madeleine let her arm fall to the table beside her, fingers nervously drumming its glossy surface. "No really, Gabriel. I want to know." She *had* to know after this morning's events. The folded note in her pocket was practically burning a hole through her dress.

The words finally drove him to look at her, one eyebrow raised in skepticism. "You're mad, you know that? Now that all the trouble we had with the Guardians is over, you want to talk about the very thing that nearly got the both of us killed?" One corner of his mouth dimpled. "It's a good thing I can't resist you, Madeleine Bertrand."

A shy smile inched onto her lips, the baron spreading a heat over her face that Madeleine hoped the blazing hearth beside her would explain away. "Is there—" She paused, knowing his answer before she dared to voice the question. "Well, is there even the smallest of chances that the treasure could be real?"

His dark eyebrows climbed higher, his arms stretching out on either side of him. "Am I not rich enough for you already? Is all this not enough?"

"Oh, stop it." Madeleine waved him off with a lighthearted swat. "You know that's not why I ask." Her mind hunted for the correct words to approach the worry looming over her. "After witnessing the lengths these men would travel, I just wonder if it could all really be a lie. How could such intricate details live on so many years without a bit of proof?"

Tossing the letter aside, Gabriel bent at the waist to meet her wandering eyes. "I'll tell you why." He straightened again before the windows, bright with midday sun. "Henri Clement was a vicious, scheming man. He probably *did* steal from King Louis, maybe as much as they say. But he likely spent it just as quickly. Nothing distracts the masses better than their own greed."

"So you think the treasure was just a cover for your ancestor's reckless spending habits." If true, old Henri had fooled even her at some point.

"Oh, I know it." Taking two sizable steps toward her, Gabriel wagged a knowing finger. "I've read the man's journals. His footprint is all over this house. *He* built the barony into the size it is today. He squandered his days with every costly indulgence you can imagine, a million ridiculous hobbies that got him nowhere."

Madeleine's arms knotted over her chest. "Such as?"

"Have you ever heard of something called the philosophers' stone?" At the shake of her head, Gabriel stood tall like a professor about to enlighten a group of new pupils. "The great Henri Clement was among a group of men referred to as alchemists. He spent decades attempting to convert base metals into gold. He thought if he could find this elusive substance, the 'elixir of life' as they called it, he could achieve immortality."

The chair beneath her moaned as Madeleine leaned tenaciously inward. "So one could assume the man needed to hoard as much treasure as he could to pay for this never-ending life he thought he might have."

"That—" Gabriel scratched his shaven chin. "Well, that's actually a valid point, but it isn't true, mark my words. Not a shred of evidence exists to validate this dreadful rumor."

"What about the key?" She extracted the intricate brass piece from beneath the collar of her work dress. Madeleine had come to view it as a symbol of their bond. She would feel naked without it dangling from her neck now.

Gabriel tossed his head back with a snort of derision, his curly locks dancing. "The key that has yet to find a door it agrees with. The blasted thing unlocks a garden shed, for all we know."

Pouting, Madeleine tucked it back beneath the gray wool at her collarbone. "Well, what about the letter? Désirée said there wasn't one, but I heard Georgette prattling on about an aunt you had, a—" She cocked her head, the name escaping her.

"Josephine Clement, *oui*," the baron finished for her. "She was my father's aunt, actually. She *did* have a letter written by Henri Clement, and she guarded the thing with her very existence."

Strangely, Madeleine's heart picked up speed. "Well, what did it say?" she asked, trying to keep her voice even.

Revolving on his heel, Gabriel sauntered to his desk. "Nothing, according to my father." He faced her again, sitting at the edge of the wood with legs unbent and ankles crossed. "It's probably still around here somewhere, a dying man's last wishes for his family. Nothing about a treasure. No coordinates. No map."

Madeleine's shoulders fell. "I suppose the map doesn't exist either."

Above her, Gabriel clicked his tongue. "Look, my darling. I know it's all very exciting to imagine the possibilities. That's exactly how this great deceiver has kept so many thrill-happy disciples panting at his heels these many years." His head wagged in pity. "I was one of them, once upon a time."

At her expression of shock, Gabriel grinned. "My great-aunt was an immense believer, you see. When she came to visit, she brought with her tales of fortune and danger, of men scouring jungles in search of our ancestor's long-lost treasure. It was all this little boy could do not to run away and hop aboard the next ship sailing to the edge of the world."

His bright eyes gleamed at the memory. "Aunt Josephine told me, with wrinkled eyes squinted and gnarled fingers pointed, about every pearl and jewel of this bounty that had propelled her lifelong obsession." He chuckled, raking a hand through his abundant hair. "She told me once that the map's secrets lay in the library, so I combed the entire thing from top to bottom. I cleared every shelf, I shook out every book. My mother had a fit when she saw the mess I made."

Madeleine imagined the child, just as compulsive as he was now, rummaging through the thousands of books within the library's walls. "Where did Josephine hear such a thing?"

Pulled from his musings, Baron Clement shook his head. "Whisperings of relatives her entire life, I'd wager. Belief is a powerful thing." He hopped off his desk and stalked around the other side, retrieving the folded parchment he'd flung there earlier.

The rustic scent of burning birch wood delighted her nose as Madeleine watched him tear open the message and scan its contents. She thought she heard horse's hooves in the drive. Glancing at the gilded clock by the fire, she noticed the late hour and rose with a languid stretch. What an indolent servant she'd turned out to be.

"I'd best get to finishing that floor," she said, starting toward the door. No matter what Gabriel said, she wouldn't leave the extra work for Cecile. As Madeleine passed by him, she noted the creases scrunching his forehead. "What is it?"

"Hmmm?" Gabriel kept perusing the letter, his eyes whizzing along the jotted ink. He glanced up at her as if momentarily unaware of her presence. "Oh, it's a dispatch from my uncle Pascal, my father's brother."

Funny, neither Clement sibling had ever mentioned having extended family. "Does he send grave news?" Whatever tidings lay on the page still pulled the master's brows in a peculiar fashion.

"No, actually. He writes that he plans to visit"—Gabriel set the unfurled letter atop his chaotic desk—"perhaps for an extended period."

"Well, you don't appear pleased with the idea. Is this Pascal an unpleasant sort of fellow?" Her cherry mouth flattened into a simper. "Should we introduce him to Georgette?"

Gabriel attempted a feeble grin but failed. "It's been almost a decade since I saw him last, but I don't remember the cheeriest of men." One hand rose to rub the back of his neck, his head shaking. "What's odd is that he—well, he writes that he's found me a wife."

Madeleine blinked. "He's found you a *what*?" Perhaps her ears played a nasty joke on her.

Shoulders rising, Gabriel released a baffled chuckle. "It's absurd, I know it. He says that he's concerned about the future of the family line and that he's determined the perfect mate for me. He's making arrangements to bring her here to meet me."

A cold, nauseating sensation burst in Madeleine's core. Setting a hand on the smooth marble hearth, she steadied herself against the wave of vertigo threatening to overpower her. Too much news had assaulted her today. Too many questions whirled around in her weary mind.

Through her anxious fog, she hardly perceived Gabriel stepping toward her, his hand outstretched. Gentle fingers squeezed her shoulder blade. "Not to worry, my love. No potential suitresses will be breaching the château. I'll simply write to my uncle and tell him the answer is no."

Madeleine smiled softly against the fingers grazing her cheek. "I hadn't imagined myself so easily driven to jealousy over your affections." In truth, Pascal Clement's declaration had scared her. She had realized, for the briefest of moments, that maybe someone better *did* deserve Gabriel's untainted heart. Surely he was worth more than a lowly woman who had plotted to harm and deceive him.

"My affections are here with you." Gabriel's thumb brushed the length of her cheekbone, his fingertips tucking the sable tendrils of hair behind her ear. "My uncle will just have to arrange to marry her himself, if she's as wonderful as he says." His face beamed bright with pride.

Just then, a knock at the door splintered the loving moment between them. Gabriel groaned, dropping his hand and reeling toward the closed double doors. "Yes?" he asked through the white-washed wood. "What is it, Georgette?"

The pudgy maid appeared a moment later, the skin beneath her frilly cap and white hair flushed. "I'm sorry to disturb you monsieur, but I—" She stumbled on her words as she noticed Madeleine standing before the fire. Clearing her throat, she smoothed her homespun skirt and recomposed herself. "Your uncle is here to see you. Would you like to visit in the parlor? I told him to wait there—"

"Yes, and I'm exasperated with waiting already." A tall, elegantly dressed man pushed past the unsuspecting maid, practically knocking her down in the process. Georgette attempted to conceal her frustration, but Madeleine couldn't miss the glint in her narrowed eyes. Pascal Clement sauntered into the study as if he owned it, arms extended in greeting. "Gabriel, my boy. It's been far too long."

Stunned, the baron accepted his estranged relative's embrace. "Uncle, I hadn't expected you so soon. I've only just received your letter this morning."

"Yes, well the couriers are sluggish these days, aren't they? I'd have had better luck with a carrier pigeon, I'd wager." The man chortled at his own joke, revealing a set of porcelain false teeth. Everything about him, from the glittering rings on his plump fingers to the fitted suede jacket and matching breaches, bespoke a man of breeding. Madeleine even spotted little tassels on his pointed shoes.

"No need to waste time with pleasantries," he said, voice booming in the small space. "We have business to attend to." His hand flipped toward Georgette, his wrinkled eyes not bothering to find her. "Tea," he ordered. "And bring plenty of cream."

Marching his way back to the entrance, the intruder volleyed Madeleine a long, dubious stare. As if jerked by a rope tied at her waist, she scampered out the door faster than the mice scurried from their barn cats. She simply shook her head when Gabriel opened his mouth to protest, the door slamming in her face at Pascal's mighty shove. Whatever a man like that had to say in a secret space, she would rather escape.

Three

Madeleine stared into the crackling flames of the parlor's alabaster fireplace, watching the fire eat away at the letter in her hand. The orange tongues thrashed and spat, curling the paper's black edges until Auguste's hastily scrawled dispatch dissolved to ash. Perhaps if she destroyed the evidence, the past lurching up to haunt her would simply cease to exist.

She glanced at the longcase clock on the wall. Nine-thirty. She had another half hour before Gabriel wanted to meet her. Throwing the last of her brother's letter into the smoldering embers, Madeleine leaned into the cushioned chair and shut her eyes. The woody scent of burning pine bathed her in its embrace as she considered what his secrecy could mean. How alluring Pascal's plan might seem—to choose a woman of breeding, to espouse convention.

Distracting herself, Madeleine let her mind travel back to the home of her youth, to the little cottage in the countryside before the greed of evil men had ripped it away. She saw herself on a tiny bed in the corner of a darkened room, lit only with the frolicking flame of a single candle. Her mother's face shone above it, soft and beautiful. Beyond her, Auguste and Jean-Paul already snuffled in pleasant slumber, the two boys cuddled together on their own hand-carved bed.

"Maman, tell me a story," her immature voice begged the woman turning to leave.

Jacqueline wagged her head, her tawny curls shimmering. "It's late, *ma chérie*." Her candle cast its glow over her two children near the opposing wall. "Your brothers are already fast asleep."

Madeleine sat up, her little hands scrunching the quilt her mother had pulled up to her chin. "Please, Maman? You always say 'tomorrow'. Papa tells me stories, but you always have to work instead."

Her mother considered the words, her tongue clicking. "Now we can't have this." She set her candlestand on the table between the beds. "You must know that you are more important than work, always." Lifting Madeleine's quilt and sheet, Maman crawled into bed beside her child and snuggled close. "Now, what is it you want to hear about?"

Excitement burst in Madeleine's chest. She wanted to know *everything* Maman would disclose. "Tell me the story of how you met Papa," she said, leaning into her mother's warmth.

With a sideways look, Maman's lips pursed into a frown. "Now, that is a complicated story." She hesitated. "Hasn't Papa told it to you?"

Madeleine shook her head. "Uh-uh."

"Not even a little bit?"

"Not even a smidge."

Sighing, Maman curled her arm around Madeleine's tiny frame. "Well, I suppose you're old enough now, aren't you, my sweet girl?" She stared into space for a quiet moment, thinking. Madeleine rested her cheek against her mother's arm, delighting in the sweet lavender scent of her skin. She would relish every moment of Maman's memories.

"Your Papa and I met at Les Fêtes de Jeanne d'Arc in the town of Orléans," Jacqueline began. "Every year, people would come from all over to remember Joan of Arc and how she liberated the city during the Hundred Years' War. There were all types of colorful parades and games. Vendors would sell food and drink and beautiful things to wear." The corners of her mouth lifted pleasantly. "That festival was the highlight of my youth."

The image of ancient, cobbled streets filled with merriment enchanted Madeleine. "Did Papa work in a booth at the festival?"

Maman took a moment to study Madeleine before she shook her head. "No, Papa was there to perform religious rites." She bit her lip. "Your Papa was a priest in those days."

Madeleine's eyebrows pinched. "But priests don't have families." Even at five years of age, she knew that much.

Her expression grave, Maman looked her square in the eye. "Oui, Papa had to renounce his vows when he met me."

Inwardly grappling with the startling information, Madeleine's gaze wandered over her mother's face. Between the tendrils of wispy blonde hair framing her face, gray eyes gleamed beneath abundant lashes. A straight, perfect nose curved above voluptuous lips and a feminine chin. "You are very beautiful, Maman." Surely that's why even a priest of God couldn't resist her.

A laugh escaped Jacqueline's lips, a melodious sound. "I dare say I was prettier then, when I was young enough to be carefree and work didn't tire me so." She held Madeleine tighter as she journeyed back to the visions of her youth. "It wasn't so much about that, though. Your father was handsome too, but I noticed that so little when compared to his character."

"We met on the street," she said, "watching dancers juggle flaming batons. I didn't even know he was a priest." Her eyes sparked. "He asked me what I thought their secret was, and I said surely the Devil had a hand in it. Then he told me the Devil didn't come to Orléans in the fall. " She smiled poignantly. "I don't think we stopped talking for all four days after that. We understood each other in a magical way. I can't explain it."

The little girl cocked her head, a bizarre picture of her father in priestly robes emerging in her mind. "Was your family angry that you wanted to marry a priest?" Surely they considered it a sin.

Jacqueline's lovely brows rose. "They were surprised, but they didn't try to hinder us. I think they saw how happy we made each other." She paused, gaze plummeting to the patchwork quilt sheltering them both. "Our community was much harder on us."

"They wanted Papa to stay a priest?"

Maman peered back at the sleeping boys, then let her eyes roam the walls flickering in shadowed candlelight. The pulse under Madeleine's cheek quickened. "He was young, but he was a very important man already. He was an advisor to Louis XVI. Many noblemen had entrusted their secrets to your father, and they were afraid of what he might reveal when he left the priesthood."

The urge to defend her beloved father erupted inside the child. "But Papa would never do that." Not the man who so gently guided his family through life's every turn.

A soft hand smoothed over Madeleine's heated face. "Of course not. He's an honorable man." Maman exhaled through her nose. "But many of these people were not. We had to move from Paris and promise never to speak their names again."

Madeleine relaxed back into her mother's arms. "I'm glad you did," she murmured. "We're safe from them now." Whoever they were. A cowardly, faceless army that couldn't possibly bother her family ever again.

Maman blinked, her expression thoughtful. "Yes, my love," she barely managed. "We are safe."

Despite her mother's reassurance, Madeleine thought she felt her tremble. A sudden wind beat against the house, rattling the shutters and scattering dry leaves outside her window.

Swinging her eyes back to her mother, peace descended over her just to look into that angelic face. "So Papa gave up everything," Madeleine said. "He became poor so that he could marry you."

Before Maman could answer, a masculine voice hailed from the open doorway. "No, ma chérie. I *gained* everything the day I met your mother."

Madeleine's gaze darted to the source, finding her father's imposing figure propped against the door frame with muscular arms knotted at his chest and a crooked smile on his lips. "Papa!" she exclaimed, inciting Jean-Paul to wriggle and flip over on his mattress.

The big man sauntered over to the bed and leaned down to capture his only daughter in a snug embrace. His dark hair, tied at his neck, smelled of iron and soot, no doubt the product of his blacksmithing. His strong hug nearly lifted her from the bed, an adoring kiss landing on her forehead. When at last he pulled back, Pierre Bertrand sat on the bed beside them, his proud stare enfolding them.

"It may seem very grand indeed to be friends with a king and the people in his court," he told the amazed little girl. "But my heart was never truly full until I married your mother, then had you"—his large hand covered hers—"and Auguste, and Jean-Paul." His brown eyes swept over the sleeping boys before settling back on Madeleine. "*You* are my riches," he said, filling the child's heart with a sense of belonging. As long as she had Papa, she could accomplish anything.

Pierre grinned, his free hand seizing Jacqueline's. "And your mother is even *more* lovely today than she was that day I first saw her, watching the fire dancers in the street."

The toll of the clock announcing the nine o'clock hour in a succession of clangs propelled Madeleine's eyes open. The parlor of the Château des Rêves surrounded her again, a cold shell of a place after basking in her childhood memories. The barony could claim riches unmatched, and yet it would never pacify her the way that pauper's cottage had.

Sighing, Madeleine pushed herself off the crimson slipper chair by the fire and started for the door. She glanced down the hallway before scurrying through the gallery, lit in patches by the moon's silvery rays. She was lucky Georgette hadn't caught her 'loafing about', as she called it. Surely, the churlish maid would demand an explanation if she saw her sneaking out.

Madeleine snatched her woolen shawl from the coat closet under the stairs and dashed across the entryway, her shoes lightly scuffing the stone. The heavy front door groaned behind her as she eased it closed. Outside, the wind whipped through the barren trees, tossing their branches in wild frenzy. Madeleine pulled her shawl high over her neck and face, shivering as she sprinted over the drawbridge and aimed herself toward the jagged silhouette of outbuildings standing against the blue-black sky.

The spicy aroma of pork curing in the smokehouse tinged the air as Madeleine wound around the barn and dairy. A quiet coach house sat beyond them in the snow-dusted moonlight. Madeleine raced past it, her boots crunching over the frigid earth and her breath swirling the frosty air in visible clouds.

The horses whinnied and kicked at their stalls as Madeleine reached the stables, out of breath but exhilarated. Even in the darkened interior of the ancient structure, she could make out Gabriel's lean form running his hand down the muzzle of an Arabian. The aroma of hay settled over her as she slowed and approached the placid pair.

At the crush of Madeleine's boots on the dry hay, he turned and welcomed her with a half-smile. "She loves the company." His fingers stroked the sable hair between the horse's eyes, prompting her long lashes to flutter and close. "I may sometimes resist the company of others, but this girl—we've hardly missed a nightly visit in the last decade."

Madeleine let her shawl dip below her shoulders, the winter winds blocked by the stone walls. "A true friend." She stretched her fingertips high, gliding them down the animal's silky nose. A giggle escaped her throat when the horse nuzzled her face for more. "All right, girl."

Gabriel watched the two of them for a prolonged moment, joy igniting in his light eyes. "She's taken with you," he said at last. He reached through the shadowed stables to grasp her hand. "I well know the sentiment."

Attempting to push back her insecurities, Madeleine pressed her fingers into his. A single lantern swinging from the rafters shed a yellow glow over his curly hair. Since dinner, he'd shed his cravat and waistcoat, donning a broad-collared cashmere jacket. She swallowed, taking him in. Perhaps their story would end as her parents' had—two people destined to unite despite a world that deemed them unsuitable. Yet still the reality of her parentage haunted her. She could never hope to be worthy of his affections.

"Why are we meeting in secret?" she asked. The question had weighed on her since receiving his invitation to speak with her only after the household had gone to bed.

Seizing her other hand, Gabriel stared at their entwined fingers. "As you might have guessed, my uncle is a strong-willed man. I don't want him making life more difficult for you." He exhaled. "I think it's best we keep our relationship a secret until he's gone."

Even at his reassurance, her stomach knotted. "And how long might that be?" She would never find comfort sharing the same roof with that man.

"I hope no longer than a fortnight. He wants this woman to stay here for the Planters' Ball." Gabriel shrugged. "Perhaps it will impress her."

Perhaps it will tear you away from me. Madeleine watched the way his contemplative brows worked, the way his jaw flexed as he mentioned this mysterious woman. Surely a hint of curiosity had budded in him, even if he didn't plan to act on it. A man like him was bred to marry an elegant woman.

"Tell me about her." The directive surprised even herself. When Gabriel angled his head uncertainly, she raised her brows. "I *know* you spoke of her." Her ignorance in the matter would only drive her mad.

In the distant forest, an owl hooted. The wind rustled the trees outside the stables, prickling her face and neck. Gabriel diverted his gaze to the blackened stalls beyond his glossy Arabian, where gentle nays and nickers filled the space above the heady alfalfa strewing the ground.

"Her name is Caroline Allaire," he said at last. "Her father is a count with thousands of acres in the Loire Valley." His gaze landed back on Madeleine, so mournful he might have been foretelling her demise. "He's eager to make an alliance."

A touch of mirth greeted her despite his gloomy tidings. "And she'll no doubt make you scores of beautiful babies to carry on this alliance."

Gabriel returned her jest with a tilted smile. "That is the hope of our most ardent uncle."

The Arabian grunted, bashing her shoed foot into the boards of her stall. Madeleine broke Gabriel's hold to reach up again, smoothing a hand over her sinewy jaw, staring into the beast's round, ebony eyes. Did she dare ask the question burning through her heart?

Madeleine kept her eyes steady with the horse's. "What did you tell him?" she asked, her voice barely audible above the whistling wind.

An agonizing string of seconds stretched between them before Gabriel cleared his throat. "I told him I would meet her." Another pause, thick with the odor of manure and horses' sweat. "I said she could come to the château and we would entertain her until the ball. I felt it was the least I could offer him."

Vision misting, Madeleine swept her fingertips in a rhythmic pattern over the Arabian's snout. A sickening ache mounted her throat. Her hands trembled. She couldn't let him peer into her soul to see her self-doubt, yet it spilled over her every surface as hard as she willed it not to.

"Madeleine, listen to me." Gabriel snatched her shoulders, pivoting her toward him. "This has nothing to do with you—or her.

24

This man is my father's brother, my blood. I owe him my every allegiance. I must respect him enough to consider his plans, at least in his eyes. I cannot simply cast him aside."

She nodded. "I understand, Gabriel." Or at least she wanted to.

"You must believe me." His fingers coiled tighter around her arms. "I will welcome this woman with hospitality. I will provide her our very best. Once the Planters' Ball is over, I will respectfully decline her father's offer and send her on her way." He brushed a rogue strand of hair from her forehead. "Then the two of us can go back to planning our lives. I promise."

Madeleine searched his face, a swarm of questions milling around her. "What about her? What about the woman who is lured into the promise of marriage, perhaps even love? Can you so easily disregard her feelings?"

He sighed, raking a hand through his curly hair. "I thought of that. Certainly this isn't ideal." His fingers splayed beside him. "Yet if she's anything close to my uncle's description, she'll find a far grander match than I before the month is out."

Madeleine crossed her arms over her chest. "I still don't like it."

"I know you don't, and neither do I." Gabriel pulled her into him, forcing her shield to lower as her arms found their place around his torso. "This will all be over in the quickest of flashes—you'll see." He bent his head to brush his nose with her cheek. His warmth encircled her.

Madeleine relaxed into his embrace, savoring his mossy scent and the steady rhythm of his heart beneath his cotton shirt. His strong arms drew her tighter, his lips finding hers. Her pulse quickened as his heated palms met her face, his fingers diving into her hair. Gabriel's kisses deepened, bewitching her, growing more passionate with his hastening breath.

The Arabian huffed with an angry smash of her hoof against the stall, ripping the couple apart and sending them both into a fit of laughter.

Gabriel covered his mouth with the back of his hand, his face ruddy. "Yes, girl. You're probably right." His other thumb moved over Madeleine's jawline. "If I shall remain a gentleman, I should go to bed now before I dishonor this fine lady any further."

Adjusting her disheveled hair, Madeleine glanced between the toes of her boots and his enamored smile. "Indeed." Her mouth lifted shyly. "We should both get some sleep, *Baron* Clement."

But the night had other plans. As Madeleine ambled back over the fields and through the frigid dark with the feel of him fresh on her tingling skin, she knew that sleep would evade her as long as thoughts of him danced in her mind.

Four

A blustery wind blew over the countryside, howling as it sent fallen leaves whirling around the air. Somewhere beyond the black silhouette of hillsides, thunder spat its angry grumble across the sky. Rain began to plummet from the midnight sky, spattering against her skin. Madeleine lowered her hooded cloak until it nearly covered her eyes and trudged on. No sense in turning back now.

Weeks had passed since she had received word from her brother—weeks to ponder his message and stew over how to respond. If he truly wanted to kill Gabriel, then she must intervene. Yet didn't she owe him the opportunity to explain himself? The very idea of him still living and breathing pumped excitement through her. The urge to hold him again overpowered her lingering fear.

The calming scent of rain wetting the earth wafted to her nose. Madeleine drank it in, attempting to ignore the aching in her back and legs. Her boots squished in deepening mud, every step a concentrated effort not to slip and soil her dress. How foolish not to have hitched a ride in a farmer's wagon, but she couldn't risk anyone seeing her out tonight.

A deafening crash overhead came again, a surge of lightning illuminating the road before her. A ribbon of sludge wound through groves of chestnut trees, leading to a tiny hamlet crowded on one side of the road. Through the sparkling veil of rain, Madeleine saw rows of thatched-roof cottages, much like the little town she'd called home in childhood. Her heartbeat picked up speed. He was there—only a stone's throw away from her.

Nestled among the shuttered businesses, one building stood out. In each of its diamond window panes, lamplight spilled over the beige stucco siding and brown trim. An indistinct roar rumbled through its iron-studded door—jovial men's voices and the tinkle of piano keys. Madeleine lifted her eyes to a sign squealing as it swung on its hinges, upon which the words "The Black Lion" were etched neatly above a carving of a painted lion standing on its back legs.

Numbness trickled from her elbows to her hands as she pressed her thumb into the door handle's lever and thrust it open. An explosion of sound rushed at Madeleine—guttural laughter, the clink of glasses, bold strains of folk music she could barely decipher in the mad swirl of the wind outside.

Madeleine's gaze swept the interior of The Black Lion, hunting for the one face she still didn't really believe existed. Most of the tables scattered throughout the establishment were ringed with men chatting or playing cards, billows of cigar smoke clouding the space around them. A plump woman in homespun cloth darted from table to table, refilling jugs of ale and taking away soiled plates.

Along the darkened walls, Madeleine glimpsed scattered girls garbed in revealing frilly gowns, their bright silks like butterflies flitting around a browning garden. Her skin pinkened as she noticed several depraved stares turned on her, but she lifted her chin and marched right through the mass of them. She had a rapier and pistol beneath her cloak if she needed them, and no disoriented drunk would deprive her of them.

"Pardonne-moi, madame," Madeleine said to a woman with curly bronze hair bent over a customer's table, sloshing alcohol

from her pitcher into their glass. Perhaps she knew Auguste's whereabouts.

The woman reached to fill several more glasses before she tucked a wad of bills into her dress pocket and turned. "Ah, hello Maddy," she said in a country brogue, killing the question on Madeleine's lips. She dipped her hand into her apron and produced a key. "There you are, dear. It's good to see you again."

Dumbfounded, Madeleine stared at the silver object now resting on her palm as the woman scampered off to help other patrons. All she needed was another key to confound her problems. Flipping it over several times, she decided not to ask any more questions. If Auguste was here, she'd find him.

Madeleine's hands slickened as she cast furtive glances around her. No one seemed to notice her now. She glided through the maze of tables and ducked into a stairwell, leaving the acrid stench of ale and body odor behind. A hallway jutted beyond her concealed position, revealing a string of closed doors. Fist clenching around her new possession, she started for the first and tried not to ponder the other side too hard.

Her key slipped into the lock but refused to turn. Madeleine sidestepped to the next door, vexxed to get a similar result, even when she jiggled the handle. With a breath of courage, she stuck the key into the third lock and gasped when it revolved with a click. Her heartbeat thumped in her eardrums. For better or worse, she'd meet whatever lay beyond.

The door creaked open, revealing the room in a slow cascade—a sloped desk, a brick fireplace, hollow save for cold ash and soot, and light from a single candle flinging shadows over the walls. When the door finally thumped the wall behind it, her breath caught. There, bent over a round table with four or five empty chairs around it, sat a man about her age, stern brows cinched as he examined a haphazard pile of papers.

He glanced up at her intrusion, feather pen paused in his inkwell. "Madeleine?"

"Auguste?" Her voice trembled, her hands rising to shield her gaping mouth.

His chair scraped the planked floor as he pushed to a stand, his pen clattering to the table and leaving an inky trail behind it. He reached her in a handful of hasty strides, his chest pumping as he looked her over. Short, disheveled brown hair poked out in every direction over his prominent ears. Beneath his dark, deep-set eyes, a severe nose hooked over his thin lips. If she saw him on the bustling streets of Paris, she might never recognize him and yet—the longer her gaze wandered over him, the more she saw that little boy peering out from his face.

"Oh, Auguste, I can't believe it's you." Madeleine rushed at him, tossing her arms around his torso and reeling him to her. Lost in his warmth, she inhaled the scent of cigar smoke clinging to his clothes. God, could this really be happening? Could the beloved companion of her childhood really be standing here, alive and well, not a mere memory but flesh and blood?

Auguste coiled his arms around her protectively before he pulled back to look at her. "Madeleine, what's wrong? What have they done to you?" His frightened gaze searched her as if hunting for her broken parts.

"I'm fine, Auguste. I'm perfectly fine." She laughed, swiping the tears peppering her cheeks. "There's much to explain, I know. Be assured, I am well."

"Well, come in from the hallway." Auguste ushered her inside, casting a furtive glance toward the tavern before thrusting the door shut. Marching past her, he pointed himself toward the table he'd abandoned. "Wine?" he asked, extending a half-drunk bottle of claret.

Madeleine shook her head. "No, thank you." She grinned, unable to squelch the childish joy she felt just looking at the brother of her youth.

Eyebrows quirking, he hauled a chair from beneath the table. "Here, have a seat, would you?" His narrowed eyes darted down her. "You seem—flushed."

Obeying, Madeleine settled herself on the simple wooden chair and lowered her hood around her shoulders. "I know I must look positively touched. There is so much to tell you. I don't even know where to begin."

After yanking a pocket square from his waistcoat, Auguste dabbed at the ink he'd dribbled on the table. "Marie will double my rent if I go staining her furniture." Frowning, he spit into the handkerchief and scrubbed harder. "Where have you been all this time, Maddy? You worried me when you didn't make your usual monthly visit. You didn't even write."

"I know, and I'm sorry." Madeleine leaned in, ready to spill the entire story to the brother she'd wished so desperately to meet again. Then the words of his letter halted her. *Kill Gabriel Clement.* Swallowing, she tried to lift her lips in reassurance. "I ran into a bit of trouble, but it's over now."

His eyes sparked as he glanced up from his work. "Clement didn't hurt you, did he?"

"No, Auguste. Of course not." Madeleine's hand instinctively flew to her throat. When her brother only cast a suspicious glare in response, she sighed. "Listen, I can't explain it. Not yet, anyway. I need to focus on *us* now. Tell me about how we met—how we reunited after the war, I mean."

Auguste's nose crinkled. "Felix was right. You really have gone daft." He sent her a playful sneer as he downed the last of his wine.

Compressing her lips, Madeleine reached out and poked him in the gut. "Don't be a pest, little brother." Her head shook. "I know it doesn't make any sense, but just tell me. Please, Auguste."

At her earnest gaze, his brows climbed his forehead. "You grow stranger by the day." Fingers clamping around the decanter, he lifted it and sloshed a fresh serving into his glass. "We met at Théâtre de la Gaîté, of course. It had to have been, oh—" His eyes rolled skyward. "05, 06? Oui, it was 1806 because I was still working for Dupont the year before that."

"Théâtre de la Gaîté? What business did I have in the Théâtre de la Gaîté?"

Her brother snorted, wine puddling at the corners of his mouth. "Must I really stoke your vanity so, sister?"

Madeleine bit her lip, her mind racing as Auguste's jests eluded her. "I don't remember. I—" The hazy vision of a theater popped into her mind's eye. Her heart thumped. "Does the Théâtre de la Gaîté have yellow seats and curtains? And a box seats with masks adorning them?"

Auguste regarded her as if she'd taken a leap into total madness. "Oui," he said slowly.

She could see it now—a sea of theater patrons stretched out in neat rows, their excited chatter quieting as the lights dimmed and the curtain rose. A tranquil moment lingered where she stood in the dark on stage, the hushed anticipation of the waiting crowd rushing through her veins. The lamplight rose, its heat slicking her skin. Her painted eyes flitted around her, searching for an invisible foe. Then—her voice alone, strong and pregnant with emotion—rang over her breathless listeners.

"I was an actress," Madeleine said. How old had she been? Eighteen, perhaps?

"Yes, is your memory really so terrible?" Auguste asked with a playful smirk.

At once, she found herself back in that beautiful theater, garbed in the flowing costume of a Greek maiden. She had laurels in her hair, a silk robe of white and blue tethered beneath her bosom in gold cords. Her sandals scuffed the stage as she marched forward and angrily delivered her final lines to Racine's *Andromache*: "Farewell. Go now. I'll stay in Epirus." Her gaze roamed to the edge of the crowd, where a shadowed man had crept near the stage. "I renounce Greece, Sparta, all my house."

As his face emerged from the dark, her heartbeat accelerated. She squinted against the glow of the stage lights. *Auguste.* Could it really be him? Blinking, she vaguely remembered the actors around her, staring expectantly back. "All my family, it is enough for me," she said, voice choked. "That she produced you, you monstrosity." She froze within the swell of applause, the lights dimming over her, gaze fixed on the face she'd thought never achieved manhood.

After the curtain fell, Madeleine grabbed up her skirts and raced backstage. Past the stuffed wardrobes and baskets of props she darted, around the milling actors and hairstylists. Ignoring their questions, she quickly descended a short flight of steps and blasted through the door to the alley. There he stood in the moonlit street, chest pumping in equal fervency with hers.

"Auguste!" she screeched, leaping into his outstretched arms. "Oh, Auguste!" Her tears mingled with his hair as she crushed him in a tight embrace. His laugh tickled her skin. The scent of bay rum lifted from his elegant clothes. Madeleine pulled back to stare at him, cupping both of his cheeks in her open palms. "How can this be real?"

"I'm not quite sure." His awestruck gaze hunted her face. "I thought you were dead. I thought they caught you when you ran off to distract them."

Her head shook in vehemence. "No, I spent the night in the woods and came to find you in the morning. The stone over the mud cave was rolled back." Her brows cinched. "The Jacobins didn't find you?"

"Jean-Paul began crying from hunger that night. A kindly old woman found us and took us to her cabin. Of course they never suspected her. She lived too deep in the woods for anyone to come looking."

Madeleine clutched his shoulder. "But Jean-Paul's shoe—I saw it in the town square." Her eyelashes fluttered against the hot tears welling there. "There were so many bodies. I just couldn't bring myself to look."

His shoulders shrugged. "The same cobbler made all the shoes for the children in town. I'm sure more than one had a similar pair."

"Yes, of course." Hope lept within as realization dawned. "So Jean-Paul, he's—"

Moonlight showered Auguste's face as a smile stretched over it. "Yes, Maddy. He's alive. And he's just like Papa. Fifteen years old and already apprenticing at a smithy in the Faubourg Saint-Antoine."

Emotion overtaking her, Madeleine clasped a hand over her mouth and let her tears cascade down her face. All these years she'd suffered on her own, believing the family of her youth dead. Now, a thousand possibilities paraded before her. She could love again, be part of a family again, lean on someone again.

"Aren't you freezing in this costume?" Auguste brushed a hand up and down her arm, spreading heat over her skin.

Madeleine chuckled, feeling the cold pierce through her thin attire for the very first time. "I really don't care. I just want to talk with you—all night if we can." Her hand squeezed his slender arm. "Please, Auguste. I've waited thirteen years for this moment."

His gaze flew past her to the back door of the theater. "I think they want you back for curtain call." She followed his pointed finger to the open door, where her director stood with arms knotted over his chest in a stream of lamplight from within.

Auguste took her hand. "I also need to say a few words to my employer. He'll be cross if I just disappear." His head flicked down the alley toward the bustling street. "Do you know the *guinguette* on the corner? The one with all the dancers? Meet me there as soon as you can get away."

Her brow hooked, her cheek dimpling. "You would take your *sister* to such an establishment?"

"You're the actress," he said as he backed away toward the theater's entrance. "Where do you expect me to take you—a church?"

An hour later, the thrill of reuniting with her brother cast aside any notion of fatigue Madeleine might have otherwise incurred. Despite the late hour and her exertions on stage, she skipped through the hibernating streets of Paris as if a child sent out to play. Garbed now in a modest gown of green muslin, she'd thrown a masculine overcoat from the theater's collection on top to block out the chilly night air.

The guinguette Auguste had mentioned lay only blocks from Théâtre de la Gaîté, a swirling cacophony of piano music and raucous laughter against the quiet streets. Madeleine felt sucked into another reality as she wound through the open-air club among drunken patrons, shouting at one another and whistling at the dancing couples as they flounced by. To the bawdy tune of a pirate's shanty, the women swished their brightly dyed skirts to and fro, kicking their legs in a lively quadrille. A distracted drunk nearly collided with her, but Madeleine managed to dodge his reeling form.

"Apologies, mademoiselle," he slurred. "Might have had one too many." He grinned down at the overflowing stein in his clumsy grasp.

"What's the night for if not celebrating?" Madeleine gave him a wink as she swiped at the acrid liquor he'd still managed to slosh on her jacket.

"Watch yourself, will you?" Auguste's face materialized from the crowd, his annoyed expression condemning the man who'd nearly toppled into her.

The inebriated man gave a pathetic attempt to stand tall. "I said I was sorry." He looked between them, as if seeing two people.

Auguste's nostrils flared. "Well, sorry isn't good enough. You shouldn't be here." His rather short, lithe form flinched at the man menacingly. "Go home before I knock you into that drink you've got there."

"Auguste, really." Madeleine tugged him back from the unkempt man who clearly shivered at his threats. "I'm fine. Let him go." Her unrelenting grip pulled until she'd hauled him all the way to the bar, his iron gaze never unhitching from the cowering drunk.

His eyes swung back, watching as she untied her jacket belt and peeled off her thick outer layer. "I just got my sister back, and now I have to see her be assaulted by a worthless street rat?" His dark gaze narrowed as she flung her coat over the back of her chair and climbed into the seat. "You still have your stage makeup on."

Indeed, her cobalt-rimmed eyes, blush-washed cheeks, and rouge-painted lips would have taken half an hour to scrub off. "I couldn't waste precious time with such trifles," she said with a chuckle. "I've waited long enough."

Auguste scowled as he slid into the stool opposite her. "What if you're mistaken for a common harlot?" he asked, glancing warily around them.

"Then I'm mistaken for a common harlot." Madeleine cocked her head, challenging him. Swiftly, she let the pang of hurt that stabbed her gut at his words mingle into the fray of the lively club. She refused to argue with him after just finding him again.

"Fine." Leaning back in his raised chair, Auguste hailed the barkeep with one hand. "You know, my employer, the *wealthy* Italian diplomat, was quite taken with you. Be nice to me and I might introduce you."

Madeleine's groomed brows lifted. "Tempting." She simpered. "And what, pray tell, my dear brother, are you doing working for a diplomat at your age? How do you even know a man like that?"

His fingertips drummed the glossy bar as he studied her for a prolonged moment. "That's rather complicated." He licked his lips, glancing away as the bartender approached. "Ah, yes, a glass of Carménère, *s'il vous plait*." The man behind the bar nodded and turned to his work as if Auguste had no companion.

Brushing off his faux pas, Madeleine inclined her body forward. "You were saying?" She recaptured her brother's attention with a gentle tap of his wrist. "The foreign diplomat. You were telling me how you got your job."

Auguste dragged a breath in through his nose. "Truly, it's not very interesting." His calculating stare flicked over her. "I'm an ambitious man, Madeleine. I've had to be, growing up alone as I did."

She nodded. Didn't she, out of everyone alive, understand this truth? A cloud of tobacco-laced smoke stung her eyes as she looked into the cavorting throng of nightlife around her. Surviving life as an orphan had changed her—into someone strong, yes. But hand-in-hand came a hardness she feared she'd never outrun.

Blinking back her haunting past, Madeleine plastered a half-hearted smile on her lips. "Well, I'm glad you're following your dreams, Auguste. Maman and Papa would be very proud." She paused, the hesitancy in his eyes so palpable she could almost taste it. "Tell me what you're working on. You're safe with me, brother."

Clearing his throat, Auguste's solemn gaze darted around the open-air cabaret before landing back on her. He leaned closer, his shaven skin glowing in the scattered candlelight. "How much do you know about Papa—before we were born, I mean. Before he married Maman."

Madeleine thought back to the tale their mother had woven for her the night she couldn't sleep. "He was a priest before he married Maman. A very celebrated priest. Papa told me he served in the court of King Louis XVI."

Auguste's head bobbed. "Oui, so I learned in my study. Jean-Paul and I were constantly tossed from house to house as children, sometimes even to the homes of aristocrats. It's amazing what one can learn with the right resources."

Her curiosity piqued, Madeleine's heartbeat hammered in her eardrums. "What more did you learn?" she asked, gulping back the rock in her gullet.

"Papa was loved in King Louis' court by all but one man. The Baron d'Avance—*Raphael Clement*." His eyes darkened as he spat the name, hatred teaming from his clenched lips. "Papa advised the king many times against the infidel's plans. He stayed true to his convictions, even when the nobles pressured him. And Raphael Clement never forgot how our father thwarted his efforts."

"Did he—" Her throat closed in on itself. "Did he send the mob that took Papa?" She could still hear their terrifying shouts and jeers, still smell the tongues of their flaming torches.

"Worse." Auguste's fists clenched at his sides. "Clement spread rumors throughout our village that Papa was holding counter-revolutionary meetings, that he was an enemy of the new republic and leading others to cling to the old regime." His nostrils ballooned, his pointed chin quivering. "They *killed* our father because of one man's lies. One man who *knew* to wait in the shadows of the revolution until people were in such a frenzy that the wildfire of terror would squelch all truth in the matter."

Tears bloomed in his angered eyes. "Think about it, Maddy. Papa could have survived. He could have gotten us to safety before the Jacobins set fire to our village." His lip snarled. "We could have been together all this time, if not for *one man.*"

She felt it, low in her gut—the seed of malice sprouting and blossoming into an all-consuming wave of enmity. "I want to kill him," she heard herself growl.

"He's already dead. His son Gabriel Clement is the Baron d'Avance now."

Madeleine's lips flattened, the culmination of so many lost dreams crashing in on her. "Then I want to kill his son."

Through the fog of her building fury, Madeleine barely perceived Auguste clutching her hands in his. "That is precisely what we'll do, but only after we find his treasure." The words snapped her attention back to her brother, whose face had brightened with his revelation. "How would you like the chance to not only rid the world of the Clement name, but to claim his family's legacy for ourselves?"

Fingers tightening around his, Madeleine fastened a determined stare on her newfound brother. "Whatever it is, I'll do it."

Five

The quaint guest room of The Black Lion settled back into focus as the door swung open and two sets of boots stomped in from the rain. Madeleine blinked, their burly forms unfamiliar until she fully slipped from the visions of her past. The first, a tall man with a long ponytail and a full beard, she knew as the one who'd delivered Auguste's letter to her at the Clements' well. The other was younger, broader. He angled his head in question as she studied him, tucking a chunk of his chin-length blonde hair behind his ear.

"Oh, *my gracious*." Realization seizing her, Madeleine jetted to her feet. Her chair toppled to the floor behind her with a thud. "Jean-Paul? Can that really be you?" In seconds, she had her arms firmly planted around his sturdy torso, her head buried in the sodden clothes of his chest.

Jean-Paul cast a dubious glance at their brother, still seated at the table.

"Don't look at me for an explanation," Auguste said, his fingers splayed on either side. "She's been staring blankly at the wall for the last twenty minutes."

Madeleine savored a long drag of his woodsy scent before lifting her gaze to his bemused face. "You're so tall. Bigger than Papa, even." Yet he had the blue eyes and light complexion of their mother.

"I couldn't have grown much since autumn," he said with a chuckle. One of his strong arms hooked her to his side. "Perhaps you've been imbibing too much of Felix's whiskey. That wouldn't be the worst of its effects."

His companion dragged his filthy satchel over his shoulder and plopped it on the table. "Nay, lad." His tousled head wagged. "She was actin' the same when I sent your brother's message. Sufferin' from a touch of lunacy. Has to be, poor girl."

"You're both wrong." Madeleine's tongue clicked. "I'll have you know, I was neither drunk nor crazy." Her playful glare latched onto this Felix fellow. "You simply surprised me, that's all. And Auguste, I was just recalling the night we found each other." She spun on him suddenly, hands on her hips. "If I remember right, you allowed the barkeep to rudely pass me over."

"Yes, then you drank my entire glass of wine and demanded I order you another."

Jean-Paul laughed again—a deep, joyful sound. "Now, that sounds like my dear sister." He smiled down at Madeleine with such affection, she wondered perhaps if they'd never separated but grown together their entire lives.

Clearing his throat obtrusively, Auguste shattered the tender moment. "Enough with wasting time." His serious gaze captured Madeleine. "You still haven't shared where you've been all this time, nor have you brought back any news of Clement's treasure."

Blood rushing in her ears, Madeleine lifted her chin. She couldn't risk exposing her escapade with the Guardians—not until she knew she could trust Auguste. "And what have you discovered about the nameless man?" she asked, recalling the mysterious pseudonym he'd penned in his letter.

Auguste's back stiffened, his cheeks flushing. "I will find him. Don't trouble yourself over that. I have several leads." Reaching for his wine glass again, he leaned back in his chair. "Now, quit changing the subject. You must have discovered something after all this time with Clement."

Madeleine glanced nervously between the three pairs of eyes bearing down on her. What could she say, really? That she loved the man they sought revenge on? That she would rather marry him than prolong their fruitless quest for his ancestor's riches? Clutching two handfuls of her woolen skirts, she sashayed toward the overturned chair still laying sideways on the plank floor.

"I have put much time and consideration into this," she said, reaching for the chair and righting it. "And I do believe"—she sank into the seat again and inhaled a breath of courage through her nose—"that there is no treasure." Her gaze landed squarely on Auguste. "I think that it never existed."

"Hogwash." Auguste slammed his glass on the table, his claret spilling over and dripping down the stem. "The letter exists. We've spoken to too many people who have seen it with their own eyes."

Had they? Her mind sprinted to remember. "Perhaps the letter exists, but the treasure does not."

Auguste swore under his breath. "This is all you have to show for a year of our time?" His tensed fingers raked through his short hair. "I don't believe it, not for a moment." Seizing his glass, he tossed back a large swig, his stormy eyes glaring over the rim.

"The baron would have told me if he had any other information." She paused, twisting a curl at the nape of her neck. "While I've been living at the château, the two of us have grown—close." Her gaze dove to her knees as she cursed the warmth threatening to seep over her face.

"No doubt you have." Auguste's suggestive retort flung her rounded stare back at him. "Clearly your efforts have proved half-hearted if the man won't even share his secrets with the woman filling his bed."

Madeleine's mouth opened to speak, but Jean-Paul stepped forward before she could. "You don't have to speak that way to her," he said, one enormous gloved hand pointed at their brother. "Maddy's doing the best she can."

Auguste's eyebrows slanted. "Perhaps you have a better idea, brother? Something beyond spending all day in that sweatshop and gambling your money away?" He sat upright, challenging the larger man who'd retreated into a sullen stance. "No? I thought not. Don't interfere with what you don't understand."

"Enough!" Madeleine stepped between her feuding brothers, one hand stretched out to each of them. "We are family and there is no need to quarrel." Fingers trembling, she flattened her mouth into a resolved line. "That said, I believe I will now take my leave. This is not what I—not what I expected, coming back here."

Fists clenched, Auguste rose to meet her. "And what did you expect? That we would praise you for flitting your time away and getting us absolutely nowhere?"

Despite the fire welling in her chest, her steady gaze hooked his. "I had hoped to find a man of honor in my brother."

"You had best find that key and that map before I ride in and find them myself," he said, unflinching. "I promise you that crooked baron of yours won't be happy if I do."

Her entire body shook, the jolting reality of Auguste's character clashing with the idealistic vision in her mind. The brass key beneath her dress melded with her skin. She could yank it out this very moment and show him just how much Gabriel had entrusted her with. Yet somehow, she had the gnawing feeling that the revelation would only put the baron in more danger.

With one last flash of her eyes, Madeleine spun to leave. Her heavy skirts brushed her legs as she hurried toward the door. She wanted only to be back in Gabriel's arms again, back where she felt safe from the cruel world hurling around them.

A hand clamped her shoulder just as she reached for the handle. Madeleine looked up into the concerned eyes of her youngest brother, his frame towering over her. "You can't go back out in that weather. It isn't safe."

Wind rattled the shutters, moaning as it lifted the tree branches outside the window. The sprinkle of rain she'd trudged through to get here had morphed into a roaring downpour. "I have to go," she said, weighted with dread at the idea of enduring more of Auguste's insults. "The head maid has strict rules on tardiness."

"He's right," Felix said, craning his neck toward the window. "Got our wheels stuck coming in when we did. Would've had to leave it if it weren't for this strong lad here."

Jean-Paul's fingers squeezed. "We'll have Marie make you a bed for the night. Surely they'd rather you find shelter than kill yourself trying to get home on time."

Glancing between the three men, Madeleine at last lifted her form and set her jaw. "Fine. But if I have to stay, I shall spend my time in the tavern." Without waiting for a reply, she turned the knob and swung the door behind her. A short bustle down the hallway brought her back to the little bar room, now crammed with patrons soaked to their core and demanding a warming stein of ale.

Madeleine found a small table in the corner and plopped onto the seat, her legs like the wilted stem of a crushed flower. The nightlife around her roared—jovial laughter, the sweet medley of piano and fiddle, the crash of fists on wood as men won or lost piquet matches. Sighing, she looked past the windowpane on the wall, peppered with pinging rain. The road to the Château de Rêves was streaked in charcoal storm clouds, a fuming tempest spewing angry bile across the night sky. Resting her arms on the table, Madeleine's head dove to bury itself in their comfort. That wondrous home in the distance and the man at its helm had never felt so elusive.

A s if a butterfly emerging from her cocoon, spring burst forth over the countryside in a brilliant array of colors. The thunder and rain clutching all of nature in its claws the night before was forgotten, save for a few scattered tree limbs along the road. Madeleine raced past them, the cheery sun warm on her back.

Dodging mud puddles this way and that, she nimbly skipped off the dirt path and into the pastures leading to the château. Jean-Paul's wagon wheels rumbled down the road behind her as she hopped a fence and surged down the hill. If not for his help, surely she would have stumbled back home barely in time for lunch preparations.

He'd come to her that night in the tavern, his careful gait dragging over the floorboards. "Mind if I sit?" he'd asked the weary Madeleine, her head still concealed in the crook of her arm.

"Look," he said, sinking into the chair across from her and folding his long legs beneath him. "Auguste is so intense that he gets carried away at times, but he still means well. You know he didn't mean what he said to you."

Madeleine saw him through a blurry patchwork of lamplight. "It didn't feel that way a moment ago." How could she know any different? How could she trust him, blood or no?

"I'm surprised you didn't serve it right back to him." Jean-Paul's full lips tilted into a smile. "He acts so high and mighty, but you're smarter. We all know it."

She couldn't help returning the gesture. "Perhaps I should have." Inhaling the musty, smoke-filled air, Madeleine gazed absently at a table of farm hands smoking cheap cigars around a game of aluette. "Why does this treasure matter so much to him? Life is full of so much more important matters for him to pursue."

Jean-Paul chuckled. "Why do you ask me? I never wanted any part of it. The two of you were bent on money and revenge, in any order you could get it."

Gaze moving over him, she silently gauged the sincerity of his words. Nothing but gentle strength shone back through his youthful features. Madeleine bit her lip. "I suppose I have no one to blame but myself." The prospect sent a shiver of fear coursing through her.

Through the haze, Jean-Paul reached out to cover her hand in his. The simple gesture swept over her like a tidal wave—the might of Papa and comfort of Mama enveloping her in sweet memories of childhood. He was so much like them both. She made up her mind on the spot to divulge what happened to her memory and swear him to secrecy.

"It's not too late to turn back," he said, his fingers gripping hers. "Auguste will understand eventually. It's never too late to change course."

Yet it is too late, Jean-Paul. Madeleine dashed through the chilly wind toward the Château des Rêves, chest aching more from the pain of this realization than the exhaustion seizing her. The spark in Auguste's dark eyes had been unmistakable. He would gain this treasure for himself or die trying. No one could stand in his way—not even his long-lost sister.

A charming medley of daffodils and purple crocuses had sprouted up along the stone wall beyond the château's moat. Madeleine wished for a moment to pluck a few for her dreary bedroom as she leaped to the gravel drive and clattered over the bridge. Sweat trickled into her hairline and her sides ached as she catapulted herself through the cold stone entryway at the house's rear.

"Madeleine, there you are." Georgette's pudgy form bustled through the elaborate house, meeting her in the gallery. "Why, it's mid-morning. Where have you been?" Her narrowed eyes surveyed the flustered Madeleine from her crooked chignon to the mud on her petticoats and shoes. Behind her, Cecile looked on with interest, her mouth lifted in a wicked smile.

"I'm sorry, Georgette. Truly I am." Madeleine put a nervous hand to the back of her neck and pulled out a clump of dead leaves from her hair. "I thought I'd journey down the road last night to purchase a few herbs from the apothecary. I didn't expect the rain to turn into a deluge. I was forced to spend the night at a roadside inn."

The older woman blinked, her stern expression softening. Despite her scowl, she couldn't curtain the genuine concern misting her gray eyes. "No doubt you've compromised your good-standing in a den of debauchery. That's all those so-called *inns* really are." Her white head shook, her tongue clicking. "I ought to throw you out on your backside."

Cecile leaned in. "Oh, please don't. Not before we've heard all her stories."

Georgette dismissed her with a swat. "I would if there weren't so much riding on today. Mademoiselle Allaire is scheduled to arrive any moment, and we *must* provide her with a dignified welcome." Gathering the maids together, she thrust them toward the open doors of the parlor. "Cecile, you assist Madeleine in changing those soiled clothes and return immediately. And *don't* get mud on my clean floors," she added, glaring at Madeleine's offending boots.

As the pair jogged through the parlor and turned the corner, Cecile coiled her fingers around Madeleine's arm. "You *must* tell me everything. Where were you last night? Who were you with? Why do you look so"—her green eyes raked Madeleine's crumpled clothes—"out of breath?"

Simpering, Madeleine hauled open the door to the servants' quarters and descended into the stairwell. "It's far less exciting than what you've imagined, I can assure you. I'll tell you everything later. Let's get me changed and back up to the gallery before Georgette loses the last of her marbles."

Only moments later, the friends emerged from the stairwell with a fresh maid's uniform on Madeleine and her dark hair repinned. "I wonder what she'll look like," Cecile said as they scampered through the parlor. "She must be ugly as a bulldog if she can't find someone of her own rank to marry."

Madeleine shook her head, eyes rolling. "The revolution did away with the feudal system, did it not?"

Cecile's incredulous smirk spoke for her. "I just hope she doesn't expect us to wait on her every whim. There was enough work for us to do around here *before* she and this pompous uncle came to—" She stopped abruptly as Georgette thrust the gallery doors open.

"Good, there you are." Georgette's keen eyes hunted Madeleine thoroughly, her lips twisting. "It's not your best presentation, but it will have to do. Come along, now. I can already hear her carriage in the drive." Spinning on her heel, she left the two maids plus Brigitte to scurry behind her.

"Now, I expect you three to be on your best behavior," Georgette threw over her shoulder as she marched toward the stairs. "Mademoiselle Allaire is a fine lady, and we *must* make a good impression. Madeleine, you will be her lady's maid. From this moment until she leaves, she is your very top priority. Do you understand?"

Madeleine halted, panic seizing her. "But I always serve the meals."

"You'll do that too." The head maid pivoted back to her, one eyebrow raised. "I expect your full cooperation in this matter. No more running around, disappearing for days at a time. I need you here."

"Yes, Georgette. Of course, but—" Her gut twisted at the idea of spending her every waking second with the approaching woman. It would be hard enough to watch Gabriel court her, no matter how artificial their relationship. "Please don't make me do it." Her clasped hands lifted in supplication.

"We're understaffed as it is, and you're the only maid I trust to have a shred of *civility* toward the poor girl." Her wrinkled eyes glared at Cecile, who made a face in response. Georgette rotated back and smoothed both hands over her crisp black dress before bobbing her way out of the gallery and into the atrium.

Casting a trepidatious look at Cecile, Madeleine dragged her feet along the polished wooden floor behind the trio of maids. The checkered atrium floor gleamed beneath strands of sunlight from the stairwell. Orange and crimson roses brightened every surface in tall glass vases, their aroma tingeing the air in sweet perfume. Madeleine forced her booted feet to stand in line beside the petite Brigitte, her gaze flitting up the double staircase, where the floorboards creaked over their heads.

Pascal appeared around the bronze horses first, the shrewd eyes beneath his bushy brows taking in the spectacle with approval. Trailing behind him, Gabriel absently fastened his cuff links. Stealing a glimpse of him, Madeleine couldn't help a sensation of pride. He looked so dapper in his gray trousers, double-breasted silk waistcoat, and knee-length jacket. For once, he'd knotted his cravat the right way and put a comb through that unruly hair. Against her better judgment, Madeleine caught herself returning the barely perceptible grin he flung her way.

The iron knocker on the château's front doors pounded the wood, prompting Georgette to strut into the entryway with back rigid and arms poised, as if an opera singer about to belt an aria. Cecile stifled a giggle, a snort escaping her nose before she could quell it. Madeleine stiffened her features as Pascal's fiery stare clamped on them.

Her heart pumped furiously as the château's doors groaned open and a dainty set of footsteps clicked on the stone behind the scuff of Georgette's slippers. Without even meaning to, Madeleine held her breath as the shadowed woman advanced into the sunlit room. Her back teeth squeezed together, jaw clenching.

"Mademoiselle Allair, how wonderful to see you again." Pascal stepped toward her, his rotund silhouette blocking Madeleine's view of their visitor. "May I present my esteemed nephew, the Baron d'Avance."

"Mademoiselle Allair." Gabriel took her hand and bent low.

An unexpected sensation twinged Madeleine's middle. She glanced at Cecile, whose eyebrows had drawn on sight of the woman. Rather than the reassurance Madeleine sought, her friend cast her a worried glance that plummeted to the floor. Huffing, Madeleine climbed to her tiptoes.

Golden hair pinned to the crown of Caroline's head, descending in wispy ringlets around her face. A yellow satin carriage dress and fitted jacket gracefully accentuated a tall, lithe figure. Madeleine gulped as Caroline's face at last shifted into her view. Wide, coffee-colored eyes peered out beneath her doe-like lashes. A slightly curved nose stopped exactly where it should have, the perfect complement to her pink bowed lips. Madeleine's stomach plunged within her. Caroline Allair was beautiful—angelic, even.

"Baron," she said, a shy smile fixing on Gabriel. "I can't tell you how wonderful it is to meet you. Your uncle has done nothing but sing your praises since our first introduction."

Gabriel dipped his curly head. "I only hope I deserve such praise."

With a deep chuckle, Pascal clapped his back. "Assuredly he does. I meant every word." The silver buttons on his waistcoat must have strained beneath his expanding chest. "We'll all sit down to lunch in an hour's time. Caroline, perhaps you'd like the chance to freshen up and acquaint yourself with your room."

"Oh, yes." The blonde woman self-consciously fluffed her pristine hair style. "I'd certainly appreciate the chance to get out of these traveling clothes."

A few moments of silence drifted over them as Madeleine tangled herself in daydreams. What if Gabriel found this new creature attractive, as any healthy young man would? What if said attraction led him to love? To abandon his feelings for her? She could picture it now—an enviable romance started this day, a day they would look back on with fondness as they told the tales to their tawny-haired, blue-eyed children.

The mad rush of her rampant thoughts stilled as Madeleine realized that every eye in the room had fastened on her. She looked from Caroline to Pascal, whose weathered face shot arrows of disgust her way. Her skin burned.

"Well, what are you waiting for, girl?" he asked. "Stop staring at the poor woman and show her to her room."

Six

"Right this way, mademoiselle." Sweeping an arm through the open door, Madeleine stepped back to allow their guest to enter her private suite.

All week, Georgette had scampered around the east wing, scrubbing and tidying every bit of imaginable space. Now, the product of her efforts dazzled as the two women crossed into Caroline's boudoir and beheld her handywork. Framed in twin sash windows with mauve drapery, a carved mahogany bed commanded the room. A lush white bedspread and plump pillows rested beneath a deep purple, gold-threaded canopy. Besides a vanity and washstand, the room offered a miniature writing desk and a porcelain tub tucked into the corner. Georgette had even sprinkled crushed lavender sprigs atop the pillows and chairs.

Flattening a hand over her chest, Caroline audibly exhaled. "Thank God that's over." She fanned her heated cheeks with delicate fingers. "I'm Caroline," she said, then shrugged. "But I suppose you must know that already."

The maid curtsied lightly. "My name is Madeleine, my lady."

"That's a lovely name." Caroline wandered to the bed, her fingertips absently strumming the spiraled bedpost. After a moment of gazing toward the windows, she spun back to Madeleine. "How do you think I did back there? I was so terribly nervous." Both hands rose to shelter her glowing cheeks.

Madeleine couldn't help the smile that dimpled her lips. "You were the picture of elegance, mademoiselle." Truly, she hadn't expected such a striking, well-bred young lady to harbor such insecurities.

"You flatter me." With a thankful expression, Caroline sank to the bed behind her. "You would think that a woman of twenty-five would have learned to compose herself by now. I'm a hopeless cause." She chuckled.

Serge appeared in the doorway, carting a hefty oak trunk in his brawny arms. "By the window, please." Caroline speared one finger toward the empty space beside an oval, full-sized standing mirror. "Thank you."

Once he had gone, Madeleine turned to her charge with hands clasped in front of her. "Perhaps you would feel better in a fresh change of clothes." Anything to distract the anxious woman, now gnawing on a thumbnail. The fact that Gabriel intended to reject her in two weeks' time already ate mercilessly at Madeleine's gut.

Caroline popped from the bed as if on springs. "Yes, I think I will." With Madeleine's guidance, she selected a white Empire waist afternoon dress with a cornflower blue floral print and stood back as the maid unfurled it.

Though unpracticed as a lady's maid, Madeleine quickly took to the meticulous art of unhooking the myriad of buttons and hooks on the lady's gown and boots. After all, she'd performed the trick on her own grander outfits enough times herself. Caroline wanted only a quick wash in the porcelain basin before she lifted her arms to receive the clean dress Madeleine suspended above her head.

"Is there not a woman in this household?" Caroline asked as she stood before the mirror, watching her reflection as Madeleine stooped to shake out the back of her skirts.

"The baron's sister Désirée resides here," Madeleine said from the floor. "She should be back in time for supper. She spent the day with the children in the village poor house."

Caroline's eyes rounded. "Truly?" She shook her head. "What a lovely woman. I can't wait to make her acquaintance. I feared an evening alone with the baron and that terrifying uncle of his." As if the thought had slipped without her consent, she covered her mouth in rigid fingers. "*Excusez-moi*, I shouldn't talk like that. It's only—well, Pascal scares me a little. I can't quite put my finger on it, but something inside tells me to run whenever he's around, ever since we first met."

Stifling a laugh, Madeleine remained silent as she finished straightening out Caroline's crêpe skirts. Several choice insults toward Pascal Clement floated through her mind, but she thought it best to keep her lips clamped shut—no matter how badly she wanted to commiserate with Caroline.

Caroline regarded her reflection for several moments, her brown eyes thoughtful. Madeleine had risen behind her, fingers busily tying the ribbons at the back of her dress. She tried to ignore when Caroline's gaze shifted to her in the mirror, quietly studying her before she spoke.

"What can you tell me about the baron?" Caroline finally asked, shivering as if coming out of a stupor. "What kind of man is he?" A mischievous sparkle glinted in her eyes. "He's certainly handsome. I don't see how you get any work done around here."

Madeleine laughed as she pulled her bow taut. "He is that." Her eyes met with Caroline's in the mirror, deliberation plaguing her. How much did she really want to reveal about the man she planned to marry herself? Did she have the confidence to tell the truth? "He's a good man, too. He's very kind." Butterflies flitted around her stomach. Hopefully the simple answer would suffice.

A contented smile stretched across Caroline's ivory skin. "Good. I believe my father will disown me if I drive away yet another of his potential suitors." She said it casually, and still Madeleine couldn't miss the sad lilt in her voice.

She paused over Caroline's jewelry box, clutching a strand of pearls. Perhaps she shouldn't entertain her curiosity, but— "Have there been many?" she asked.

Caroline sighed as Madeleine slipped the pearls beneath her curling wisps of hair. "Far too many, I'm afraid." Her slender shoulders lifted. "My father thinks I am too particular for a woman my age, but what else can I be? He sees only a business transaction where I see a lifelong commitment."

Gazing into the mirror, she gently fingered the necklace Madeleine had clasped at the nape of her neck. "I refuse to be tethered for a lifetime to someone as pompous, dull, downright *insipid* as some of these men my father has thrown at me." Her perfect brows gathered, her chin thrusting outward. "I deserve my intellectual equal—a man who isn't afraid of a woman who *thinks.*"

Madeleine swallowed, her hands falling limp behind Caroline. Hadn't Gabriel once uttered such similar words to her? He wanted a woman with her own opinions, someone who would discuss life with him rather than merely hang on his arm and look pretty. She swiped at her collarbone, where sweat had begun to pool.

Revolving to face her, Caroline cocked her head. "But listen to me prattling on about my miniscule problems." She shook her head, grinning. "You must think me terribly selfish to have so much and still want more."

Something hard stuck in Madeleine's gullet. She blinked, the rays of sunlight from the window casting Caroline in a light she hadn't anticipated. She was beautiful, yes. But beyond the silky hair and angelic features, her heart teemed from the vulnerable pools of her eyes. She was *good,* too. A better match for Gabriel than she'd imagined would waltz through the château's front doors.

"I think you deserve to be happy," she managed, her voice strangled. She could not deny the truth parading before her.

Caroline reached out to touch the hand Madeleine tried to keep from quivering. "Thank you, Madeleine." She straightened to her full, statuesque height. "Now, how do I look? Ready to meet my fate?" Her chin playfully swung right and then left, displaying both sides of her flawless face.

With a weighted heart, Madeleine wagged her head. "No. You look ready to make your own fate." As she followed Caroline out the door, she halted at the threshold and closed her eyes. Her knuckles blanched as her fingers curled around the wood. Perhaps God had sent Caroline to the Château des Rêves for a reason—one she couldn't yet consider without her spirit crumbling within her.

The château's kitchen buzzed with the din of supper preparations by the time Madeleine finished dressing Caroline yet again and stumbled into the fray. At Georgette's bidding, she assumed her place at the stone fireplace. Amid the clash of pots and scurry of feet, Madeleine took up a ladle and stirred the reddish bisque bubbling over the crackling flames.

"So?" a voice lit the air behind her. "What is she like?"

Madeleine jumped at the sound, splashing the scalding soup on her hand. "Ow." Her ladle sloshed into the iron pot as she yanked her hand back and winced. Her skin pulsed and reddened where a burning sensation had spread.

"Sorry." Cecile cast her a concerned frown. "Should I get you a cool towel?"

"It's quite all right." Madeleine brought the offending finger to her lips and bit it. "I suppose I was lost in my own revelries," she said out the side of her mouth.

Her friend tossed her long braid over her shoulder as she bent to pull a loaf of bread from the oven. The scent of yeast and rosemary instantly mingled with the tomato soup already filling her senses. "It's that bad?" Cecile asked.

"So much worse." Groaning, Madeleine nearly launched into the whole story before spying Georgette at the cutting board, furiously slamming her knife into a defenseless carrot. "I'll tell you about it later. If I don't fish that ladle out of the bisque, I have a sneaking suspicion that *I'll* be the main course."

"Brigitte! Bring the soup tureen!" Georgette chirped, propelling the petite servant girl toward the fire.

The little brunette thing looked curiously from Madeleine with her hand still propped in her mouth, to Cecile, who glanced around them for some sort of makeshift tool. "Here." Setting her steaming loaves of bread on the table, she retrieved a long wooden spoon from among Georgette's hand-carved collection and dipped it into the pot suspended over the flames. The hook above it squealed as the pot tipped dangerously on its side. "There we are," Cecile said, holding up the ladle triumphantly, as if a prize won at the local fair.

Madeleine wiped the ladle clean with a towel while Brigitte gaped at them in wonder. "I—I thought for certain that you were going to flood the kitchen floor in soup," she stuttered. "Georgette would have killed us all, then." Her mouth juddered as if she actually believed the words.

"It wouldn't be the first time she's tried," Cecile said with a wink.

"Here, bring your tray closer," Madeleine said. Hot steam misted her face as she bent over the thin soup and gingerly poured it into the tureen on Brigitte's tray. Covering one of the girl's shivering hands, she smiled. "Be careful when you take this to Georgette. She'll want to sprinkle it in chopped basil."

With a visible gulp, Brigitte hastily nodded and turned to the head maid with the grace of a baby giraffe learning to walk.

A hand squeezed Madeleine's shoulder blade. "This new woman—she'll be gone before you know it." Cecile's lips curled wryly. "And if not, I do know where we can find some poison." The green eyes beneath her feathery lashes sparkled as the two shared a furtive laugh.

Minutes later, Madeleine found herself tiptoeing down the upper corridor toward the dining room with the tray in her hands. Georgette had certainly spared no expense. The hallway, normally unused and lit with a single candelabra, danced with the flickering light of clustered candles every few steps. The airy scent of rosewater reached every corner. The floral tapestry beneath her feet had brightened several shades with the round of washings Georgette had insisted every piece of cloth in the house undergo.

Distracted, Madeleine barely heard the hushed voice beckoning her from a darkened room along her path. "Psst! Madeleine." She rotated her head to find Gabriel hiding in the shadows.

"What are you doing?" She ducked into the parlor illuminated only with a patch of white moonlight streaming through the window.

"Waiting for you, of course." Gabriel lifted her tray from her grasp, depositing it on a cushioned bench along the wall. With one swoop, he anchored an arm around her waist and drew her to him. His balmy kisses pacified Madeleine as she melted against him, lost in the robust scent of his cologne. The warmth of his body encircled her, *protected* her against all the fear and uncertainty this day had assailed her with. He pulled her close, sighing against her neck. "How I've longed to embrace you this whole day through."

Gabriel's curly hair brushed her face as she withdrew enough to look at him. "You're going to get us caught," she teased, even as an eerie premonition gripped her. Something told her this might be the last embrace they ever shared.

"Would that be such a bad thing?" His soft thumb moved over her cheekbone. "It would at least save me the trouble of explaining to Caroline why I can't marry her."

The words unexpectedly wrenched at her. "Listen, Gabriel." Madeleine stared into the fingertips she'd rested on his chest before looking into his shadowed face. "Be gentle with her, please. Don't prolong this charade longer than necessary."

"Of course. We needn't wait until the Planters' Ball if you think it's best." He studied her, his dark eyebrows furrowing. "You're worried about her."

Madeleine nodded once. "As a servant, I see things. A side of people the world doesn't always get to." She paused, her mind wandering to the heartache she'd seen brimming on Caroline's beautiful face. "This woman doesn't deserve more pain."

Seeming to comprehend, Gabriel lifted her fingertips to his mouth and kissed them. "Then I shall do my best not to compound it." Above her fingers, his light eyes sparked.

Madeleine met his adoring gaze with a smirk. "I'm aware I'm the servant, Baron Clement, but I must insist you go in to dinner at once." Her gaze pitched to the tureen abandoned on the bench beside them. "That soup will not stay warm forever, and I will not be blamed for delaying its presentation any longer."

"Fine." Gabriel kissed her again, holding her to him as if savoring the taste of her. At last he retreated, stepping backward out the door. "I'll go, but I refuse to enjoy it. Not while you're serving the food rather than sharing it with me."

The silver scrolled wall paper of the château's dining room sparkled in reflected light as Madeleine traversed the doorway, tureen nested in her hands. All along the walls, Cecile had lit sconces now splashing quivering shadows over the mirror and opposing row of portraits. Atop a snowy linen tablecloth, Georgette had arranged a centerpiece of spring flowers accentuated by silver candlestands and dipped candles. Madeleine rounded the table and set her tray next to Caroline, the guest of honor.

"My charity work often takes me far away," Désirée was saying from her spot across from Caroline at the table's center. "But Paris has so many who need help, I would feel remiss if I did not stay home for the time being."

"Thank you, Madeleine," Caroline said to the maid lifting the tureen's lid. Her gaze swept back to Désirée as Madeleine began to ladle bisque into her bowl. "I would love to go with you sometime, if you would not mind my company."

From far down the table, Pascal snorted. Madeleine stole a glance at him, decked in his finest furs and jewels, his greased hair tethered behind his bulging neck. "We have plenty of amusements planned for your stay, my dear. No need to bother with my niece's trifles."

Désirée volleyed a playful glare at Pascal as Madeleine approached him. "Caring for the poor is not a trifle, Uncle."

"Indeed," Caroline said. "If we, the wealthy, do not help our fellow countrymen, then who will? It's both our duty and our privilege."

Pascal clutched his bowl as Madeleine filled it, brows lifting. "I had no idea you were such a philanthropist, Mademoiselle Allair. What do you think of that, Gabriel?"

"Hmmm?" From the opposite end near the fireplace, the baron snapped to attention. All eyes pinned to him. Madeleine couldn't stop the smile that flicked over her lips. Too engrossed in watching her serve dinner, he hadn't been paying them a lick of attention.

"I said what do you think of Mademoiselle Allair's proclivity for charity?" Pascal shouted across the room, as if Gabriel's hearing had faltered.

The baron's eyes darted sheepishly around the table, landing briefly on his sister, who produced a warm smile and an arm squeeze for Madeleine. "Oh yes, very nice." He cast a curt smile toward Caroline as Madeleine lifted the ladle from her tureen. With the porcelain vessel shielding his guests' view, he let one finger of his free hand caress Madeleine's wrist as she poured him a ladleful.

Flushed, Madeleine quickly turned to set her tray atop the serving table before anybody saw the color seeping onto her face. She found it ridiculous that such a simple gesture could launch her heartbeat into a frenzy. Yet glancing at her blushing reflection in the gilded mirror, she couldn't deny the truth. She needed him, even when her warring heart bayed that someone might need him more.

"This soup is delicious," Caroline said just as Madeleine had collected herself and begun to distribute white wine into their long-stemmed glasses. The clatter of spoons rang over the small gathering, the rich medley of spiced tomatoes, cream, and basil from the garden waltzing around the air.

"I prefer mine hot." Pascal emphasized his remark with an irritated scowl Gabriel's way. Madeleine froze over his wine glass, feeling his beady eyes move up her arm. Did he already suspect a relationship between the two of them?

"Oh, pay him no mind." Désirée elegantly swiped her spoon toward the older man. "This is marvelous. Madeleine, do give Georgette our sincerest compliments on her cooking."

With a nod, the servant woman used the distraction to escape Pascal's leering glare. Yet still, she couldn't shake him, even after Cecile had appeared with the evening's entrée on a silver platter and left with their used bowls. Her fingers trembled as she served him, moisture springing to her browline. No matter where she stood in the lavish dining room, that stare bore through her, exposing her beneath his scrutiny.

"Tell us about your family," Désirée said to their guest. "Do you have brothers and sisters?"

Caroline finished her dainty bite of chicken fricassée before dabbing at her chin with her linen napkin. "I am the eldest of seven."

"Seven?" Désirée let out an airy chuckle. "My, you must be used to having children around everywhere you go."

"Yes. The youngest are seven and ten." Caroline paused, her hand on her wine glass. "And then there are my nieces and nephews," she said finally, quieter this time.

Pascal's chair groaned as he leaned inward, scratching his chin. "You have a sibling who is married?" The question sounded more like an accusation.

A prolonged moment stretched over them, thick with the scents of butter and thyme. Caroline swallowed, a forced smile lifting the corners of her lovely mouth. "A brother and two sisters, actually." She inhaled, her dark eyes tumbling to her half-eaten meal. "I realize it is not conventional for the eldest to remain unmarried, but marriage is a blessing that has thus far passed me by."

From her place in the corner, Madeleine couldn't help aching for the woman. Caroline's slender arms self-consciously hugged her body. Loneliness teemed from her every pore. Madeleine looked beyond her to Gabriel, who had fixed Caroline with an empathic expression. Something low inside her tremored.

"Well, we are not so conventional here," Désirée mercifully shattered the silence.

Caroline blinked back the tears that glistened in the candlelight. "My father is a winemaker," she said, masterfully shifting topics. "I brought bottles of his most prized port if you'd all like to try it."

"Excellent." Pascal raised his empty glass, eyes swinging to Madeleine. "Well, bring it here, girl. Hurry up, now." His head shook with his booming laugh. "If she had any intelligence, she would have served your wine first," he said to Caroline.

She bristled. "It's not her fault. She didn't know."

Gabriel's eyes rolled apologetically up to Madeleine's as she sloshed Caroline's family port into his glass, but she refused to meet his gaze. Better not to toss fuel onto the inferno raging in Pascal's face every time he looked at her.

The evening went on in a whirlwind of chatter and the clink of crystal. Madeleine did her best to keep her hands busy, only allowing a few stolen glances Gabriel's way when Pascal was otherwise entertained. The ardor in her master's sky-blue eyes weakened her resolve to steel herself against him. His gaze burned into her even when she tried to warn him to look away.

61

"Your father tells me you recently had tea with the empress," Pascal said to Caroline over the last few bites of pots de crème.

"Yes." Caroline's headband glittered as she nodded. "She was delightful. Very demure."

Pascal grunted. "It's a shame the emperor is busy on foreign soil." His attention switched to Gabriel. "Have you ever had occasion to meet him?"

"I regret that I have not, Uncle."

"Hmmm," he said, almost beneath his breath. "Strange to have two such distinguished families under one roof and yet nobody here has yet met our leader."

Madeleine nearly burst with laughter at the smirk on Gabriel's lips as he stared into his empty plate. Would his uncle believe it if he spoke the truth and told him the servant woman he'd insulted all night had not only met Napoleon, but saved his life? Certainly not.

Désirée caught the play between them and thumped her knuckles on the table. "I say it's high time to move this gathering to the drawing room, shall we?"

The shuffle of shoes on the floral rug filtered past her as Madeleine bent to retrieve the Clements' soiled dishes. Her feet ached from standing so long, and all she could envision as she piled forks atop her stack of plates was dipping her toes into the château's moat.

Muscles burning, she turned to leave and yelped as she nearly collided with a tall figure. Her vision focused, spearing her with dread. There, standing before her like a planted tree, was Pascal. His narrowed eyes ripped through her, tearing flesh until they reached her bones.

"I have just one question," he said. "How long has my nephew been in love with you?"

Seven

"I —" Madeleine gripped the dishes in tremulous hands, their bone china faces starting to clatter. The dining room suddenly felt like the inside of Georgette's iron soup pot. Her cotton dress clung to her, cleaving to her damp skin. Madeleine took a step back and bumped into a dining chair. "I don't know where you—"

"*Don't* lie to me, girl." Pascal's barked order stilled her. In two commanding strides, he was over her, his towering frame trapping her against the empty table. "I saw the two of you, grinning at each other all night, *touching* when you thought no one was looking. If I didn't want to scandalize our guest, I would have tossed you out that window myself." His salt-and-pepper head indicated the wall of sash windows beyond.

Her fingers now juddering beyond her control, Madeleine pivoted sideways enough to deposit the china on the table. Allowing a moment to collect herself, she sucked in a breath through her nose and tried to think of something, *anything* that might explain their behavior. Yet when she turned back, his angered, ruddy face thrust her words back down her throat.

"I could understand if my nephew's interest in you existed only to fulfill his lust," he said, his hawk-like eyes slithering down her.

"What man hasn't bedded a servant or two in his youth?" Coldness entered his dark gaze, a promise that she would never mean anything. "But no. This is so much more than that. Gabriel is convinced that he loves you. It was written across his foolish face every time he looked at you tonight." His thick nose snarled, as if the very idea repulsed him.

From deep within, a fire erupted. How many times this week had she been told she mattered as nothing but a body to warm a man's bed? Madeleine stood taller, her chin lifting despite the fear still knotting her middle. "And what if I love him, too?"

Pascal chortled mockingly, his rounded belly quaking. "Oh, that really is quite amusing. Come, now." His head angled, his lips pursing. "A woman like you sees only opportunity in a man like my nephew. How clever of you to try and rise above your station, to try and *be* someone the world actually lends a second glance to. I might admire you if you weren't the very dirt beneath my shoes."

Madeleine's teeth clenched in her closed mouth, her quickened breaths rushing through flared nostrils. She wanted to scream at him, to beat her fists on his ornamented chest and tell him he'd never rend the bond of love she shared with Gabriel. But glaring into his face now, so close the stench of his tobacco blanketed her skin, she had no rebuttal. Hadn't she sought out Gabriel for this very purpose—to seduce him into supplying her riches beyond her dreams? The cold irony of it nauseated her.

"Now, I'm going to say this once, so listen carefully," Pascal said, his mouth a stern line. "You will end whatever dalliance you have with my nephew at once. You will encourage him to marry Caroline Allair. You will stay as far away from him as possible at all times, and you will *not* lead him astray again."

She stared into the yellowed, false teeth beneath his curling lips. "Or *what*?"

His brows narrowed, his mouth lifting wickedly. "Or I will kill you in your sleep."

The truth of his threat emptied from every pore of his weathered skin and yet Madeleine couldn't help but scoff. "I lived through a revolution, monsieur," she said, her voice growing in confidence. "Do you really think you can frighten me with death?"

Pascal searched her face, his devilish eyes shining like two wells of black ink. "Perhaps not your own." He paused a second, like his mind still churned with ideas. Then his expression transformed to stone. "If you do not end your affair with Gabriel now, then I will kill *him*."

His promise plunked into her gut like a stone drifting to the bottom of a lake. *Kill Gabriel?* The very thought, even if she'd harbored it at one time, flung chills down her limbs and spine. Her blood ran cold. She'd sooner open her own veins than see him harmed.

"You couldn't do that." She hunted the plains of his face. "Not to your own flesh and blood."

"I assure you, girl—I can, and I *will*." Pascal's chest broadened, his hateful gaze unrelenting. "This alliance with Compte Allair will bring me hundreds of acres and an immense amount of power. But make no mistake. This barony is my home, my ancestral right. I will gladly seize it back from my brother's selfish children if you force my hand. With no heirs, it would only take one"—he held up a finger, then another—"two deaths. Then everything you see is mine."

Madeleine scrunched herself against the chair back, gulping the bile climbing her throat. Gabriel's rich baritone drifted down the hall, mingled with Désirée's sweet laughter. Her heart stampeded against her chest wall. Her throat collapsed on itself. How could she put either of them in danger, even for a moment? This madman would stop at nothing to see his plans flourish.

Before she could finish her thought, his fingers clamped on her chin. She tried to withdraw, but his fingernails drove painfully into her skin. Madeleine's world rattled in delirious frenzy but the face leering back remained cool, calculated, *murderous*.

"Do we have a deal?" he asked.

Through the fog, she could hear only one reverberated response. "Yes, monsieur." *Yes, I will save the man I love, even if it means forsaking him.*

"**M**addy, what is it? Why are we in such a rush?" Cecile's breath hastened as she sprinted to keep up.

With a furtive glance down the dual staircases, Madeleine raced across the corridor, her boots thumping the marble. Pascal had just joined the others in the parlor. They might have only moments before Caroline expected her help undressing. Without bothering to answer her friend, Madeleine aimed herself at a small door at the hallway's end and blasted toward it.

"Did you bring the lantern?" she asked between breaths, one side below her ribcage already beginning to ache.

Cecile held up the iron and glass item in question. "Yes, but I don't see why we'll need it in the house—"

Already, Madeleine had snatched it from her, seizing a candle from the sconce on the wall and lighting the wick inside. A flame sparked to life, glowing orange within the four glass panels. Madeleine lifted it high in one hand while grabbing the door's wooden handle with the other.

The ancient door groaned as if awakened rudely from a long winter's nap. Clutching a fistful of skirts, Madeleine began the steep ascent up the stairway before them. Every stair creaked beneath her weight, threatening to give way.

Behind her, Cecile pushed her hands against both walls. "I don't know if I like this. There's a reason we never go up here."

"It's just an attic, Cecile." Yet even as she said it, the wind outside howled, knocking the shutters against the house in an ominous rhythm.

"An attic of a very old house where the ghosts have most likely congregated to murder anyone who trespasses."

"If there are ghosts in this house, wouldn't they choose to live in the most lavish of rooms, rather than a stinky old attic?" Madeleine slowly propelled the door at the top of the staircase open, a phantom-like squeal issuing from its rusty hinges.

The small space flooded with light as Madeleine stretched to her tiptoes and hung their lantern on a hook in the ceiling's center. Streams of yellow candlelight thrust away the shadows, illuminating a room crammed with dusty bookshelves and forgotten chests. In the corners, items had been piled above their heads—blankets, pillows, decorative brass—all diffusing the musty scent of mildew.

"A rich man's graveyard," Cecile said with a shiver, buffing her upper arms with her crossed hands. "Tell me again why we had to come up here?"

Madeleine looked at her through the murky light, biting back her tears. "Because it's the only place in the house we can talk alone. Even in the servants' quarters, Georgette or Brigitte could overhear."

Cecile's braided red hair shimmered as her head angled. "Maddy, what's wrong? You look like a ghost yourself, your skin is so pale." Stepping forward, she brushed the unruly hair from Madeleine's face, her hand falling to her shoulder.

Within the dank, forgotten walls of the château's attic, Madeleine told her everything: how Pascal had cornered her in the dining room, how he'd threatened to take Gabriel and Désirée's lives. How Caroline made a more perfect mate for Gabriel in every way. She even divulged the part of her past she'd learned at the Black Lion—that they'd all trusted a liar, a sinner, a woman filled with such malice, she'd wished death upon their master.

Her knees giving way, Madeleine collapsed with a thud onto a carved cedar trunk and stirred up a cloud of dust. "I have to leave here." She moaned, rubbing her face with her outstretched fingers. "I have to go before I make his life any worse."

Cecile had listened with rapt attention, her luminous emerald eyes considering every word. Now, she knelt before the trunk. "You know that isn't the answer. You can't leave him alone with his uncle—not after what Pascal has told you." Her head wagged. "You can't abandon him to your brother's devices, either. One or the other of them will kill him."

Her vision crystallized with tears, Madeleine sniffed. "What am I supposed to do, then? I've spent the last few months trying to save him, and now he's buried deeper than I ever imagined." Her gaze sauntered to the miniature window, its dirty panes affording a view of the blustery twilight. "Gabriel Clement is nothing but trouble to love."

Fingers gently squeezed hers. "But you love him anyway," Cecile spoke the words on her heart.

"Yes." Madeleine pivoted back to her, droplets streaming down her cheeks and dribbling from her chin. "Sometimes I wish so desperately that I didn't, but I could no sooner live without breath than deny my love for him."

Cecile's lips arched faintly. "Then you will survive this. Forget about your past and who you once were. Now you are a woman willing to sacrifice anything for the people you hold dear."

The wind wailed again, rushing down the hilly terrain and crashing against the stone house. Madeleine stared down at their entwined hands, the thick gray cotton of her work dress. Was she really the heroic person Cecile described, or had it all been for show? Pascal's words, the chilling feel of his fingers on her chin, still raised gooseflesh on her arms. He'd meant to rile her. He'd wanted the sickening twinge in her stomach to grow until she lost her will to fight.

Just the thought rammed her anger to the surface again. Dropping Cecile's comforting grip, Madeleine launched up and stormed to the doorway. "*How* could a person be willing even to say such despicable things?" She whirled, pacing back to her friend.

"You should have seen him, Cecile. The sheer glee in his eyes as he sentenced me to keep away from the man I love."

Rising, Cecile crossed her arms over her torso. "I'm not surprised. I had him pegged the minute I saw him. Or rather, the minute he shoved his noxious shoes in my face for cleaning." Her fingertip tapped her jawline. "Perhaps this isn't the crisis you imagine. Have you thought of going straight to the baron with the information? Surely he will take your word over this uncle he hasn't seen in a decade."

"Surely he will chalk it up to one of his uncle's whims," Madeleine said as she heatedly paced, her boots hammering the loose floorboards. "He feels he owes Pascal so much simply for being his family. He will never take his threats seriously. And besides"—her fingers splayed on either side, flinging spidery shadows on the wall—"I can't take the chance that Pascal is bluffing. He could hurt Gabriel or Désirée, *both* of them."

Cecile shook her head ruefully. "Pascal Clement, Raphael, Henri. How wicked a family roamed these halls before our time?"

"And now we must pay the price for their crimes. All of us." Her frustration at a boiling point, Madeleine halted before the trunk she'd used as a seat and kicked it with a guttural grunt. The force of her swing capsized the heavy wooden box, crashing it against the floorboards and spilling its contents into the layer of dust.

"Oh, no." Plunging to her knees, Madeleine hurriedly gathered an armful of papers and trinkets. "They're bound to catch us up here now with the racket that must have made."

Together, the women righted the trunk and stuffed it again with its former valuables. Letters passed through Madeleine's hands, damaged toys, handkerchiefs laced with the spicy odor of cedar. A host of family memorabilia existed up here that the Clements most likely knew nothing about.

Then a particular item caught her eye, a tri-folded scrap of parchment scribbled in heavy ink writing. Plucking it from among the possessions she'd wedged inside the trunk, Madeleine examined the words to no avail. "Cecile," she said, drawing her attention. "What does this say?"

Leaning closer, Cecile squinted through the lantern light. "To my family upon my death."

Madeleine's fingers quivered as she turned it over and inserted her fingers beneath its already broken seal. Inside, two elegantly scrawled pages unfurled in her hands. Ignoring the script she couldn't read anyway, she scanned until she found the signature. "And this?"

Cecile carefully folded the pages in her hands, their edges already crumbling from age. Her brows scrunched as she concentrated in the waning light. When they relaxed again, the truth was etched across her face. "Henri Clement."

"The letter." There, scratched in bold black ink, were the words of Gabriel's ancestor, breathing air for the first time in years. Madeleine swallowed, her throat stinging as reality settled over her. "This could change everything."

Eight

The brittle pages of Henri Clement's letter to his heirs fluttered in Madeleine's trembling fingers. Holding it to her bosom, she climbed the stairs from the servants' quarters and rounded the bend to the hall leading to the salon. The afternoon sun poured in from every window, bathing the glossy plank flooring in radiant light. Madeleine drew a cathartic breath through her nose, Georgette's cinnamon and clove potpourri rushing through her senses.

Her fate had been twisted in this letter before. Years ago, when she made her money entertaining crowds of Paris's theater patrons, Henri Clement's ancient message to his family had fueled her. Madeleine could see herself standing under the sizzling lights, sashaying across the vast stage in the deep purple robes of a queen. Lifting her bejeweled fingers, she summoned the actors playing her subordinates to wait on her every whim.

Madeleine's rings and bejeweled clothes sparkled amid the quivering stage lamps as she faced her audience to deliver her final oratory. *You'll find him in the first row, two seats to your left from center stage,* Auguste's voice echoed in her mind. Her eyes swept the throng coolly, settling on a man in his forties with sandy close-cropped hair and thick sideburns. His lips twisted suggestively, and she knew she'd spotted her target. *He's an utter fool, a rogue. But he's the only one who will admit to seeing that letter. You must do everything in your power to find out what he knows.*

With her brother's command stampeding through her every muscle, Madeleine let her gaze tangle with the man's. She would deliver her every line to him, dripping with seduction. She would make him the star, the most honored among her admirers. She would leave the world behind if it meant opening a door to the Moon King's treasure.

The man's lips parted, his devilish brow hooking. He sat back and took her in, his thumb roving up and down his fingertips as his eyes wandered her body. Her lines came hard, forced. Madeleine gulped back the bile climbing her throat and kept on with her imposing dialogue. The past had delivered worse than this. She could withstand him. How many times she reminded herself before the lights dimmed and the theater swelled with applause, she could never have counted.

It took not ten minutes, sitting alone in the quiet of her dressing room, for the man she'd ensnared like a fish to come knocking at her door. He appeared out of breath when she answered, his broad chest rising frantically, his cheeks ruddy. "Pardon my intrusion, mademoiselle." He stood tall, his lips puckered as if she'd begged for a moment of his presence. "I am Marcel Toutain. Might I—come in for a moment? Perhaps we could share a drink?" He held up a bottle of champagne in one clenched fist.

With only the hint of a provocative smile, Madeleine opened the door wider and stood back to admit him. A wave of bay rum assaulted her as he passed, his leering eyes refusing to rip from the curves of her bodice. Directly after the final curtain call, Madeleine had rushed to her dressing room and shed her costume in favor of her undergarments. Over her petticoats and stays, she'd tossed on a silk robe that did little to mask her feminine qualities beneath.

"You are quite the actress," he said, his gaze roaming her open wardrobe crammed with clothes, lace, and feathers sticking out.

"I don't believe I've ever seen Catherine de' Medici played with such—fire." The word bounded off his darkened smirk, its meaning unmistakable.

"*Merci.* You are too kind." Madeleine lithely indicated a chair across from her vanity and turned away while Toutain seated himself. She had two champagne flutes ready for the occasion. *He's a drunk, and a lousy one at that,* Auguste had told her. *Get him drinking and he'll tell you anything. There is nothing he loves more than bragging about himself.*

Madeleine coerced her lips upward as she offered both glasses for Monsieur Toutain to fill. The champagne bubbled out and their glasses clinked together. Sitting at the vanity with her legs crossed and her robe falling loose off her shoulder, Madeleine allowed him to drink and to talk. Auguste was right. The more Toutain guzzled down his gullet, the louder and faster his stories came.

"That is fascinating," she said, clutching her half-drunk glass that she had yet to refill. "Tell me, Monsieur Toutain. What did she have to say to *that?*"

"If I remember correctly, she said, 'dear God, now you've done it'. Then she fainted face-first into the hedges." Toutain burst into a fit of laughter, slapping his knee and waving the empty bottle of champagne.

Employing her practiced acting skills, Madeleine joined in feigned laughter. Amid his grandiose tales, she'd spilled glass after glass into his crystal flute. Now, she reached beside her dressing table to retrieve a bottle of Merlot she'd stashed away. Would he find it odd that she had it there, just waiting for his company? Madeleine distracted him with a sly grin as she uncorked the new bottle and leaned in to replenish his glass.

"You must have some stories of your own, Mademoiselle LaRivière," he said, gaze tumbling down her throat. "You're a woman of the world, after all."

Her lips compressed as she set the bottle in front of her vanity mirror. *A woman of the world.* She was well aware that much of society thought of her as nothing more than a strumpet. Perhaps in this instance, she would use such fallacies to her advantage.

"Now, now." She wagged her finger. "I want to hear more about you." Her bottom lip caught in her teeth. "I want to hear adventure. Tell me your most *exciting* story."

Toutain smiled wickedly. "Well, that's quite an impossible task, my dear. You see, my entire life is an adventure."

"Name one," she purred.

"I once spent the night in the dressing room of the most beautiful actress in Paris."

Madeleine chuckled—a hollow, grating sound. "That does not count."

"I have attended a costume gala where the hostess wore nothing but a powdered wig."

"Interesting, but I know you can do better, monsieur."

Toutain stared into his glass, whirling the burgundy liquid. "I know where the Moon King's treasure is."

Her stomach flip-flopped. Madeleine gestured casually with her fingers, attempting to force down any outward sign of her excitement. "The Moon King? I've never heard of him."

Pride crept over his features as his spread fingers cast shadows on the wall. "He was a powerful baron who lived long ago. He buried one of the greatest treasures ever known to man where he thought no one would ever find it again."

Madeleine leaned closer, deciding to tempt fate. "So where is it?"

His eyelids fluttered, his throat visibly swallowing above his knotted cravat. "On a remote island in the Atlantic," he said, the confidence in his voice waning.

She threw her gaze to her mirrored image in the vanity as if dropping all interest. "So you don't know."

Toutain slammed his glass down, wine sloshing over the rim. "I saw the treasure's coordinates, written in the baron's own hand. I can't be expected to recall every number." Already, his words had begun to slur.

"And who would have shown you such a thing?" Madeleine retrieved a puff off her dressing table and began to powder her nose in talc.

From the corner of her eye, she could see him scrambling to remember, desperate to impress her. "He would only tell me his initials. J.C., I think it was. Some avaricious mariner trying to convince me in the back of a seedy tavern to shell out my hard-earned money for his ill-fated exploits."

Madeleine sighed in disinterest. "And I suppose you didn't give it to him."

Scoffing, he picked up his drink again. "Of course not. Not to a treasure seeker with nothing but a pair of initials and an associate called 'the nameless man'." His eyes rolled upward mockingly.

Despite the thrill leaping through her veins, Madeleine distractedly combed her brows with her fingertip. "The nameless man? What kind of a moniker is that?"

"Precisely." Toutain gulped a swig of Merlot and wagged his head. "He claimed his ancestors helped hide the treasure." His face scrunched. "*Ugliest* fellow I've ever seen. Huge, leering eyes and a long, hooked nose. He looked more like a crow than a man."

"He didn't say where in the Atlantic they hid it?" Madeleine asked, impatience biting at her. "Where did you meet these strange men?"

When her questions met with silence, she swung her gaze back to Marcel Toutain. For the first time, he studied her carefully, the lust in his eyes melting into suspicion. "Why do you want to know so badly?" His stare plummeted to the empty glass in his hand, his impaired mental cogs churning to life.

Madeleine had to reel him back in, quickly. Pivoting toward him, she let her robe slide farther down her bare shoulder. "No reason, really."

His eyes narrowed, prompting her to rise and strut several feet until she stood over him. Toutain let his gaze wander her openly as she bent and plucked the flute from his grasp, discarding it on the floor. Easing onto his lap, she felt the tension dissolve from his every muscle. "I just wanted to picture it, is all." Her eyes looked straight into his, feigned innocence teeming from them.

The predator reentered his face as his grin tilted. "I doubt you've ever been there. The docks in Bordeaux are no place for a fine lady like yourself."

"I can't say that I have." The stench of his liquored breath impaled her.

Madeleine's stomach lurched as he lifted her arm to his mouth, laying a trail of slow kisses from her wrist to the inside of her elbow. "I'm weary of talking about other men." His impish grin deepened, transforming him into the Devil himself. "I'm weary of *talking*. My townhouse is only blocks from here. I can assure you, we'll be quite comfortable there."

"Of course," she said, compelling her rebellious lips upward. "I would like to share one more drink, if that's all right." Madeleine pushed off of him, collecting his glass and her own before spilling the last of the wine into them. Mindful to keep her back turned, she cautiously flicked back the base of her ring and scattered its powdered contents into Toutain's wine. Thanks to Auguste's purchase at the village apothecary and two bottles of alcohol, Toutain would soon be asleep in his chair.

Back in the Château des Rêve's gallery, Madeleine shook as the vision of her soiled past played out in her mind's eye. At what point she'd quelled her sinful nature, she couldn't yet pinpoint. But now, with the very pages in her hand she had once nearly sold her soul to acquire, none of it really mattered. She had a duty to perform.

Outside the salon's double doors, she could barely control the rhythm of her labored breath. Gabriel's broad voice drifted through, touching a smile to her lips. Then came Caroline's giggle and the booming cackle of the uncle he unwittingly trusted. Her stomach roiled. How could she give up everything she held dear just to placate him? Then the dismal answer echoed back, as it had so often since the night Pascal threatened her. *If I don't obey, I'll lose everything regardless.*

Madeleine gripped the silver door handle beneath her fingers a moment longer before she thrust it open, converging with her fate. All three pairs of eyes immediately lifted toward the intrusion. The trio sat in crimson slipper chairs around a tea table, cards strewn over it. Caroline held a pair of dice in her hand, posed as if ready to roll them.

"Madeleine." Gabriel spoke her name in a reverent tone, exciting her middle in ways she had commanded it not to.

"Forgive the imposition," she said, forcing her arid throat to speak. She looked past the annoyance on Pascal's wrinkled face to the man she'd come for. "Baron Clement, might I have a word?"

"Of course." Rising from their game, Gabriel glanced at his companions. "I won't be but a moment." His hand nearly met the small of her back as they passed through the outer doors, Pascal's expression of mingled haughtiness and suspicion trailing their every step.

While Gabriel turned to close the windowed door behind him, Madeleine wandered to a spot on the veranda safe from any prying eyes inside. Beyond the railing of carved stone, the moat trickled past them to the river. An expanse of lawn dotted in lush elm trees dazzled between the water's edge and the pastures, their abundant leaves dancing in the sunshine.

Drinking in the scent of lilies and primroses, Madeleine clutched the chilling rail. Gabriel's boots on the stone patio only quickened her thundering heartbeat. With a whispered prayer for strength, she pivoted toward him and gasped at his nearness. Madeleine drove a hand to his chest and stepped backward, colliding with the rail.

"There is but a curtain between us." Her cautious gaze flew to the salon doors, heat ramming to her cheeks. "Please, Baron. Behave yourself."

Gabriel cast her a slanted grin. "I am quite ready for this whole charade to be over." He lifted both hands in compliance. "But if you so insist, I shall practice my utmost decorum."

"*Merci.*" Madeleine looked at the toes of her work boots peeking out from her skirts. Every part of her wanted to find safety in his arms. With great effort, she hampered her feelings and extended the letter in her grasp. "Here. I have something for you."

Hooking an eyebrow, Gabriel let his fingers brush hers as he accepted the offering. "What could it be?" He lent her one last smile before his eyes fell to the paper, his brows promptly gathering as he took in the words. He glanced up. "Is this what I—" Shock overtook his features. "Where did you find this?"

"In the attic in an old chest."

After gingerly unfurling the pages, Gabriel scanned the letter, his light eyes zipping along every line until they landed at its conclusion. "Did you read this?" he asked finally.

Madeleine cocked her head, the absurdity of his statement clear on her pursed lips.

His open palm flopped in midair. "All right, did Cecile read this?"

"I will admit that curiosity got the better of me." She had deliberated only a handful of minutes before her mischievous friend had convinced her to delve in.

Gabriel's dark head shook. "Well, then you know." He shrugged. "It's nothing. No coordinates, no clues. My father was right all along."

Just as she had believed at first. "Oui, but do you notice anything strange about it?"

"The seal." His thumb moved over the red wax circle, broken across the middle. "It says Arcadia. This isn't the Clement family crest. I've never seen it before."

Madeleine leaned inward, catching a whiff of his musky cologne. "Look at the writing." She drew one pointed finger to the text of the letter, then the words etched on its outer layer.

Gabriel examined them closely before nodding. "You're right, they are written by a different hand." He held the two in the sunlight, the papers fluttering in the light breeze. "This one," he said, indicating the heavy script on the front. "This is Henri's writing. I've read enough of his journals. The other is familiar, but I cannot place it off hand."

Anticipation bubbled inside Madeleine to imagine the possibilities. "If someone went through the trouble to forge a letter, it stands to reason that the treasure might be real after all."

A dubious look had already settled across his proud brow. "Perhaps, but I would need a lot more evidence than this to believe it." He shot her a pensive smile. "The absence of the true letter doesn't mean it says what you think it does."

"But it certainly gives one reason to wonder."

"Aye, it does." Gabriel refolded the letter and tucked it in his waistcoat pocket. "Thank you, Madeleine. I'll do my best to try and identify the author of this letter."

Madeleine clasped her hands behind her back, suddenly wishing she could hop over the veranda and swim until the river carried her to the distant, battering ocean. "There—" Her voice choked. "There is something else I need to speak with you about." The roiling ache in her stomach screamed at her to stop while she still could, then Pascal Clement's insidious voice rang through her again. *Two deaths. Then everything you see is mine.*

"Come now, it can't be all that dire." Gabriel chuckled, trying to hook her downturned gaze with his.

Swallowing back her weakness, Madeleine met his gaze. She saw acceptance there, concern. How could she possibly tell him she didn't want his love? Knees wobbling, she steadied herself on the rail. "I have been thinking a great deal about the two of us. About Caroline." She paused, forcing herself to plunge ahead. "I think it will suit us all if you don't dismiss your uncle's proposition so quickly."

A trite laugh escaped him, though his brows cinched together. "I admit I don't always comprehend your jests, but this one I don't find the least bit of humor in."

Madeleine angled her head, attempting to display her sincerity. "I'm not jesting, Gabriel." Her stomach tautened at the confusion that glinted in his eyes. "Caroline is a good woman. I think she could make you happy."

Gabriel stared through her, his expression indecipherable. A light breeze blew past them, lifting his curly locks. He took several moments to study her as if still judging her sobriety. Then his voice came—wounded, raw. "How could she make me happy? She isn't *you*."

The words punched her square in the gut. Fortifying her resolve, Madeleine gazed into the green landscape beyond his head, her eyes roaming the hilly meadows and fields of lavender. "We can't keep pretending that we're suited for one another. You are a baron, and my parents were nothing but peasants."

"You know I don't care about that." His frustration groaned through his every word.

Madeleine hugged her arms as the wind whipped her hair into her face. "But society does. Think about the ridicule our children would endure, what *we* would have to face. You would have to explain why you married me for the rest of our lives."

"Blast what they think!" Redness had climbed up his clenched throat, spilling onto his face. A storm raged on his usually calm visage. "Do you think I am going to base my life decisions on the vain opinions of people I hardly know?" His look softened, the chest beneath his silk embroidered waistcoat still pumping. "I don't want any of that. I just want *you*." Eyes pleading, he reached out to tuck the rogue strands of her hair behind her ear.

His gentle touch pacified her. Madeleine locked her gaze with his, pulled in by the promise there, the intense longing. Then Pascal's wicked face flashed through her mind again and she recoiled. "Please—don't."

Gabriel stared at her, his fingers suspended in midair. Then realization dawned, trickling from his wrinkled brow to his flared nostrils and parted lips. "You don't *want* me anymore—is that what I am to understand?"

The pain in his eyes sliced through her. "Of course not, Gabriel." The words barely squeezed from her vocal cords. "Please, this isn't about that."

"Then, praytell, what is it about?" His voice rose, biting with anger. "How can I not be confused? Just last week, we were planning—" He paused, hunting her face. "Did my uncle speak with you?"

Her head shook desperately. "No, this is all me. This is my idea." Better he think such an awful lie than to place himself in the path of Pascal's vengeance. "I can leave if you'd like. I'd loathe my presence here to be a constant reminder." *But oh, how will I protect you if I'm gone?*

"No. I won't deprive you of your livelihood simply to protect my feelings."

Planting two open hands on his thin hips, Gabriel looked over the rolling countryside for several moments before speaking. The wind whistled and the robins tweeted in the branches over their heads, yet here below, the world stopped. His sullen eyes glistened when they found her again. "Everything in me is screaming at me to fall on my knees and beg you to reconsider." His square jaw tensed. "But it won't do any good, will it? You've already made your decision."

His defeated words rammed her emotions to the surface. She wanted to rush into his arms, to wrap herself in his warm hold and promise she would never depart from it. Yet she could feel the malicious glare searing through the curtains of the salon. Pascal would not release his talons until he had what he wanted or someone was dead. So she simply nodded, tears flooding her eyes and choking any decent response from her lips.

He drank her in for a minute longer before his shoulders lifted. "I suppose I shall leave you be, then."

Every step he took away from her as he languidly moved toward the house felt like an anchor lugging her downward, casting her to the bottom of the sea. Throwing one last glance over his shoulder, Gabriel disappeared behind the double doors. Madeleine grabbed her skirts and sprinted over the veranda. A broad set of steps led her to the stone bridge that traversed the château's moat. She raced across it, her tears flowing freely, her chest on fire. Soon, the meadow enveloped her, her boots pummeling the slick grass. She would run until she had numbed her body—and her heart.

Nine

The intricate dance of cello and violin reverberated off the château's walls, a welcome boost in tone from its usual silence. Everywhere one looked, the lavish papered walls and gilded trimmings had been splashed with spring. Garlands of rosebuds, peonies, and poppies adorned the hallways. Bouquets of lilies peppered the ballroom. Laughter and chatter bounded from room to room.

Blowing a strand of hair from her face, Madeleine weaved among the sea of guests with a tray in each hand. At least a hundred people churned around the house, sharing conversation over a glass of brandy, admiring the oil paintings, taking a turn on the dance floor. She had just finished hauling away the dinner plates and already her back and shoulders ached. Now, the enticing aroma of Georgette's confections filled the entrance to the ballroom as she plunked her trays onto the dessert table.

Gabriel's guests milling nearby swarmed to the display like a cloud of moths with rounded eyes and wetted lips. Madeleine presented fruit tarts and miniature cheesecakes, and the trays Cecile set down next offered mousse-filled pastries and petit fours. The beautiful selections Georgette had painstakingly arranged nearly disappeared within minutes. Madeleine absently rubbed a hand at her lower back, plastering on a smile despite the pangs radiating from her legs.

"Don't worry, Georgette and Brigitte should be along shortly with more," Cecile said, leaning close. "I've never seen people eat like this, the greedy misers. These trays alone had enough to satisfy them all had they taken just one."

Madeleine's gaze shifted warily to the guests standing within earshot. "Let them enjoy themselves. Most of them probably don't have a cook like Georgette at their beck and call."

Indeed, it did her heart good to see the château crammed with ordinary people. The aristocracy from neighboring lands attended, of course, but most of the baron's guests hailed from farms across Avance. Perhaps that's why she had worked with Désirée so tirelessly to make tonight a success. Those who toiled, not just those who inherited, basked in the merriment this evening.

"I'd wager *she* has a better one." Cecile motioned with a nod toward the archway that Gabriel, Pascal, Caroline, and her father had just passed through. "Even with all of that finery, she isn't half as lovely as you."

Madeleine shot her a warning look. "Stop it. You know she's beautiful, too." So beautiful it put a lump in her throat. Caroline's cap sleeve gown of peacock blue and silver brocade only enhanced her statuesque figure. Her blonde hair, knotted at the back and cascading in ringlets around her face, glittered as her diamond tiered headband caught the light. She and Gabriel, standing side by side in the midst of such a decadent party, looked like they belonged together.

"Can I help it if I feel the need to defend my friend?" Cecile bent to stack the dessert trays atop one another. "Everything was perfect before she waltzed in here, intent on stealing the baron's affections. She had better go right back where she came from, if you ask me."

"You mean, ever since Pascal came to Avance."

As if sensing his name on her lips, the man turned his face toward the pair. His ugly, bulging eyes raked over her once before reverting back to his conversation. Madeleine couldn't quite tell whether he met to ogle her or threaten her, but either way she felt demeaned.

"So good of you to join us, Comte," he was saying as they neared the refreshment table. "I had feared you would find yourself too busy this time of year to attend our country soirée."

"Nonsense," Caroline's father said, his gray head shaking. "As a grower myself, I know that farmers are the lifeblood of a man's holdings. I only wish Caroline and I were able to stay long enough to witness the spring planting."

Madeleine set to rearranging what few desserts still remained on her tray, ignoring the curious look Gabriel launched her way. Caroline had informed her days ago that the Planters' Ball would mark her return home, and Madeleine would not let Gabriel crawl back to her the moment his suitress had gone. No doubt, Pascal hoped for an engagement that very night.

"Of course, we would love for you to attend some of our festivals at home," Caroline said cheerily, her hopeful gaze falling on Gabriel. "Perhaps in the fall, when the valley is showered in autumn colors."

The baron opened his mouth to speak, but Pascal's voice overpowered his. "The summer would be even more ideal, I think. I have heard that the Loire Valley is unmatched under the warm sun."

Comte Allair chuckled. "Alas, it is beautiful all year long. You are welcome any time you wish to explore it."

"You heard the invitation." Pascal clapped Gabriel's back. "What say you, my boy?"

Cheeks reddening, Gabriel looked a moment at the drink in his hand before he forced a weak smile. "It would be an honor, Comte," he said with a dip of his head.

"The honor is mine, Baron Clement." Comte Allair beamed a broad smile, catching Gabriel and Caroline together in his approval. "You have been such a gracious host to my daughter, it is truly the least I can do for you."

"Oh, she is a delight." Pascal leaned toward the count and spoke behind his hand, his artificial friendliness nauseating Madeleine. "As has been watching the saplings of young love grow."

Gabriel stiffened. "Uncle, please."

Pascal shrugged a response. "'Tis nothing to be ashamed of, Gabriel. Take it from an old man like me. Enjoy the advantages of your youth while you still can." As if inspired, his gaze swept the ballroom beyond them, where couples whisked around the parquet floor. "Speaking of romance, perhaps Caroline would like to dance."

Lodging a look of irritation in his uncle's skull, Gabriel awkwardly turned to the blushing woman beside him. "Would you, Caroline?"

"Of course." Her shy smile shone down at him as he took her hand and bowed before her. Gabriel allowed one stray glance to skitter over Madeleine as they passed her, then let it tumble beneath the rhythm of his shoes as he led Caroline into the mass of whirling dancers.

"Don't just stand there gaping all night. The master isn't paying you to daydream."

Madeleine jumped at Georgette's brash voice, yanked from her dangerous tarrying into long-lost hopes. *"Désolée,"* she murmured, gathering the trays that Cecile had piled and handing them to her friend. The warm scent of freshly baked apples and cherries wafted to her as she helped Georgette and Brigitte lay out the new creations.

"Well." Georgette stood back to admire her work, swiping a wrist on her temple. Her hefty bosom rose and fell in labored breaths. "Cecile, Brigitte, go get the last of the desserts. I need to teach Madeleine a thing or two about serving the public."

Meeting the housekeeper's glare with a crooked smile, Madeleine returned to distributing her delectable sweets. Even in her advanced age, Georgette would never admit to being worn out. Instead, she took another breath and stood shoulder-to-shoulder with the younger maid, placing silver forks upon the tiny china plates and handing them out with a kind word.

As the lively waltz wore on and her interested patrons dwindled, Madeleine struggled not to watch the one person still commanding her thoughts. Instead, she focused on the quartet in the corner, their polished wooden instruments singing the notes of Haydn's "Quartet in G major". The elegant pull of the bow over the violin's neck mesmerized her, yet all too soon, she found her gaze wandering to the couple her mind refused to release.

Standing tall, Gabriel led Caroline around the dance floor in a triangular pattern with ease. His right hand grasped her gloved one, while he kept the left tucked behind his back. He wore a black cashmere tailcoat cut short in front, his chest sheathed in a high-collared shirt and crimson waistcoat. Despite her resolve to forget him, Madeleine couldn't deny the effect he still had on her. She almost neglected to breathe as she watched him warm in the grips of another woman.

Caroline giggled at something he said, tossing her head back. A hard knot grew in Madeleine's stomach as Gabriel joined in Caroline's laughter. Jealousy raged within against her most stalwart will. *She* wanted to be the woman safe in his arms, the woman who shared his most intimate jests. Her breath came hard, as if two unseen hands dug their thumbs into her throat.

Then her body went numb as she realized her desperate gawking at him hadn't gone unnoticed. Still revolving Caroline effortlessly around, Gabriel had locked his gaze on Madeleine. Turn after turn, he aimed his stare back at her like a ghostly force had cemented it to her face. Warmth trickled down her arms and into her frozen fingers. Her cheeks filled with color, her lips fiercely begging to curl.

"You need to come back to Earth, girl." Bemused, she turned to see Georgette also watching Caroline and the baron. "Get your head out of the clouds."

"I—" Madeleine cleared her throat. "I am here with you, Georgette. I can assure you."

"No, you are not." Georgette plopped a hand on her robust hip. "I see that look in your eye and it is dangerous. You may think his attraction to you means something. That he'll somehow fall head over heels in love with you and forget his duty to the Clement house. Trust me, he won't."

The words stung more than she expected them to. "Forgive me, but I don't believe you know what you're saying." What did Georgette know about love, anyway?

"I know more than you think." Georgette had sidled closer, emanating the scent of yeast and flour. "You are *nothing*, Madeleine Bertrand. The sooner you make peace with that, the better. Look around you." Her plump wrist swept the ballroom. "The members of nobility here—they will never see you as an equal. They all know you are lesser. It's ingrained in them. In *him*." Her chin thrust out to indicate Baron Clement, still staring in earnest their way. "He may look at you in lust, but he will never look at you the way he sees Mademoiselle Allair—a true lady. You are nothing but a passing fancy."

Nausea seizing her, Madeleine stepped backward. Her vision teetered, everything around her awhirl. The shimmering walls and frescoed ceilings closed in on her like the crags of a fathomless cave. She stole a glance at Gabriel to see that he had halted his dance and dropped Caroline's hand. Georgette was right. She could never hope to be good enough for him, and the longer she stood here confusing him, the more danger she put him in.

Madeleine grasped two handfuls of her heavy black skirts and reeled toward the back stairwell. Painful breaths wheezed from her lungs as she darted across the swirled marble floor. Pascal's wicked glare judged her from among the milling throng. Several guests shot her looks of surprise as she raced past them. "Madeleine," she heard Gabriel call from behind her, but she kept on. "Madeleine, wait."

Chest heaving, she slowed at the base of the stairs, one hand on the carved wooden banister. The baron's command made any other action an act of defiance in such a public space. She turned to him, head drooping and eyes pinned to the floor.

"I'm sorry, Baron. I didn't mean to cause such a stir. I shall comport myself properly in the future."

Gabriel glanced over his shoulder before moving closer, into the shadows of the stairwell. "Are you all right, Madeleine?" His fingers flinched as if to touch her, then retreated beside him.

"Oui, I am fine." She forced herself to nod, to let her eyes entangle with his worried gaze. "This is all just harder than I imagined."

His jaw clenched, his voice lowering. "Say the word and we can end this. I will tell her father tonight—"

"No." The sudden word quieted him. "No, it's just an adjustment—that's all." Her trembling fingers covered her middle. "You and Caroline—you look perfect out there. Like you were meant to find each other." Did it hurt worse that she spoke the truth?

He stepped closer, so close that his amber and vanilla spiced cologne showered over her. The tiny flecks of green in his light eyes sparkled as his gaze inched over her face, anchoring on her lips. "I already found *you*. There is not room in my heart for you both."

His nearness launched warm shivers down her extremities. Madeleine swallowed, battling the urge to fold herself within his embrace. "You will change your mind with time. I know you will."

When his lips opened to protest, she backed away. "I can't stay. Cecile needs me in the kitchen." With that, she bound around the banister and down the stairs, ignoring both his attempts to call her back and the prodding of her own heart.

Night had long fallen and the moon climbed high over the treetops by the time the Planters' Ball waned into a few scattered guests stumbling toward the exits. Like a bunch of scurrying rats, servants bustled around the château, lugging away trays full of dirty glasses or rearranging furniture. The kitchen clanged with the din of copper pots being scrubbed in sudsy water.

Madeleine ascended the back stairs, her arms weighed down by two enormous wooden buckets of water. Through the window, she caught glimpses of townsfolk merrily chatting about their evening as their boots crunched the drive. The earthy scent of moss and grass traveled on the breeze, a comfort amid the trials storming within.

The burden of her cumbersome load hardly allowed Madeleine to traverse the upstairs hall. When at last she reached Caroline's door, her forearms burned and her shoulders ached. After plunking her buckets down on the hardwood floor, she knocked softly. "Mademoiselle Allair?"

"Yes, Madeleine. Please come in."

Her trepidation at seeing Caroline again after her behavior that night quickly vanished with her struggle to lift the teeming buckets again. "Cecile—said you—requested a bath." Her second bucket barely made it across the threshold, scraping along the polished floor as she dragged it in against its will.

"Please." Stationed at the open window, Caroline hardly seemed to notice her. Instead, she gazed down the winding drive, where a string of carriage lanterns bobbed into the murky distance.

Madeleine hauled the porcelain tub from the corner, silently cursing the muscles protesting against its weight. The water she had heated over the kitchen fire rose in swirls of steam as she emptied it into the tub. Returning to the vanity, she selected a bar of cassia-scented soap, a brush, and two small terry cloth towels to set out on the table she had positioned beside the tub.

Seemingly lost in her musings, Caroline limply allowed Madeleine to unknot the silver ties of her dress and lift the beautiful ensemble over her head. She held her breath as the maid undid the strings of her stays, then put a hand to Madeleine's wrist when she moved to discard her shift.

"I'll do it. Thank you, Madeleine." A sadness had overcome Caroline's usually jovial face, a deep sort of melancholy.

Madeleine stepped away, her gut twisting to realize she was probably responsible. "Perhaps I should leave you to soak for a while."

"No, please stay." Caroline kicked her undergarments aside and eased herself into the hot water, an immediate look of calm descending on her features as she leaned back and closed her eyes. "There now, that's better."

"Did you dance your feet into an angry condition?" Madeleine bent to retrieve the clothes strewn on the floor, setting Caroline's narrow-toed slippers neatly beside her chest. "These shoes don't look like the easiest to dance around in."

Caroline let out a blithe laugh. "Women's designers certainly don't aim for comfort." Her eyes slipped open again, finding Madeleine folding her silk undergarments by the mirror. "But I had a lovely time tonight. These lands are filled with truly good people."

"I'm glad." Madeleine could say nothing else before a lump materialized in her throat. This woman deserved every bit of happiness life could possibly bring her way. How could she have stolen precious moments from her time with Gabriel? Madeleine busied her hands stacking and straightening Caroline's clothes in her cedar chest before guilt could squeeze the very life out of her.

"Madeleine?" Caroline's sweet voice stilled her. "Might we speak for a moment, the two of us? There is something I feel we need to discuss."

Hands like icicles, Madeleine revolved on her heel to face Caroline. "Of course." It took every bit of strength inside to pull a chair from the writing desk and set it beside the tub. Somehow, she felt like a schoolchild in need of a scolding, even as she looked into the kindest eyes she'd ever beheld.

Caroline forced a stiff smile, then grabbed the bar of soap and stared at it in her palm. "I want to be frank with you. From our time together, I can see that you are a genuine person. I don't believe you'd ever wish to hurt or to deceive."

"I—" The words stuck in Madeleine's throat. "I thank you for that." If only Caroline could peel back the curtain of her past and peer into the true depths of her depravity.

"If you were to ask my father, he'd tell you that a woman my age has no room to be choosy about a mate." She sighed, the bathwater swirling around her as she folded her knees in. "But I say a woman must guard her heart, no matter her age. So I need to know if I'm going back home tomorrow to pine after a man who could one day be my husband, or a man who will never return my affections."

Madeleine shivered, stunned by the vulnerability in Caroline's gaze as their eyes met amid the steamy air. "I cannot lie to you." Her arms hooked protectively around her body. "The baron and I did share a romantic bond, but it's all in the past." Perhaps if she repeated it enough out loud, she might convince herself.

"Are you sure?" Caroline asked, dragging her wet bar of soap up the length of her arm. "You can't deny the way he looked at you tonight. The way he *looks* at you any chance he gets. I'd have to suffer blindness not to notice as much."

A warm wind blew through the open window, fanning the drapery and prickling Madeleine's skin. Outside, the bullfrogs' nightly song chirped above the rumble of carriage wheels trundling down the drive. She set her chin atop her fingers and truly thought about Caroline's question. Either possibility drove her to terror or misery.

"I don't know," she said at last. "Baron Clement is a grown man with a will of his own, and as much as I wish I could steer his feelings in the matter, I cannot." Leaning inward, she angled her head. "I can assure you, however, that I will not pursue him. The barriers between us are too high. I have every faith that with time, his heart will heal enough to see you the way he looks at me now."

Cheeks flushed, Caroline played at the bubbles jouncing along the surface of her bath. "My pride hurts to say it, but I certainly hope you're right." Her lips stretched thoughtfully. "I like him, perhaps too much for my own good. He's so unlike the other men I've met. He's interested in medicine, science, philosophy. I'll wait for him, but only if there exists a real chance that he is serious about me."

Even as her gut wrenched to imagine Gabriel loving someone else, Madeleine reached a comforting hand to the tub's ceramic rim. "Of all the people I could ever envision him courting, *you* are the perfect match. You must give him time. He's a recluse. He isn't used to other humans."

Caroline shared a chuckle at the observation. "I suppose I can relate to that." Drenched tendrils of hair clung to her neck as she nodded resolutely. "Very well, then. I shall give him another chance, if he wishes to take it. Perhaps I'll write to him when I arrive home."

Bittersweet joy mingled with Madeleine's heartache. At least Gabriel would be safe with Caroline. At least he'd have a good woman by his side who would give him everything she so desperately wished she could provide. Standing, she reminded herself again that this stabbing pain within her was but a temporary ailment. When she saw him in his new life, happy again despite the obstacles life had hurled his way, the agony of losing him would dissolve. Her yearning would fly away on the wind.

Just as she turned to fetch Caroline's nightclothes, a voice halted her. "Thank you, Madeleine." Caroline smiled despite the worried lines between her brows. "Thank you for being honest with me. I will not forget your kindness."

Ten

The midmorning sun cast warming rays on the kitchen's walnut oak table as Madeleine bent over it, pounding and kneading at the dough she had concocted. Sweat beaded at her hairline, her lower back screaming in protest, but on she worked, folding and shaping. She couldn't read or write. She didn't know the first thing about the ways of the gentry like Caroline or Désirée did. But for all the world, life had at least taught her how to make a proper brioche.

Pausing to allow herself a breath, Madeleine swiped a wrist over her forehead before forging ahead. Her fingers squeezed, her knuckles popped, and the savory odor of yeast filled the kitchen. The image of Caroline in Gabriel's arms surfaced again, torturing her. Leaning into her dough, she pushed her palms to the wood until she thought the table might buckle.

Since that night, the days had meandered by like a funeral procession. Every morning, she woke from agonizing dreams of him into a bleak reality where their love would never exist again. Every day, she threw herself into cooking, baking, laundering the sheets, scrubbing the floors, keeping as far from him as she could. With a streak of dread, she pictured the time she would be cooking for *them*, laundering *their* sheets, learning to love *their* children.

"That looks like a fine brioche," Georgette said as she approached, eyeing Madeleine's creation like an art connoisseur might admire an oil painting. "You must teach me how you get your dough so light. I loathe to admit that mine needs work."

From her spot at the butter churn, Brigitte sat up straight. "I would love to learn, as well. Would you teach me, Madeleine?"

"Keep up with your work, girl." Georgette snapped her fingers at the inquisitive young maid. "When I decide you're ready to help with the cooking, you will know."

Madeleine tossed a sympathetic look the girl's way. "I would be happy to show you both. It really isn't all that hard. I must have made it a thousand times when I worked in the bakery in Paris." Those were such lonely days, and yet sometimes she yearned for their simplicity.

"I would be grateful for the instruction." Reaching high, Georgette pulled a silver tray from a shelf on the wall and began filling it. "I must say, I am impressed with your work ethic of late. You had me worried that you'd never amount to much, but for the last few weeks, you've put in double the effort."

Remaining silent, Madeleine watched the old woman set a willow pattern tea cup and saucer on the tray, then a small plate loaded with biscuits and fruit. Could Georgette have once been like her—plagued with dreams she could never fulfill? The thought sent an icy shiver down her spine. She would rather die young than become the cranky, work-obsessed woman standing before her.

"Brigitte, are you nearly done with that butter?" Georgette asked, cleaving Madeleine from her ponderings. "It's time to take the master his morning tea."

"Oh, Georgette, might I do it today?" Madeleine wiped her oil-soaked fingers on her apron, then yanked it over her head.

Georgette lifted a curious brow. "I thought you'd requested Brigitte serve the baron his tea from now on. Something about being of better use down here?" Even as she feigned ignorance, her shrewd eyes said she knew Madeleine's true reasons.

"I know, but there is something I must ask of him. Just for today."

"He hardly ever touches the food anyway," Brigitte said. "Drinks only half his tea on a good day."

"That doesn't give us leeway to shirk our responsibilities," Georgette said with a scowl. "I suppose it won't hurt to alter the routine for one day, as long as you don't forget your place."

"Never." Madeleine accepted the tray from Georgette, butterflies flitting around her middle. She had barely seen the baron in the last few weeks. Cecile had assumed her duties in the dining room, and every time she heard footsteps in the house, Madeleine darted into another room for cover. She hoped their separation would help them both to move on, but even more, she feared facing him again after their last encounter.

Madeleine's fingers trembled as she climbed the stairs and traversed the hallway, Gabriel's teacup and saucer jangling. The cathartic blend of lemon and camomile did nothing to calm her agitated nerves. Part of her wanted nothing more than to declare her love for him again, while the other half begged her feet to run away forever.

He barely acknowledged her with a grunt when Madeleine's knuckles rapped on his door. Despite her hard work tidying his study, their weeks apart had overthrown her efforts. Books were piled all around, papers haphazardly strewn across the floor and bookshelves. The beautiful mahogany of his desk was splashed with ink, fingerprints and broken quill pens everywhere.

Oblivious to her presence, Gabriel sat hunched over his desk, his pen flying across the page. A stack of open books lay beside him, diagrams of the body outlined amid the text. His clothes looked soiled and stained, his rebellious hair unbrushed. His square jaw was peppered with the beginnings of a beard.

"I've brought you your tea, Baron," Madeleine squeezed from her throat, driving his head up.

"Madeleine." He still spoke the name with reverence, as if she hadn't stomped on his heart like a child's toy.

Madeleine ambled into the room, praying her legs would keep her upright long enough to deliver her offering. Setting the tray atop his desk, she never let her eyes leave his tortured gaze. He had deep lines beneath his eyes, fatigue lacing his face.

"Thank you." He raked a hand through his disheveled hair. "I had expected Brigitte. Is she ill?"

"No. I requested to serve you today, my lord." At the gleam of hope in his gaze, Madeleine hurried on. "You see, Désirée has been away these past few weeks and she asked that we catch up in the music room this afternoon. Georgette said I must have your approval to visit her."

"Oh, I see." Gabriel's forlorn gaze dove to his lap. "Of course you may visit with Désirée. You may see her whenever you like."

"I thank you, Baron." Madeleine meant to go, but somehow her feet refused to carry her away. The sight of him, obviously broken because of her, twisted her gut. It was so much easier to pretend only her heart mourned for what could have been between them.

"Will Caroline be visiting soon?" she asked. "I do hope to see you happy again."

Raising his weary eyes, Gabriel only stared in return. His wilted shoulders and labored breath spoke for him.

"Perhaps I could bring you a new shaving brush and razor," she said. "I can help if you—"

"Is there something else I can help you with, Madeleine?" he asked, quieting her. When she ruefully shook her head, he focused back on his work as if she no longer stood before him, aching to share just one conversation.

Swallowing back her tears, Madeleine found her footing and left him alone again.

"It feels so good to be home again." Désirée led Madeleine into the music room, a welcome sight in her high-waisted lavender gown. Her recent jaunt into the local impoverished villages had tinted her skin a shade darker. Pascal had called her endeavors foolish, but Madeleine couldn't help noting how happy her friend looked whenever she returned from such an excursion.

With an added bounce in her step, Désirée crossed the room and seated herself on a recamier of royal blue velvet. One elbow resting on the sofa's arm, she neatly curled her legs behind her. Madeleine chose a matching tufted armchair and settled into it, well aware she could never make lounging look so graceful.

"This was my favorite room as a child," Désirée said, her blue eyes roving lovingly across the sunlit space. Beside them, a fortepiano of cherry wood commanded the entire corner. Beyond a circular floral rug, a gilded harp sat in quiet elegance next to a guitar and a lyre, each on their own stands. "I used to love to bring my toys in here and just play on the floor, listening to my mother make beautiful music."

Madeleine gazed with her into the vision of her childhood. "Your brother told me about her skill on the harp." She glanced around at the other instruments. "Did she play all of these, as well?"

"Every one." Désirée looked at the harp with a sad smile. "Our mother could play any instrument she picked up, but the harp—that was her favorite. She would sit here for hours, singing to the walls, pouring out her heart." Her blonde head shook. "I only regret that I didn't learn from her when I had the chance."

"We never quite realize what we have until it's out of our grasp, do we?" Hadn't Madeleine herself neglected her father's reading lessons and found herself an illiterate adult? What she wouldn't give to have a second shot at it.

Lost in distant memories of her scholarly father, Madeleine flinched when she noticed Désirée keenly watching her. "It's unnerving when you look at me like that, Désirée," she said, crossing her ankles below her black skirts. It usually meant she had something to say.

"I'm only curious. It's interesting that you would say that after the situation I walked into today."

Cheeks flaming with color, Madeleine focused on the hands working in her lap. "That isn't the same."

"Oh, really?" Désirée's recamier groaned as she shifted her weight forward. "When I left, you two were closer than a pair of turtledoves in a little love nest. Now, I come back to find you not speaking, and Gabriel looking like he crawled out of a cave. I admit I was caught up in preparations for the Planters' Ball, but I hadn't expected the world to turn upside down in that time."

Madeleine bit her lip, daring to look back into Désirée's searching eyes. What could she say that would make any sense? "We had a disagreement—an irremediable disagreement."

"So serious a difference of opinion that you would throw your relationship away?" Désirée clicked her tongue. "Madeleine, we walked together through the Guardians' plot to overthrow Napoleon. I saw how much Gabriel loved you and how much you loved him back. What you would sacrifice for his well-being."

That sinking feeling had grabbed hold again—the slow descending dread that promised Madeleine she'd never escape it. She *did* love him, more than she could ever put into words. She loved him enough to leave him be.

"I wish I could explain, but it would only bring harm." To Gabriel *and* his passionate sister.

Désirée released a disappointed sigh. "I wish you could, too. My heart was at peace knowing that my brother had found the true love of his life and now—now I find him hulled up in his office again, writing letters to this Caroline Allair." She gestured with her arm, seeming not to notice the effect her revelation had produced in Madeleine. "I adore the woman, but he doesn't love her like he loves you. He made that clear during our breakfast this morning."

Jaw clenched, Madeleine swallowed back her sudden emotion. "What did he say?" As if she really wanted to know. As if she needed to open that wound wider.

"Nothing. He never does." Désirée's slender fingers drummed her bare arm. "I asked him what had possibly gone wrong with the two of you and he would only say it was not his choice. Then he went silent for the rest of the meal and jumped to attention any time he heard footsteps in the hall or saw movement outside the window." Her head angled in petition. "He's still captivated by you, Madeleine. Isn't there any way you could work out whatever happened?"

Madeleine wagged her head, forcing words from her dry throat. "I'm afraid not. This is not something I decided lightly. And I didn't throw him over in hopes of reeling him back in."

"Of course not; that isn't like you." Désirée reached out, severing the space between them. "But I had so looked forward to calling you 'sister'."

Their fingers entwined on the arm of the recamier. "You can still call me 'friend'. I'm not leaving here, as much as it tempts me." At least not until she knew Pascal was too far away to hurt the family she adored ever again.

"Good." Swinging her legs to the floor, Désirée sat upright. She dusted her palms on her crêpe dress as if brushing off their distasteful conversation. "Let us talk about something else, shall we? Are there any happier bits of news I missed while I was gone? Other than my *dear* uncle leaving to attend to business at his own estate?"

Her mind wandering the past few weeks, Madeleine tapped her jaw with her fingertip. In truth, she had thought of little else since cutting ties with Gabriel. "Not unless you count Georgette hounding the new maid until she nearly quit several days ago."

"Cecile informed me of that," Désirée said with a short laugh. "It's a good thing you're both here to catch her, poor girl."

"Yes, well I'm certain she'll survive. She has already proven she can withstand the worst of Georgette. There's little more to the old woman than a loud bark."

"And a keen ability to argue." Désirée put one finger in the air. "Oh, did my novel arrive from the British book sellers? *Sense and Sensibility.* It's the newest romance from London, and I was dying to read it my whole trip."

"Now that you mention it, I do recall a series of books arriving in the post." Madeleine rose to a stand. "I tucked them in the library shelves. Wait a moment and I'll fetch them."

Désirée popped to her feet, clapping her hands together. "Oh, I do love the feel of fresh books beneath my fingers. It's just like Christmas." Her excitement swept her to the fortepiano, where her fingertips grazed the keys. "I suppose I should spend more time here and not between the covers of romantic books—that's what my father would have said. 'True romance will only find you if you practice what matters most: music and needlepoint, of course,'" she said in the lowest register she could muster, sinking to the piano bench.

Madeleine stepped into the hallway just as the first notes of Désirée's lively melody rang from the fortepiano. The woman had more skill than she would admit to. Her charming song echoed through the hall as Madeleine passed an oil landscape depicting Napoleon's coronation and rounded the doorway of the library. Sharing a wall with the music room, the lonely library filled with the dainty dance capering beneath Désirée's fingers.

The volumes in question stood upright alongside Désirée's other cherished novels—three brown spines with gold lettering that Madeleine couldn't decipher. Apparently, English eluded her as much as French. She had just clamped her fingers around all three books when the shelf beneath them slightly retreated. Startled, Madeleine yanked her hand back and stared wide-eyed at the mahogany ledge.

Nothing. The shelf stood still as it had faithfully done for hundreds of years, its polished wood gleaming in the sunlight. Madeleine shook her head to expel whatever strange magic her mind had conjured. She reached for the books again, but before her fingers could ever touch Désirée's new novel, the shelf moved back again with a click. Nay, the entire bookcase retreated several centimeters.

Stepping backward, Madeleine took in the massive floor-to-ceiling bookcase stationed in the corner. It looked as ordinary as all the others, but every so often it shifted back and then forward again. Brows cinching, she placed two palms on the nearest shelf and pushed. The bookcase held firm. With a grunt, she tried harder, but not even her full body weight would cause it to budge even a little.

"Désirée!" she called over her jaunty performance. When she went unheard, she raced to the entrance of the music room and poked her head in. "Désirée, come quickly. You must see this."

With a bemused expression, Désirée jogged after Madeleine, out of breath when she stumbled to a stop before the mysterious shelves. "What is it?" she asked, her bright eyes scanning the book titles.

"I'm not quite sure." Madeleine stretched an open palm into the air. "This whole bookcase snapped backward, then into place again." Her hand pushed forward and toward her face again. "It has happened at least five times since I've been standing here."

Désirée surveyed the piece of furniture with wonderment, as if a ghost might jump out at any moment. Silence hung around the tepid library as they both anticipated a deviation that never came. "Are you sure you really saw it move?" Désirée asked finally. "Perhaps it's just old and about to tip over."

"I swear it. The entire case moved." Madeleine's fingertips brushed the smooth wood. "I tried with all my might to shove it back myself, and it's solid. This is fine craftsmanship, no matter its age."

Frowning, Désirée bent to inspect the underside of the shelves. "What changed, then? Why won't it move now?" She rattled the edge of the bookcase to no avail. "And why wouldn't someone have noticed it shifting before? Gabriel and I have spent hours in this library."

Madeleine's eyes rushed over the case's every detail. What made this one special, among all the others? Then realization dawned, tingling down the lengths of her fingers. "The fortepiano," she said. "This is just on the other side of it. Désirée, would you go back and play that tune again?"

Désirée shrugged. "I suppose so, but I doubt *that* will have any effect." She simpered at Madeleine's pleading face. "Oh, all right, I'll count it as an adventure."

The seconds ticked by as Désirée disappeared into the music room and her buoyant tune lit the air again. Madeleine held her breath, willing the case into motion. Then, as Désirée's hands climbed the fortepiano's keys into the upper octaves, the books before her clicked back. "There!" she screeched, loud enough for the whole estate to hear. "Play that part again!" To her delight, the repeated set of notes produced the same result.

Désirée appeared in the doorframe again, her normally pallid cheeks ruddy with excitement and her chest pitching. "What happened?"

"The fortepiano must be coupled with this bookcase somehow. Each time you hit a specific key, it moves back. When you remove your finger, it goes back to its original position."

"So I'll play them, one by one," Désirée said, Madeleine's elation mirrored in her enormous grin. "Is it this one?" she yelled, one strident note clanging through the rooms.

"No, try again."

"What about this?" One note higher and still no movement. After an octave and a half of Désirée playing and Madeleine shouting back at her through the wall, the familiar click sounded again, followed by the scrape of wood as the case shifted slower this time.

"That's it! Hold that key down, Désirée!" Sprinting forward, Madeleine seized both sides and propelled the bookcase farther in. Once it sat behind its neighbors, a rolling motion took hold. "I need your help! I can't push it all the way by myself!"

In moments, Désirée emerged beside her, mirth playing on the lines of her feminine face. The bookcase had not swung back out.

"What did you use to hold down the key?" Madeleine asked.

"Just an old onyx stone. It's always on the fortepiano. It's been there since"—the light in Désirée's eyes erupted—"since the days of Henri Clement. They say he'd get terribly cross if anyone touched it. And so it's rested there ever since."

The declaration compelled both women to stand side by side and prepare to push. On Désirée's count, they pressed their bodies into the wood, mesmerized when it rolled to the side and vanished behind the other shelves. In its empty chasm, a blackened staircase crossed in spiderwebs plummeted into the earth.

Désirée audibly swallowed. "Could it really be true?" Her quaking fingers found Madeleine's. "Do you think the treasure is down there?"

Pulse racing, Madeleine tore her awestruck gaze away from the stairwell to meet her friend's rounded eyes. "The secret lies in the library, right? There's only one way to find out." Her lips curled.

As if she had springs in her feet, Désirée bounced up and hurried from the room. When she returned, she had a lit candelabra in one hand and a parasol in the other, presumably to clear away cobwebs. A dimple dented her cheek as she peered down the ancient, dusty stairwell. "Let's go find the Moon King's bounty."

Eleven

The wooden staircase groaned beneath their feet as the pair of women descended. The glowing orbs of Désirée's candelabra splashed light only a short distance around them, flinging their elongated shadows over the stone walls on either side. A dank odor encompassed them as Madeleine maneuvered the lacy parasol in front of her, clearing away the tangle of cobwebs that hundreds of years had allowed to fester. Still, silky webs managed to float around the thick air, finding only the women to cling to.

"How far do you think this goes?" Désirée asked after they had traversed at least twenty stairs. She stretched her candelabra over the inky dark, the space below them fathomless.

Madeleine pressed her palm into the cold stone to her right, careful to keep her balance. "I think it's safe to assume we're bypassing the first floor. Whatever he hid down here has to be underground."

The idea sparked a thrill in Désirée's blue eyes, glimmering in the candlelight. "I can't wait to see what it is." She paused on one particularly angry-sounding step. "I do hope he didn't set any traps to deter interlopers like us. I would hate to fall prey to one and die down here because no one can hear us yelling for help."

Shaking off an involuntary shiver, Madeleine pressed a hand to Désirée's shoulder. "More likely these stairs are so old that they've rotted and we fall through. Let's not think too hard about it, shall we?"

A handful of stairs remained before the women reached solid ground. Madeleine exhaled in relief, her palms finding the surface of a rough wooden door with a steel post barring it shut. "We've come this far. Do we tempt fate?"

Désirée nudged her with an elbow. "Open it before you drive me mad." She stood back as Madeleine thrust the steel bar onto its hooks and a rush of air tunneled down the stairwell. "The bookcase," she said, panic rising in her voice for the first time. "He must have had it wired somehow to move back into place when you unbolt the door. Now we really are trapped."

Madeleine steadied her trembling hands on the length of freezing steel. "There has to be another way out," she reassured herself more than her companion. "He probably put that mechanism in place so that no one could follow him down here."

Hastily nodding, Désirée swallowed and indicated the door with her head. "Well, let's find out whether this little descent into the abyss was worth it, shall we?"

Comforted by Désirée's familiar sarcasm, Madeleine gripped the iron handle until it clunked and pushed the door in. Nothing but a well of black stood beyond the doorway, creating a sensation like icy fingers grabbing hold as she trailed Désirée's stream of light. Immediately, she had to reel her arms close to her body and blow into her hands. The musty scent of age and neglect hung damply around the chilling air.

Désirée moved her candelabra in an arch over her head, revealing bits of the forgotten room. A small desk, rife with papers, nestled in one corner with a birdcage dangling over it. Several steps forward led them to a pile of ash with several rods tented over it and an iron kettle suspended from their middle. Beyond that, a series of shelves with what looked like art supplies adorned the far wall.

"No treasure after all." Désirée let out an exasperated sigh. "I feel foolish now, thinking Henri might have actually hidden something down here. He was always a disappointment."

Madeleine smiled through the murky light. "You searched the house as a child just like Gabriel, didn't you?"

"Of course I did. We spent our childhood believing the fanciful stories." Désirée set her candelabra on the desk and whirled at the center of the room with her arms wide. "If a treasure map *did* exist, it probably led here—to the grand cave of nothingness. A private office space for a deranged man." Her forehead crinkled. "That's what this is, right? An office? With a—firepit? Nothing about him makes sense."

"I think so." Madeleine crouched low to examine the iron pot. Some type of hard, dry residue had solidified within.

"He's mocking us," Désirée said, knotting her arms over her chest. "I can't believe I fell for his tricks yet again."

Rocking back on her heels, Madeleine let her gaze wander the dim, flittering light. "But why would he want to taunt his descendants so? And why would a man go through so much trouble to protect a room if it had no meaning?" Surely he could have conducted his business in any of the hundreds of rooms above their heads.

"I suppose you're right. Perhaps there is more here than meets the eye."

Lifting the pot from its hinge, Madeleine pulled the iron vessel into both hands and sniffed its solid contents. "This smells like metal. Désirée, didn't Gabriel say that Henri was an alchemist? This could have been his laboratory if he didn't want anybody to witness his work."

"That is the most sense I've heard all day." Kneeling, Désirée joined her on the hard stone floor. "Alchemists weren't respected in his time. They were ridiculed, punished even. If the people at court knew what he was doing down here, they might have had him thrown out. The king could have taken his title and lands."

The metal in his pot shone dully beneath the candlelight. "It seems he never reached his goal. This certainly isn't gold."

Désirée chuckled. "Or maybe he chose instead to use the stone to make an immortal elixir, and he's still just sitting there at his desk, watching us."

Their shoes scuffed the floor as they rose from their hunched spot by the firepit and explored the tiny room. Madeleine drifted toward the shelves on the wall where the candle's rays barely touched the assortment of jars and bowls. The acrid odor of turpentine met her nose as she brushed her fingers over the smooth glass. Many of them had varying levels of a paint-like substance. On the bottom shelf, she found a stack of wooden bowls with the substance brushed over them and several cups of paintbrushes.

"Your brother didn't mention that Henri was a painter," she said to Désirée, who now pushed on the stone walls as if one of them might reveal a secret passage.

Désirée's shoulders lifted. "I don't know that he was. None of the paintings upstairs bear his name."

"That's odd." Madeleine gripped a jar of clearly used brushes, clanking together as she inspected it. "He has a plethora of painting supplies over here, though I don't see the canvas he would have practiced on."

"Who could paint in a place with this kind of lighting?" Désirée asked, sauntering toward Henri's desk.

Giving up her musings, Madeleine followed her friend. While Désirée sank into Henri's surprisingly plain wooden chair, Madeleine's fingers swept the birdcage. A thick layer of dust adhered to her fingertips, scattering in the air and choking her. How could a bird have survived in a place like this, anyway?

"Madeleine, look at this." Désirée rifled through the piles of papers strewn across Henri's desk, her feet tapping hurriedly on the stone floor. "These are all letters written to Henri over a huge span of years. I recognize some of these names. Statesmen, aristocrats"—she sucked in a sharp breath— "the king himself. What a treasury must exist here."

Heart thumping, Madeleine leaned over the desk, where an assortment of stained quills littered the wood. "Perhaps there is something about the treasure in there. Maybe even the real letter he wrote to your family."

Désirée flattened her fingers over the scrawled pages, taking another breath. "Now, I'm not going to let myself get carried away like last time. There also might be nothing." She couldn't hide the grin pinching the corners of her mouth. "But it's worth the effort to look through all of these. Let's collect them and get out of here before we freeze to death."

Eagerly snatching up every last paper on Henri's desk, the women folded them into their arms and turned to leave. Désirée seized her melting candles before stopping short behind Madeleine. "I almost forgot the bookcase had closed on us. What do we do now?"

But already Madeleine was poised on her tiptoes, reaching for the birdcage swinging from the ceiling. With a bit of hunting, her fingers located a lever inside and flipped it down. From up the stairs, a faint rumbling quaked the door. "I knew he couldn't have put a bird down here." She shook her head. "This Henri of yours was a wonder."

"A wonder or a madman—one of the two." Désirée ducked through the doorway, one arm full of Henri's letters and the other clenching her candlestand.

The pair clattered up the stairs, gasping when they surmounted them. Madeleine's chest burned from running in such cramped quarters. Her lungs felt like they might explode. Yet joy leapt within as sunlight flooded the stairwell and they found the gap open again for them to pass through. In a fit of giggles, the women floundered into the library, arms full of pages from the house's hidden depths.

"I can't believe we just did that!" Désirée shrieked. "Oh, Madeleine, my heart is bounding out of my chest." Puckering her lips, she blew out the candles not extinguished by her lively declaration.

"I told you we wouldn't die," Madeleine said with a wink.

"Madeleine? Désirée?" Just then, a figure careened through the doorway, stumbling to a stop in front of them. In contrast with his earlier melancholy, Gabriel wore nothing but a worried gape. His unkempt hair flew around his face, his sullied shirt hanging loosely off his thin body. His aghast gaze shifted from his sister to his former love.

"What's happened? I came running when I heard you screaming at each other from my study, but no one was around—" His inquisitive stare washed over the pages in their hold, then to the missing bookcase and wall. He blinked once, like he'd just stepped into a bizarre dream. "What on earth?"

"We will explain everything, dear brother." Désirée shoved around him, capering toward the hallway. "It seems our dear Henri had more secrets than we could have guessed."

Madeleine's face heated as Gabriel's eyes pinned on her. An awkward moment passed between them as they stood alone in the library, Désirée still chattering as she disappeared down the corridor. He raked a hand through his abundant hair, then stepped aside with a sweep of his arm.

Even as they left the library in miserable silence, Madeleine harbored her first bit of hope since crushing Gabriel's heart on that sunny afternoon. Nothing might come of the papers in Henri's covert study, but at least the baron had something else to think about now. She hurried on to the rhythm of his footsteps falling behind her, praying this would prove the distraction they both so desperately needed.

T he black curtain of night had fallen over the Château des Rêves when Cecile shoved a letter into Madeleine's hand. "Apparently I'm supposed to give you this and I'm *not* supposed to read it." She bustled around Madeleine, who stood at the kitchen wash basins with Brigitte, rinsing the pots and dishes the little maid scrubbed.

Mopping her free hand on her apron, Madeleine scurried after her. "Wait, who gave you this?" The ink-scrawled contents already blotted with drips of soapy water.

"Some imbecile with a lot of nerve," Cecile said over her shoulder, her fiery braid swishing as she walked. "He told me that if I dared to read his note, he would slit my throat. I promise you this. If you've taken up with that lout, I'll disown you."

"Cecile, please. This is important." Lurching forward, Madeleine caught her by her wrist and spun her back. "I'm sorry for what he said to you, but I need to know. When did he give you this? Where?"

The redhead's brow arched in curiosity. "About an hour past, in the village. Why are you so bothered over it?" Awareness emerging on her pretty features, she stepped closer and lowered her voice. "He wasn't a suitor, was he? Was that Auguste?"

Madeleine sighed. "I fear it could be none other. My brother doesn't exactly aim to make friends when he is about a task." She took one last glance at Brigitte, still working away with a towel and bowl of white brick dust, before she popped the seal with her thumb.

Her eyes rapidly scanned the page, every muscle in her body tense.

"I suppose your illiteracy was all a ploy to get me to read and write your correspondences for you," Cecile said with a laugh.

Madeleine revolved the damaged letter to face the other maid. "Can you read this?"

A full smile cracked over Cecile's lightly freckled face. "Well, aren't you just full of surprises." She leaned over the page in

Madeleine's hand. "Now you must tell me everything it says. That's not a throat-slitting offense, is it?"

Gripping the page, Madeleine pivoted toward the kitchen fire and used the flames to read by. Her lips briskly whispered the words so only Cecile could hear.

"Dear Madeleine, it is with the utmost urgency that I write to you today. Firstly, I must apologize for my behavior toward you when last you visited The Black Lion. I have been under much pressure to locate this treasure before our funds run dry. That is no excuse for how I treated you, and I wish I could take back what I said to you."

Cecile huffed. "What about what you said to me, you lout?"

With a playful roll of her eyes, Madeleine returned to the letter. "Felix has been closely surveying the dispatches coming to and from Avance. He informs me that the baron has written quite a few letters to the daughter of a Comte in the Loire Valley. I do not wish to burden you, dear sister, but I must know now if I need to seek alternate arrangements in this regard. It seems you are not as close to the baron as you once were. There are several women I know of who might replace you if the baron has lost interest in you."

Madeleine hurried on as Cecile swore under her breath. "I have made a promising lead in the case of the nameless man. In fact, I am preparing to travel as I write this. A close confidant has revealed the patterns of a mercenary ship that could very well be in collusion with the nameless man. We believe his last port was the nameless man's home. If I find him, I know I can convince him to share his information with us. Until then, please take care and be safe. Come to The Black Lion when I return on the nineteenth. We have much to discuss. Auguste."

"Do you really take orders from him like that?" Cecile leaned against the stone hearth, nostrils fuming. "Now I wish I could go back in time and clock him like he deserves."

"Yes, well I don't have the luxury at the moment." Turning toward the raging fire, Madeleine held out Auguste's letter and felt the rush of heat funnel up her arm. "I must keep up this charade until Pascal and Auguste are both somehow appeased." The edges of the page began to singe and curl as the fire devoured them.

Flames danced in Cecile's green eyes as she stared into the snapping embers. "It isn't fair. You're just a pawn in all of their games."

"All the more reason to find that treasure as soon as we possibly can." Madeleine threw the uncharred remains of Auguste's letter into the fire, relieved when the inferno hissed and converged around it. "The rest will mend itself with time. Then I will be free to leave, knowing my brothers have a future in this world and Gabriel is in love again."

"Oh, Madeleine." A bitter sadness had crept over Cecile's face. She bent to kiss Madeleine's warm cheek. "God will repay you for this tenfold. You are a far better person than you let yourself believe."

Across the kitchen, a pan crashed to the floor. Madeleine and Cecile both jumped, their stunned gazes volleying to Brigitte. The poor girl paled and stuttered as she crouched to retrieve the offending pan. "I—I'm awfully sorry."

"It's all right, Brigitte." Madeleine squeezed Cecile's hand before she marched back to the half-washed dishes. "I should have been helping you, anyway."

The diminutive young maid averted her eyes, grabbing the copper pan again in ever-so-slightly trembling hands. Madeleine silently wondered at her jumpiness, but joined her again at the basins, dipping her clean dishes in pure water. Weeks on end with Georgette as her guide could make anyone nervous.

"Goodnight, scullery maids!" Cecile called as she disappeared around the corner.

And what a long night it would be. Until Désirée or Gabriel made a discovery in Henri's letters, Madeleine would work her bones dry at whatever job she could find. She would hold her head high and forget Gabriel Clement. She would not turn back.

Twelve

M adeleine stood at the window of the upstairs salon, hugging her arms around her torso. Behind her, Gabriel and Désirée bickered about Henri's letters. Before her, the world was perfect. Every shade of green painted the landscape, each more dazzling than the last. The crepe myrtles had bloomed, their pink blossoms sweeping the sky amid a whirlwind of white almond tree petals cascading on the breeze.

Under the guise of aiding in a very important manner, Désirée had excused Madeleine from work again. Really, she wanted to sit around the round rosewood table by the white marble fireplace and debate whether the Moon King's treasure could actually exist. She and Gabriel had gone about several rounds before Madeleine excused herself to find comfort in the nature outside the château's tall sash windows. The treasure was important indeed, but how could she take another second of sitting next to him—his face in front of her, his cologne in the air she breathed?

Shivering, Madeleine drowned out the din of their competing voices and watched the red-breasted robins hopping from one tree limb to the next. How could Henri Clement's letter have vanished from his house when clearly he knew how to keep whatever secret he wished? She would never forget Auguste's reaction when she had left Marcel Toutain's company without the infamous letter.

Théâtre de la Gaîté had emptied out and Madeleine had hardly been given the time to don a proper dress when Auguste marched up the intricate aisle runner toward the stage. "Well? What did you find out from Toutain?"

Madeleine glanced furtively over her shoulder, afraid Toutain might miraculously wake from his drunken stupor so soon. Grabbing hold of the handrail, she daintily descended the steps at stage left and crossed in front of the first row of seats. "Very little, I'm afraid. Whoever he did business with told him nothing."

With a low growl, her brother shoved one hand through his short hair. "I knew I should have interrogated him myself. I can't believe you didn't get the letter."

"It isn't like Toutain has the letter anyway." Tying a crocheted shawl over her muslin gown, Madeleine strutted to a stop between the rows of yellow seats. "The man with the letter was a ship captain with the initials J.C. He wanted Toutain to fund his expedition to find the treasure."

Auguste hooked an interested eyebrow. "Did this captain tell Toutain how he acquired Clement's letter?"

"No, but he had an associate who goes by 'the nameless man'. This mysterious fellow claims his family hid the treasure wherever the coordinates lead. He wouldn't divulge his name, but he lives there at the tavern, on the docks of Bordeaux."

"Well, at least it's something." Auguste held a leatherbound journal close to his chest, jotting down the information as Madeleine dispensed it. "Perhaps I'll go to Bordeaux when given the chance. He may not have a name, but any man can be found."

Without thought, Madeleine found her hand on his wrist. "Please, Auguste, would you let me do it? I feel as if I must finish what I started."

Auguste's thin lips twisted as he considered her proposal. "I suppose it makes more sense for you to take time off from your *job,* what with the precarious nature of acting posts." The chest beneath his fanciful tweed suit swelled and then deflated. "It doesn't matter right now anyway. We don't have the money to afford a trip to Bordeaux."

A nudging voice tempted Madeleine to mention the modest amount of money she had collected from her *steady* work in the theater, but her good sense won out. "How much do we need?" she asked.

"Too much." Auguste flipped his journal closed and slapped it on his palm. "I do have an idea, though. If you're willing to hear me out." At Madeleine's receptive expression, he gestured to the vacant seats along the aisle. Madeleine chose one five rows back, still scattered with sequins from its recent occupant.

The seat beside hers creaked as Auguste slipped into it and gave her a long look before speaking. "I need to know how committed you are to this endeavor. Our situation is about to get a lot more complicated."

"Auguste, I told you." Madeleine gripped his hand, her head cocking. "I am willing to do *anything* to avenge Maman and Papa. Just say the word and I will go to the ends of the earth for you."

His steely eyes darkened. "I know you would. You proved that tonight. But swindling a man into giving information is child's play compared to what I may need of you."

Madeleine set her jaw, narrowing her impassioned gaze on him. "I told you. Whatever it is, I will do it."

"Good girl." His free hand rose to pat her blanched fingers. "First, we will need the money, of course. I have quite the scheme in place for that. But once we have it, you will go to Avance. You will use any means necessary to get Clement to tell you where the treasure is hidden, and then you will take him down."

Her heartbeat stampeded, the idea both thrilling and terrifying at once. "But how will we accomplish such a feat?"

Auguste's mouth curled wickedly. "I've hired a local named Felix to watch the goings-on at Clement's château. He has discovered a maid there carrying on a dalliance with one of the local nobles for months now." His nostrils flared above his pinched lips. "It won't be hard to create an opening in their staff when I decide to write to the man's wife, detailing his affair."

The thought planted a cold ache in Madeleine's middle, but still she found herself nodding. She could not deny the beloved brother of her childhood whom she'd lost for so many years. Besides, these rich, profligate people deserved what they got. She would spill her own blood if it meant pleasing her brother.

The memory faded, Désirée's insistent voice invading her thoughts. "I wanted this treasure to be as real as you did, Gabriel Clement. I had just as much faith as you." Madeleine pivoted back to find them squaring off at the tea table, each with a mess of pages before them and scowls on their lips.

"Perhaps, but you were distracted by any little concern that came your way," the baron said from his opposing spot on a plush yellow slipper chair. "Parties, games, boys—"

"Fun, you mean." Désirée's normally pallid skin burned red. "Pardon me for wanting to live my life. No, I didn't wither away in the library scouring every book. I wasn't made to make life into an island like you do."

A glint of pain crossed Gabriel's bright eyes, but he fastened his lips and took up the next letter. "If it were real, *I* would have found it already."

"Typical man's response." Huffing, Désirée narrowed her eyes on the letter in her hand and scanned it like the words were falling off the pages.

Stifling her amusement behind the back of her hand, Madeleine strutted from the window and sank onto a settee nearby. She watched the two of them, her fingertips traveling the smooth rosewood armrest before meeting one of the gilded swans stationed at the settee's sides. After emerging from such unpleasant memories, it pacified her to see that every sibling pair fought from time to time, even the seemingly perfect ones.

"What do you think of all this, Madeleine?" Désirée asked as she flipped over one brown page and picked up another. "Would Henri Clement have gone through all the trouble of building a secret room into his library if he wasn't up to something? My brother here seems to think that he only wanted a little solitude." She rolled her eyes.

Gabriel's face shot up. "You said it yourself that he used that room for his alchemy. Of course he wanted secrecy."

Désirée's palm flattened toward her brother. "I was asking Madeleine only, if you don't mind."

Glancing between the two, Madeleine gripped the cool head of a swan in one hand. No answer would appease them both. "I think that depends on what he was hiding," she said at last, "and why."

Désirée sat up straight, one eyebrow arching. "What do you mean by that?"

"Well—" Madeleine swallowed, feeling the weight of Gabriel's gaze on her. "If he really did hide a treasure as some think he did, he could have very easily just placed it in the secret room we found. Judging by the cobwebs alone, nobody has found that place since Henri died." She held up one finger. "But maybe he had another reason for hiding it. An ulterior motive. In that case, his home alone would never do."

"I like this idea." Désirée's lips curled. "Tell me, what other motive might our old Henri have had in stashing away his treasure?"

"Oh, I don't know." Madeleine shrugged. "Perhaps he did concoct the elixir of life. Maybe a pirate king in a far-off land needed it for a sickly daughter, so he traded his every possession to get his hands on one vial. Only, Henri didn't know that the treasure was actually cursed. So he had to hide it in the earth's most remote location so that no one would ever find it." She could see it all playing out in her mind's eye, a glittering stage play bursting with intrigue.

Gabriel stared at her blankly. "So, why leave clues behind if nobody is ever supposed to find it? Surely he wouldn't murder his offspring."

Madeleine searched her brain, her creativity stretching across the void. "The curse must have expired upon his death. That's why he put it in his final message to his family. So they could find it only when it was safe to do so."

The tiniest of smiles edged Gabriel's mouth, though he said nothing. Behind him, Désirée clapped her hands. "Bravo, Madeleine. You have a fanciful imagination."

Accepting her accolades with a bow, Madeleine swept her arm in a wide arc, much like she had on stage so many times before. "It is my pleasure to entertain." She lifted her head to find the smile creeping so far up Gabriel's unshaven lips that he could barely contain it.

"Or maybe a rival knew his secret," Désirée said with a far-off look in her eye. "The only way to keep him from reaching the treasure first was to hide it somewhere he didn't expect."

Sighing, Gabriel tented his fingers. "Or perhaps he needed a safe haven from the women in his life."

Désirée glowered at him. "He should have counted himself lucky to have women in his life at all." Her chin lifted defiantly. "Don't behave so callously, brother. We know you love us." She sucked in a breath as if trying to retrieve her tactless comment, but the damage had already crept over Gabriel's skin in a changing array of colors.

He swallowed, his gaze flitting to his working fingers before he cleared his throat. "Yes, well, Henri must have acquired some knowledge that I am not privy to." His forlorn eyes swept over Madeleine before plummeting back again, twisting her stomach in raw guilt.

"Well, thus far my search has been nothing but a fruitless endeavor," Désirée swooped in to change the subject. Her elbows thudded atop her neat stack of papers as she turned to her brother. "What about you? Have you found anything?"

Gabriel shook his head. "Nothing but a collection of dry correspondence and military orders." Hanging a paper beside him in his thumb and forefinger, he lifted it to the sunlight. "There is a fascinating account of the sale of a cow."

From her spot on the settee, Madeleine shrugged. "It was significant to the cow, at least."

Matching her clever simper, Gabriel let the page drift like a fallen leaf to the others before stretching his long fingers over his pile. "You would think that a man who had hidden an enormous fortune somewhere would have *someone* who needed to write to him about it."

"Perhaps he destroyed those letters," Désirée said, plucking up her next letter, "so no one would find them."

"As opposed to all of these extremely easy-to-find letters in his secret underground lair?" Gabriel asked, expression dubious.

"Or he had *another* hideaway," Madeleine said. "A covert place within this house where he hid anything relating to the treasure."

"Yet another secret room?" Gabriel glanced at Désirée, but she was absorbed in the letter before her. He scratched his bristly chin. "I would say you were as crazy as my sister, but you might be on to something. After all, I never would have believed that this—"

"Hold on just a moment." Désirée's order sliced through the conversation, flinging both stares on her. Her eyes wildly flew over the scrawled words in her grasp, her skin morphing from pink to red. "I might have found something."

Gabriel's chair tumbled behind him as he shot up. "What is it?" His long legs carried him quickly to her side, Madeleine not far behind as she scampered after them.

Drawing close to his side, she peered over Désirée's shoulder at the delicate brown paper in her hand. Gabriel smelled of stale clothes and yesterday's lunch, yet still every fiber in her body felt drawn to him. With a steadying hand on Désirée's chair back, she tried to focus on the message that had Désirée so clearly enthralled.

Désirée inhaled sharply, her quivering fingers fluttering the page. "Most esteemed Baron Clement, thank you for your recent inquiry. I have placed it where you requested, and there it will safely stay. Please write again if I can assist you further. Sincerely, Louis Colbert."

Silence settled over them as the trio gazed dumbstruck at the letter, each considering its contents. Then Gabriel stepped backward, pushing a hand through his tangled hair. "This is nothing. That message could mean anything."

Désirée whirled, her blue eyes alight. "Or it could be *something*." She bit her lip, brow furrowed. "I wonder what Henri asked him to hide. Maybe part of the treasure?"

"He didn't say '*hid*'. He said 'placed'," Gabriel said with an exasperated sigh.

"Well, it was clearly something he wanted to keep safe." Désirée's nostrils fumed.

With a light touch on her friend's heated skin, Madeleine pointed to the aged letter. "More importantly, who is Louis Colbert?"

Désirée wagged her head. "It sounds familiar, but I—I can't seem to place it." Even through her rage, she silently implored the brother above her.

Gaze landing hesitantly back, Gabriel finally unlatched his clamped lips. "He was a prominent man in Paris at the time this letter was written. He oversaw the Bibliotheque Nationale."

Shooting to her feet, Désirée beamed back a smile that stretched nearly to her ears. "The National Library? Henri asked the director of the National Library to hide an important relic?"

Excitement stirring her middle, Madeleine couldn't keep the joy off her own face. "The secret lies in the library," she repeated the oft-spoken phrase so dear to the Clements' legacy.

"Now hold on just a minute." Gabriel poked one finger up, but his companions hardly heard him over their flurry of laughter and anxious whispers.

Already, Désirée had snatched Louis Colbert's dispatch from the table and donned a knit shawl across her shoulders. "Come on, I'll bet we can reach Paris before it closes." She seized Madeleine's hand, tugging her along as she jogged toward the door.

"You don't even know what you're looking for," Gabriel called after them, sprinting over the flowered rug to keep up. "You can't just waltz in there demanding that the librarian produce whatever it is Colbert put there hundreds of years ago. It's probably not even there anymore. The books have moved since the time of this letter. They survived a war, for pity's sake."

By now, the group had reached the wrought iron rail overlooking the checkered vestibule. Spinning back on the marble floor, Désirée stared her brother down through slitted eyes. "First, you said there was nothing special about our library. Then, you insisted Henri's correspondences were nothing but business transactions." One of her thin fingers speared his chest. "Now, we're going to find whatever it is Henri Clement asked Louis Colbert to place in his library. If you really think it isn't there, what do you have to lose? Prove us wrong."

With a visible gulp, Baron Clement looked between the two women staring expectantly back. Curiosity and fear battled in his gaze as it swept past them, down the stone entryway and out the sash windows to the fields beyond. His hands dove into his pockets. Then, with an air of determination locking his square jaw, he nodded. "All right, then. Let's be on with it."

Thirteen

T he brilliant spring countryside greeted the Clement family coach as its robust pair of mares clomped their way over the dusty roads. Madeleine drew back the curtain in her little window to see the parade of flowering dogwoods and bushy apple trees ripe for picking. The sweet scents of peach blossom and wildflowers mingled on the breeze, delighting her as she watched the warbling wood thrushes bouncing from limb to limb among the treetops.

A rut in the roadway jolted the jostling carriage, forcing Madeleine to steady herself on the velvet cushioned bench. Her attention swung back to the interior in which she sat, to Désirée beside her, voraciously rereading Henri's letter as if for the first time. Sensing a pair of eyes on her, Madeleine dared a glimpse at Gabriel seated across the carriage, his sad expression enfolding her. He held her gaze a painful moment before rubbing his hands together between his knees and reverting his eyes to his own window.

The winding road to Paris carried them in solemn silence, save for the occasional exclamation on Désirée's part, when she thought of a new possibility in their search. So different it was from the last time they'd taken this journey together, with Gabriel's strong, warm frame cuddled beside her. With their tender kisses and shared promises to love each other forever. Madeleine hugged her arms around her torso as a lonely chill coursed through her. Her stomach lurched. All that beauty was just a memory now.

After what felt like days inside such cramped quarters, the horses' hooves slowed on the cobblestone, and the carriage deposited the trio before a simple white stone building with circular windows dotting its upper edge. Madeleine tried desperately not to let her hand tremble when Gabriel helped her down to the street, his balmy fingers lingering a moment longer than they needed to.

"Here we are," Désirée said with a hopeful breath, her twinkling eyes surveying the stone railings and arched windows. She tossed her brother a smirk as she took his hand to climb down the carriage steps. "So good of you to dress for the occasion."

Indeed, with the time Désirée had taken to gather her findings and order Serge to ready their journey, Gabriel had righted his offensive appearance. He stood before them now with a shaven jawline and a fresh linen shirt beneath his jacket and embroidered waistcoat. Georgette's homemade lemon soap even emanated off his skin.

"Yes, well I couldn't very well go out in public looking like a street urchin." A dimple creased his cheek, and Madeleine had to glance away to keep her wits. How was she ever to forget him if even the simplest of his gestures made her heart skitter?

Désirée nudged him with her elbow. "It's not a sin to clean yourself up at home, you know."

The brother and sister pair wandered into the building while politely bickering, with Madeleine following at a respectable distance behind. Clad in her black cotton maid's uniform, she knew any more familiarity with the Clement siblings would appear suspicious to the scattered patrons milling around the library's interior. Already, a handful of curious glances had been launched their way, particularly directed on her hermit of an employer.

After traversing a wide marble hallway, the group found themselves within a grand circular room with bookshelves lining the walls and row after row of reading desks. Stone pillars adorned the room, tall archways rising up to domes in the roof where ocular windows allowed sunlight to spill over the splendid room. Madeleine's eyes traveled the daunting collection of books. This room alone would take them years to scour if they planned to pull out every book.

"All right, our fearless leader." The baron revolved to his sister, who bit her lip as she stood gaping at the impressive display. "Where shall we start? You were convinced you could find whatever it is Colbert placed here. Lead the way."

With a slow spin, Désirée looked from one bookcase to the next. "It's here; I can feel it." Yet the longer she stood there, the more desperation crept over her lovely features. "Perhaps if we have a closer look."

Casting a cautious glance Madeleine's way, Gabriel trailed his sister to a polished bookcase that stretched nearly to the ceiling. Désirée's lithe fingers swept over the leather bindings and gold embossed titles, vainly searching for a treasure as elusive as a leaf amid a roiling ocean.

Désirée's bright eyes closed as if in prayer. When she opened them again, plump tears laced her lashes. "What did you want us to find, Henri?"

Behind her, Gabriel opened his mouth to speak but left it hinged open at the look of sorrow crowding his sister's face. Madeleine felt her pain deep in her gut. How excruciating to have hoped for something to be real all these years and then come so close to discovering it, only to find oneself trapped.

Her hand reached out to cover Désirée's trembling fingers. "From all your years of searching for this treasure, there isn't one other clue to help us now?" Panic sprouted in Madeleine's middle to imagine what Auguste might do if their search yielded nothing.

Désirée shook her head, swiping at a tear. "Nothing that I can think of." She turned hopeful eyes to Gabriel. "Did Papa ever tell you anything?"

Pity plagued his gaze. "I'm sorry, he didn't." Gabriel inhaled deeply. "Papa had given up any hope of finding Henri's treasure by the time I was old enough to really pursue it."

Staring into the ocean of books, Désirée brought both hands to her heart. "It really is our family's curse, isn't it? We're all a bunch of fools." She smiled wistfully. Her companions joined in the poignant silence for several moments as the world went on around them, oblivious to their private sorrows.

Then, a spark lit in Madeleine's memory. She turned to Gabriel. "Baron," she asked, her cheeks filling with color to address him so formally. "What did the outside of that letter we found say? What was the word?"

A crinkle dented the skin between his eyes as Gabriel pondered her question. "On the seal? Arcadia, I believe it was. Why do you ask?"

Feverish joy whirled within Madeleine. "Could that be a clue?" she asked. Désirée grabbed her wrist, hope spilling over her face. "Is that the name of a book? Arcadia?"

Pursing his lips, Gabriel let a stern look wash over the pair of women as if determining his next move. Then, without a word, he rotated on his heel and marched over to a man seated at a high desk nearby. "Where might I find 16th century Italian literature?" he asked. "Specifically pastoral poetry?"

The bearded librarian lifted his quill pen and jotted something down on a slip of paper. Handing it to Gabriel, he aimed one pointed finger to a doorway the three hadn't yet traversed. With a nod, the baron thanked him and hesitantly turned back to the waiting women.

Even Gabriel couldn't force down the grin that dimpled his cheek as he looked from Désirée to Madeleine's expectant faces. "Keep in mind, this could be nothing. I don't want you two getting into another frenzy only to have your hearts broken."

Désirée emitted an exasperated grunt. "You are the most vexing creature on this planet. Out with it already!" Though her nostrils flared and color bloomed on her fair skin, her eyes sparkled buoy-antly.

Gabriel held up one pacifying hand. "Arcadia is a poem written by Jacopo Sannazaro about a man who discovers a perfect world amid his own personal sorrows. It influenced so much of Euro-pean literature that it will never be forgotten." Mischief played on the lines of his handsome face. "I'm sure it's here in this library. There's no doubt."

Hopping on the soles of her slippers, Désirée clapped her hands. "Let's not waste any more time. Let's go find it."

A massive oval-shaped room lay beyond the doorway the librar-ian had indicated. The trio passed beneath the grand doorway in awe, taking in the tiered bookshelves that adorned every wall, each within its own arch. Sunlight filtered over the enormous assem-blage, spilling in from an egg-shaped skylight overhead, surround-ed by ocular windows.

Following Gabriel's snaking path amongst rows of impossibly long tables, Madeleine soon found herself next to Désirée before a towering series of bookcases. "It should be here, somewhere in this section," Gabriel said. Mesmerized, she drifted toward the captivating sight, drawn by their ancient beauty. Before this, she'd thought perhaps the Clement family owned every book known to man.

The musty scent of age touched her nose as Madeleine pulled a book out here and there, admiring their worn covers and sweep-ing her fingertips over the stamped titles. Unlike the library at the château, she could read these words—*The Prince, The Man-drake, The Book of the Courtier.* Somehow, comfort and warmth enveloped her to feel so small amid thousands of books. Surely Papa had familiarized himself with this library during his time in Louis's court. Madeleine closed her eyes and inhaled the sweet, chocolate-like odor wafting off the open book in her hands and felt closer to her departed father than ever before.

Her eyelids fluttered open to find Gabriel only steps away, watching her curiously. Madeleine's cheeks warmed against her will and she shoved the book alongside the others. As if yanked from a trance, he reeled back to the bookshelves and raked a hand through his mass of curly locks. Madeleine returned to her work, wondering if they would ever be able to live side by side without the silent glances and awkward moments.

For a quiet stretch of minutes, Madeleine combed the gathering of books alongside her companions. The titles began to blur together as her eyes jumped from one to the next. Smooth leather met her fingertips, then linen and even metal. Unconsciously drifting closer to the baron, she was soon shoulder-to-shoulder with him, their arms occasionally brushing as they reached up to scour the library's collection. Despite herself, her heart thumped to feel his warmth beside her, to breathe his vanilla-tinged cologne. More than once, Madeleine had to stop herself from looking into his eyes, knowing the vulnerable soul behind them would reel her back to him.

At last, like a dream, the one word she sought sprung before her eyes. Madeleine gasped, slipping the treasured book from among the others. "I think I've found it," she said, commanding the immediate attention of the Clement siblings. Flipping the front cover back, she scanned the inner inscription. "Arcadia, by Jacopo Sannazaro, a pastoral poem," she read.

When her words met with silence, Madeleine glanced up into two stunned expressions. "How did you—" Gabriel's forehead wrinkled, his surprise converting to mirth on his freshly shaven lips. "But I thought you couldn't—"

Madeleine smiled shyly. "There are many things you don't know about me, Baron Clement." With a pang of sadness, she realized he would never know them now that another woman would fill his life.

"Apparently so." Gabriel shook his head and chuckled, a blithe sound in the expansive room.

"Well?" Désirée asked, her shoes clicking on the floor as she moved closer. "Does it say anything else? Is there something hidden within the book's pages?"

Frowning, Madeleine perused the rest of the page and several after it. Finding nothing, she carefully flipped through page after page of neatly printed text until the empty back cover stared back. "I don't see anything unusual."

"Let me have a look." Désirée's jittery fingers hunted the book next, her search revealing nothing but a few motes of dust that floated around the sunlit air.

An air of bitter disappointment encircled them as Désirée slumped against the bookcase, leaning her head on a shelf. "I really thought this would lead us somewhere." She gazed at the book sadly, her palm brushing the age-worn cover. "I guess I should know not to expect more from Henri Clement. Just more games to occupy his witless descendants."

Madeleine stepped closer while Gabriel looked on with dark eyebrows drawn. "You are anything but witless." She squeezed Désirée's silk-clad shoulder. "I know you thought it would be here, but maybe it's somewhere else. We won't stop looking."

Désirée cast her a half-hearted smile, but the joy had drained from her blue eyes.

"It doesn't make sense that he would leave behind clues in such a public spot, anyhow," Gabriel said. "What did he expect to happen when somebody wanted to read this book? Whatever Colbert put in there would just fall to the random reader?"

"I don't know." Sighing, Désirée hugged her arms around her frame. "Perhaps we'll never know." She passed the book to her brother, who implored her with an open palm.

Watching Gabriel carefully examine the book's print, Madeleine let her mind run wild. "There has to be more to it. Something we're missing. Why would Henri lead us here, of all places?" She focused on the large clock above the doorway, its hands incessantly ticking, feeling the hours dwindling before Auguste stormed in with swords drawn.

Désirée stared listlessly into the panorama of books around the room, at the library patrons stationed here and there, searching for a book or seated over one at a desk. "Henri loved books. That's one reason we have so many. He was a proud patron of this library." Her forlorn smile tilted sideways. "So maybe we do have something in common, however small. Our family carried that love through the generations."

Resting her head on Désirée's shoulder, Madeleine tried to still her racing nerves. "Perhaps that's his treasure. His legacy. He left you all with a profound love that no amount of years could erase."

"Wouldn't that be a disappointment to all the treasure hunters he has inspired?" Désirée's shoulders shook with laughter. "It wasn't money after all. It was books. The treasure was out in the open all along. Come hoard your fill of literature and better yourself through the written word."

Madeleine joined her in hushed giggles. "You never know. Henri was a trickster, after all."

"Oh, Maddy." Désirée buried her face in her perfumed shawl. "I just want this day to be over. Let's go back to the château and demand ice cream. Bowls and bowls of it."

"Agreed." Pushing off the bookcase, Madeleine fanned out her crinkled skirts. "I'll make it myself if I must."

Just as the women had prepared themselves to leave, Gabriel held up a detaining hand. "Wait one moment." With Arcadia opened to the back page, he squinted hard at the lining inside the cover.

Curious, Madeleine and Désirée tailed him to a table within a darkened alcove. Reaching in his back pocket, Gabriel glanced furtively around them before producing a pocketknife and releasing the blade. He bent over the book with riveted concentration, pointing the tip of the blade to the paper meeting the cover's edge.

Désirée gasped. "What are you doing? That book is hundreds of years old."

"It's nothing that can't be pasted." His knife tip indicated the subtle swells on the surface of the inner cover. "This page here has been torn off and glued back before." Gabriel shrugged. "Perhaps it was a mere mishap, but perhaps not."

Holding her breath, Madeleine leaned over the book with the other two. The knife blade squealed as Gabriel cautiously ran it beneath the tacked-on paper, prying until it released from the cover. His blade slid easier then, uncleaving the page from its book until he'd created an opening large enough to slip his fingers through. Madeleine gripped the table's edge as Gabriel's fingertips disappeared into the pocket he'd made, returning with a small slip of paper.

Her heartbeat hammered in her ears as she crowded close to Gabriel, peering down to find words she didn't recognize. Her own language.

"It's a riddle," he said, breath heavy with excitement. "'Let evening stars be your guide. Beyond the waters, endless treasures hide.'" He stood back with a surprised chuckle, clutching the back of his neck like he couldn't quite believe what they'd uncovered.

"What are all these numbers?" Désirée asked, her fingertip skimming a row of writing beneath Henri's riddle.

Gabriel shook his head. "I haven't a clue. But Désirée—" His eyes met his sister's, more joyful and full of life than Madeleine had ever seen them. "It's real. The treasure is real. All these years, nobody has been able to crack his code, and here we are with actual proof."

Grasping his wrist, she smiled back through her tears. "I told you, brother. It's good to see that you believe me now."

Light shone through his tears as his eyes turned to Madeleine. "Thank you, Madeleine." Her pulse quickened as his adoring gaze swept her face. "Thank you for believing in us enough to help us find this clue. I know we're not always the easiest lot." He laughed as Désirée bumped him with her side.

Throat dry, the maid could merely nod in reply. What would happen when he discovered her clandestine motives, her despicable greed? Would these two beautiful creatures still love her when Auguste came raging through their door, ready to kill in order to steal their rightful inheritance? How much easier the world seemed when the treasure simply didn't exist.

"I wonder what waters Henri could be referring to here," Désirée said. "He couldn't have left us with an easier clue? It was difficult enough to find this one."

Loosening his cravat, Gabriel wagged his head. "I can't begin to guess now, but we shall figure it out. I know we will." His eyes sparkled as they connected with Madeleine's. "Today my hope has been restored. It's a new beginning."

Fourteen

Night bathed the barony in darkness, the silver moon casting a creamy glow across the countryside. Crickets chirped, their strident song reverberating over the hills and down the valleys. Here in the dew-soaked grass, Madeleine pulled her knees against her chest and listened to the river as it trickled past, tumbling over its rocky bends and carrying the scent of lilacs.

Two other faces glowed in the light of the campfire. Désirée sat staring with sanguine trust into the black sky as if the stars overhead would at any moment reveal their secrets. Beside her, Cecile had a devilish smile plastered on her face as she imbibed a bottle of Georgette's spring cider.

It had seemed like a good idea when the three of them had concocted a plan over *babas au rhum* in the kitchen. They would take Henri's words literally and plant themselves beneath the stars near a body of water. Surely, an honest, uncomplicated attempt to interpret his hidden message would yield results. Now, seated on thin wool blankets atop the hard earth with the wind whipping through her hair, Madeleine allowed second thoughts to creep in.

"What, exactly, are we looking for?" she asked, wrapping her hand-crocheted shawl tighter around her shivering arms.

Garbed in a deep blue cashmere cloak, Désirée peeked back from within her fur-trimmed hood. "It said evening stars will be your guide." She dragged in a long breath, her look inspired as she lifted it to the twinkling sky. "Perhaps if we look long enough, the answer will come to us."

Cecile snorted. "So, apparently, we are looking for her sanity." With her hearty chuckle, she tossed back a slug of cider.

Though she glared in return, a hint of mirth played on Désirée's lips. "It isn't insanity to believe in something."

"I believe we're going to catch our deaths out here," Cecile said as the wind picked up again, stirring the trees along the riverbank into a wild frenzy.

"Oh, don't be so dramatic." Désirée snatched the bottle out of Cecile's hand. "It's nearly summer. It's barely cold out here." She looked like a fish on dry land as she clutched the bottle in an awkward hold and drank a swig of cider.

Madeleine shook her head. "I do believe we are a bad influence on you, Mademoiselle Clement. Here you are, a well-bred woman, lurking around the fields at night, drinking straight from the bottle."

"Trust me, this is not the most unladylike venture of my life by far." Corking the bottle, Désirée set it before the fire. "I have stories that would make your head spin." Despite her words, she daintily dabbed at the corners of her mouth with her thumb and forefinger.

"Oh, really?" Cecile leaned in, her brow hooked and her skin illumined by firelight. "Do any of these stories involve *men*?" A mischievous look skittered over her face as her laugh lifted into the void of night.

Désirée's eyes gleamed as she smirked in return. "Would I be out here with the two of you if they did?" Her shoulders lifted. "If only there were men so worthy of our poor, lonely souls."

"It won't last forever." Cecile angled forward to strategically add a few more sticks to the fire. "I have big plans for a hog reeve down the way."

Her comment sparked a fit of laughter among the women, their giggles mingling with the gush of river water running past.

"What about Serge?" Madeleine asked.

Cecile stuck out her tongue in disgust. "Serge makes a superb friend, but a romantic partner?" Her bronze head wagged. "I think I'd have better luck with that hog reeve."

"The right one will come for both of us, I know it." Désirée swung her gaze to Madeleine. "Of course, you *could* be part of the most idyllic relationship of all time, but you refuse to be."

Though they were spoken in good humor, Désirée's words still wrenched at Madeleine. How could she explain her deal with Pascal without putting Désirée in danger? Even in the older man's absence, he had left servants to watch her every move. Fastening her lips, Madeleine stared into the glowing embers spitting from the fire and retreated into silence.

"She has good reason," Cecile said gently.

With a mild frown, Désirée crossed her arms over her cloaked chest. "And *you* know what that is. I see who the better friend is here."

Cecile cast a cautious glance at Madeleine. "There are some things in life you can't share with everyone."

"I'm sorry. I don't mean to push, I just—" Désirée sighed, her face drawing sadly. "I just wish I could help somehow. I thought the two of you would never separate. You both made each other so happy."

The fire popped and fizzed as Madeleine gazed into its capering depths. Though its warmth showered her arms and face, a cold ache still spread inside of her. Désirée deserved better answers than she could provide. With each passing day, new memories sprouted, some she cherished, others she wanted nothing more than to escape. Would Désirée still want to be her friend when she discovered her unsavory past? How could she?

"To be honest," Madeleine said at last, her throat sore, "Gabriel is better off without me. Each new memory I have of myself affirms this." Her arms protectively encircled her bent knees. "He could never truly be happy with a person like me."

"Don't say that." Désirée's forehead wrinkled in concern. "After all you did to save him, to bring him home, I know who you really are. What in your past could possibly make you feel so unworthy?"

Madeleine's gaze veered from Cecile to Désirée, her fear and desire to do right by her friends waging war in her mind. Drinking in a cathartic breath of fresh grass and smoke, she plunged ahead. "The fact that I knew about the treasure before I came here. That I arrived in hopes of taking it from you. That I nearly killed a man to lay my hands on it."

Skin blanching, Désirée watched her in silence for a prolonged moment, her fingers gripping a rock beside her. "Tell me—" Her voice faltered as her eyelashes fluttered. "Tell me more. Please, Madeleine."

The entire ugly story paraded before Madeleine's eyes, a swirling cacophony. A voice deep within begged her to stop, warned her that the Clement family would cast her out and never allow her to return if she proceeded. Yet staring into Désirée's expectant face across the fire, Madeleine knew her guilt would never ease unless she admitted the truth.

Inhaling a breath of courage that sank low in her body, Madeleine diverted her eyes to the shivering treetops overhead. "My brothers are alive. I did not remember that until recent months." She pulled her legs in closer, shivers skittering along her skin. "My brother Auguste—he has pursued Henri's treasure with singular focus. He charged me with finding someone called 'the nameless man', a man who claimed that his family hid your ancestors' treasure."

The memory captured her senses, transporting her to another time. Madeleine saw herself standing on the docks of Bordeaux, gazing at a collection of ramshackle buildings, their worn paint and broken roofs bleak in the rising moon. Behind her, the ancient town stood proud, its stone walls tossing candlelight across the river. Here, a baby screamed. Two men yelled and scuffled somewhere in the darkness. Madeleine suppressed a shiver as she urged her legs forward.

Her every step on the decaying wood moaned beneath her boot-ed feet. The briny wind fluttered her hooded cape as Madeleine wandered past riverboats of every variety caporing in the waves. A light rain trickled from the chasm of rolling skies, plunking in tiny splashes over the algae-laden wood.

Most of the dismal buildings crowding the docks were dark inside, their inhabitants tucked into bed, she assumed. Here and there, where yellow candlelight glittered in a window, Madeleine could make out the crude shapes of a kitchen or living space. One square dwelling stood out from within them, its two-story structure flooding the river in light and notes from an accordion. It had to be the seedy bar Toutain had spoken of.

Despite Auguste's lack of faith in her, Madeleine was proud she'd come this far. Heart beating out of her chest, she reached for the iron handle to a little door on the side. She would prove herself, no matter what this eerie place forced her to do. She owed Auguste that much.

Before her thumb could compress the handle, out of the dark-ness a hand gripped her wrist. Madeleine leaped backward, collid-ing with the solid frame behind her. Spinning, she forced her gaze to climb a linen-garbed chest until they met with the cold, sneering face of a young man.

His leering eyes descended her slowly, as if they might dig be-neath her cloak. "What have we here?" His whiskey-laced breath showered her in little droplets. A second, bear-like hand clamped on her other wrist.

Though fear bit at her middle, Madeleine cast him her fiercest expression. "Monsieur, you will unhand me at once." She tried to jerk one arm free of him, but his fingers only squeezed tighter.

"Monsieur." The man chortled, revealing a mess of stained and crooked teeth. "No need for formalities, my dear. I'm no gentleman." Yanking her to him, one hand swung around to grip the back of her cloak.

Madeleine planted both palms on his chest and gritted her teeth, pushing with all her might. His laughter echoed in her ears, the energy draining from her body as he stood there unmoved, pawing at her clothes. If only she could reach the pistol she had tucked in her knapsack. If only she could remember the instruction on fighting her father had once tried to instill in her.

"You shouldn't have been wandering around these parts all by yourself," he said in her ear, his breath hot on her neck. "Don't you know this is no place for a lady?" One hand dove beneath her cloak, anchoring at her waist.

Over the rush of blood in her ears, his callous words sunk a quiet resolve through her. Hadn't she been thrown on the street as a child? Hadn't she learned to survive, one hard lesson at a time, *against* the type of miscreant who held her captive now? Her eyes narrowed, producing a grin on the man's smarmy face as his hands moved to explore her.

"I may go wherever I please," she said through curled lips. With all the force she could muster, her knee jetted up between his legs.

Yowling, the man released her. Before he could reel back any farther, Madeleine caught him by the collar of his soiled shirt and rammed her fist into his eye. The man flew backward, landing with a crash on the wooden boards of the dock. Madeleine stood over his body as he doubled over in pain, rolling around. Her chest rose in frantic waves and her reddened fingers screamed at her, but she would bask a moment in her victory. She didn't turn away until his pleading eyes begged her to.

The little tavern on the docks teemed with cigar smoke when Madeleine marched through its rickety door. The caustic odor singed her nostrils and down her throat. She swore she felt the floor sway beneath her. Steeling herself, she straightened her back and wound through the fray. Everywhere she looked, unkempt men in tattered clothes guzzled liquor by the stein. Some bickered over a game of cards or the arm-wrestling match set up in the corner. Others merely slumped in their chairs, as if lifting a glass to their mouths were the only action they had the strength to perform.

Madeleine found the bartender beyond a row of half-awake clientele, a couple about to tumble from their chairs by the looks of it. Even the bar had dirt caked on its surface, droplets of ale making pools of mud on the wood. Affronted by the smell, mingled in body odor, she held her breath as she signaled for the barman.

"Glass of ale?" he asked, tossing a foaming cup atop his filthy bar.

"No, thank you." Madeleine wondered if that's all this place really had to offer—a glass of strong ale to wash your troubles away. "I'm looking for an old friend, actually. I used to see him here. Big eyes, long nose, looks a bit like a crow." She threw him a charming smile, the description Toutain had provided sounding ridiculous on her lips.

The bartender released a throaty chuckle, his rotund belly shaking. "Now, what's a pretty thing like you doing looking for a troll like François?"

François. Madeleine tried to control the rapid thump of her heart as she kept her smile painted on and shrugged innocently. "Like I said, just an old friend." Letting just enough mischief show on her face, she knew he wouldn't be able to discern the truth from her playfulness.

Seeming to enjoy her game, the bearded man laughed deeper, his head wagging. "I ain't seen the man around these parts in ages, but you can check upstairs." One thick finger jabbed toward the ceiling. "Stairs are right outside. François used to live in the apartment up there—but perhaps you know that already." He cocked his head, one brow lifting comically.

With merely a simper, Madeleine turned and retreated from the bar. Better the barkeep think whatever lewd imaginings he wanted about her than to guess her true intentions. Outside, the salty wind sliced through her, sending her cloak flapping and hair whipping from its pins. Her attacker had long ago slunk back into the shadows, no doubt licking his wounds.

Gripping a wobbly railing in white fingers, she climbed an uneven set of stairs on the tavern's side. High above the river, she looked down at the lights glowing across the lapping water. Just like her life—beauty always existed, even in the depths of deprivation.

Her gentle knock on the apartment door brought a short man with graying dark hair and spectacles to her. He pitched her a guarded look, rounded eyes sweeping her face.

"*Pardonnez-moi,*" Madeleine said with her kindest smile. "I am looking for François. He's an old friend. I haven't seen him around here in quite some time, and I was hoping I might check in on his well-being." Bile climbed her throat just to spew the dishonest words. When had she converted from Christian-born girl to master deceiver?

"Please, come in." The man stood aside to admit her, though his nervous glance darted every which way along the docks. "Might I take your cloak?" His weathered hands opened to accept it.

"Yes, thank you." Sweeping the soaked piece of clothing from her shoulders, she gave it to the man and watched him hang it on a homemade coat tree by the window. Through a tiny kitchen, he led her into an office-like room warm with the scents of clementine and cinnamon.

The man shifted from one foot to another. "Have a seat," he said with a flourish of his hand. "I regret I don't have a better place to entertain. There isn't much space in my home, I'm afraid." His forehead crinkled warily as he watched her sit in the plush armchair opposite his desk. "I'll get us some tea."

Despite the rain and wind raging outside the man's window, his little cocoon from the outside world felt cozy. Papers were strewn across a worn oak desk alongside an inkwell and whale oil lamp casting light into the small space. From within a small brick-laid hearth in the corner, firelight illuminated a wall full of books and an elk head fixed beside them. Madeleine sucked in a breath, spying an oval portrait just visible in the fire's capering flames.

Careful not to let her steps creak on the floorboards, Madeleine pushed off her chair and crept toward the gilded frame, glittering in the balmy firelight. The oil-painted face staring back had a hooked, bird-like nose. Dark, beady eyes looked out from beneath bushy brows, accentuated by the wild hair sticking out over his sizeable ears. She swallowed, taking in the homely creature. Realization dawned as her host clattered beyond her in the kitchen. This man was François's *father.*

Her breath rose in heavy waves as Madeleine snuck to the man's desk and began to rifle through his papers. If anyone knew the nameless man's location, his father would. Footsteps groaned on the floorboards beyond the partially open door. Between her rummaging, Madeleine glanced up, her pulse rushing faster and sweat emerging at her hairline.

At last, one letter stood out among the others. Lifting it in the lamplight, Madeleine gulped at the two words scrawled above the rest—*dear papa.* She whirled the piece of parchment around, eyes scanning for any sign of its origin. The answer glared back at her in heavy-handed script—Capri. Joy leaped inside of her as she imagined bringing this back to Auguste, seeing approval spread over his features.

Then, the click of a pistol's hammer made her throat go dry.

Fifteen

Madeleine's skirt fluttered in the breeze as she sat on the riverbank telling her story, Désirée and Cecile peering back through the dark with rapt attention. "I just remember the letter slipping through my fingers," she said, lost in the vision of that tiny apartment on the River Garonne. "I couldn't think of anything to do in that moment but to turn and look at him."

She could still hear the crackling fire in his miniature hearth, could still feel its heat rushing down her skin as she reeled back, the barrel of his silver musket coming into focus. Their eyes met over the top of it, fear brimming in the dark irises behind his gleaming spectacles.

"I knew you were trouble the first moment I saw you. Anyone who comes looking for François always is." He stepped back, the hand posing his gun outward quaking.

Gulping back her rising panic, Madeleine splayed her fingers in the air. "Please, I don't wish to harm him. I only wish to join him on his quest to find what is rightfully his."

A low, mirthless chuckle issued from the man's throat. "Join him long enough to learn his secrets and then try to kill him is what you mean."

Her brows gathered, her mind racing through the conversation she'd shared with Toutain in her dressing room. "The captain, you mean? The one who met with potential investors downstairs in the bar?"

"Captain, pirate, whatever you wish to call him." His mouth curved downward in disgust. "He told my son that if he led his crew to the treasure, they would split it evenly—the two of them."

"I'd wager that was a lie," she said.

"Of course it was a lie. François would never listen to me, but I could discern that filthy mercenary's duplicity the minute he stepped through these doors. He *looked* believable. He looked sophisticated and refined. But he was barbaric. He wanted nothing but to take that treasure for himself."

Searching his wounded gaze, Madeleine deduced the conclusion to his story. "Did he hurt your son?" she asked, voice quiet beneath the rain tinkling on the window.

He swallowed, tears brimming behind his glasses. "He certainly tried." The hand clutching his pistol slowly descended. "He knew the place to look for. My son knew *where*, in that vast space, his ancestors had buried it. Throughout the course of their relationship, it became apparent to my son that this pirate planned to kill him the moment they found the treasure." His shoulders wilted. "He barely escaped with his life and has been running ever since."

Even with the threat of danger, Madeleine's heart stretched across the void between them, compassion stirring her soul to watch this injured creature turn his lonely gaze to the distant horizon. Her own parents' faces haunted her shattered memories. Hadn't the hands of greedy opportunists ripped them apart, too? The same sting that never left her day and night reflected back in the man's firelit eyes.

"That must weigh on you a great deal, to be separated from your son," she said at last.

Blinking back his tears, he nodded slowly. "It is my constant companion." His diminutive frame shivered, as if the very thought of it chilled him. Traces of the elderberry tea he had brewed wafted in from the kitchen. "This treasure has added a burden to my shoulders I'm no longer sure I can carry."

His words echoed through her, resonating from somewhere deep within. Auguste had only been back in her life for mere months, and already the Moon King's bounty had monopolized most of that time. Listening to the rain patter on the river beneath their feet, Madeleine wondered if this treasure would indeed prove worthy in the end. How much would it rip asunder in the meantime?

"Perhaps we are all cursed," she said, inciting the man to look at her. "Anyone who learns of this treasure seems to abandon all thought of their former life in search of it. How valuable is a life spent alone, even if riches surround you?"

"That is precisely what I told my son." His head shook sadly. "But he refused to listen to me. François has his mother's spirit. He will pursue this venture with singular focus until that treasure either rests in his hands or kills him."

Without thought, Madeleine stepped toward him. "But François is safe now, isn't he? If he stays in hiding."

As if she'd lit a spark inside him, his gaze snapped with fire. "Until people like you come rooting him out." He lifted his pistol again, its round, ominous barrel trained on her face. "Who sent you, anyway? This pirate? I thought I'd run enough of his minions off."

Madeleine tried to ignore the chilling ache in her gut as she stepped back and collided with the desk. "Of course not. I would never work for such a man." She cocked her head, pleading eyes appealing to him. "I swear to you, I speak the truth. I have no desire to hurt François."

"Maybe you do, but I can't take that chance." His nostrils flared as his finger hooked the trigger.

"Someone will hear you!" she blurted, desperate. "There are dozens of people in the tavern downstairs. Surely the sound of your gun will bring them to your door."

A derisive puff of air escaped his lips. "Have you taken a look around since you've been here? The roughest criminals in Bordeaux fill that tavern. Do you think they will spare a second thought for one gunshot? I can toss you in the river tonight, and nobody will even care when your body washes up." His own words forced him to swallow. "Though I never thought I would have to kill a woman to keep my son safe."

Madeleine's knees buckled, her body swaying. She steadied herself against his desk, her trembling fingers barely gripping the edge. Nausea in the pit of her stomach spread through her body until ice encased her extremities. Staring into the barrel of his gun, she realized with a bitter pang that it would be the last thing she saw unless she took action. And Henri Clement would steal yet another life with his hidden treasure.

Forcing power into her legs, Madeleine sprung from the desk, aimed at her foe. She gritted her teeth, arms extended like a cat about to claw a neighborhood bully. The man's eyes broadened, though he hadn't the time to react before she crashed into him, arms encircling him.

The pair grunted and huffed as they wrestled before the fire, Madeleine frantically grabbing for the gun in his grasp. Deadlocked between them, the pistol fired, an ear-splitting shot blasting through the apartment. The bullet pinged off the man's spectacles, shattering them as they tumbled to the floor. Seizing his wrist, she squeezed until he was forced to drop it with a yelp, depositing the decorative hilt into Madeleine's open hand.

Out of breath and ears ringing, she stood up within the cloud of pungent gunsmoke. François's father was bent before a swirl of firelight, chest pitching and hands on his knees. Shards of glass from his spectacles littered his braided rug. Despite the turmoil that had just transpired, the study reassumed its tranquil quality.

The roar of the patrons downstairs carried on, unaffected by the fight that had just ensued.

He glanced at her wearily as she leveled the pistol at him, her thumb clicking the hammer down again and depositing another bullet into the chamber. "I suppose you're going to kill me now. It's the sensible thing to do." He said it without a hint of mourning, just quiet resolve.

Madeleine blinked, her grip tightening on the pistol. Yes, perhaps it was the sensible thing, but could she ever really murder an innocent man?

"Just tell me where the treasure is," she said. "Both you and François will be safe. Nobody has to die."

His yearning gaze traveled to the window, where the wind beat against the building's side. "That's just it. Had I known, I would have told someone long ago." He sighed, his whole body sagging beneath an unseen weight. "His mother's family hid that God-forsaken treasure, not mine. She refused to share their secret even with me, only François. Only her own flesh and blood."

Heart aching, Madeleine turned to snatch François's letter from the desk and stuff it into her pocket. How badly she wished she could promise this man that she wouldn't pursue his son, but Auguste would never hear it. Instead, she kept the pistol trained on his small frame and backed away.

"I will only go there to speak with him," she said. "I promise you, monsieur."

His head shook with vehemence. "Please, mademoiselle." His wrinkled hands folded in supplication.

"I won't hurt him." She nearly tripped as she stepped through the doorway and retrieved her cloak from the hook, the pistol's aim never leaving him. "I swear it. I swear to you." Grappling for the door handle behind her, she volleyed him one last silent vow before ducking out the door and hurrying down the stairs.

The bullfrogs' throaty groans brought her mind back to the present. Madeleine stared into the fire, where orange flames ate at fresh-cut birch logs. The wind whistled over them, rustling the bushes along the rivers' edge, throwing smoke into her stinging eyes. Coughing, she fanned the air with her shawl before setting her forearms atop her knees.

"By the time we journeyed to Capri, the nameless man had fled," she said, the memory tasting bitter on her tongue. "By letting that man live, I gave him the opportunity to warn his son. Auguste was furious with me." The ire in his gaze, his incensed words that day, still haunted her.

Cecile huffed. "Of course he was. Is he so heartless that he could have killed a man who did nothing to deserve it?"

An owl's strident hoot echoed from the woods as Madeleine thought on her question. "I've often asked myself the very same." Her voice trembled. "I would like to imagine he wouldn't, yet with how this treasure has possessed him of late—I honestly don't know."

The memory of him tortured her—standing over her with fists clenched and veins popping from his muscles. "He told me I was good for nothing now, save for my looks. That if I didn't have a brain, at least my body could still be of some service." The words barely choked from her arid throat. Madeleine tucked her head against her knees, blocking it all out—the disgust on Auguste's face that day, the horror in Désirée's eyes when she learned the truth about her.

With her head buried and eyes closed, her body gave way to sobs. Two arms came around her quaking frame, attempting to pacify her. Salty tears rushed in abundance down her face, wetting her quivering lips. How good of Cecile to comfort her even when her actions merited nothing but castigation. Yet all she wanted was to depart this place, to run so far that she could never hurt another soul again.

"Hush, now. It's all over." A soothing hand brushed back her rebellious hair.

Madeleine started, peeking up through her clouded gaze at Désirée's face, her pallid skin glowing like bronze in the firelight. "You don't hate me?" Madeleine's eyes searched the compassionate ones staring back. "After everything I've done to you—to your family? How can you even look at me now?"

Désirée's eyes twinkled, the hint of a smile edging her lips. "Did you really come here to seduce my brother into giving you his treasure?"

Shame heating her cheeks, Madeleine nodded. "I loathe to admit it, but I did."

"But you don't feel that way anymore," Désirée said.

"Of course not." The notion seemed preposterous now—that she had ever sought to take from the most benevolent creature she had ever met. "I love him more than anything in the world. I love you, too." So much, her stomach ached to imagine anyone bringing a speck of harm on the Clement house.

Sheltering both of Madeleine's hands in hers, Désirée gripped them tightly and looked her squarely in the eye. "Then I forgive you, Madeleine Bertrand. Whoever you were no longer matters. It is who you *are* that counts." Her head angled, mercy alive in her blue eyes. "And if you marry my brother, or if you don't, you are still my sister. Forever."

Madeleine's shoulders shook as Désirée enfolded her again. "Thank you," she whispered against Désirée's velvet cloak, breathing in her floral scent. "Thank you for that, Désirée. I shall never forget your kindness."

Pulling back, Désirée let humor play on the soft lines of her face before she broke into full-on laughter. "Look at you. My poor, unsuspecting brother didn't stand a chance, now did he?"

"He had better hope of becoming an orator," Cecile said, her laughter mingling with Désirée's.

Madeleine glanced from one woman to the other. "It just happened, I swear it." Her hands opened in defense. "I didn't even try to attract him as I was supposed to."

Désirée pressed her fingers over her curled lips. "Oh, Maddy, of course you didn't. One look was all he needed to begin falling in love with you."

"And what will it take for him to forget me?" Sucking in a shaky breath, Madeleine swiped at the balmy tears dotting her cheekbones.

"That, I don't know." Désirée planted one arm around her. "I doubt this is pleasant to hear, but Uncle Pascal plans to bring Caroline back here soon. She and Gabriel have grown—close through correspondence. Perhaps he *has* found love again, despite my hopes for the two of you. Perhaps it's for the best."

The statement pierced Madeleine clear through. Laying her head on Désirée's downy shoulder, she blinked away the tears rimming her eyelids and basked in the river's churning sound. Somewhere deep within, hope sprouted and entwined with her misery. Gabriel would have a good woman to love him always. They both would be safe, despite malicious uncles and long-lost brothers. What more could she ask for?

"How will you handle Auguste?" Cecile asked as she prodded the fire with a fallen branch. "I expect he will be angry when Caroline returns and he sees the two of them together."

Désirée made an involuntary shiver, her gaze darting across the darkened countryside. "It chills me to know someone is out there watching our every move."

"It's only Felix. The man is harmless." Madeleine sighed, knowing her brother was anything but. "I suppose I'll have to give him something. Some portion of the clues we've found so far to keep him pacified for now."

"Or you could tell him everything," Désirée said.

Madeleine rolled her gaze up to her face. "Have you taken leave of your senses?" She chuckled.

"Think about it." Désirée's fingers flung long shadows over the earth as she extended them. "You displayed your loyalty to Gabriel over Auguste when you gave him the letter you found instead of your brother. So far, you've brought him nothing. Of course he is going to be wary of your actions here, especially when he sees a new woman commanding Gabriel's life."

Pushing up to sit beside her, Madeleine wagged her head. "So what do you suggest we do about it?"

"This family needs that treasure about as badly as I need an extra gown in my wardrobe. It's just a bit of fun to pass the time and certainly not worth losing each other over." Désirée clapped her hands together. "What do you say you invite him here in person, and we can discuss it. We'll show him the clues we've found thus far, and we can all find the treasure together. Everyone wins."

Cecile plopped her hands on her hips, her brows gathered. "Are you insane? You want to bring that lunatic under our roof?"

"I appreciate the idea," Madeleine said, "but that's riskier than I would prefer, especially with Pascal around. The pair of them would certainly set each other off."

Désirée's shoulders wilted. "Well, does anyone have a better idea?"

"You could trick him." Cecile poked one finger up, excitement fueling her coy expression. "Make up some fraudulent clues to throw him off track. Even if he finds this nameless man, he still won't know where to find the treasure unless he knows who that pirate was."

The memory of that cozy apartment above the tavern flashed in Madeleine's mind. "I read the name on that letter I found in Bordeaux. I never told Auguste, but I—" Her hand scrunched at her chin, the image refusing to budge. "I can't remember it for the life of me."

"Precisely." Cecile's voice yanked her back to the present. "You didn't show him that letter because you didn't trust him, even then. Tell him the pirate's name is Jean Carpentier or Jaspar Chasse. It doesn't matter, just give him something to keep him busy."

"She might be right about this," Désirée said. "A distraction could help, at least until we figure out Henri's clue about water and stars."

Madeleine draped her arms over her body, the image of Auguste's rage when he discovered that she had double-crossed him injecting ice in her bones. "Do you think it will work? What do I do when he finds out I lied to him?"

The night answered in the soft medley of the cricket's chirp and bullfrog's croak. Neither woman could offer her a suggestion, but as Madeleine gazed into the glowing embers of their dying fire, she found both had drawn near.

"We're a team, Maddy." Cecile placed Madeleine's hand in her two warm palms while Désirée took the other. "We will figure this out together."

"We won't leave you alone, ever," Désirée said.

And in those two loving faces, Madeleine knew she'd found the true family her heart had always longed for.

Sixteen

T he first signs of summer flaunted their robust beauty along the roadway as Madeleine rode a farmer's cart to The Black Lion. Beneath pleasant streams of sunlight, the verdant hills dipped and swelled as far as her eye could see, their tall grasses rolling strands of silver over the countryside. Reclining atop her bed of straw, Madeleine breathed in the earthy scent of alfalfa and watched the ash trees flutter in the wildflower-tinged breeze.

With every lurch of the wagon over the bumpy road, her heart jumped higher in her throat. What would Auguste have found in his quest for the nameless man? Would it alleviate her worry over the Clements' fate or merely complicate it? Looking out over pastures spotted with cows and baying sheep, she tried to let her anxiety tumble beneath the churn of the wagon wheels. It would do no good to fret, after all.

The dusty yard of The Black Lion was teeming with people when the wagon swayed to a stop in the unkempt grass. With a word of thanks to the farmer, Madeleine scrambled over the splintery bed and hopped over the tailgate. At once, she found herself amid the milling group—townspeople gossiping and trading amongst themselves, delivery men carting crates of clinking bottles into the back of the establishment. At the far end of the crowd,

Madeleine spotted a familiar form towering over the others and grabbed up her skirts.

"Jean-Paul!" she called, weaving her way to the stables. He turned at the sound of her voice, a pensive smile stretching across his face.

"Big sister." His words sounded ridiculous when he enfolded her in his bear-like embrace, his giant hands cradling her. There was nothing big about her next to him.

Madeleine sighed, dragging in the odor of molten iron clinging to his linen shirt. He smelled like their father, coming in from a long day in his blacksmith's shop, all metal and sweat. For a brief moment, she was that little girl again, swathed in comfort with a world of dreams spread before her. Then she opened her eyes and reality snatched her in its ugly claws.

"What is it?" Pushing away, she hunted the depths of his troubled expression. "What haven't you said yet?"

Chest expanding, Jean-Paul glanced down at his gloved hands. "I wish I could tell you there will be a warm welcome after all this time we've spent apart." His eyes brimmed with regret as they rose to meet hers. "You deserve that much after what you've been through."

Her throat closed in on itself. "Things didn't go well for Auguste on his journey?"

Jean-Paul shook his head. "He arrived home in a rage. Ordered me to come out here and prepare his horse." His eyebrows knit. "I think he plans to confront the baron now, before anyone else can get to the treasure."

"No." Panic welled in Madeleine's chest, rushing down her arms and stiffening her fingers. "We can't let him do that." Not when they were so close to deciphering Henri's clues. Gabriel would have no answer for her brother, and Auguste would kill him.

A large hand anchored on her shoulder. "I don't know that we can stop him," Jean-Paul said. "The longer he looks for this treasure, the more obsessed he becomes. I'm concerned for his mental state."

Without another word, Madeleine whirled in the dust and seized two handfuls of skirts. Ignoring the throng of townspeople, she jogged toward The Black Lion. Jean-Paul might cower at the thought of hindering their brother's plans, but she would put a stop to this. She would fight him, if need be, if it meant protecting Gabriel Clement.

The tavern's studded front door swung open just before Madeleine could reach it. She hopped backward, coming face-to-face with Auguste. Fire propelled his steps as he swiftly walked past her, not even sparing a second glance. Madeleine raced to catch up, her cantering feet matching his wide gate.

"Auguste, what do you plan on doing?" she asked.

"What I should have done all along." He kept up his ominous march, fists clenching and unfurling in repetition.

"You *can't* hurt him. He doesn't know where the treasure is. Not yet." Desperate, she threw herself into his path.

Auguste attempted to sidestep her one way and then another, but Madeleine's agile feet moved faster, blocking him. "Out of my way, sister," he said with a grunt, "unless you want me to take you down with him."

Her palms jetted out in front of her. "Auguste, listen to me. Listen for just a moment." What could she possibly say to detain him? Tell him everything, like Désirée had suggested? Make something up, as Cecile said? Looking now at his reddened skin and flared nostrils, the absolute hate in his eyes, she doubted either would suffice.

"We have creditors moving in from every direction. Running around the continent has soaked up all of our money. I don't have the time to stop and listen." With one solid swipe, Auguste shoved her out of his path.

Madeleine trailed him, choking on the dust his pounding boots littered in the air. "*Please*, Auguste. This will do us no good. We will find another way." She lunged for his arm, but he easily avoided her.

"I thought I told you to make ready my horse," he said to Jean-Paul as he strode past him and into the stables, Madeleine close at his heels.

While Auguste threw his saddle over his black mare's sinowy back, Madeleine's mind raced to procure *something* that would keep her brother from attacking the man she loved. Her hand hovered over the chain tucked safely beneath her collar, but no. Gabriel had entrusted her with it.

"I remembered something—something new." Her heart thudded. "A letter I found when I spoke with the nameless man's father." If only she could remember what she'd done with it.

Auguste squatted to buckle the horse's saddle around her stomach. "He isn't nameless. His name is François Martine."

She gasped. "So you found him."

"Yes, I found him." He spat the words as if they tasted of molding bread. "He was hiding with a family on a farm in Cornwall."

When he reached for the horse's bridle from a hook on the wall and kept up his work, she stepped toward him. "Well, what did he say? Will he help us find the treasure?" Her forehead scrunched. How could he reveal such a massive breakthrough with such flippancy?

Sighing, Auguste turned to her. A remorseful gaze flicked over her before he unhinged his lips. "He's dead, Madeleine." He brushed an open hand through his hair. "I found him on the floor, stabbed to death in the stomach."

An icy chill seized her. "He's—" The words refused to come, her throat constricting. "Who would do such a wretched thing?"

"Many people would for the amount of money we're seeking." Auguste returned to draping the bridle over the mare's head and placed the bit between her teeth. "In this case, it had to have been that blasted pirate. It was fresh. Martine couldn't have been dead for more than a day." He paused, his hand clenching the bridle. "If only I had been a little bit faster."

Madeleine looked on in horror, unsure whether he regretted failing to save a man's life or losing a clue to his beloved treasure. "What about the family you mentioned?" she asked. "Did he kill them, too?"

As if snapped from a dream, Auguste straightened and shook his head. "No, they were unharmed. He was living in one of their outbuildings. They never even saw his attacker or knew he had passed." Gathering the reins, he flung them over the horse's back.

Relief flooding her, Madeleine plastered a hand over her hammering heart. At least more innocent people weren't murdered in the name of greed. Her father's face flashed through her mind, his muscular form being dragged from their cottage. She saw Maman, helpless in the arms of evil, desirous men. When would it end? When would the quest for money and power cease to triumph over decency?

While Madeleine stood aching for the old man on the docks of Bordeaux, Auguste unhitched the stable gate and led his horse from her stall. The clop of her shoed feet on the slab floor barely ripped Madeleine from her musings. She looked up just as her brother planted one foot in a stirrup, preparing to swing his other over the animal's broad back.

"Auguste, wait." She rushed forward and gripped his hand on the saddle's pommel. "You *must* listen to me before you run blindly into what you do not know."

Auguste flicked her hand away with a rough swat. "I have no choice now. If that mercenary felt confident enough to murder Martine, he must know where the treasure is. We have to beat him there, or everything we've worked for is in vain."

Madeleine tried again, her hand firm on the saddle as she blocked him from mounting it. "We found clues," she blurted, desperate to stop him. "Clues that this pirate *doesn't* have." Her chest pitched and sweat moistened her skin as he turned back to her, searching her face.

"What do you mean *we?*" His dark eyes narrowed, suspicion sparked in their stormy depths.

Dry, trodden hay and manure filled her senses as Madeleine inhaled a long breath. How much could she tell him without endangering Gabriel? "The baron and I," she said, hurrying on when his brows flinched. "He trusts me. He told me of his ancestor's treasure, and we've been looking for it together."

Curiosity skittered over his brow, yet still he flexed his jaw defiantly. "Well, what did you find?"

"First, we found what appeared to be Henri's letter." She bit her lip. Best not to tell him she'd discovered it herself and shared it with Gabriel. "It didn't provide any direction on the treasure's location, but it turned out to be a forgery."

"Most likely planted by *him*," Auguste said with a roll of his eyes.

"His sister Désirée and I—we found a secret room under his library filled with letters Henri received and his alchemy supplies. It was amazing to see."

Madeleine tucked a strand of hair behind her ear. Already, her brother's gaze had begun to glaze over. "That led us to the National Library, where we found a clue Henri had left there. A real clue, Auguste."

Triumph lifted inside her as he shifted into a beam of light pouring through the ceiling, the sun illuminating the hard swallow of his throat. "What did it say?" he asked in a reverent tone.

"'Let evening stars be your guide. Beyond the waters, endless treasures hide.'" Madeleine smiled at the tears sprouting in her brother's eyes. "I don't know what it means yet, but it's a start. The treasure is real, Auguste. And it *has* to be discoverable if Henri had confidence that his family would find it with the bread crumbs he left behind."

Auguste stared at the floor for a prolonged moment. Chatter from the townspeople outside the stables lit the air. Behind him,

Jean-Paul moved from foot to foot, his expression uneasy. When Auguste's gaze swung back to Madeleine's face, a bizarre mixture of rage, hope, and unease resided there.

"Why didn't you tell me the two of you were following these clues together?" he asked. "Don't you think I might have given him a little bit more clemency, knowing he had let you so far into his confidence?"

Her shoulders lifted. "I didn't know what to believe. I was afraid you would only think the worst of him, that you would be angry if you knew." She shook her head. "Honestly, you hated him long before you sent me to the château. I didn't want to upset you any more than necessary."

His keen eyes dissected her like a vulture hunting fresh meat. Madeleine recoiled, feeling naked beneath his scrutiny. A string of excruciating moments passed, nothing but the whinny of horses filling the space. Then, reality dawned in his brown eyes.

"You love him," he said, advancing on her when Madeleine only blinked in response. "You actually think you love this man."

She sucked in a shaky breath, knowing she couldn't deny it without the truth seeping over her face. "Would it be so wrong?"

A mirthless chuckle flew from his mouth. "For a poor country girl to get swept up in the fantasy that a rich scoundrel like Clement could actually want her? Yes." His head angled in pity, condescending her very existence. "Come now, sister. This is the son of Raphael Clement. You *remember* what that man did to our father, do you not?"

"Yes, and I also know that a man's substance does not consist of his father's sins." Against her will, ire rammed through her body. Her nostrils flared and her skin flamed. "Just as I know a father's benevolence does not always transfer to his sons."

Her words quieted him, injured sorrow piercing his countenance. His eyelids fluttered, his hand reaching up to rub the back of his neck. When his gaze entangled with hers, their hollow resilience told her she would never truly reach him. "I have fought my whole life to reach this point. I fight for my father. I fight for his legacy. What a shame you are so weak-minded that one man's charms can cause you to doubt that."

Madeleine opened her mouth to speak, but he was swifter. "I have placed much faith in you, sister. I have sent you into the front lines, hoping you would put yourself aside for once and emerge victorious." His head wagged sadly. "I see now where your loyalties lie. They are as easily blown about as a fallen leaf in the wind."

Her entire body trembling, Madeleine gritted her teeth. If only he knew what she had endured for him. If only he could peer into the expanse of her soul and witness the daily sacrifice and torture she lived. Would he care? Would he even understand it? Somewhere in time, the little boy she had known in childhood had transformed into the iniquitous, jaded man standing before her.

"My loyalties remain where they always have." She fought to keep her voice even. "I want to do what is right. I will not let innocent people be hurt, no matter how greatly I've been hurt in the past."

Auguste scowled. "And you suppose he's innocent? A person raised by Raphael Clement, the Devil himself?"

"He *is* innocent." Her fists tightened at his guffaw. "I *know* him, Auguste. He is nothing like his father. He is nothing like the man you depict him to be."

Her brother's eyes rolled skyward. "Blinded by love. You always were a victim to it, even in Italy." Before she could comprehend his strange words, he had stepped toward her, looming. "Do you know how many letters Felix saw passing between your precious baron and Caroline Allair? Fanciful envelopes, perfumed stationary—love notes, Madeleine. Make no mistake. Felix says her household is preparing for an impending marriage, even now."

The truth sank through her body like a stone slowly descending the depths of a lake. Madeleine steadied herself on the wall, sweat emerging from her every pore. She had witnessed reality for so long—had steered it, even, yet the words plunged her into a despair she wasn't sure she could claw her way out of. Gabriel would marry another woman, and she—well, she would go as far away as she possibly could as soon as the threats had retreated. She had no other choice.

"Poor Maddy." Auguste's words chafed her already broken heart. "You always did believe the best in others, even after the world hardened you." He slipped a strand of her hair behind her ear, launching a shiver through her. "It's a good thing you have your brother to watch over you. I will expose this liar for who he is. I will make him pay for hurting you."

"No." Madeleine swallowed back the pain engulfing her. "Don't hurt him, I beg you. What happened between Gabriel Clement and I is so much more complicated than I can explain right now. Just give me a little bit more time, and I will produce the treasure's location." She cocked her head, eyes imploring him. "I know I can. Then you will never have to worry about money *or* the Clement family again. We will leave them behind to whatever devices they choose." Her hand flattened on her stomach, the prospect stabbing her with a raw ache.

Auguste considered her proposal, his hawk-like stare boring into her. At last, he seized the mare's reins in one hand. "One month, Madeleine. You have one month. Then I'm coming for that baron, treasure or no." With one more serious glare aimed her way, he led his horse back into her stall and began to shed her bridle and saddle.

Muscles relaxing and heartbeat slowing, Madeleine tiptoed from the stables, as if the mere sound of her footsteps might set him off again. Outside, the sunlight blinded her. She raised her fingers to block it out, the harsh rays warm on her goose-pimpled skin. Jean-Paul stood under a tree not far away, a sullen look plastered over his masculine features. Madeleine started toward him, but the big man shook his head and covered the space between them in several monstrous strides.

"Not now, sister," he murmured as he passed her, shoving a slip of paper into her hand.

Madeleine watched him disappear into the stables before unfurling the note he'd slipped to her. Sloppily written in Italian read the words *meet me in Solomon's Meadow, on Tuesday at 4 p.m.* With a furtive glance toward the stables, Madeleine crammed the note in her dress pocket and bustled back to the road. She had only one month to decipher Henri's message and not a clue where to begin.

Seventeen

"Let's keep going. It can't be much farther." Désirée held a lantern high, casting yellow rays of light over the mysterious walls of the cave into which they'd ventured.

Behind her, two women huddled close—Madeleine, eyes scanning every nook within the cave for signs of a clue, and Cecile, complaining about the cold. The rocky floor crunched beneath their feet as they ventured into the earth's belly, the squeak of an occasional scurrying rat or nesting bat reverberating off the walls.

"Tell me again why we are doing this." Cecile ducked as one such bat winged over her head. She glared at the offending creature who would dare disturb her peace of mind.

"We've searched near every other bit of water in the whole barony," Désirée threw over her shoulder. "This has to be it. I don't know why I didn't think of it sooner. Where else would Henri have hidden something precious but a secretive place like a cave on his own land?"

Cecile shivered, though she kept pace behind Désirée. "I remember the last time you led us into a place like this. We were nearly lost without even a light to direct us."

"Well, it's a good thing I'm along on this trip, then," said a booming male voice behind them.

Pinching her lips together, Madeleine focused on keeping steady over the uneven ground. She had tried to forget he was behind her, that every thump of boots filling her eardrums belonged to the man she couldn't have. Désirée had insisted he join them, not only for safety, but a helping hand.

"How can you possibly associate Henri's clue with this place?" Cecile asked. "Did it not say we would find it by the stars? Forgive me, but there is little hope of seeing stars from here, especially in the day."

Huffing, Désirée led them up an incline. "I don't know. Perhaps the stars would have brought us here had we studied the night sky."

"This valley *was* once known as Stargazer's Field," Gabriel offered.

"See? It was providence that I thought of it." Désirée's lantern bobbed as she commandeered them through a snaking tunnel.

Madeleine cupped her hands over her mouth, breathing balmy air over her frozen fingers. "How do you even know this place, Désirée?" Raphael Clement couldn't have approved of his only daughter traipsing through the filthy underground.

"Don't you remember the catacombs, Maddy?" Cecile released a blithe laugh that echoed in the cramped space. "Rich people are oddly fascinated with exploring disgusting places."

Désirée paused a moment to swat at Cecile before she carefully traversed a particularly narrow passage. "I had a youth, once upon a time," she said, turning sideways to fit through the opening. "One of my beaus was the adventurous sort. The two of us came down here all the time—" Her voice drifted off, perhaps as she remembered the person trailing their party.

"Please, Désirée. Do go on." From Gabriel's sarcastic tone, Madeleine could sense him turning every color known to man.

"Relax, it was all perfectly innocent. He never even tried to kiss me." A snort accompanied her pleasant giggle. "Though I doubt Papa would have allowed him to court me had he known we were sneaking off."

"Didn't his grandmother used to chaperone the two of you?" Gabriel asked.

"If by chaperone, you mean fall asleep in her chair, then yes. We were always back before she awoke."

Gabriel pierced the darkness with a long whistle. "I always knew that Eugene Pinchon was up to no good. I told Papa as much."

"Would you have liked any of her suitors?" Madeleine asked.

A moment passed over them with only the crunch of their boots sating the chilly air. "No, you're right," he said quietly. "I would have condemned every one."

Silence overtook them as each retreated into their own revelries. Madeleine's legs and feet ached from trying so hard to keep upright. Her fingertips brushed the craggy walls around them, their stone faces rough against her skin. The damp odor of mud and rock clung to every surface. Her body tremored in the cold, her foot dislodging a stone and sending her careening forward. The earth rushed toward her face as her every muscle screamed in alert.

Just before she hit the ground, one arm looped beneath her armpit, tugging her backward. "Woah, now." Gabriel's voice hummed in her ear, his breath hot on her neck as he pulled her upright, his stalwart form supporting her. Fighting to regain her footing, Madeleine seized his torso in both hands. When at last she had her feet planted firmly beneath her again, she found herself pinned against him, their faces a mere breath apart.

Chest pumping wildly from shock, Madeleine could do nothing but stare into the crystal eyes fixed down on her. Lantern light sputtered over his shadowed face, illumining his flared nostrils and flexing jaw. His arm still hooked around her waist. Her hands still clutched him. The dizzying scent of his musky aftershave satiated her every sense.

For a moment, no time had passed. No malicious uncle existed, no women waited in the wings to take him from her. His heart thudded against hers, his eyes soft as they roamed her face, landing on her trembling lips. Electric surges pulsed through her extremities, luring her to him, begging her to end her agony and press her lips to his. His fingers curled at her back, urging her.

"I see it!" Désirée announced, snapping Madeleine from her daydream.

Gabriel's grip loosened, his gaze still entwined with hers a quiet moment before conformity overtook him. He stepped backward, sweeping an arm toward the blackened space the others had disappeared into. Shaken, Madeleine followed the stream of his lantern until they reached a spot where water leaked in from the roof and cascaded over the rocks.

"Isn't it beautiful?" Désirée asked, gazing in awe over the cascading water.

"I thought you said it was a waterfall." Cecile approached it with arms crossed over her chest. "This is nothing more than a trickle. Why would Henri bother to hide anything here?"

Ignoring her, Désirée set her lantern next to the thin stream of water and wetted her hand. "I'll admit, it was more impressive in my teenage years." She shook her fingers of liquid. "We must have come here during the rainy season, when the fall was much thicker."

"Did you ever find anything when you were down here?" Gabriel moved around Madeleine, causing her breath to catch as he passed.

"No—but then, I didn't know to look." Désirée heaved a weary sigh. "Perhaps if we move some of these rocks. Certainly the entirety of his treasure isn't down here, but he might have left something."

Alongside the others, Madeleine silently got to work digging into the walls, plucking at rocks and roots embedded in the earth. Kneeling, she examined the cave floor, stealing glances at Gabriel's toiling frame every chance she got. She cursed herself for the power she still allowed him over her. Her heart galloped within her, the curve of her back burning where he had touched her.

"Look! What are these?" Désirée's excited exclamation provided a welcome relief from Madeleine's excavating. Already, her fingers stung from the cold dirt. Drawing near to the others, she followed Désirée's pointed fingers to a portion of the wall strewn with letters. "Could this have something to do with the code we found in Henri's book?"

Gabriel pushed past his sister; his brows cinched as he examined the chalky text. "I believe these are initials. See?" His finger jabbed at one pair of letters and then another. A faded cross joined the two. "Désirée, these are nothing but lovers' declarations. It seems you two weren't the only ones who snuck down here."

Shoulders falling, Désirée slumped against the rock. "Perhaps I'm merely grasping at straws. I had really hoped we would find something down here."

"I know." Cecile threw a comforting arm over her shoulder. "We are just looking in the wrong place—that's all. It will come to you, I know it."

The climb out of Désirée's secret cave felt twice as long as their descent. A gentle breeze whistled over the valley as the group of four emerged, haggard and out of breath. As she shook dirt from her skirts into the wild grass, Madeleine couldn't help feeling Gabriel's eyes on her. Her cheeks flushed to recall his arms around her, his breath on her skin. Refusing to look at him, she continued to dust off her clothes until all the dirt freed from the black cotton folds of her work dress.

The trundle of carriage wheels attracted her attention toward a coach meandering up the winding path. Gabriel and Désirée glanced at each other curiously as it rolled to a stop beside their own and the door popped open. The rotund figure who emerged planted the taste of bile in Madeleine's mouth.

"At last, I have found you." Pascal sauntered through the tall grass, his arms extended. "We have been looking all over the country-side for you. That presumptuous old maid at the château was little help."

Désirée laughed. "Forgive her, Uncle. She is too busy for pleasantries."

The intruder's beady stare darted past his relations to the young maids behind them. "And what, may I ask, are all of you doing out here in the middle of the day, looking like street ruffians?" His dark eyes tightened on Madeleine, peering into her.

"Just a little excursion," Gabriel said, clapping Pascal's shoulder. "Désirée had a craving for revisiting one of her childhood haunts."

Pascal's brow hooked as he examined his shoulder for any dirt Gabriel's touch could have left there. "Not the most delicate behavior, but you are both adults." He straightened, his sinister smile widening. "It's bound to be a joyous day, for I have brought the grandest surprise with me."

Pivoting toward the waiting carriage, he cupped both hands around his mouth. "Come on out, dear."

Madeleine's spirit sank as two slippered feet descended the carriage steps, silk beaded skirts rustling above them. Caroline glowed with sheepish excitement, her skin pink and lips a cherry hue. Blonde curls framed her face, cascading from a center part, the rest of her hair pinned at the crown of her head in an intricate weave.

Snapping to attention, Gabriel brushed off his dirtied trousers and adjusted his disheveled collar. "Caroline, how good of you to return. We weren't sure when to expect you back again." He advanced forward, bowing to kiss her extended fingers.

Caroline's adoring gaze encompassed him as he rose to face her. "Pardon me. I should have made the proper arrangements. Your uncle was just so keen to surprise you."

"No, not at all." Gabriel's unruly hair tossed with his wagging head. "I—we love to have you here." He glanced down at his hands, his boyish anxiety driving a dagger into Madeleine's heart.

"Well, come now." Pascal ushered Caroline toward his carriage. "It has been a long journey. What say the two of you sit down for a nice tea, hmmm?"

With Cecile's comforting arm wound around her waist, Madeleine trailed Désirée to the Clement family coach. Before she could climb in behind her, a hand clamped on her wrist. Startled, she looked up into a furrowed brow and snarled lips.

"What do you think you are doing?" Pascal growled. "You cannot ride with the family as if you are one of them."

Désirée poked a perturbed face out the carriage window. "It's quite all right, Uncle. Madeleine and Cecile rode with us here. We do not mind sharing our coach with our servants."

"But I mind." He shoved Madeleine's arm away. "You and your friend can walk from here."

Cecile stepped up, hands on her hips. "That would take nigh an hour. Who do you expect will fetch your tea if the two of us are still hiking our way home?"

Pascal's glare rounded on her, but before he could answer, Gabriel flung himself in the way. "This is absurd. We do not treat our servants like animals." He turned an apologetic expression on Madeleine. "Why don't you and Cecile take our coach and Désirée and I will ride with Uncle Pascal?"

Désirée let out a breathless laugh. "Forgive me, Uncle, but I am not rearranging myself for your silly whims. I will ride with the servants." She sat back on her bench, arms folded.

Fire danced in Pascal's eyes before an idea brightened them. "Better yet, I will ride with you. That way, Gabriel and Caroline may ride alone. Each of the servant girls can hop up next to a driver. Does that suit everyone?" He delivered a wicked, triumphant look Madeleine's way.

Gabriel hesitated a moment before walking backward toward Pascal's coach. "Fine. I will see you all at home, then." He held out a hand to assist Caroline into the carriage before ascending after her.

Sighing, Madeleine stepped to the wheel and heaved herself up next to Serge. The driver made fine conversation the whole journey home, but it couldn't rip her from thoughts of Gabriel and

Caroline together, *alone* as Pascal had so indelicately put it. The possibilities ran rampant through her mind like a pack of wild dogs, ripping every dream she'd ever had of him to shreds.

When the carriage train rumbled up the château's drive, Madeleine jumped down before they had even fully stopped. The horses nayed and stomped as she jogged past them, desperate to remove herself from the Clements' presence.

Georgette turned several hues of red when she heard the news, hands jetting up to her flabby cheeks. "Oh dear, I have so much to do." She bustled through the kitchen toward the cupboards, nearly knocking Brigitte on her backside. "It's a blessed thing I just happened to tidy her room today. I had a feeling she would grace us with her presence again soon."

In sullen silence, Madeleine watched her fill a copper kettle and hang it over the fire before selecting a few fresh pastries from her ever-replenishing collection. Careful not to spill, she lumped two glass dishes with fruit jam, then wobbled to the pantry and took a wedge of brie from inside a terra-cotta pot. The arrangement looked perfect as she emptied a silver tray into Madeleine's hands, topping it with a pot of steaming hot tea.

"Now, are you sure you want to do the serving?" Georgette's wary gaze washed over her as she tucked two linen napkins beneath the flowered plates. "Brigitte may suffice if you prefer. She only manages to spill *some* of the time." She threw an irritated scowl at the petite young maid, who kept up her floor scrubbing with a dismal sigh.

"No, thank you. I will serve them on my own." Madeleine's hands blanched around the tray's edge, determination fueling her. She could not avoid seeing them together forever.

Georgette's brow arched, her eyes saying she knew so much more than Madeleine would tell her. "You're sure?" she asked again.

"I am quite sure."

Tilting her chin up, Madeleine carted her tray up the stairs and down the hall toward the grand salon. Despite protesting arms that threatened to give way, she clenched her teeth and forced her tray to remain steady. Just footsteps from the door, a familiar face emerged.

"Oh, Madeleine, there you are." Caroline greeted her with a cheery smile. Since departing Pascal's carriage, she had shed her fitted traveling jacket and straw hat, a lavender cap sleeve gown complimenting her slender figure.

"Forgive me, mademoiselle. I should have helped you with your clothes."

"Not at all." Caroline lightly touched her elbow. "I had a chance to freshen up at a roadside inn not far from here. I know how busy the work around here keeps you."

Casting a furtive glance toward the closed salon door, Caroline stepped closer. Her skin emanated violet posies as she leveled a thoughtful look on Madeleine. "I wanted to thank you." She bit her lip. "When I left here last, I hadn't made up my mind about the baron. I thought he was too embroiled in the past to even consider."

Madeleine's stomach twisted at the bashful light that spread over Caroline's delicate features. "But you were right. He is intelligent, and gentle, and kind. He's—different from any other man I've made acquaintance with." Her fingers absently toyed with the string of pearls at her throat. "I might not have written to him had you not encouraged me. So thank you, Madeleine."

A hard lump materializing in her throat, Madeleine forced her mouth into a frozen smile. "I take it your correspondence has gone well?" As if she desired to know a single detail of it.

Caroline's porcelain skin deepened a shade darker. "So much better than I could have envisioned." Her listless gaze floated to the door, as if she looked upon her future. "I suppose I should go inside, then. I've kept him waiting long enough."

"Please, allow me." Balancing her tray in one arm, Madeleine twisted the ancient knob and pulled back the door for Caroline to enter.

The château's grand salon glittered with sunlight as Madeleine followed their guest around the settee. Ignoring the tall frame stationed by the empty fireplace, Madeleine set her tray on the tea table and busied herself with preparing their afternoon snack. Snippets of their conversation touched her ears as she poured steaming mint tea into each of their cups. Their laughter tunneled through her head.

Forcing her throbbing hands to keep steady, Madeleine set a china plate filled with pastries and macarons between them. Gabriel glanced up from his armchair, his quiet discourse with Caroline halted. "Thank you, Madeleine."

Refusing to meet his gaze, she simply nodded before dispensing their teacups beside the plate and snatching up her empty tray. Though the couple had commenced with their pleasantries, she could still feel his eyes on her until she slipped out the door. Finally able to breathe again, Madeleine let her aching head fall back against the door and closed her eyes. The mingled voices inside the salon planted a stinging pain in her throat. She had to get away before it ate her away.

"Sleeping on the job?" A voice like steel snapped Madeleine's eyes open. There, garbed in his pretentious silk clothes and jewels, stood Pascal Clement, eyeing her like evening supper.

"Pardon me, monsieur." Shielding herself with her tray, Madeleine attempted to step around him. When he blocked her path, her gaze reluctantly climbed to his. "Please, monsieur. I must be about my work."

"Your work is whatever I say it is." An amused light lit in his stony gaze. Pascal stepped closer, the sweet, smoky odor of pipe tobacco lifting off his embroidered waistcoat. "I do believe I hear the stirrings of new love bounding off those walls." His wicked stare drifted to the closed salon doors.

Madeleine attempted to escape again, but one hand caught her around the ribcage. His ragged breath hissed in her ear, his nearness churning a nauseous ache in her stomach. Caroline's beautiful laugh floated into the hall, driving the knife deeper into Madeleine's gut. Tears squeezed from her eyes. "Please, monsieur, let me go."

"Just listen." His warm breath on her ear launched shivers down her spine. Caroline's laughter intensified, joined with Gabriel's masculine chuckles. "That is the sound of two people falling madly in love with one another. What a beautiful sound, is it not?"

Pascal's fingers restricted on her torso. "See? He has no need of you anymore. You were nothing but a trifle to be discarded on a whim. A snack before dinner." His finger brushed her cheek, triggering her face to whip away from him. "If I catch you sneaking off with him again like you did today, you know what will happen."

The clammy feel of his spittle lingered on Madeleine's skin long after he retreated, his footsteps vanishing down the hall. When at last she unfroze her icy extremities and stumbled back to the kitchen, Madeleine comprehended the truth. She must leave this place not only for Gabriel's safety, but her own.

Eighteen

Madeleine swept her fingertips over a bright display of scarves, the glossy silks and woven foulards tangling around each other in a gorgeous patchwork of red, yellow, and blue. Behind them, a long table displayed chunks of lavender quartz and polished jade. Seizing one in her fist, she ran her fingers over its smooth, rounded surface before plopping it back with the others.

A gentle breeze lifted the wisps of hair framing her face as she moved on to a jeweler's table. Madeleine always loved coming to market—the jovial exchange of merchants and buyers, the scent of fresh fruit wafting on the wind, the feeling of community. But today it meant escape—from Pascal and Caroline, from Auguste and the colossal weights upon her heart.

"A trinket to match your spirit?" A woman seller with curly auburn hair under a handkerchief beckoned her with a wrinkled hand.

Smiling, Madeleine took the jaspar bracelet she extended. "You know me well, Margeaux." She shook her head, passing the lovely piece of jewelry back to its maker. "Yet how would I pay for such an indulgence?"

The merchant let her creation dangle from Madeleine's fingers a moment longer. "That baron pays you, does he not?" she asked with a keen smirk.

"Not enough for trinkets." Madeleine chuckled at Margeaux's persistence. "Besides, who would I wear it for?" It certainly wouldn't match the gloomy maid's uniform that had become her constant companion.

"You never know who you may meet." Margeaux's eyes sparkled, her finger wagging. "I have seen some *dangerously* handsome men about the market today."

Madeleine laughed, the sound lifting into the open air. Lightly catching Margeaux's hand, she deposited the bracelet on her veined palm. "Then I should take every precaution to defend myself, shouldn't I?" Her chest lifted in a heavy sigh. "Alas, I am under strict orders to buy fresh fish and be home before the sun can sink any farther." Already, the blazing orb sagged in the afternoon sky.

"Whatever your prerogative is, my dear." Margeaux hung the jaspar bracelet alongside one strung with garnet. "Just be sure to enjoy your youth. You won't get it back."

Wandering on, Madeleine passed to the stands pedaling every type of produce imaginable. Bunches of lettuce and chard were bundled like bouquets of flowers beside purple heads of cabbage and freshly picked carrots. Fruits of every shade fashioned a rainbow of colors and scents across the wide tables.

"Here you are, mademoiselle." A rumpled old man in dirty clothing offered her a peach from among his selection. Madeleine had told him her favorite fruit once, and now every time he saw her, he refused to let her go without one.

"*Merci*, Gustave." She admired the soft, purpled skin of the flawlessly ripe fruit before bringing it to her lips. A burst of sweet nectar flooded her mouth as her teeth sank into its flesh. Madeleine closed her eyes, savoring it. "Divine, as always." Her patron clapped his gnarled hands together, delighted at her reaction.

Farther down the cobbled street, a group of unkempt local fisherman hawked their latest catch. Madeleine ordered several Dover sole from their usual supplier and stood back as he pulled them down from his stand and wrapped them in butcher paper. Her nose plugged with the scent of raw fish, Madeleine's eyes wandered the rolling landscape beyond the fields. Where would she go when she left this place? Who would she be? The prospect made her stomach lurch.

"Madeleine!" a voice beckoned her. "Pssst, Madeleine!"

Whipping her head around, Madeleine examined the direction the voice had called her from. All that lay beyond the table was a butcher, beyond which an abandoned alleyway tunneled a crooked path through town. "Madeleine!" she heard again, a female voice if she wasn't mistaken.

Curious, she crept toward the source of the voice, eyes darting to and fro. The chatter of the marketplace faded as she stepped into the narrow alley. Goose pimples emerged on her skin in the cold, dark space between the buildings. Madeleine spun around, searching for whomever had called her here. Yet as far down the crooked alley as she could spy, not a soul ventured from the stone structures.

Just when she had given up and set her sights back on the market, a long scrape drew her attention upward. Before she could comprehend it, a figure had leaped from a low rooftop and flung themselves across her back. Madeleine hit the ground beneath the attacker with an angry thud. Instantly, her palms stung and her cheekbone pulsed in pain.

Fingers wildly grappled at her neckline, yanking out stray strands of hair. Madeleine pushed off the ground, attempting to roll the assailant off her back, just as their fingers closed around the chain on her neck. With a fierce tug, the chain snapped. The attacker went sprawling over the ground at Madeleine's resistance.

Madeleine scrambled over the stone, aimed at the key dangling from a small hand. All she could see of her foe was dark trousers and a black cape sheltering their identity. She descended on the figure with every bit of ferocity life had built in her, desperate to claim Gabriel's key back.

A few moments passed beneath the disorienting chaos of struggle. Madeleine panted, her frantic breaths mingling with equally weary breaths from her partner. The two wrestled for possession of the key, grunting and shoving. Though Madeleine proved her superior strength, her opponent was quick. Just as she released an arm to grab the stolen item, they rolled to their knees and sprinted down the alley.

Gritting her teeth, Madeleine rose and gave chase. Her boots pounded after the fleeing form, her legs pumping beneath her flurrying skirts. Ahead of her, the cloaked subject deftly bounded through the shadows, putting space between them. Madeleine forced her aching legs to run harder, determination fueling her every movement. She couldn't lose that key. She just couldn't. Not after Gabriel had entrusted her with its safekeeping.

Her heart thumped like an anvil as she raced through town, her skirts brushing the buildings in the cramped space. Just as she'd closed the gap between herself and the retreating figure, her skirt snagged on a jagged wall, hauling her backward. Seething, Madeleine crouched down to jerk it free. She could still see the staircase her attacker had ascended in the dim light. Whatever fool had the audacity to steal Henri's key would not so easily slip through her fingers.

She stood, taking a moment to catch her breath, planning to launch herself up the stairs. Then, two hands clamped around her arms, pinning them behind her. Madeleine tried to twist in this new person's grasp, but could only see the edge of another hooded cloak. Fear budded inside her at the strong hands and solid, muscular body pressed to her back. She could not so easily wrestle this one to the ground.

"You have what you want. Leave me be." The reality of her defeat sank through her like the slow, agonizing descent of the sun at dusk. What if this loss cost her everything? Auguste would never forgive her. Gabriel never should.

Without a word, the man detaining Madeleine led her down the shadowed alley. Her boots plopped over the cobblestone, reluctant to abandon the escape route her attacker had employed. His hold on her wrists had slackened. He didn't prod her as she expected. Yet somehow, she knew resisting him would only work against her.

Madeleine hoped perhaps someone would pop out from a doorway and help her, but only destitute silence answered back. The man halted before an impressive wooden door and lifted the steel bar. She could only glimpse dark blond stubble on his chin before he shoved her inside and locked her in with a loud clang.

"Hey!" Immersed in a room of pure black, she smashed herself against the door and pounded on the wood. "You can't just leave me here!" Despite her protests, his footsteps faded down the alley. Madeleine sighed. The marketplace wouldn't disband for hours, and no one else seemed to be around this time of day. So much for Georgette's fancy dinner.

Groping the empty dark, Madeleine ventured farther into the room. The distinct scent of hay lifted off the floor, her boots crunching it as she crept onward. She collided with something solid, her hands detecting the shape of barrels and crates. *A storehouse.* She slid her fingers over every surface, prying at the wood, but found nothing that might help her escape.

Wallowing in her failure, Madeleine sat cross-legged on the stone floor and leaned against the door. The day's events whirled through her mind, the possibilities torturing her. Perhaps one of the disbanded Guardians had summoned their allies from within their prison cells. Or maybe this pirate they were chasing had decided to turn the tables on Auguste. *Auguste.* Was he capable of having her attacked so he could find the treasure without her? Her kidnapper was admittedly gentle in capturing and imprisoning her.

The hours ticked on, nothing but the roar of distant voices and the hiss of wind funneling down the alley. The cold air seeped into her work dress, compelling her to pull her knees in and hug them tightly. Here in the quiet, she had no choice but to think—about her own choices, about Gabriel and her daunting future without him. Would the parents she held so sacred in her memory be proud of the woman she had become? The answer frightened her.

The tiny slit of daylight under the door had long melted to black before the alley stirred with activity. Madeleine jetted to her feet, thumping the door with her fists and yelling. The open wounds on her palms burned anew as she bashed them into the wood without care. At last, the bar stretching across the threshold lifted, the door creaking open to reveal Gustave's terrified face.

"Oh, Gustave, thank God for you." Madeleine rushed forward, throwing her arms around the old man's neck.

Gustave sheepishly patted her shoulder in reply. "It's my pleasure. What were you doing locked inside a storehouse?" he asked as she pulled away.

"Two men ambushed me. They robbed me and threw me in there." Her gaze flitted to the stairwell her attacker had vanished into. They both were no doubt long gone by now. "Have you seen any strangers about lately? A small man and a larger one, perhaps blond?"

Tapping his chin, Gustave shook his white head. "No, mademoiselle. No one peculiar." He gestured down the street with a frail arm. "We should take you down to the *gendarmes* if there are criminals roaming around town."

"No, Gustave, but thank you." Madeleine glanced around at the band of curious faces she had already attracted. "They took nothing of great importance, and I am quite unharmed." If the law got involved, she would have to explain why the thieves took only the key from around her neck and left a reticule full of coins dangling at her waistband.

The road to the Château des Rêves was empty at so late an hour. Normally, Madeleine could have summoned a ride from a farmer or sympathetic traveler. As she hobbled down the dirt path, the night enveloped her in eerie darkness. An owl hooted from the rustling treetops. Animals scurried through the roadside bushes, making her jump every time their rushing feet disturbed the leaves. Ignoring the throbbing pain in her knee and every horror story she'd ever heard about highway robbery, she pressed on.

When the lights of the château rose into view, Madeleine's shoulders shook with relieved laughter. How long had she held her breath, scared of the ghostly unknown about her? Even in the knowledge that she could defend herself, her attack had rattled her nerves. The comfort of home lured her in, candlelight flickering in every window of the stone walls, casting their luminescent beauty over the moat.

"Oh, Madeleine, there you are." Cecile raced out to meet her before she had even breached the stone wall separating the fields from the drive. Chest pitching, Cecile doubled over and held her side. "We were so worried. We've been looking everywhere for you."

"Well, I'm sorry to have caused such a fuss."

Cecile's eyes widened as the two passed into the waves of candlelight. "My word, what happened to you?" She lightly touched Madeleine's cheek below her stinging skin. "Are you hurt? Who did this?"

Pulling gently from her hand, Madeleine started for the house. "I'm perfectly fine, just a little scraped up." A sudden thought jolted her. "I didn't ruin dinner, did I? Georgette had her heart set on making Caroline *sole meunière*."

"Oh, don't fret about that. She served lamb chops instead." Cecile fell in step beside her. "You should see the fuss she's made over you, though. Once dinner was on the table, she had every servant in the entire estate out looking for you."

Madeleine arched a skeptical brow. "I'm surprised she didn't throw my belongings out for being late again." She paused before they reached the drawbridge. "She didn't tell the baron, did she? About my tardiness?" She could only imagine the trouble that might brew if Pascal found out.

Cecile shook her head. "I told him you were indisposed at dinner. A kitchen emergency. If I had told him you were sick, he would have insisted on checking on you." Her smile faded. "He and Caroline left for the opera hours ago."

"Good." Shoving down the ache Cecile's words produced, Madeleine traversed the creaking drawbridge. "That should give me ample time to clean up. I'm sure Georgette will know what to do." Spotting a bucket left beside the door, she scooped it up. "I will go fetch some water. Would you tell Georgette I've returned? I don't want her fretting another moment over me."

After Cecile squeezed her arm and disappeared into the château, Madeleine turned at the sound of carriage wheels rumbling up the drive. The Clement coach bobbed under the moonlight, two glossy black horses elegantly trotting up the winding path. Madeleine instinctively retreated into the shadows as the carriage swayed to a stop before the drawbridge. She reached for the handle behind her, but already the carriage door had punched open and Gabriel descended.

Madeleine watched in silence as his hand swept out to assist Caroline. She looked like a queen in the thin strands of moonlight, her velvet cloak cascading over a high-waisted brocade gown of green and silver. Her porcelain skin blushed at Gabriel's touch, her shy eyes twinkling as she passed him and started for the house.

"Caroline, wait." Gabriel retained her hand, reeling her back to him. Nausea churned in Madeleine's middle to see him take both of Caroline's hands in his. He spoke to her in low tones for several moments, Caroline nodding and smiling demurely. Then he leaned in, his lips capturing hers, his kiss gentle in the glowing light.

Clapping a hand over her mouth, Madeleine stepped back before she teetered sideways. Ever since Pascal had first threatened her, she knew this would happen, and yet the sight of it still flushed her veins with ice water. She took another step back, the wood groaning beneath her boots. The sound alerted both spellbound lovers to look her way.

"Madeleine?" Gabriel squinted down the bridge. "Madeleine, is that you?"

Face burning hot, Madeleine emerged from the threshold with her bucket in hand. "*Oui*, Baron. I—I didn't mean to disturb you. I was just going to the well for some water."

Caroline hugged one arm around her body, her awkward gaze averting to the ground. Gabriel rubbed the back of his neck. Neither of them would look at her until Madeleine had crept in humiliation over the bridge and stepped to the drive beyond.

A quick glance from Caroline converted to a worried stare. She sucked in a breath. "Madeleine, what happened to your face?" Her fingers lifted as if to touch it, suspending in midair. "Your skin is scratched and bruising."

"It's nothing, really." Madeleine flushed as Gabriel stepped around Caroline to examine her. "I had an encounter in town today. A pair of thieves." Her eyes darted to his. "They stole your key, Baron. I'm sorry."

A tide of emotions rolled over his face, his concerned gaze trickling down her wounded cheekbone before locking with her eyes. He searched them a quiet moment before his lips unfastened. "That's quite all right," he said, voice husky. "As long as you are safe, that is all that matters to me."

Madeleine swallowed, the words echoing in her heart. It was all she wanted for him—safety and happiness.

"Come with me to my study. I'll clean you up." Gabriel nodded toward the château.

"Oh, no." Madeleine shook her head, clutching her bucket to her chest. "Georgette is phenomenal with cuts and bruises. She will have me all better in no time."

Gabriel caught her by the elbow before she could move past him. "That may be, but I learned a thing or two in medical school." His fingers tightened softly. "I would prefer to handle it myself, if you don't mind."

Unable to speak, Madeleine looked from Gabriel to Caroline. Despite her intrusion, Caroline's face only exuded kindness. Madeleine nodded, heart pounding in her ears as she marched toward the château ahead of the pair. A new day had dawned, one in which she would have to leave Gabriel Clement behind for good.

Nineteen

Just breathe. Madeleine closed her eyes, the warm summer air infusing with her skin. The world spun around her, but here in the quiet, she could imagine herself floating on the lapping waves of a lake, all of it forgotten. No troubles, no family to contend with, no treasure. Just the soft breeze gliding through her hair, kissing her face, carrying her to a foreign world.

The image of her beautiful mother filled her mind's eye, bent over her loom, weaving bright strands of wool over one another. Of her father, reading the holy scriptures by candlelight late into the opaque night. *I will find a way to honor you. To carry on your legacy.* She would find a way to undo all the wrong she had wished on the world in the dark hours of her life.

The wind swelled, rushing over the tall grass around her ankles. Madeleine opened her eyes to a still grove of ash trees, the birds flitting from branch to branch her only companions. Sunlight winked through the twirling leaves. As far as her eyes could behold, empty fields stretched beyond her miniature haven. Solomon's Meadow, they called it. She glanced up at the golden sun. It had to be four o'clock by now.

Memories of the previous night flooded her, of Gabriel's soothing hands as he cleansed her wounds, the intensity of his focused gaze. He had sat her down in a plush blue slipper chair by the hearth in his study, setting a whale oil lamp on the table beside her. The light had flamed her already sweltering skin, bathing her in a thin layer of sweat.

"Are you comfortable?" Gabriel asked as he pulled another chair alongside hers.

"Yes." The lie barely squeezed from her bone-dry throat. How could she possibly be comfortable in such close quarters after watching him kiss another woman?

He leaned close, cerulean eyes perusing her battered face before he began dabbing her skin with a wet cloth. Madeleine winced at the sudden surge of pain. She allowed her eyes to sweep his face once, then quickly diverted them to the shadowed bookshelves lining the wall.

"The Guardians are all still imprisoned except Cousteau, aren't they?" she asked. "Whomever attacked me cared solely about the key. They didn't even attempt to steal my money. They knew my name."

"As far as I know, that's true." Gabriel continued to softly smear her scratches with water, tilting her chin up to get a better view. "But many more people are in search of this treasure. They always have been."

"I suppose you're right." Madeleine watched him fold a clean cloth and douse it with a clear substance from a bottle. "I shouldn't have still been wearing that key." Could she admit to him that it had comforted her, made her feel close to him despite the giant gulf she'd wedged between them?

Gabriel recorked the bottle and pivoted back to her. "I gave it to you, didn't I?"

She sucked a sharp breath through her teeth as he patted her skin with the cold, stringent liquid. "For safekeeping." Her hand absently drifted to her throat, almost expecting to find the treasured item there. "Besides, things are—things are different between us now."

His eyes shifted from her cheekbone to her tortured gaze, tender in the glinting lamplight. Here in the solitude of his study, she could almost forget what she'd beheld in the drive, squelch the constant ache gnawing at her. The tick of his longcase clock filled the space, the sound so soft, she could still hear each of his quiet breaths. Gabriel held her gaze for an agonizing string of seconds, never wavering.

"That may be true, but I meant what I said down there." Fervency lit his unflappable stare. "You are worth more than a million ridiculous treasures. To damnation with Henri's clues and riddles. You are safe and it's all that concerns me."

Madeleine swallowed, managing a feeble nod. His words sparked a warm trickle down her arms, her heart yearning for him against her will. Her gaze plunged to her lap as he returned to his supplies on the tea table.

"Now then, lift up your skirt for me, please."

Her cheeks reddened, her bewildered stare hurtling to his now crouched position on the rug before her.

Gabriel jabbed a finger toward her sheltered legs. "I need to have a look at your knee."

"My knee is perfectly fine and in no need of your assistance." Her ankles crossed beneath her chair as if to shield her from his probing hands.

A nearly imperceptible smile tugged at one corner of his mouth. "This pool of blood on your dress would suggest otherwise." He gently seized one of her booted feet in his hands, his head angled imploringly. "Come now, it will only take a moment. I won't be able to rest tonight if I ignore it."

Sighing, Madeleine gingerly grabbed the hem of her skirt and lifted it the length of her shin until it rested on her thigh. Pain reverberated down her skin as the fabric peeled away to reveal an open gash with blackened blood clotting at the edges. Gabriel cupped her calf in his gentle hand while he cleaned her injury, his fingertips sweeping her skin, his pulse warm against her.

Madeleine's breath hitched, her eyelids fluttering closed against the feeling his touch invoked. She had to remain strong—for his sake, if nothing else.

"You look like you could use a brother's embrace," another male voice whipped Madeleine from her daydream. She blinked, Gabriel's study dissolved, a field of unkempt grass rising at her ankles. Turning, she spotted Jean-Paul strutting across the meadow toward her, a jovial grin on his handsome face.

"Forgive my tardiness. I hope you weren't waiting long." Her brother's arms closed around her, trapping her against his solid chest. The mingling of sweat and molten iron filled her senses, calming her. If anyone could ease the pain of last night's troubles, Jean-Paul stood the greatest chance.

"You have no idea how wonderful it is to see you, brother." Madeleine drank in his comforting scent a minute longer before she unlatched herself from him. "You're looking well. I take it you were able to leave without Auguste knowing?"

A cloud passed over Jean-Paul's face as he led her deeper into the grove of ash trees. "He was drinking today—too much to notice my coming or going." His large hand swung toward a group of rocks clustered around a tree trunk. "Come, let's sit and I'll tell you everything."

Perched on the flattened edge of a mossy rock, Madeleine listened with her chin in her splayed fingers as Jean-Paul told her all the forbidden things Auguste would never allow. Jean-Paul explained with hands dancing in the air, his booming voice carrying on the light breeze. As his story unfolded, understanding dawned, plugging the gaps in her memories of Auguste.

"So he hasn't always been like this?" Madeleine's brows narrowed, her fingers twirling a shoot of grass she'd plucked from the earth. "When did it change for him? When did he become so obsessive?"

Jean-Paul's broad shoulders lifted. "He was always passionate, even when we were children. But after he found out why Maman and Papa were killed, something snapped." Sadness plagued his bright eyes. "Over the years, it has only grown worse. He hardly sleeps anymore. He drinks wine more than he eats. He—he talks to them."

Her forehead scrunched. "Papa and Maman?"

"He sees them when he drinks. He thinks they're appearing to him from beyond the grave." Jean-Paul swallowed, a bitter frown lacing his bristly lips. "I hear him speaking to them at night sometimes, telling them he'll make everything right."

Madeleine sucked in a ragged breath. "Dear God, it's so much worse than I thought." All this time, she had thought if she found enough clues, she might reason with Auguste. How could one reason with a man who was already halfway to madness?

"I'm afraid of what he'll do, Maddy." Jean-Paul's deep baritone lured her eyes to lock with his. "Not just to the baron, but to you and anyone else who might stand in his way. Maybe even to those who are simply nearby when he finally explodes."

Grasping his giant hand in both of hers, Madeleine brought it to her chin. "We won't let that happen, all right? We will work together to stop this before anyone gets hurt. I refuse to lose my dear brothers after all this time apart. We *will* find a solution."

Yet looking into Jean-Paul's dejected gaze, the truth speared even the most hopeful reaches of her soul. Her two brothers had never parted. He understood better than anyone the lengths Auguste would travel to avenge their departed parents.

She offered him a wry smile. "I'm sorry I ever embroiled myself in this plot with Auguste. You deserved more from me."

Jean-Paul shook his head. "It was another time. You were—you were different then."

"Yes, I suppose so. Though I still don't truly know who that person was." She laughed, the pain of their predicament blending with its absurdity. "Somewhere in the space of my darkened memories, I learned to act and to fence and to fight for myself. I have a scar I don't remember ever putting there. I can't read my native tongue, but I read and speak fluent Italian. How can this be?"

"You don't remember living in Italy?" he asked.

"Auguste mentioned something about it, but I—" Her head wagged, the memories refusing to loosen. "I don't have any recollection of it. What happened there?"

His fingers curled around hers, his look soft. "Some things are better left in the past."

Despite her curiosity, Madeleine nodded. If whatever happened there was truly so troublesome, she couldn't burden her shoulders with it now. She needed all the strength and focus she could muster to face Auguste and Pascal and whatever other obstacles life chose to throw her way.

"Do you really love him, Maddy?" Jean-Paul's question yanked her back to the present. "Auguste said that you fell in love with the baron. He was very torn up about it."

"Yes, well he believes that Gabriel could never truly love someone like me. Auguste thinks he's deceiving me."

Her brother searched her gaze. "But he does love you, doesn't he?"

She blinked back the tears springing to her eyes. "He did. Before I pushed him away." The scent of lilacs and honeysuckle dragged through her nose. "It's complicated, but it—it wasn't meant to be." The words hardly spilled from her choked throat. She hadn't expected the pain admitting it would invoke.

"If you love him, you should tell him." A smile dimpled his cheek. "In the end, love is all we really have in this world."

Madeleine smiled back through her tears at the baby brother of her youth. How wise he was beyond his years. "Yes, well—it's too late now. I shall be happy to share in the love of my family." Her chest ached, the vision of Gabriel and Caroline kissing in the moonlight still vivid in her memory.

"Auguste isn't the only reason I wanted to meet, you know." With a mischievous grin, Jean-Paul twisted around and reached into his knapsack. Producing a small wrapped bundle tied in string, he dropped it into her hands. "Happy birthday."

"It's my—" Madeleine stared at the present in awe. "I didn't even know. How old am I, anyway?"

Jean-Paul emitted a hearty chuckle. "Twenty-three. Though much older in life experience, I'd wager."

Gingerly taking the string bow in her fingertips, Madeleine tugged until it gave way. She unwrapped the brown paper beneath, finding two combs within the folds. Holding one up to the sunlight, she delighted to watch the gold teeth glimmering. Atop each of them, gem-studded dragonflies glimmered green and blue.

"I bought them from that crazy woman you always talk to in town. The one who thinks all her jewelry is good luck." Jean-Paul took one from her, brushing his thumb over the stones. "They suit you, I think. I wanted to make something in my shop, but what woman wants to wear chains of iron?"

"They're perfect, Jean-Paul. I will wear them the first chance I get." Madeleine leaned in to plant a kiss on her brother's cheek. "You're the very best parts of Maman and Papa rolled into one person, you know that?"

He blushed. "I hope that's true. I wish I remembered them, even a little." He glanced up at Madeleine, that vulnerable little boy alive in his eyes again. "We're going to make it through this, aren't we?"

Hooking her arm around his neck, Madeleine pulled his blond head against her cheek. "Of course we are, little brother. If there is one thing our parents taught me, it's that we can make it through anything as long as we have each other."

Hours later, Madeleine sat atop her narrow bed, unraveling the chignon in her hair. In her view out the open window, swans waddled over the footbridge leading to the fields, their feathers wet from their nocturnal swim in the moat. Madeleine smiled to herself as she brushed out her thick sable locks and began weaving them into a single braid. She would miss the swans and their regal beauty when she left this place.

Her chest constricted when she imagined journeying into the unknown, leaving the château behind, leaving *him* behind. A mild breeze rattled the shutters, sweeping in the scent of apple and plum from the neighboring orchard. Madeleine tied off a simple black ribbon at the end of her braid, pushing back her memories of trekking through that field and meeting Gabriel in the church ruins. His kisses belonged to somebody else now.

A knock on her door drew her attention upward. She frowned, kicking off the bed and tossing her braid to her back. Georgette usually yelled through the door when she wanted something, and Cecile wouldn't have bothered to knock. When she saw the expectant face on the other side, Madeleine instinctively crossed her arms over her thin nightdress.

"Baron," she said. "To what do I owe this pleasure?"

Gabriel smiled sheepishly, an unreadable gaze taking her in before responding. "Forgive me for the intrusion. I looked for you before dinner, but I couldn't find you."

Because she had sneaked off to meet Jean-Paul, of course. Madeleine's fingers tightened around the door. "That's quite all right." Did he know something? Had he seen her escaping the château?

Reaching into his waistcoat, he produced a small package and held it out in the spidery light of his candle. "Here. For your birthday."

Their fingers brushed as Madeleine accepted his offering. Brussels lace met her fingertips. "It seems everyone knows it's my birthday but me." Pulling away the lace, she found a small book with leather binding inside. *"Letters from a Peruvian Woman,"* she read the Italian title.

"I found it in a bookshop in Paris. I had been searching for the Italian translation since I discovered you—" He glanced down, running a hand through his thick mop of hair. "It's the story of a strong, brave young woman. I think you will like her."

Awestruck, Madeleine allowed herself to look into the hopeful eyes staring back at her. "Thank you, Gabriel." The name rolled off her tongue so naturally, she hardly perceived saying it. "This is incredibly thoughtful."

"Yes, well I couldn't let your birthday go by without celebrating a little." He held her gaze for an agonizing moment, everything unspoken between them lingering in the quiet hallway. Then, he cleared his throat and turned to go. Madeleine had nearly dipped back into her bedroom when his voice halted her.

"Oh, I almost forgot. I had one more thing to tell you." Candle-light bobbed over the walls as he took two steps closer and lowered his voice. "I deciphered the code Henri left at the end of his clue. The string of numbers under his riddle. It was a book cipher, with every number corresponding to a page, line, and letter of *Arcadia*."

Madeleine's heart leaped into her throat. "What did it say?"

A smile lifted one corner of his mouth and then the other. "It said, 'it lies in the very heart.'"

"That's all?" Madeleine's shoulders fell. "He certainly was a trickster, wasn't he? Leaving clues with so little information to help us. Sometimes I think it was all a joke."

"Perhaps." Eyes shooting to the ceiling, he tapped his chin with one finger. "But I have to wonder—the very heart of what? The place he hid it, maybe? Or the barony itself? Perhaps the very heart of his existence."

"And what do you think that was?" she asked.

Gabriel's eyes danced with brilliant light when they met hers. "This home, of course. When he inherited it, the house had fallen into disrepair. He put everything he had into rebuilding it into the beautiful place you see today. Of all his endeavors, I believe that was the most important to him."

She laughed. "There isn't exactly a river running through the halls, now is there?"

"That might have negated the reconstruction." He shared in her mirth with a quiet chuckle. "We'll both think on it. The answer must be attainable."

"I certainly hope so."

It felt so good to laugh with him again. Their distant relations these last few months had buried a cold ache inside of her. Now, the soft lines around his eyes and mouth emerged as he gave her another long look before shrugging his broad shoulders.

"Well, good night, Madeleine. I hope it was a good day."

"Thank you. And good night."

Madeleine watched him turn and march down the darkened hallway, his candle creating a halo around him. Reluctantly, she closed her door and leaned against it, inhaling through her nose. *Forget him. Forget you ever shared anything more.* Yet deep down, an ominous voice told her she never would until she left him.

Opening the book he'd gifted her with, Madeleine ambled to her bed and plopped down on the pillows. Her life might rage like a chaotic storm around her, but tonight she would immerse herself in Princess Zilia and her harrowing adventures.

Twenty

"There. Shining like a new franc." Cecile held a freshly polished silver platter at arm's length, her proud reflection smiling back at her.

Behind her, Madeleine plunked an ornate fork into a sectioned drawer. "That's the last of it, then. I'll gather all of this up and take it back to the dining hall," she said, tossing a spent rag over her shoulder.

"I'll do it." Already, Cecile had stacked several platters atop the silverware drawer and hoisted them into her arms. "You just finish the dusting in here, and I'll meet you downstairs afterward."

"If you insist." Madeleine simpered at her friend's retreating form before turning to face the tangle of wooden furnishings clustered in the ballroom's corner. Even a modest get-together meant hours of added work for the household staff.

First, she rearranged the fiddleback chairs until they made a perfect line against the ballroom's enormous arched windows. Sunlight streamed between the heavy bunches of claret drapes, bathing her as she bent to glide her cloth over the chairs' intricate cherrywood arms and legs. There was something cathartic about such detailed work, a welcome distraction from the frenzy of her current reality.

Engrossed in the simple act of wiping away the previous evening's remains, Madeleine hardly heard the footsteps trudging in behind her. By then, she knelt on the hardwood floor, rag buffing the scrolled legs of an armchair. A cold lump rose in her throat as she realized someone had merely sidled into the ballroom to watch her, their unseen form silent in the vast room.

Madeleine glanced over her shoulder, catching a glimpse of Pascal over the fortepiano's lid. "Might I help you, monsieur?" Pivoting back to her work, she let her eyes roll in disgust. Of all the people she needed to invade her daily chores, he was the last.

"Oh no, I'm just enjoying myself." Pascal sauntered toward her, kicking one of the perfectly arranged chairs out of place before plopping himself into it. His lascivious stare slid down her approvingly. "After last night's activities, I'm quite bored. Everyone is tucked away in some corner of the house, busy with their own affairs."

After finishing the last of her dusting, Madeleine swiped a hand over her perspiring brow. "Surely you have affairs of your own, monsieur. Watching me clean can't be the most fascinating endeavor this house has to offer."

He let out a weary huff. "Truly, it's as tedious as all the rest. But in desperation, one must reduce one's standards." His jeweled fingers caught the light, flapping with his every stomach-churning word.

"Well, I'm afraid I must withdraw my services. I have more work waiting for me downstairs." Pushing off the floor, Madeleine rose and collected her dirty rags from the edge of the fortepiano.

"You would choose housework when you could idle here and converse with a nobleman?" His wicked grin mocked her. "I expected more, even from a girl as simpleminded as yourself."

Swallowing back her rage, Madeleine simply lifted her chin. "I am but a slave to my humble position, monsieur. I would not think to rise above my station to occupy your time." A hundred insults rammed into her throat, but she calmly held them at bay.

Pascal glanced away, a streak of irritation arching his brow. "You had best do well to remember your station." He sighed, his beaded waistcoat swelling and dropping. "But today is horribly mundane and I have nothing better to do." His fingers gestured toward the hall. "You know where my chamber is."

He spoke the words so indifferently that Madeleine nearly missed them. She froze in place, an icy chill tunneling down her arms and fingers. When she dared to meet his pernicious eyes, he scowled. "Well, don't just stand there gaping. It's not every day you get to share the bed of a man like me."

Nausea roiling her midsection, she somehow managed to unhinge her jaw. "Indeed it is not, and I certainly never shall." Forcing her legs to move, she started for the door.

Pascal spurted from his chair and blocked her path. "You will do whatever I tell you. I thought we had established that fact by now." His spidery fingers crawled up her arm and throat, nesting beneath her chin. He stepped closer, his breath hot on her ear as he murmured into it. "You may think you belong to him, but you are *mine*. Mine to use however I please."

So close his spittle doused her skin, Madeleine's gaze entwined with the evil glaring back at her. "I belong to no man, and I promise you, I never will." Her teeth gritted. "You will unhand me at once."

His bone-chilling laugh overwhelmed her senses. "No. I will do what I should have the moment I stepped foot into this house—teach you your proper place here." He clamped one hand around her wrist, but Madeleine yanked free of him. Undeterred, he hooked an arm behind her back and dragged her to him. He laughed again, his wine-laced breath creeping across her skin like a bed of worms. "Now you can march up to my bedchamber this moment or I will take you right here."

Madeleine went still in his arms, taking him in from his flushed face to the fleshy neck beneath his lacy collar. She could fight him, she knew it. It wouldn't be difficult to wrench herself free of his grasp and run to freedom. Yet what manner of torture would he devise if she chose to defy him? Who might he endanger in his quest to control her? There had to be a more fruitful solution.

Her steely gaze fastened on his, her voice hard. "Monsieur, I will *never* allow you to have any part of me." Her stomach lurched at the vicious curl of his lips. "Now, you will let me go before I tell Gabriel *every* wicked deed you've performed in the last few months. I am certain he will be quite interested."

His fingers dug into her throat. "You wouldn't," he fumed. "You *can't*."

"I assure you, I can and I will." She set her jaw, determined to convince him of her lie. "Your nephew will learn of your deceit if it's the last thing I do on this earth."

Pascal's nostrils ballooned, his wild eyes transforming from wicked to violent. "You little witch!" he shrieked, seizing the back of her neck. Madeleine had no time to react before he shoved her downward. Surprised by his strength, she hurtled to the floor, her injured knee instantly screaming in pain. She blinked, horrified by the blurry image of Pascal standing over her, face contorted in maniacal rage.

"Monsieur Clement, what is the meaning of this?" a new voice joined the fray, breathless and outraged. Madeleine peered up from the floor to see Caroline, skin pinkened and lithe fingers clenched into fists.

"Mademoiselle Allair," Pascal greeted her as if she were a welcome visitor popping in for tea. The twisted ire on his face melted to congeniality, his chest still pumping in exhaustion. "Rest assured, this is nothing of your concern. Just the discipline of an indolent servant." He spit the last few words, his glare narrowing again on Madeleine.

Caroline knelt beside her, cradling Madeleine's face in gentle hands. "Discipline or violence? It sounded from the hallway as if you were hurting her." Her brown eyes swept Madeleine's face, inspecting it.

"She is unharmed." Pascal straightened, clearing his throat. "A fine lady such as yourself will appreciate that I cannot allow a wayward insubordinate to defy me without penalty."

Caroline's nostrils flared as she looked from Madeleine to the unholy man above them. "That well may be, but where I was raised, there is *never* cause to raise your hand to another human being. Servants are not toys. I believe the baron would agree with me."

His hand flew to his ornamented chest. "Mademoiselle, that was not my intention—"

"Yes, I *heard* your intention very clearly." Caroline angrily flicked a lock of hair from her forehead. "Now I *insist* you make some better use of your valuable time." Revolving back to Madeleine, she blocked him from further contact.

Dumbfounded, Pascal teetered, rocking on his heels. Then with the slightest huff from his lips, the click of his shoes carried him out of the ballroom.

Righteous fury converting to tender concern, Caroline thrust out a hand and helped Madeleine to her feet. "Are you all right? He didn't hurt you?" Her eyes still roamed the maid's every plane in search of a nonexistent injury.

"No, mistress. I am fine." In body, perhaps. Madeleine absently hugged one arm around herself, her skin still crawling with Pascal's smarmy touch.

A moment of silence drifted over them, Caroline's dented brow and pursed lips saying she wanted to help so badly and didn't know how. "Perhaps you might style my hair before we dress for dinner," she finally suggested. A distraction to serve a greater purpose.

Madeleine nodded. "Of course, mademoiselle. It would be an honor."

The two women crossed the ballroom in silence, Madeleine's hands gnawing at the dirty rags she had reacquired. She tossed them down the laundry chute on their way, fixing the door in the wall back in place and trailing Caroline up the winding stairs. The noblewoman paused at the landing, fingers gripping one of the tall bronze horses standing guard.

"Madeleine, forgive me, but I heard more than I cared to of that conversation." Her worried gaze soaked into Madeleine's very soul. "Are you sure there isn't anything you need?"

Madeleine steadied herself on the wrought iron rail, fearful of tumbling down the stairs in her present state. "Thank you, but I am quite fine." She forced her lips upward, knowing her smile must look as artificial as the empty words Pascal had dismissed her with. Caroline perused her face for a long string of seconds before nodding and continuing up the staircase.

Caroline's bedchamber was fresh and full of sunlight when they entered. A brand-new bouquet of flowers greeted her bedside every few days, hand-picked and arranged by an adoring Georgette. Today, a crystal vase of poppies adorned her bedside table, their cheerful orange faces accentuated by sprigs of lavender and baby's breath.

Determined not to let her weakness show, Madeleine marched straight to Caroline's washstand and doused her hands with cold water. After flipping a bar of lemon soap over and again in her hands, she rinsed them and swiped them on the rose-adorned towels hanging on the rack. She inhaled a ragged breath, content to have washed the feel of him away, at least for the moment.

Back rigid and legs tucked demurely beneath her stool, Caroline looked like a queen when Madeleine began pulling out her simple chignon and placing the pins on her dressing table. The idea poured a comforting warmth through Madeleine. Gabriel would have a fine woman to accompany him through life. She would make him proud, bless him with her kind heart and sharp mind. Despite the pain it wrenched within her, that's all she really wanted for him.

A long time passed while Madeleine brushed out Caroline's silky strands of blonde hair and began weaving them into a more intricate pattern. Since Caroline's last visit, she had practiced often on Cecile, attempting to remedy the meager abilities she possessed. Now, her fingers nimbly laced through Caroline's mane, braiding and pinning a creation she could be proud of.

"He had no right to speak with you that way," Caroline said at last, shattering the wall of silence between them. "I'm just sorry I didn't come by sooner to stop it."

Madeleine shrugged, keeping on with her work. "It's nothing I haven't encountered a dozen times before."

Caroline frowned, rubbing Milk of Roses into her hands and forearms, littering the whimsical scent into the air. "Well, that is rather disheartening. No woman should ever have to endure such harassment from a man, verbal or otherwise." She sighed, screwing the lid back on her lotion. "I suppose my title has shielded me from having to face such atrocities. No one dares to speak to a highborn woman like that."

What a luxury. Madeleine reached for the pearl-studded pins she had found in Caroline's luggage, imagining every man in her existing memory who had belittled her. Men of title, street urchins, anyone who could summon the words to turn her God-given beauty into shame. Even Auguste treated her like nothing more than a body to entice his prey.

"If you don't mind my asking—" Caroline's eyes met hers in the mirror, fear fueling them more than idle curiosity. "You told Pascal that you would reveal his secrets to the baron. I appreciate that it isn't my place, but I can't help wondering to what you referred."

Madeleine shook her head, feigning indifference. "Nothing more than a mere bluff. A man like Pascal Clement has to harbor his fair share of indiscretions. I hoped that I might protect myself by pretending to know one of them."

Astute eyes followed her in the mirror. The look on Caroline's lovely face said she didn't quite believe it, but she kept such thoughts locked within her rosy lips. "Madeleine, I—" She glanced away from the mirror. "I can't help but notice your discomfort around Gabriel and myself. When last we spoke on it, you said what the two of you had was in the distant past, but your face tells a different story every time he is near."

The frantic need to defend herself thundered through Madeleine's veins. "Mademoiselle, I assure you, nothing of the sort is transpiring between us—"

"Relax, Madeleine. I know." Caroline's head tilted as she studied the maid's flushed skin in the mirror. "Gabriel would never treat me that way, and you have proven yourself to be nothing but a professional and devoted servant to this household." She lightly rubbed her brow with a knuckle. "But still I cannot dismiss what passes silently between you two. You have a history. You can't control it."

Fingers suspended in midair, Madeleine squelched her impulse to deny Caroline's very accurate conclusions and just listened.

Caroline sat regally, her head held high. "I have every reason to trust that Gabriel feels for me as I do for him. But I cannot erase what the two of you shared. It's impossible for me to make him forget it, either." Her gaze latched with Madeleine's, resolute in the sunlit mirror. "Neither will I choose to join myself with a man only to be disgraced by extramarital affairs."

Madeleine's heart plummeted within her. "Surely you know I would never—"

"I do." Caroline breathed, blinking back her sprouting tears. "Women of my rank may not have to face men harassing them from street corners, but we are taught our inferiority from an early age." Her hands blanched on the vanity table. "We are expected to marry whomever our fathers decide and to smile in heart-wrenching silence when our husbands bed whatever woman they truly long for. But I demand more for my life."

The pain of her cruel reality spilled over her face, her brows tapered and lips trembling. "Though I know Gabriel would never put me in such a terrible spot, still I worry. I don't want your life to be miserable, watching the two of us together, raising a family. I won't pretend to know what transpired between you, but I suspect you would hate it here."

Throat sore, Madeleine barely managed to swallow. She could not deny Caroline's words. Her very presence in Gabriel's life meant ceaseless torture. But she couldn't be ripped from this place—not yet. Not until she had secured safety for both of them.

"Are you telling me you want me to leave?" she asked shakily.

"Heavens, no." Caroline flashed her a sad smile. "I simply want you to know that when you are ready, there are options available should you desire them. My family has several country estates. I can provide you with a comfortable, prestigious position far away from these walls. You would be respected and sheltered from attacks like the one you just had to face downstairs." Brown eyes solemn in the mirror, she wagged her head. "I won't let it happen again, Madeleine. I want to take care of you."

Touched, Madeleine placed a hand on Caroline's shoulder. "Thank you, mademoiselle." After a lifetime of running away, of scouring the streets as a child and battling to stay alive in adulthood, the offer showered her with indescribable warmth.

Caroline reached up to take her hand. "We women have to stick together. We all rise or fall as one."

The two stayed there in silence for a long moment, understanding passing between them. Both stood down tremendous foes in their lives, but their enemy was not each other. Against her every impulse and desire, Madeleine thanked God for the woman of integrity she was most certain would one day become Baroness Clement.

Twenty One

A tranquil breeze swirled through the orchards, fluttering the sunlit leaves, brushing their faces against one another. Songbirds hopped from branch to branch, infusing the endless rows of fruit trees with their harmonious whistles. The air lit with the crisp scents of ripened apples and pears, of cherry blossoms floating in the late afternoon sky.

With a sigh, Madeleine stretched high to pluck another low-hanging apple, the stepstool beneath her feet groaning. Smooth beneath her fingertips, the sweet-smelling fruit plunked into her basket with ease. She picked two more before eyeing the rounded collection she'd already amassed. Two bushels should be enough for Georgette's satisfaction. She doubted she could carry more.

Seizing one basket handle in each clenched fist, Madeleine started back across the orchard toward the château. The sooner she left this place, the better. Memories plagued her—of another day as gorgeous as this one, a day she had gathered apples with excitement fluttering in her chest. The day Gabriel Clement had first kissed her.

Shuddering against the intruding vision of her own happiness, Madeleine trekked over the verdant field with muscles straining beneath the heavy load she transported. Already, the patchy blue sky had given way to strands of yellow tinged in pink. Soon it would be nightfall, Georgette eager to put supper on the table and to finish her apple tart.

Her arms pleaded with her for relief by the time she dropped both of her baskets on the terra-cotta floor of Georgette's kitchen. The old woman hardly spared her a second glance, choosing instead to slap poor Brigitte's hand and reprimand her for braiding the dough crooked. Breathing heavily, Madeleine leaned against the stucco wall and washed a dirt-caked arm over her forehead.

"There's no time to dawdle," Georgette said. "I had hoped for your help with dinner, but it seems you're wanted upstairs."

Madeleine pushed off the wall, frowning. "Is Caroline ready to dress already?"

With an exasperated huff, Georgette's eyes snapped her way. "Am I to know the intimate affairs of everyone in this house? Just go and see what they want."

Upstairs, the tick of the longcase clock echoed through the halls, Madeleine's dirty boots the only other sound filling the space. The parlor the Clements so often occupied was empty, along with the dining room and grand salon. Frowning, she swiveled toward the soft murmur of voices drifting from down the hall.

Even before Madeleine had reached the library, Cecile leaped out as if she'd skulked in the shadows for this moment. "Oh Madeleine, there you are. Thank heavens."

Madeleine jumped, half expecting a burglar. Before she could open her mouth, Cecile had seized both of her hands and led her beneath a sconce on the wall already bleeding candlelight into the darkened hallway.

"Oh, dear." Cecile clicked her tongue, green eyes assessing her friend. A hushed laugh danced in the air around them. "Were you out wrestling sheep? I will fix you."

As Cecile began to pluck leaves from her hair, Madeleine glared at the closed library door. "Cecile, what is all this? Why is everyone in the library, and *why* do they want to see me?" Her heartbeat picked up speed to imagine some new clue she and Désirée had somehow missed within the mysterious room.

Cecile shrugged. "They must have been in the library already when your guest arrived." Bending, she shook an alarming amount of dirt from the folds of Madeleine's dress.

"*My* guest? What on earth do you mean?" Madeleine twisted to look at Cecile, but already her friend had ducked around her other side, adjusting the gnarled bow at her waist.

At last satisfied with Madeleine's clothes, Cecile bounced to her feet. Before Madeleine could react, she licked her thumb and swiped it across Madeleine's cheekbone, pulling it back to reveal a muddy smear. Her eyes lit with humor. "All I know is the most handsome man I've ever laid eyes on is in that room calling on you. If you don't run away with him tonight, *I will*." With a playful shove, she propelled Madeleine toward the library.

Bemused, Madeleine caught herself before she stumbled into the door. Her hand fairly shook as she reached for the knob, fearing what lay beyond. Who could possibly be calling on her? Jean-Paul? He was certainly handsome enough for Cecile to entertain such thoughts. But why would he come here unless serious trouble brewed on the horizon?

The dusky light of the library was punctuated by orbs of flickering candles. The room smelled of roses tinged with sweet cigar smoke. Madeleine dipped her head as she entered, hardly able to glimpse Gabriel, Désirée, and Caroline seated across from a commanding form. "You called for me, *madames et messieurs*?" At her disruption, both men jetted to their feet.

"Yes, Madeleine. Do come in." Gabriel hesitated, gaze flitting to their visitor. "You have a guest."

Allowing her eyes to finally journey across the room to the newcomer's imposing form, Madeleine sucked in a sharp breath. Indeed, Cecile hadn't steered her astray. He was perhaps more handsome than she remembered, with his blond hair neatly tied at the nape of his neck, his chiseled jaw shaved clean, his stalwart chest garbed in a blue corduroy waistcoat with gold buttons. He looked exactly like the venturesome sailor who had left her at the port of Marseilles and yet like a polished gentleman at the very same moment.

Madeleine clamped a hand over her pulsing throat. "Christophe." The single word fused the air with energy.

He took a step toward her. "Ja—Madeleine." Of course he would still call her Jacqueline. How rotten of her to have given him a false identity.

The pair stared in wonder at each other for a solid moment. How long had it been since they'd shared a comradery aboard ship, since her heart had yearned for him among the churning waves of the Atlantic? And yet it felt like no time had passed. His rugged face and sharp blue eyes lured her every instinct his way.

"Ahem." She glanced away to find Gabriel still standing with his hand awkwardly posed on his hip. "This is the captain who helped you off that island, no doubt."

Madeleine swallowed, suddenly aware of the other three people still occupying the room. "Yes, Baron. Captain Roux was most generous to me. I doubt I would have survived if not for his aid."

"Nonsense." Christophe kept his eyes trained on her. "Having you aboard my ship was nothing but a pleasure for me."

Gabriel's nose expanded, but he said nothing. In contrast to his paling skin, Madeleine couldn't stop the heat pouring into hers.

"Captain Roux has been regaling us with stories of his adventures at sea," Désirée rescued her with a clever smirk.

"They have been most fascinating," Caroline added.

"Indeed." Gabriel's mouth had converted to a straight line as his dubious stare darted between Madeleine and the harrowing ship captain.

Caroline shot to her feet, touching one delicate hand to Gabriel's arm. "Perhaps we should leave now. Give these two a chance to talk."

"I agree." Désirée followed suit. "Let's get in a game of piquet before dinner begins."

"But we've only just met the man." A hint of panic edged the calm expression Gabriel maintained. "Don't you want to hear more of his riveting stories?"

Leaning close, Caroline spoke low. "Darling," she said, the word twisting Madeleine's gut, "they haven't seen each other in a long while. I'm sure they would appreciate the privacy."

Before he could protest, Caroline gently took his arm and hauled him toward the door. She and Désirée both hurled knowing smiles Madeleine's way, chattering together as they passed the threshold. From the hallway, Gabriel's worried gaze drank her in, his hand raking through his dark hair. Then the door snapped shut, blocking him from view.

Hugging an arm around herself, Madeleine let her eyes wander the shimmering wood floor and intricate floral rug before rising to find him staring pleasantly back at her. The afternoon had seeped into dusk, a bluish hue from the window casting its glow around them. The colossal two-story bookshelves on every wall stood like sentries watching them, reveling in her discomfort.

In contrast, Christophe looked nothing but self-assured as he took her in from his spot before a glittering set of gold and crimson books. Cocking his head, a roguish smile skittered over his lips. "Hello," he said, the single word launching a shiver of thrill over her skin.

Madeleine tucked a strand of hair behind her ear, wishing she could keep her face from flushing. "Hello." She pressed a hand over her surging belly, suddenly aware of the undecorated black dress clothing her. "I'm not quite what you were expecting, am I?"

His approving gaze washed over her. "I was rather surprised when I called on Jacqueline Michel and was told you didn't exist." His eyebrow hooked. "Luckily for me, your *very* accommodating maid quickly deduced who I meant and took pity on me."

"I'm sorry I lied to you." How many people had she treated similarly in her adult life? Deception had become a cancer within her. "I—"

"Please." He held up a hand. "You owe me no explanation. You were a woman alone on a deserted island. I could have been a common criminal, for all you knew. You were right to protect yourself."

She nodded tentatively. "I should have at least told you once I knew you better." Her shoulders lifted, the unvoiced truth between them gnawing at her. "I suppose I was just scared."

Christophe studied her in thoughtful silence. "Scared I would see you differently if I knew who you truly were?" His light blue eyes blazed in the shifting candlelight, searing through to her core.

She swallowed against the heat of his gaze, fingers fanning out her skirts on either side. "You came here expecting a noblewoman, and here stands before you a mere humble servant." How small it made her feel, to have feigned great wealth and been discovered for a woman of inferior birth.

A smile edged the corner of his mouth. "Your manners are rather practiced for a domestic." His head shook, compassion filling his gaze. "But you shouldn't be ashamed of your station in life. It only means you work hard for everything you have. I am no stranger to that."

Relief streamed over her. Auguste's words had plagued her of late, replaying over and again in her mind, reminding her that she would never mean anything to anyone of value. Perhaps she had convinced herself of it as the days wore on, burying her in a dizzying parade of scrubbing and laundering.

Madeleine returned the smile glowing back at her, the unease she felt in his presence slowly melting. "How did you even find me after all this time?"

"It wasn't hard." Christophe gestured with his large hands, flinging shadows over the bookshelves. "I disembarked in Marseilles after months in the Caribbean, weary and weather-beaten, only to find your letter waiting for me. It took just a few inquiries into the seal to discover its origin."

"I see." Madeleine glanced down, newly on edge. She had nearly forgotten about the letter she'd asked Cecile to pen for her, dismissing him from her life. In her wildest dreams, she'd never expected to face him again.

"Would you like to sit down?" Madeleine gestured toward the chairs left abandoned by Caroline and the Clement siblings. "I don't often have the chance to rest between my chores, but in this case, I believe they will make an exception for me."

Captain Roux clamped an arm behind his back. "No, I have only a few minutes to stay. A sailor never sleeps, after all. I just came by to—to see you." His gaze softened, the broad shoulders beneath his gold-trimmed jacket squaring. "When I received your letter, I thought you had married the baron of this estate. I had to see for myself."

"It would appear my actions are not so easily predicted." Madeleine inwardly recoiled, knowing full well that was her exact intention when dictating that letter.

His smile widened, eyes shining. "Luckily for me."

Madeleine glanced down at her fingers nervously intertwining around each other. "I was feeling rather bold when I wrote that letter." Bold enough to believe she could actually one day be the mistress of Avance.

"'Business relationship,' you said." Christophe shook his head. "I confess, my pride was damaged when I read those words. I did not spend nigh a year with you living in my head to settle for a *business relationship.*"

Eyes shooting back to him, she searched his face. How deeply she had longed to hear a word of affection from him aboard ship. Each day that had passed with no such endearments, she had convinced herself their connection was but a product of her overzealous imagination.

"What are you saying, Captain?" she finally asked, heart in her throat.

He ambled forward, eyes pinned to her. "Christophe," he said, stopping only a breath away. "I'm saying the same thing I scrawled in the pages of that silly book." He chuckled, mirth lighting his gaze. "I was so sure of myself, so certain I could sweep you off your feet with so little effort. Rather than tell you to your face, I let my arrogance lead. I won't make that mistake again."

Madeleine swallowed, the nearness of his body sending her heartbeat into frenzy. Details of his face emerged that she'd forgotten—the soft smile lines around his full lips, the small scar above his right brow. His sky-like eyes wandered her face, his chest rising in fervent waves. If only she had been able to read what he'd written to her, she might never have left his side.

The scents of cinnamon and saffron intoxicated her as his fingertips rose to trace her cheekbone. "We had a companionship on board the *Faucon*. You made me feel things I never felt before." He sighed, a dreamy look clouding his down-turned eyes. "Tell me I wasn't alone in these sentiments."

"Of course not. I—"

Yet before her lips could utter another word, he had covered them with his own. One muscular arm bound her to him, his other hand slipping into her hair. Shocked at first by his sudden action, Madeleine soon melted into his sturdy arms, the glorious feel of his lips caressing hers. His warmth encircled her, the rhythm of his thudding heart pressed to hers. She could have lost herself in his kisses forever, abandoning the cruel world around them.

When at last he pulled away, Christophe rested his forehead on hers, his hot, impassioned breath sprinkling her skin. "I have longed to do that since I first laid eyes on you." Both of his hands anchored at her waist, pulling her against his solid body. "Oh, how I've missed you, Madeleine."

She smiled against him, a sense of belonging flooding her. "Truly?"

His head pulled back just enough for his eyes to entangle with hers. She saw hope there, the promise that everything would be okay if only she trusted him. "Come away with me," he said, the unexpected words thrilling her. "I only have but a few days in Paris, and then I set sail for North America. After that, I'll take you anywhere you want to go. Anywhere in the world."

The idea set her imagination on fire. She'd heard tales of exotic foreign lands, people of every shade with customs so distant from her own. How she'd longed to pull the curtain back, to explore places like China, India, the vast plains of Africa. Now, the possibility stood before her in the form of this impossibly handsome, adoring man.

"I—I don't quite know what to say." Could she really leave her brothers behind, Désirée and Gabriel, Cecile? "France is my home. I'm not certain I could so easily abandon it."

Christophe studied her face, his gaze warm. "What could possibly be keeping you here?" He glanced around at the books tinged in trembling light, the ornate mahogany furnishings. "Do you honestly want to spend your whole life in this place, waiting on these people's every whim, washing this man's undergarments." She grinned shyly at the image as his hand swept her arm. "Wherever we go, I will take care of you. Anything you want, you'll have it."

Inhaling a quivering breath, Madeleine stared into the hands she'd pressed to his muscled chest. He was right. She couldn't let her life pass by, pining after a man who belonged to someone else. Gabriel would marry, build a life apart from her. Instead of wallowing in that miserable truth, she could be free, sailing across endless ocean waters with a man who truly wanted her.

His fingers hooked at her chin, propelling it upward. His thumb brushed her jawline, his burning eyes roaming the curve of her neck to her lips and into her conflicted gaze. "Just tell me you will consider my offer. I must leave in three days, but I will wait until then."

She swallowed, nodding. How beautiful a dream paraded before her mind's eye—standing at the helm of the *Faucon*, blasting through the waters of the Atlantic, the spray on her face and his brawny arms around her. Yet something deep in her heart ached to consider it.

"Oh, Madeleine, *please* say you'll come." Christophe nuzzled his face in the crook of her neck, flinging delightful shivers through her. "You belong with me. I won't let you go without a fight, not this time." He held her close for a quiet moment, the tree branches outside scraping the château's side, his breath curling in her ears.

Emboldened, Madeleine lifted his head in her hands. His tethered blond hair slid like silk under her fingertips. His jaw tensed beneath her palm. She drank in a breath of courage before lifting on her toes and pressing her lips to his. His skin heated as he returned her kiss, slow and soft, his hands squeezing the arched plain of her lower back.

Just when she was ready to surrender her entire world for him, a knock at the door yanked her from her delirium. Madeleine sprang backward, nearly colliding with the bookshelves as the door swung inward. At the sight of Gabriel's face on the other side, she turned a darker shade of red than she knew she could.

"Pardon the interruption." His suspicious gaze tumbled to the narrow space between them, where Christophe still gripped her hand. Gabriel cleared his throat. "Georgette has just announced that dinner will shortly be served. Would you be so kind as to grace as with your presence, Captain? You too, of course, Madeleine." His solemn gaze pinned her in place, daring her to wilt onto the floor.

"I regret I must decline your invitation, Baron." Christophe reached for the tricorne hat he'd left atop a bookshelf, not bothering to drop her hand. "I was just telling Madeleine that I have business in Paris tonight. I just dropped by to say hello." His fingers gently tightened around hers.

"What a pity," Gabriel said, sarcasm lacing his dry tone. "The ladies will be so disappointed that your stories of sea life are going with you." His eyes narrowed on the captain, prompting Christophe to shoot unseen daggers back at him.

"Come along, Captain. I'll walk you out." Madeleine let go of his hand, wedging herself between the two distrustful men.

Their retreat down the maze of hallways transpired in silence, Gabriel diverting to the dining room with one last flash of his eyes. Christophe watched him go, the hint of a smile edging his lips. The pair said nothing until they'd reached the front door, where Christophe's gold-trimmed coach waited for him. Madeleine waved to Matthieu in the driver's seat as they crossed the drawbridge.

Before he ascended the carriage steps, Christophe spun to face her. Adoration had retaken his gaze as he let it pour over her. He twisted on his tricorne hat, smoothing the hair beneath it, then let his hand cup her cheek. She blushed, knowing the dining room faced their way and almost feeling the prying eyes from within.

"Think about it, Madeleine," Christophe's soulful baritone hummed through her musings. "I'll be at that tavern down the way. The Black—" The word eluded him, his forehead wrinkling.

"Lion." Madeleine smiled against his hand. "Yes, I know it well. I will bring you my answer before you go."

Christophe grinned, leaning close to plant a peck on her forehead before he disappeared into his coach. He watched her from the window as the horses began to trot, tugging him and Matthieu away. The carriage wheels rumbled, sprinkling a cloud of dust behind them, leaving Madeleine to a decision she wasn't yet sure she could face. She marched back to the château, her spirit dismal in the knowledge that she may very soon leave it behind for good.

Twenty Two

"What is the rush? What happened?" Cecile panted between her words, barely keeping up as Madeleine dragged her by the arm down the narrow hallway.

"I can't explain here." Darting around a corner, Madeleine ignored her aching side and sprinted down the corridor. Down here in the servants' quarters, no oil or candles were expended unless absolutely necessary. Yet even in the dark, her confidence guided her. She had traversed these halls enough to run them in her sleep.

When they reached her door, Madeleine punched it open. A blithe ribbon of moonlight trickled over the small space, but she raced to the candle at her bedside and made quick work of igniting it with her tinderbox. Its yellow glow created a beautiful orb around it, flinging shadows over the walls. Madeleine had just enough light to kneel at her bedside and rummage through her tiny collection of books.

Rising to her feet, she held a blue leatherbound specimen at arm's length. "Please, Cecile. You must read me the inscription inside before I go mad."

Still catching her breath, Cecile accepted the offering, then turned it over in her hands. "Where did this come from?"

"Captain Roux gave it to me while I was on board his ship." Madeleine paced the room, her boots thudding over the worn plank floor. "Before I foolishly left him without even knowing how he felt about me."

Cecile eyed the book with one eyebrow arched. "Why does every man seem to think you need a book? Next time, tell them *jewelry* is what we really want."

Despite her anxiety, Madeleine chuckled. "Please just read it, Cecile. I have to know what it says."

Pulling the book toward her lightly freckled face, Cecile squinted in the dim light. She shook her head, advancing toward Madeleine's candle and plopping on the bed. "My dearest Jacqueline." She smirked up at the woman desperately marching past her. "I have not the words to express how greatly I've enjoyed having you aboard the *Faucon* these past few weeks. You have filled it with light and joy, things I have largely forgotten living a lonely sailor's life. I cannot let you go without you knowing that I'm—" Cecile paused, eyes widening. "I'm falling in love with you. I wish for you to stay with me, always. Christophe."

Their eyes met over the letter, Madeleine frozen in her tracks and mouth agape. Cecile squealed in excitement, clamping her hand over her mouth. "That gorgeous man has wanted you all this time and you were here scrubbing floors?" She looked at Madeleine as if she'd taken a complete leave of her senses.

"Yes, well I didn't exactly know that. I couldn't read what he wrote." Madeleine pushed a hand into her hair. "Cecile, what am I going to do?"

"Is there even a question? You run immediately to wherever he is and admit you were the biggest nincompoop who ever lived for leaving him." Cecile laughed, setting the book beside her on the bed. "What did he even say to you tonight? I wanted so badly to ask you as soon as he'd gone, but they were so slow at dinner, I thought the food would take on mold."

Madeleine turned to her, hand shielding her surging stomach. "He still cares for me. He wants me to leave with him for North America, then anywhere I can dream after that."

Clapping her hands together, Cecile sprang from the bed. "I can't believe it—you traveling the world with that handsome Atlas of a man? You must send me back trinkets from wherever you go." She gasped. "Better yet, take me with you. There's bound to be other acceptable males on board his ship."

Madeleine couldn't resist the slow smile her friend's enthusiasm etched on her face. "I haven't given him an answer yet. I still haven't decided what I'll do."

Two hands captured her shoulders. "Maddy, you must be jesting." Cecile's green eyes darted between hers. "You can't stay here all your life, slowly transforming into Georgette. There is a life waiting for you out there, a grand adventure that most people can't even dream of."

Sighing, Madeleine let her gaze drift to the window, where the tranquil moat glittered beneath the moon. "I know, but what about—" The very name arrested in her throat, choking her.

"Gabriel Clement?" Cecile's head angled, pity tracing the candlelit lines of her face. "He's with Caroline now. They're happy. Leave them be and go chase a little happiness for yourself." Her fingers swept the wisps of hair falling from Madeleine's bun. "You deserve a life of joy, of truly being loved."

A quiet moment drifted over them, Madeleine considering her words. "I can't leave him before I know he is safe from Auguste's clutches. My brother is not well."

Cecile shook her head. "There will always be treasure hunters eager to steal whatever fortune the Clement family sits upon." Her green eyes drove into Madeleine's soul. "You can't live your whole life protecting everyone around you. At some point you must fly away and pursue your own dreams."

Just then, a hurried knock startled them both before the door swung inward. Désirée's flushed face emerged from behind it, illuminated by her candle. "I came as soon as I could." She snapped the door closed. "I love that woman to death, but Caroline eats slower than my poor grandmother did in her old age."

Cecile pivoted toward her with hands on her thin hips. "Could it have something to do with the display Madeleine was putting on outside with her gentleman friend?"

Wincing, Madeleine threw her palm over her face. "You all really saw that?" She groaned.

"Yes, and I couldn't wait to run down here and find out what happened." Désirée leaned down to set her candlestand on the windowsill. "He's deliciously handsome, Madeleine. And so cultured. Caroline and I simply could not stop chatting about it at supper."

With a toss of her bronze head, Cecile emitted a throaty laugh. "I thought the baron's head was going to explode with all the praise these two were laying on him. Especially once the captain kissed you."

Glaring at Cecile, Désirée took Madeleine's hands into her warm grasp. Her baby pink crêpe gown smelled of the sweetest rose petals as her kind eyes wandered into Madeleine's. "He appeared to adore you. What did he say?"

Madeleine's breath hitched. Could she really tell the truth to this woman who had harbored dreams of them becoming sisters? Sailing away would not only mean leaving Avance but leaving her and the friendship they had fashioned while hunting for Gabriel together.

"He told her he's in love with her," Cecile spoke for her, beaming at the news. "He asked her to run away with him aboard his ship."

Désirée's brows climbed her forehead. "He asked you to marry him?"

"Well, not exactly." Madeleine caught her lip in her teeth. "I suppose I hadn't thought that far into it yet."

"You need to know before you decide anything." Désirée squeezed her hands. "Your reputation is at stake, after all."

Cecile clicked her tongue. "What reputation? She isn't some wealthy debutante who will be ruined if her departure is leaked to society."

At Désirée's bemused expression, Madeleine brought her hands between them. "She's right; it's different for us. I was an actress, for goodness' sake. Nobody cares about what we do or who we're seen with. They would only care if I married someone like—" She blinked, realizing too late who she spoke to.

"Like my brother?" Désirée's lovely face had turned somber. "I've given up hopes for the two of you, but still. Madeleine, this isn't just about your reputation. It's about morality. Could you really live with yourself before God knowing you're dwelling in sin with that man?"

Madeleine blushed. "I wouldn't necessarily be living in sin with him. I'd like to believe I can control myself, thank you."

"But can he?" Cecile said with a snort. Her hand swiped the air. "Leave her alone, Désirée. It's a new era, haven't you heard? Women are free to love whom they choose without constraint."

Désirée's lips pressed together as she turned a troubled look back on Madeleine. "I desire more for you than that. You deserve a man who loves you and wants to honor you in marriage. We both know what would happen if you go sailing across the sea with a man like that." Her skin pinkened.

"I appreciate the concern," Madeleine said. "I promise I won't go anywhere with him without a proper union." The image of her father flashed through her mind, on his knees before a raging hearth, lost in prayer deep into the night. He would chide her with a similar sentiment, she knew.

"Good." Désirée smiled, her eyes shining in the dancing candle-light. "I know you have been through a great deal these past few months. Don't go just because you need to escape Caroline and my brother. Go because you *want* to." Her gaze leveled squarely on the other woman. "Do you want to go with him, Madeleine?"

As she glanced between her two expectant friends, Madeleine's mind raced with images. She saw Christophe, standing at the helm of the *Faucon*, wind whipping through his golden locks. How she'd longed for him to take her in his arms and kiss her as he had tonight. Now, his touch lingered on her face, his kiss still leaving an electric tingle on her lips. She could enjoy that sensation again and again—*forever*, he'd said. She could throw off her cares for the fathomless waters of the Atlantic, never having to toil again, only to relax in the arms of a man who adored her.

Then Gabriel crept into that vision, weakening its blinding light. She remembered the first time their eyes locked in the parlor, the first time his hand swept hers. His gentle gaze encompassed her as they lay together on the floor of his study, breathless from the fall they'd just endured. A hundred moments entangled around each other—tender kisses, embraces, conversations that had thrust her so much deeper into loving him than physical passion ever could.

Eyes misting, she looked into Cecile's hopeful face, and then to Désirée. "I haven't a clue what I really want," she said finally, her breath quivering. "But one thing I know. Whatever happens to me, I shall never abandon the love of my friends." She smiled through her tears. "This may well be our last adventure together, and I'm not going to waste it. Let's go celebrate."

Désirée's eyes sparked as she turned a mischievous grin on Cecile. "Berry tart in the kitchen?"

"Georgette will kill us." Cecile rubbed her hands together. "Let's go."

G abriel's study rested in lonely silence when Madeleine strode into it, her nightly duties nearly complete. A fire crackled in the white marble fireplace, filling the small space with warmth and a lustrous glow. She sighed, her gaze roaming the unkempt shelves stretching to the ceiling. Did Brigitte really think this was clean? Some days, she regretted turning over the master's study to her inexperienced hands.

Madeleine shuddered, realizing she already sounded like Georgette in her head. Rebelling against the notion, she reminded herself that Brigitte was still learning as she moved to collect the baron's half-eaten lunch tray. The poor girl had enough to endure downstairs with Georgette insisting she stay until every last dish and kettle sparkled.

Reaching for the baron's fallen teacup, Madeleine righted it in its saucer and swiped at the liquid that had spilled on the wood. She stacked one china plate beneath another, the dishes still bearing half a small loaf of bread and remnants of jam. Lifting the tray in her hands, she couldn't help but explore his scattered desk with a forlorn smile. It still looked as messy as ever—papers strewn over every surface, inky fingerprints dotting the desk. A shimmer caught her eye, pulling them to the center of the desk, where a lone ring rested within the rolling waves of firelight.

Gasping, Madeleine dropped her tray with a rattle, her hand clamping over her open mouth. The reality of the ring's resurgence sunk low in her gut, sickening her. Almost without thinking, she lifted it reverently in trembling fingers. A brilliant medley of diamonds and topaz met her gaze, winking in the shifting light. His mother's ring, the one he had offered to *her* when he assumed himself as good as dead. Madeleine's eyes filled to imagine it on Caroline's hand, greeting her every time the woman waltzed into a room.

Footsteps in the hall stiffened her. Madeleine jumped, setting the white gold ring in its place. She whirled to find Gabriel watching her solemnly from the doorway. "Forgive me, Baron. I didn't mean to pry." Madeleine couldn't stop the heat from gushing into her face as her gaze dove to the floor.

Gabriel stood in silence for a prolonged moment, agonizing her. Then his every step toward her quickened her already hammering heart. He stopped only an arm's length away. "Allow me to explain—"

"There is nothing to explain. Your life is your own and I should not have been snooping." Madeleine tried to launch herself toward the door before she could humiliate herself any further, but he caught her gently by the waist.

"Please, Madeleine, I think we need to talk about this." His gentle voice hummed in her ear, the smell of his musky cologne tantalizing her every sense. She dared to lift her gaze and found sincere, vulnerable eyes looking back.

Madeleine swallowed. Even such a simple touch blazed the skin where he held her. "What is there to say?" she asked, the pain on his face impaling her. "You will marry another woman and be free of me. She has replaced everything I once was to you." Her stomach roiled. Had she really just expressed the deepest fear in her heart, out loud for him to consider?

Gabriel's brows cinched. "Is that what you think?" He stepped back, one hand on his hip while the other raked through his hair. "Madeleine, you forced this situation on me. I *wanted* only you, and you pushed me away. You *told* me to pursue Caroline."

"I know, and I'm sorry." Her chest surged painfully. "None of this is your fault. You *should* marry Caroline. You should be happy. Forget what we shared together. It's easier that way."

He wagged his head slowly, a thousand emotions passing over his face. "Madeleine, I could never forget what we shared. It will be a part of me, always." His weary gaze wandered to his mother's ring still glittering atop his desk. "But I must move on from it for Caroline's sake. I care for her very deeply."

A hard ache implanted in her chest and spread outward to hear him utter the words. Madeleine pushed back her tears but still they flooded her eyes. "I am happy for you," she said with a quivering smile, trying to reassure her joyless heart.

Gabriel cocked his head, studying her. The fireplace sizzled, sprinkling the air with the aroma of cedar. At last, he heaved a long sigh. "But can I be happy for you?"

Madeleine frowned. "With the captain, you mean?"

For the first time, irritation flashed in his steely gaze. "Of course I mean the captain. *Captain Roux.* This vagabond from God-knows-where who just trounced in here acting like he owned everything in sight." He gestured around him, shadows dancing on the far wall.

"Owned me, more precisely." An angry impulse bit at her. "Forgive me, Baron, but nobody owns me. Not even you."

His hand balled into a fist at his forehead. "Oh, don't I know it," he blurted. Softening, Gabriel lowered his hand and stepped toward her. "I am quite aware that you are not mine to control, but when I saw the two of you together, when I saw him kiss you—" His words trailed off, their unspoken meaning clear in the quiet room.

"You were jealous." Hadn't she experienced the same sensation every time he and Caroline shared even a smile?

Gabriel opened his mouth to speak, then exhaled, nodding. "Forgive me, Madeleine. It isn't my place to protect you. I just want to see you live a good life."

"And you don't think I can live such a life with Christophe Roux? You don't think he would make me happy?" Fueled by her indignation, her questions sounded more like accusations.

"Living aboard a ship for the rest of your life, surrounded by a group of lonely, women-starved men?" He shook his curly head. "No, I don't believe you would be safe or happy."

Madeleine blinked, the reality of his words driving fear into her core. Christophe had protected her aboard the *Faucon* on her last journey, but surely danger would snatch her in its claws at some point.

Thrusting the notion aside, she lifted her chin. "Well, as you say, I am not yours to protect." She steeled herself against the hurt her words produced on his face. "If I decide that Christophe Roux is the man I want to spend my life with, then it shouldn't be any concern of yours, Baron. You'll simply have to employ a new maid."

Gabriel's eyes searched hers, the firelight moving over the robust planes of his face. "We both know this is so much more complicated than that." He stepped closer, so close she could see the gentle flecks of green in his shimmering eyes. His shaven skin emanated vanilla and musk.

Her breath hitched, her vision hazing the closer he came. He hovered over her, so near she could have stretched onto her tiptoes and kissed him. But standing there, a mere breath away from shattering everything she'd worked for these many months, reality seized her. To embrace him meant destroying him. Dizzy, Madeleine took a step back, and then another.

"Madeleine, wait." Gabriel's hand shot out to detain her, but already she had retreated to the space beyond his tea table and chairs.

"I'm sorry, Gabriel—Baron." She nearly tripped as she stumbled to the doorway. "We can't keep doing this. I must go."

"At least let me explain the ring," he called, shoving his hands into his pockets.

She shook her head, her blurred vision hardly making him out. "She will make a beautiful bride." With that, she shoved her aching body into the hallway and ran until the comfort of her room encircled her.

Twenty Three

"Submerge them all, just like this." Madeleine demonstrated the action to Brigitte, thrusting her paddle into one of the giant copper urns of the washhouse. She watched with approval as the tiny maid duplicated her movements. "Good. Now swirl it around. Keep them moving."

Muscles protesting, Madeleine took a brief rest to swipe an arm over her perspiring forehead. The steamy air crowding the squat stone building infused with her body, sticking her hair to the sides of her face and seeping beads of sweat into the handkerchief she'd tied around her head. Wisps of boiling lye burned her skin as she bent to push the linens around again. Forcing her weary arms to work, she reminded herself this was the last time she would ever have to launder sheets for a great house again.

"How do you know when they're done?" Brigitte asked from beside her. She grunted, propelling her paddle around only with great effort. The copper urn before her looked like it could swallow her whole.

"It takes some time," Madeleine said. "After churning in the soapy water for a while, the dirt will come out." She recalled her first lesson in the art of laundry with little fondness. Georgette had stood back and let her figure out how to man every pot alone.

"Can it rest a minute?" A masculine voice made her jump. Madeleine pivoted back to find that the baron had soundlessly crept up behind them. "I'm sorry, I didn't mean to startle you."

"That's quite all right." She glanced self-consciously down at her wet, crumpled apron and dress. "What brings you to the wash-house this time of day, Baron?"

"I wondered if I might have a word"—he leaned close—"in private."

Madeleine looked up at Brigitte, who quickly glanced away, nearly dropping her paddle in her feigned indifference. "Certain-ly." Propping her paddle against her urn, Madeleine wiped her pruney hands on her apron. "Brigitte, I'll only be a moment. Keep the boilers going, would you?"

Outside, a summer wind swept the barony and rustled the ver-dant trees. Even the heat of the day felt so much nicer than that stuffy washhouse. She could breathe again, fresh air free of acrid cleaning agents. Gabriel's hand invited her to walk beside him.

Falling comfortably into his relaxed stride, she stole a sideways glance his way. He looked happy today, so much cheerier than how she had left him the night before. "Forgive me for my peculiar odor," she said with a laugh. "I've been bathing in lye and sweat all morning."

A smile jerked the corner of his mouth as Gabriel rolled his sleeves to his elbows. "If you're implying that you smell bad, you are mistaken."

Madeleine's gaze fell to her well-worn boots crunching a dirty path toward the château. "Now, what is this all about? If you mention that ring, I'll run back to that washhouse so fast—"

"I shall never mention the ring again. I promise." Gabriel's fin-gers spread out before them. "It's about Henri, actually. I believe I've figured out his clue." Pride beamed off his face, a mysterious bit of humor puckering his lips.

"That's amazing. We should go tell Désirée."

"I don't want her to know just yet." The couple had reached the moat, which trickled past a bed of grass and cattails. "I don't want to excite her hopes if I'm wrong. You know how eager she gets and how fast disappointment will make her spirit crash."

Madeleine squinted out the sun's rays. "That's true. She is such an optimistic creature." Not like her, jaded from a life of repeated setbacks. Her eyes swept the babbling water coursing past their feet. "Henri's clue led you here?"

"You led me here, actually. What you said about a river running through the château." Proudly plopping his fists on his hips, the chest beneath his double-breasted waistcoat swelled. "I believe I know exactly where to look, if you will come with me."

A chill skittered up her arms to imagine going anywhere alone with him. She glanced back at the washhouse, now a distant image beneath the swaying trees. "As long as I'm not gone too long. Brigitte has never done the laundry before. She's liable to blow the place up."

Returning her smile, Gabriel motioned toward the footbridge crossing over the moat. "We'll hurry. Right this way."

Trailing behind his determined form, Madeleine traversed the creaking footbridge and approached the château's monstrous stone walls. Gabriel led her to a side of the house she had rarely found occasion to visit, where he yanked open a wooden door to a mysterious porthole. Stealing a furtive glance in every direction, Madeleine passed him and stepped through the opening. It would do her no good to have obeyed Pascal's every demand only for him to see her sneaking off with his nephew.

Ahead of her, the dark stone corridor dipped in a set of stairs descending into blackness. An icy sensation seized her, the same feeling she'd encountered when journeying into the depths of the catacombs. "I thought you said this had to do with the moat," she said, whirling to face him. "The moat is outside."

Kneeling on the dirt-sprinkled ground, Gabriel lit a lantern he had presumably left there. "There is more to it than meets the eye." He stood and pulled the door closed, a glowing orb of yellow candlelight encircling them both. The couple shared a long look before he gestured to the stairwell.

Madeleine held her skirts high and carefully took the stairs, stepping through the ribbon of light cast by Gabriel's lantern. At first, she could make out very little, then her eyes slowly adjusted to her murky surroundings. At the base of the staircase, she blinked, making out a stone walkway stretching before her, beside which a still pool of water sat.

"What is this place?" she asked, eyes following the trail of water until it disappeared into the shadows.

Gabriel held his lantern high, advancing into the ancient-looking room. "It's a continuation of the moat you see outside," he said, spearing his finger toward an iron gate through which water passed. "Back in Henri's time, this was a working farm. They used the gates to bring supplies in from the river on boats."

She took in the vast space, littered with tiny nooks and shadowed bends in the wall. "How will we know where to look? It's so big. There are so many places he could have hid something down here."

Grinning, he led her down the corridor, aimed at a large circular object she couldn't make out. As they approached, the contours of a waterwheel revealed themselves. "For many years, they ran a working mill down here. They used this to power it. And if I'm not mistaken—" Wandering forward, he set his lantern on the floor and reached for a lever on the wall. He thrust it downward with a mighty shove, inciting a series of creaks and clangs as the gears began to churn to life. "It still works," he said with a satisfied smile.

The two of them stood back, watching in awe as the waterwheel cranked into motion, dumping small bits of water at first, then more as it picked up speed. Soon, a cascade thundered over the spinning contraption, pushing the once steady pool of water into a frothing river.

Madeleine smirked up at Gabriel. "Beyond the water," she said.

"In the very heart." He looked back at the falling water, excitement capturing his gaze.

"Do you think he would hide it here? Could there really have been unimaginable treasure tucked beneath our feet this whole time?"

"There's only one way to find out." Already, he marched toward the swirling wheel, bright eyes hunting. "I can't see behind it," he shouted over the water's commotion. "We'll have to get closer."

Plastering her body to the wall, Madeleine trailed him down a narrow passage with only a thin strip of floor for her boots to grapple. Water sprinkled her arms and face as they passed the wheel, finding a quiet alcove nestled beside it. Gabriel pushed at every wall, but only unyielding dirt and stone answered his prods.

"There's nothing back here." His chest heaved, disappointment tugging the corners of his mouth.

"Maybe it's on the other side," she suggested, pointing up the base of the waterwheel.

Gabriel's eyes ascended to the spot she indicated. "I don't think there's any other way over there but to climb this." His gaze met hers, searching for approval.

Madeleine shrugged. "This ancestor of yours certainly was an adventurer. I'm willing if you are."

He surveyed the colossal structure for a few moments before crouching to expel the candle from his lantern. "I can't climb this thing without both of my hands," he said before gingerly placing the candle's end between his teeth.

Wincing, Madeleine watched him stretch his arms wide and take hold of the wooden parts, heaving himself upward. "Please be careful." She could just see him setting his bobbing hair on fire, but, incredibly, he clamored up the wheel without harming a single strand. At the top, he seized the candle in one hand and crouched low to dangle his arm toward her.

Finding her footing, Madeleine climbed to the spot his hand waited and allowed him to drag her up behind him. A similar alcove rested on the waterwheel's opposing side. Madeleine easily dropped into it, hands quick to search the tiny space as Gabriel worked his way toward her.

Madeleine's heart leaped into her throat as her fingertips brushed wood. "I think I found something!" Her hands groped for a handle but found none. When she jammed her body against it, the door wouldn't budge.

The light from the baron's candle soon illuminated a small wooden door set in the stone. It had no decoration, no markings, not even a handle or knob to indicate its purpose.

She frowned, slumping against it. "This has to be it, but how do we get in?"

Gabriel braced his hands against the door, groaning as he forced his body weight against it. The impressive door didn't even shift. "This thing would take a battering ram," he said, glaring at the offending object.

As he turned, a ray of his candle illuminated a strange shape on the wall. "Look!" Madeleine charged toward the darkened space, her hands finding a cut-out compartment with several wooden knobs inside. When he held the candle close, a collection of objects lined up before them—a square, a circle, a rose, a moon and a star, a cross, and a heart.

"Why do these look so familiar?" Gabriel cocked his head.

"Because some of them were on the end of that key you gave me." She could scarcely hear herself over the rush of blood in her ears. Pulling at the rose, she yelped with delight as it shifted outward. "Look, they move. This appears to be a puzzle."

Gabriel blinked, seemingly immobilized. "You mean even though we no longer have the key, we still might use it?"

She watched in shock as the pieces clicked this way and that. "Your Henri must have been brilliant to think of something like this. A key that doesn't need an actual lock." Conjuring the image of the beautiful chunk of brass that once lived around her neck,

Madeleine moved the circle into place first. Next, she pulled the rose over it, followed by the cross.

When nothing happened, Madeleine's brows gathered. "I don't understand. That's it. That's the symbol on the end of the key."

Gabriel licked his lips. "Try pushing it in."

Nodding, Madeleine covered the newly-formed symbol in her palm and pushed until it retreated into the wall. Her fingers twisted just as they would a doorknob, producing a loud clank in the wall, like a steel bar lifting. To her amazement, the door growled inward, uncovering another blackened corridor.

She turned to her companion, mouth falling open. "We did it. I can't believe we did it. We're really here."

A contented smile lifted his lips as his gaze wandered over her candlelit face. "Are you ready to go find the Moon King's bounty?"

Nodding, she hardly perceived her feet moving beneath her. Their shoes scuffed the stone floor, only a short space before them visible in the candle's flickering light. The deeper they journeyed, the harder her heart stampeded within her. Gabriel's hand found hers in the dark, and Madeleine laced her fingers with his, grateful for his comfort against the trepidation eating at her every part.

At the end of the hallway, they emptied into a small, rectangular room. Madeleine's heart plummeted, the hand holding hers dropping limply at his side. Only four silent stone walls encircled them, fixed with torches on every side.

"This doesn't make sense," Gabriel said, approaching the far wall. His hands braced against the stone. "Do you see a hidden door somewhere, another puzzle, perhaps?"

Madeleine scoured every surface—the walls, the floor, the low ceiling, but wherever her eyes landed, they met only the same gray stone. The two of them kicked and pushed at the immovable walls until they both breathed heavy from exhaustion.

"It's no use," she said between breaths. "There's nothing here. It's just an empty room."

Gabriel thrust a fist to the wall above his head, leaning on it wearily. "Why would Henri lead us all this way for nothing? What good could this have possibly done him?"

"Perhaps there was once something here and it was moved."

"Who could have moved it?" he asked, candlelight moving over his face as he gazed despondently back down the hall. "We're clearly the only two people who have passed through this place in centuries."

Fingertips brushing the cold, uneven walls, Madeleine squinted in the murky light. "What about these torches? Maybe they have something to do with it."

"You're right." Gabriel pushed off the wall, twisting to touch his candle to the kindling inside the nearest torch. "Henri wouldn't have put these here without a purpose. Everything he did was deliberate." Methodically, he moved from one torch to the next until every one blazed with a mighty orange flame. He blew out his candle and cast it aside, the room aglow in frolicking light.

Half expecting something magical to appear, Madeleine held her breath. When nothing did, her brow scrunched. "I had hoped that would work."

"It did." He wagged his finger as if indicating an unseen clue. "I don't know what it is yet, but we'll find it. Henri was too smart to leave his treasure out in the open for just anyone to find."

Madeleine's arms swung around her. "Though we're not exactly in the middle of a wide-open field here."

A smile touched his lips as Gabriel looked back at her through the blazing torch light. "Let evening stars be your guide," he recited. "I'll bet whatever it is doesn't become apparent until nightfall." With that, he sank to the floor and sat cross-legged atop it.

"So you're just going to sit in here for hours?" She knotted her arms over her chest, the frigid temperatures already seeping through her work dress. "They're bound to wonder where we are and come looking for us."

Gabriel flashed her a grin. "I doubt they'll find us in here." After unbuttoning his waistcoat, he pulled it off his torso and rolled it into a ball. "I'm not bargaining on the fact that the door out there will open for us again. I'll lay here and wait until whatever Henri wanted us to find becomes apparent." Rolling his sleeves to his wrists, he reclined on the floor and shoved his rolled waistcoat beneath his neck.

"How did I ever get mixed up with this crazy family?" Madeleine sighed as she slid down the wall to sit on the hard, bumpy floor. She couldn't help watching the baron, lacing his fingers beneath his head and staring up at the ceiling with a contented look on his handsome face. The hunt for this elusive treasure was surely this family's passion, the fuel that kept it going even in the face of seeming defeat. She'd never seen him happier than he was on that dusty floor.

With the cold burrowing to her very bones, Madeleine tucked her knees against her chest and wound her arms around them. "You seem different," she said to Gabriel, who now laid back with his eyes closed. "More relaxed. Like you don't have a care in the world."

"I'm practicing the art of letting things go," he said, crossing one ankle over another.

"You will have to teach me that someday. I've never quite been able to master it." Another shiver coursed through her, knocking her teeth together.

"Oh, I'm far from having it mastered." Gabriel opened one eye, squinting at her from his reclined position. "You look like you're freezing. Perhaps my waistcoat might help."

Before he could extract it from beneath him, Madeleine's hand shot out. "No, please don't trouble yourself. I'd hate to spoil your comfort." And what good would a garment with holes for arms actually do for her?

"Then come over here and lie down with me." He gestured with his arm. "I'll keep you warm."

Madeleine stilled, the idea both thrilling and terrifying. "No, I couldn't possibly—"

"I'm not going to let you sit there and freeze to death when I have enough body heat for the both of us. Now come here." Rising up on his elbows, he suspended a hand midair toward her.

Heart thumping in her throat, Madeleine crawled to him and took his outstretched hand. She could barely breathe as he pulled her in beside him, fitting her perfectly against his side, his arm curling around her and anchoring her to him. Her head fell to his chest, her ear pressed above the steady rhythm of his heart. Finding nowhere else to go, her palm lay gently on the ridge of buttons climbing his torso.

The couple lay there in silence for what felt like ages, nothing but the distant roar of the waterwheel touching the space. Against her every effort, Madeleine felt safe in his arms, drinking in the smell of him, watching her hand rise and fall with the pattern of his breathing. Slowly, her reticence thawed, her body relaxing into his as his warmth percolated through her chilled skin.

"I'm glad we have the chance to be alone, actually," he said at last. "I need to apologize for what I said to you last night."

The memory of it sparked a twinge of pain. "Please, you don't need to—"

"But I do, Madeleine." His arm tautened slightly against her. "I have no right to dictate who you consort with, or even to know, for that matter. I behaved like a fool, and I'm sorry."

She said nothing, only nodded against the crook of his neck.

Gabriel inhaled a prolonged breath, his chest swelling beneath her fingertips. "You must know you are more than a servant here. You are family to Désirée and I. No matter where you go and who you are with, that fact will not change."

His words struck something deep within her, an emotion she almost didn't recognize. How fiercely had she longed for her kin when wandering the streets as a child, hungry and alone? How hard had she prayed to hear that very phrase again—*you are family?*

And yet, the reality of their true relationship pummeled her back to earth.

"Will you feel the same when I'm waltzing around the high seas, dwelling in sin, as Désirée calls it?"

He waited a few beats before replying. "So you're going then, with Christophe Roux?" His jaw tightened beneath her.

Madeleine stared into the orange flames capering high on the wall, the agony of leaving him nearly pulling her backward. "I have nothing keeping me here," she reminded herself. "I could stay here and be a maid all my life, or I can go lead a life of adventure."

"And you considered your own personal safety?" he asked.

"I can handle myself. You saw what I did to your mighty swordsman friend, Justin Aubert."

A deep, masculine chuckle reverberated throughout the room, delighting Madeleine's weary soul. "That's right, I'd nearly forgotten. He didn't say much, but the poor man was rubbing his shoulder for days."

The two shared a laugh, the distance they had erected waning in that peaceful, secret room, tucked below a bustling house. Madeleine couldn't contain the joy spearing through her to see his chest ripple with laughter, to hear his low baritone lifted in merriment. It could almost make her forget the fact that she had just promised to leave him behind for somebody else, forever.

Soon, the quiet had settled over them once more. Unexpectedly, Gabriel's hand rose to twist a few loose strands of her hair around his finger. He sighed, a gratified sound. "I wish you every bit of joy you could ever dream of." Shifting, his sparkling eyes angled downward to meet hers. "I only want you to be happy, Madeleine. That's all I could ever wish for."

Gaze intertwining with his, she searched his face. Could it really be that easy? Could they just let each other go, watch as the other began a new life with someone else? She clutched his shirt, the linen smooth beneath her fingertips. How desperately she wanted to pull him close, to admit she would only ever harbor true love for him. And yet, her fingers relaxed against his chest.

"And I you." It was all she could say before her words failed. She closed her eyes, sinking within his embrace and holding him closer. Gabriel's strong arms coiled around her, cradling her, a shield of protection within a perilous world. The two clung to each other for hours, Madeleine counting the beating of his heart until sleep overcame her.

Twenty Four

Madeleine opened her bleary eyes, the world coming into focus one detail at a time. A stone wall, splashed in shifting light. An empty floor. A strong hand fixed on her arm. Dizzying warmth trickled over her to comprehend that she still lay within Gabriel's hold. She blinked, letting her eyes travel the length of his linen-garbed chest to the placid eyes looking down on her.

His mouth inched into a smile. "It appears we both fell asleep," he said, not making an attempt to move.

Rising on her elbow, Madeleine yanked off the crooked handkerchief barely cleaving to her hair. "How long has it been? Did you wake up before me?"

"Only by fifteen minutes or so. You looked so peaceful, I didn't want to wake you." Gabriel revolved to his side, pulling a fob watch from his crinkled waistcoat and squinting at the glass. "We've been down here for over three hours. Surely whatever is supposed to happen has transpired already."

Crawling to her hands and knees, Madeleine pushed off the jagged stone floor and stood ahead of her companion. The two approached the walls, looking between the torches for anything that had changed, some type of passage that might have revealed itself. Yet the longer her eyes strained against the flashing walls, the deeper her hopes sank.

"Nothing has changed." She flattened her hand on the fire-warmed stone. "Everything looks just as it always did."

Gabriel's broad shoulders wilted. "It would appear we are chasing fairies again." His head shook woefully as he spun in a circle, still searching. "I had really hoped this would be the place. He left such intricate clues and took the time to hide it so well. Did someone get here before us?"

Madeleine's fingers splayed on either side of her. "How desperately I want to know that, too. Every mystery Henri presents us seems to lead to another mystery." Seizing her rumpled skirt, she started for the corridor. "It's past time to begin supper now. Georgette will be furious with me, and poor Brigitte could still be stuck in the washhouse."

"Madeleine, wait." A soft hand caught her wrist to detain her.

Spinning back, she found Gabriel staring up at the ceiling, his other hand speared toward a peculiar glow above him.

"Do you see that? Above the torch that has gone out?" Letting her go, he marched toward the spot and studied it for several seconds. "It appears to be some type of picture. A diagram of stars."

Stomach flip-flopping, Madeleine drew near. Above her, a pathway of painted stars wound from the wall to the space above them, where it abruptly stopped. The artwork had an ethereal quality, unlike anything Madeleine had ever seen before. "Why do they glow?" she asked, still taking in the awe-inspiring sight.

Gabriel reached toward the mural, his fingers falling just short of it. "He must have figured out a way to concoct phosphorescent paint," he said, a fascinated lilt to his voice. "He probably knew Henning Brand, the man who discovered phosphorus. They were both alchemists searching for the elixir of life. Only Brand found something much more useful in his studies."

Memories of Henri's hidden den flashed through her mind, of the mysterious supplies they'd found adorning the wall. "I understand why he had paintbrushes and crusted bowls in his secret room now."

He nodded. "He couldn't practice alchemy out in the open. People would have considered him a madman. And during the 17th century, knowing how to make phosphorus *was* alchemy."

"But how does it work?" Her gaze darted to the rest of the blank ceiling, still illumined with torchlight. "Why is it only visible in this place where the torch has gone out?"

"As far as I understand it, white phosphorus reacts to oxygen and creates light." His pointed finger indicated the cold torch. "The glow of this torch's fire infused light into the paint, but it's only visible in a dark environment."

Their gazes met, his eyes bright with flame. No words had to pass between them to understand the other. Quickly, they both set to work, tugging torches off the wall and snuffing them on the stone. When at last the final flame had sizzled to ash, Madeleine scampered back to the center of the room and stretched out beside Gabriel on the hard floor.

The image above dazzled her every sense. Thousands of stars sprinkled the ceiling's face, their white glow encasing the room in celestial light. Soon, patterns emerged among the swirling stars, pictures of objects you might see in real life—a tree here, a boulder there, an intricate depiction of a place its artist surely knew well.

"It's a map," Gabriel said with an amazed laugh. "All this time people were looking for a paper treasure map somewhere, and he painted it down here, tucked under our feet all these years."

"He was incredible," Madeleine said, lost in the stunning array of twisting stars. "The key and the map were easily stolen, but this remains."

Gabriel's finger aimed at the waves of stars surrounding the map. "What is that—water? An island, perhaps?" Madeleine's eyes trailed the path of his finger as it swept over the glittering picture. "With cliffs on the western edge and a river flowing through it. Look, the treasure is there, behind that waterfall." His finger indicated a predominant "x" behind a curtain of stars painted like cascading water.

"So his clue in the library is twofold. 'Let evening stars be your guide, beyond the water endless treasures hide.' Both here, under his painted stars, and on the island he depicted here."

Gabriel looked at her, overwhelmed. "I suppose you're right. And 'it lies in the very heart' fits, too. This waterfall is situated in the very center of the island."

His words sparked a memory in Madeleine's mind, chilling her. She recalled waking up on Traitor Isle, of climbing the cliffs for safety. She saw herself stumbling into the jungle, wandering through a field of ferns, finding a plummeting waterfall and Alec Brassard at its base. Her eyes scanned the map, taking in every detail, all of its components falling into sync with the picture in her mind.

"I know where this is," she said. "I've been here."

Gabriel's head whipped her way. "What do you mean? You've been to the island where Henri hid his treasure? How is that possible?"

Madeleine nodded, her voice thick with emotion. "I have stood near that very waterfall." Her fingertip pinned the "x" Henri had brushed across the stone. "This is the place the Guardians left me for dead after I warned Napoleon of their plot to murder him. They call it Traitor Isle. Christophe told me that sea captains send their errant sailors there to punish them. I met his ship's former steward there, who had been caught stealing goods."

Gabriel's brows narrowed. "Why would they send you to a place like that? They wouldn't dare if they knew what lay in the depths of it."

She shrugged. "Maybe they wanted me to find it for them. They don't have this map, after all." Her mind raced back to that dank room the Guardians had hog-tied her in, their angered voices growling above her blindfolded face. "I heard them say they want-ed me alive somewhere, in case I could tell them more. They didn't want Napoleon's men finding me dead in the river and confirming the truth of what I told him."

Pain radiated from his crystal eyes. Gabriel reached out to find hers in the dark, his fingers constricting gently. "I'm so sorry for all of that. How desperately I wish I could have been there to protect you." His gaze swept the glowing planes of her face a quiet moment before anchoring at her eyes.

"You couldn't have," she said, throat compressing. She held his gaze a few seconds longer before propelling hers up to the ceiling. "Anyway, it's in the past now. There's no use dwelling on what is already done." Or wallowing in her unrequited love. Already, the touch of his hand burned a trail of fire from her wrist to her arm.

Gabriel was silent a few beats before his fingers tensed against hers. "And this is the place your Captain Roux knew to find you?" The words dangled in the air, more accusation than statement.

"What are you implying?" She frowned.

"Not a thing, I just find it interesting that the island Roux's ship chose to dump their thieving sailor was the same place that Henri hid his treasure. What are the chances of that happening by sheer coincidence?"

Madeleine thought back to the ominous beach upon which she had first opened her eyes. "It was not only that man; there were hundreds of them. The entire beach was filled with the bones of traitors they had cast upon the shore. Captains have used that island for years."

"The question remains: is there a reason they chose that partic-ular island, or was it simply ideal in its isolation?" Gabriel released a long breath. "I would be interested to know how the Guardians learned of it, why they would employ it so readily."

"I don't know." Letting go of his hand, Madeleine sat up and crossed her arms over her knees. "In any case, I don't think Christophe knows anything about Henri's treasure. He was not even the captain of the *Faucon* when Brassard was left on the island, and Christophe saved both me and him from its shores."

Sitting up slowly beside her, Gabriel cast her a cautious glance. "Just be careful, please. Remember that you barely know the man. You don't really know what he's capable of or what his true aims are."

She glanced away, her cheeks heating. What right did Gabriel Clement have to caution her against a benevolent man like Christophe Roux? If not for him, she could have been killed by the madman already dwelling there. He had rescued her, clothed her, given her money, and lent her his driver. The envy-born notion that he could be anything but wonderful made her want to race into his arms this very moment.

Without a word, Gabriel rose and extended his hand to her. Reluctantly, Madeleine took it, dusting her skirts as she straightened to her feet. Her eyes flashed as they tangled with his and dashed away again. She would begin her journey with Captain Roux before the week was out and end this foolishness between them. The baron would just have to get used to the idea.

"I suppose we should go," Gabriel's voice tickled her ears. "They are bound to be worried about us upstairs. It's the middle of dinnertime now."

Madeleine nodded, stealing one last look at Henri's beautiful map before following Gabriel to the passageway. Thoughts of Pascal wrung her gut. She would have to think of a lie to avoid whatever violence he could concoct against them.

"We should have kept at least one lantern burning," Gabriel said as they traversed the blackened corridor, hands sweeping the walls to guide them.

"It's more adventurous this way," she said with a short laugh. "At least we know the way out."

"There's another door that leads to the cellar. We can climb up to the kitchen that way."

The rushing sound of the waterwheel led them back to the moat. Madeleine grabbed hold of its base, easily scaling the side ahead of Gabriel. Gingerly feeling their way over the wheel and along the passageways, the couple soon found themselves near where they started. Night had overtaken the château, the sunlight that had once poured through the moat's iron gate replaced by the glimmer of the moon.

Gabriel sought her arm, pulling her through a narrow flight of stairs hewn between two walls. Soon, a door creaked open to the root cellar, surrounding them in the aroma of hand-picked vegetables and cured meats. Holding tight to Gabriel's waist, Madeleine stumbled through the cramped space until another stairwell deposited them in the kitchen.

The familiar room was nearly empty when the pair burst through the door, weary and relieved. Only Brigitte stood near the stone hearth, hands frozen in midair and mouth hinged open at the sight of them. Both Madeleine and Gabriel burst into a fit of giggles at the sight of each other.

"Oh dear." She swiped at his crumpled waistcoat where a flakey white substance coated him from shoulder to shoes. "I got lye all over you."

Unconcerned, he grinned through the veil of his disheveled hair. "You look like you've been crawling through the fields." He lightly touched her soiled skirt. "We will have to wash up before we make an appearance."

"Yes, that would be the sensible thing." A new voice swiveled their attention to the doorway. There, Pascal stood with arms knotted and searing gaze descending their dirtied attire. Beside him, Caroline pressed her lips together, blinking in confusion.

"Caroline. Uncle." Gabriel stepped forward, hand extended. "What are you doing down here in the kitchen?"

"We were *looking* for the two of you." Pascal's foot tapped the terra-cotta floor. "I suppose you believe it's appropriate to go wandering off for hours at a time without telling anyone? You had us all ill with worry."

The baron moved close, laying a hand on both newcomers' arms. "Certainly not. I apologize." Glancing over his shoulder, he gestured toward his filthy companion. "Madeleine was helping me with a personal project and we lost track of the hour. I'm very sorry for any alarm we might have caused."

"I see." His intense gaze flinging from his nephew to the maid, Pascal perused her every part with a glower that both belittled her and promised certain vengeance.

Squirming beneath his scrutiny, Madeleine swung her attention to Caroline. Her heart plunged at the sight of her. The poor woman could hardly keep her lips from trembling, tears edging her blue eyes and skin several shades paler than normal. Madeleine twisted her fingers awkwardly at her middle, trying to think of a plausible explanation that might salvage the couple's bond.

"I hope you didn't let supper get cold on my account," Gabriel's artificially cheerful voice broke into her thoughts. "I will just run upstairs and change. I'm sure you'd like to do the same, Madeleine."

Reluctantly lifting her feet, Madeleine felt the heat of Pascal's stare on her as she passed him for the hallway. Everything in her ached with embarrassment and fear. Her path down the narrow passages felt like a punishment, the low ceiling and walls closing in around her. When she reached the door to her bedroom, she barely possessed the energy to twist the handle.

Madeleine had just lit the candle on her bedside table when her door burst open without a knock. She jumped backward, hand over her heart, a sickening feeling grabbing hold. There, in the feral wave of candlelight, Pascal's wicked face sneered back.

"You've played your little games for the last time," he said, thundering toward her, his every muscle daring her to cower.

Instead, Madeleine swallowed her fear and forced herself to stand tall. "None of this is a game, and I certainly am not engaging with you." Her finger indicated the door he'd left open. "You will leave my room at once."

He leaned over, nostrils fuming. "I will go nowhere until you admit what you've done, you little harlot."

A kindling rage inside begged her to match his fury, but she shoved it below the surface. This madman could kill Gabriel if she didn't select her words carefully. "I know it looked suspicious, but I can assure you nothing happened—"

"I'm not daft, girl," Pascal shouted, spewing her with saliva. "The two of you are gone for hours, and when you do finally drag yourselves out of the root cellar, you're both covered from head to foot in dirt." The noxious scent of pipe tobacco assailed her as he angled closer. "Now, you might be able to convince that naive girl out there of your lies, but I know *exactly* what you were doing down there."

Madeleine's lips flattened into a thin line, anger bubbling just beneath her skin. How many men could she allow to treat her as a mere object before she fought back? "You know nothing," she hissed, teeth gritted. "You *are* nothing."

"How dare you speak to me in such a manner?" Eyes widening, he seized her wrist in clenched fingers.

"Let me go." She attempted to wrench her arm away, but his hand clamped harder, launching shock waves of pain to her elbow.

Despite her flailing body, Pascal managed to hook his free arm around her waist and yank her to him. Torso pressed against his, Madeleine found herself trapped in a cocoon of his stale odor, his wet, panting breaths along her neck. "I'm going to teach you a lesson you'll never forget." His hand unclamped from her wrist, diving for her soiled skirts, hunting for the hem.

"No!" Desperate, Madeleine maneuvered both of her hands to his chest, pushing against him with all her might. His arm merely tightened at her lower back, his assault on her clothing growing more frantic. Madeleine tried to lift a knee to drive between his legs, but he'd pinned her so tight, she could barely move. Out of breath, she writhed within his hold, the violent fear of a caged animal budding within her.

I can't let him do this to me. I can't. Tears crowded her eyes, pain racking her body, her arms growing weak from struggling.

His hand worked at her dress, bunching the fabric higher, higher. Nausea climbed her chest to peer through her hazy vision at Pascal pulling at his own tunic, but she would use any distraction presented to her. With the tiny amount of slack he gave her, Madeleine reared back and drove a fist into his eye.

Her attacker yelped, freeing her to plaster a hand over his face. "Why you little—" He lunged for her, but Madeleine darted for the space by the window. Chest pitching and face red, Pascal squared off with her, his menacing gaze converting to hysteria.

Through the fog of her fatigued breaths, she barely heard another voice join the fray. "Madeleine, I nearly forgot. I picked this up off the floor—" Gabriel stopped short at the threshold of her room, her handkerchief dangling from his open hand. "What's going on in here?" he asked, his confused glance ricocheting between them.

Yet in his crazed condition, Pascal didn't even seem to hear his nephew. Seething, he tugged a dagger from his belt and posed it by his ear. The smooth steel glimmered in the candlelight, a terrifying, maniacal rage burning in his dark eyes. With an unholy wail, he lurched toward Madeleine, blade aimed at her trembling body. Before she could react, Gabriel had lurched himself between them, blocking the path of Pascal's knife.

"No!" she shrieked, reaching to pull him back. But already the dagger had pierced his flesh, sinking deep into his chest and spewing a pool of crimson around the wound. Pascal yanked the knife back, slick with blood. The weapon clattered to the floor as he stumbled backward, seemingly ripped from his trance. Face white, Gabriel teetered and sagged to his knees, clutching his bleeding chest.

Blood pumping furiously, Madeleine leaped for Pascal's discarded dagger and shoved it in his face. "Leave!" She thrust the blade higher, trained on his vile throat. "I swear on everything I've ever held dear that if you don't turn and run this very moment, I will gut you."

Pascal's horrified face looked from his own bloodied knife to Gabriel, collapsed on the floor at his feet. Already, the sound of rushing footsteps pounded the hall outside the little room. He deliberated a moment, hand rubbing the back of his neck, before he twisted around and bolted for the door.

The knife slipped through Madeleine's quaking fingers, bashing against the stone floor once again. Breath high in her throat, she sank to Gabriel's side. A stunned expression had overtaken his features, sweat leaking from his pale skin. Ripping his shirt open, Madeleine revealed a hole between his pectoral muscle and his shoulder blade, a well of blood gushing from within.

"It's all right. It'll be all right." Shakily, her hands hunted her petticoats for clean fabric she could employ to stop the blood. The rush of footsteps neared, Cecile and Georgette spilling into the room just as Madeleine pressed a heap of her torn petticoats over his stab wound. Gabriel bellowed in pain, his face scrunched and teeth gritted.

"What happened here?" Georgette gasped at the sight of him, immediately whirling toward Cecile. "Fetch the surgeon. *Now!*" The old woman struggled to her knees, shoving Madeleine out of the way. "You're doing it wrong. Let me work."

Madeleine sat back in horror as Georgette expertly tended to Gabriel, her hands steady and quick. A dazed look had entered his eyes, his eyelids blinking lazily. "Please don't go anywhere," she whispered, her fingers tangling with his curly hair, her tears peppering his skin.

"This is no time for sentiment. I need you to get me some fresh water and alcohol. And more clean cloth. Go now." Georgette split his shirt open further, exposing his abdomen, where his breaths came shallower and less frequent by the moment.

With great effort, Madeleine pushed herself off the floor. Her legs felt like bricks as she floundered to the door, covered in the blood of the man her heart still desperately clung to. Stealing one last glance at his form lying broken on her bedroom floor, Madeleine summoned her inner strength and forged ahead.

Twenty Five

All night long, a cloud of dread clung to Madeleine. She paced the hallway outside Gabriel's room, where two servants had carried him on a homemade litter. The surgeon had come and gone, promising they'd know more in the morning. In the wee hours before dawn, she knelt with Caroline and Désirée to join hands and beg the Lord for his life. They embraced one another, their tears mingling, united like sisters under a single mission.

Yet as the agonizing hours stretched on, her company dwindled. Caroline stumbled off to bed some time after three o'clock with Désirée reluctantly following soon after. Madeleine knelt on the silk fiber rug, hands folded and sodden eyes fixed on the lions adorning his bedroom door. *Please, God.* Her whispered pleas came again and again, spiraling through her entire body. *Please save him.*

The candle on the hallway table eventually sputtered and died until it was only a hot pool of wax. A ray of moonlight glowed around her, comforting her amid her racking sobs and gnawing fears. Georgette hadn't even allowed her in the room after they'd moved him. She said only Cecile could remain detached enough to help her tend him.

And so, she poured out her heart to an unseen God, a God she had barely spoken to since her childhood. Her father's prayers echoed on her lips, the words he'd taught her blossoming with meaning. Fatigue plagued her, stinging her eyes and blanketing her frame in the pull to rest. But still she kept on, her words fervent, her mind focused on the man within those gilded walls.

A harsh click sprang Madeleine's eyes open. Confused, she pushed off the floor, now illuminated in a sunlit sparkle. Her joints ached and one side of her body felt numb. Looking up into Georgette's weary face, she realized she must have drifted off to sleep at some point before dawn.

"You really do care about him, don't you?" Georgette sighed, plunking a fist on her rotund hip. "I suppose you can go in and see him."

Hope leaped in Madeleine's heart as she clamored to her feet, still swiping drool from her face. "How is he? The surgeon wouldn't tell us anything."

A rare sparkle lit Georgette's crinkled eyes. "Go on and see for yourself. Just be quiet." Her hand reached out to squeeze Madeleine's shoulder. "Remember what I said. Guard your heart."

Her heartbeat thumped in her ears as Madeleine reached for the ornate silver knob and languidly pushed the door inward. Closing it behind her, she turned and crept over the hardwood floor, her blood quickening at the sight of his sleeping form lying in a stream of sunlight. Plump white pillows supported his head and neck, his satin sheets and velvet blankets pulled chest-high across him. His bare chest revealed a bandage wrapped around his torso, the spot Pascal had stabbed him loaded with gauze and free of any visible blood.

Madeleine ducked below the canopy of gold and blue tenting his bed, easing herself onto the edge of his mattress. He looked so peaceful lying there still, his chest rising and falling, his skin a healthy color again. Everything in her longed to touch him, but instead she simply watched him draw breath, something she'd wondered if he would ever do again.

Soon his eyelids fluttered again, a small smile curving his lips. "Not a bad sight to wake up to," he said, voice thin.

Her heart somersaulted, her love for him uncontainable. She reached for his hand, wrapping her fingers around it. "How are you feeling?"

"Honestly? Like I was stabbed in the chest." He laughed weakly, then winced. "But I hear I should pull through. Thanks to you, I didn't lose too much blood."

Madeleine shook her head. "It was all Georgette. She's an angel when she's not acting like the devil." Joy sprouted within her to see the light spreading over his features.

After a moment, Gabriel's face fell serious. "What I walked in on, with you and Uncle Pascal—it certainly didn't look like you were having a friendly discussion." His thick brows lifted. "Would you tell me what happened?"

The urge to deny their connection rose in Madeleine. Yet looking into his bright, soul-searching eyes, she knew nothing but truth would suffice. All of it. She owed it to him after he'd literally stepped in front of a knife for her.

"He was trying to rape me," she said finally, watching the color drain from Gabriel's face.

His jaw tensed, the fingers entwined with hers coiling. "He didn't hurt you—"

"No, no. Nothing like that." Madeleine forced her lips into a reassuring smile, even as reliving the moment chilled her to the core. "I fought him off. But he would have killed me if you hadn't come in when you did."

Gabriel's head angled on his pillow, a flood of emotions sweeping his face. "Oh, Madeleine." His free hand lifted to cup her face, his thumb brushing her cheekbone. "I'm so sorry. I had no idea what my uncle was capable of. If I had, I would never have allowed him to dwell under my roof, never have let him near you."

"I know." She looked down at their laced fingers, wondering if he'd still want to touch her once he knew the whole story. "I'm afraid that part is my fault."

At his cinched eyebrows, Madeleine inhaled a breath that reached her legs. "Your uncle threatened me. Long ago when Caroline first came to the château. He noticed the relationship between us, and he told me that if I didn't step back and allow your bond with Caroline to flourish, he would kill me." She bit her lip. "Worse yet, he would kill you and Désirée to inherit the estate in your stead."

A flash of anger lit his intense gaze. "Why didn't you tell me? I would have cast him out. How dare he threaten you in such a manner?"

"I didn't want to take the chance that he would hurt you." Her eyes drifted to his wrapped chest. It all seemed silly now. Pascal would have hurt someone no matter what she chose to do.

A quiet moment encased them, his chiseled face falling placid again. "So you never really stopped caring about me? You didn't really want what we had to end?"

She wagged her head, tears forming in her eyes. "Of course not. I could never stop loving you." Her heart wrenched at the hope stirring on his visage. "But Gabriel, you must know everything. By then I knew the painful truth about myself. That I could never really deserve you."

His mouth flattened. "That sounds like Pascal talking. He made you believe that."

"No." Madeleine took another shaky breath, praying for courage. "It was no mistake that I came here. You see, when we were just children, your father sought revenge on my father by having him killed. They were old rivals in the court of King Louis." She braced herself, forcing her next words. "My brother Auguste and I—we concocted a plan. I was to come here, find Henri's treasure, and—exact vengeance on your house for your father's sins."

Gabriel's vulnerable gaze hunted hers a painful string of seconds. "So it was all a lie? Everything we shared was just an act you performed to get the treasure?" His fingers holding hers slipped away, torturing her.

"Of course not." Madeleine brought both hands to her face in a prayer-like pose. "I came here to steal your treasure, to rip everything your family held dear away from you." Her head shook, her disheveled hair cascading from its loose pins. "But instead I fell in love with you—truly fell in love. The kind of love I never thought I could ever have or deserve. I didn't care a whit about that treasure once I really knew you."

The man swallowed, a disillusioned look misting his eyes. "But still you lied to me."

She nodded. "So many times and for far too long. I was so afraid of losing you, I convinced myself that you were better off not knowing the truth—about me, about your uncle. I thought I could fix everything myself."

"Instead of trusting me." Sunlight filtered through his lace curtains, highlighting the pain teeming from his ocean-like eyes.

"I'm so sorry." The words stuck in her arid throat. They would never suffice. "I had planned to leave with Captain Roux. But when I saw you laying on the floor, clinging to life, I knew I couldn't go without telling you the truth."

Madeleine sucked in a breath, daring herself to drive onward despite the hard quality overtaking his face. "The truth is—I love you. I fell in love with you despite never planning to or even wanting to. All of the anger and deceit inside of me melted away when I encountered your gentle spirit." Tears stung her eyes. "And no matter what happens, even if you cast me out and never speak with me again, I will love you always."

In the quiet moment that followed, Madeleine's heart fluttered against her ribcage. She held her breath, longing to know what was transpiring in his head. Gabriel swept his eyes to the mirrored wall, his expression distant, indecipherable. His fingers worked at the plush blankets tucked around his bare chest. When he looked back at her, the adoration he'd once reserved only for her had drained from his face.

"I need some time to think about what you've said." He blinked, casting her the cold look of someone she'd barely just met.

"Of course." Madeleine dipped her head, anxiety freckling her entire body as she rose and awkwardly marched toward the door. She stole one last glance at Gabriel, his lonely form washed in the morning light, before yanking the door open and finding Georgette on the other side.

The old maid's shrewd eyes skittered down Madeleine before stepping around her. "The gendarmes are here, Baron. Are you ready to make a statement regarding the incident?"

Gabriel's attention snapped to the doorway. "In a little while, Georgette. Is Caroline there?"

At the sound of her name, the blonde woman bolted from a chair in the hallway. She looked as if she'd slept only a handful of minutes, her silk dress crumpled and hair barely adhering to yesterday's chignon. She stepped to the doorway, dark circles rimming her eyes.

"I'm here," she said, tone chipper despite her fatigue.

Gabriel visibly relaxed within his blanketed cocoon. "Caroline," he spoke the name with reverence, as if it breathed life to his soul. "Caroline, please join me."

Madeleine watched her bustle into the room and sink to the same spot she had just occupied. Gabriel reached for her hand, clasping it within both of his as if his life depended on her presence. She saw Caroline lean in to brush her fingertips over his forehead before Georgette swung the door inward, clicking it shut.

Avoiding the maid's judicious stare, Madeleine whirled and aimed herself toward the kitchen. She couldn't go back to her room to change. Not with his blood still staining her floor. She would work until her hands went raw if it meant forgetting all that she had forfeited when she chose to wander a path of deceit.

The Black Lion was particularly raucous when Madeleine stepped through its doors. An arm-wrestling match had commenced in the corner, drawing half its patrons into a focused circle around a pair of men locked in a vicious battle of strength. All around them, onlookers laughed and jeered, howling when their chosen opponent gained an advantage, swearing when they failed.

Madeleine descended into a cloud of tobacco smoke, eyes scanning the room. Everywhere she looked, alcohol flowed. Patrons clashed their steins together, sloshing the tables in amber liquor. They guzzled it by the jug, swiping their arms over their inebriated faces before picking up dice and casting them over the soggy wood. A spirit of gaiety had seized the tavern, its wild merriment in such stark contrast to the bitterness plaguing her soul.

Beyond a ring of more serious men with cards stationed before their wrinkled brows, Madeleine spotted Christophe watching a pair of fiddlers lifting a jaunty tune around the room. The ship captain smacked his large hands together, chuckling at a half-drunk village man attempting to tap out a dizzy jig.

Summoning her courage, Madeleine wound through the riotous crowd and touched a hand to his muscular arm. Christophe turned with a start, his surprise converting to joy at the sight of her.

"Madeleine, you came." His warm hand found hers beneath her cloak, hauling her to his side.

"Yes, but—only for a moment." She could barely hear herself over the tavern's roar or the rush of her own hammering heart. He smelled of saffron and black cardamom, the spicy, smoked scent of his clothes thrilling her senses. Every time she was near him, she lost herself, even when her mind was made up.

"Why don't the two of you have a dance?" the flailing villager slurred. "It's mighty lonely dancing out here on your own."

Madeleine flushed. "Oh no, I couldn't—" But already, Christophe tugged her along.

"It will be fun," he said, white teeth glimmering with his hearty laugh.

Attempting to keep her breath even, Madeleine allowed him to draw her close. His arm muscles flexed as he led her in a circle, kicking his feet with the energy of a scampering rabbit. Soon, the couple whirled this way and that, their frolicking legs stomping out a syncopated rhythm.

Madeleine gazed up at Christophe, skin flushed. "You aren't half bad." She giggled as he twirled her in a circle and pulled her back to him.

"I've been to lots of places with all kinds of people, but they have one thing in common." His eyes twinkled as he commandeered her to the chirping violin. "They all dance."

The lively song's final notes strained from the violin, the fiddlers finishing with a flourish. Madeleine peered up into Christophe's face, flush with laughter and exertion. Their chests pitched against one another, the thudding of their hearts bounding back and forth. With great effort, she dropped her hold on him and stepped away.

"I just came to give you my answer," she said, still convincing herself. "I can't go with you."

Christophe swept a hand through his loose blond hair, glancing at his boots before fixing her with a knowing look. "I figured as much when I saw you without any luggage."

A lump crowded her throat. "I'm sorry, Christophe. I truly wanted to go with you." The call of the open sea still lured her with its mystic voice. *He* still tempted every part of her.

"But you can't leave *him*." At her questioning look, he shot her a tilted smile. "I would have to be a complete imbecile to have missed the daggers that baron of yours had for me when he thought I might steal you away." His mouth flattened, his mirth converting to solemnity. "But Madeleine, you must know that men like him marry women of breeding. From what I gathered, I supposed he and that woman with him had already reached an arrangement."

As often as she'd considered it, the truth still caged Madeleine in an icy chill. Had Gabriel already asked Caroline, even before she found the ring on his desk? Perhaps that is precisely what he'd wanted to tell her that night when she'd refused to hear him. How foolish her words to him that morning must have seemed if he'd already promised himself to another.

Thrusting her worry aside, Madeleine hugged her arms protectively around herself. "It doesn't matter, really. I can't leave when my heart belongs here." Her shoulders lifted. "You wouldn't be happy with a woman who is constantly pining after somebody else."

Christophe stepped closer, his warm hand reaching up to tip her chin. He studied her a tantalizing moment, their faces a breath apart, before giving her a clever smirk. "I believe I can convince you otherwise."

His confidence sparked a chuckle from her lips. She shook her head, taking in his fervent eyes and straight nose, the way his square jaw flexed as he searched her face. "You deserve so much more than that." Her gaze fluttered into his. "I hope you find it."

With one last look, Madeleine stepped back again. Just as she prepared to turn away, a memory struck her. "Oh, Christophe?" The word incited his head to turn up. "Do you happen to know of a pirate with the initials J.C.?" she asked, summoning her vision of poor François Martine's father, echoing the only fact he knew about his son's attacker.

Strong chin cradled in his fingers, Christophe's brow hooked as he considered her question. "Not that I can recall just now," he said finally. "Should I be on the lookout?"

Madeleine shook her head. "No. I was only curious." A malicious seaman like the one who killed François would not so easily be identified. She could only pray that Auguste did not meet a similar fate at his hands. She had just revolved on her heel, readying herself to pass through the thunderous crowd again, but Christophe's voice halted her.

"Madeleine, wait." Before she could look back at him, a large hand covered hers. Christophe reeled her to him in one quick motion, plastering her form to his. Fingers diving into her hair, he kissed her ardently. His lips tasted of honey as they moved against hers, his impassioned breath hot on her skin. Despite her intentions, Madeleine melted against his solid body, his exotic scent thrilling her to the very core.

When at last he pulled away, Christophe's eyes wandered her face as if surveying a priceless relic. "I told you I wouldn't let you go without a fight." A grin tickled his full lips. "You know how to contact me when you change your mind."

Dizzy, Madeleine walked backward, eyes locked with his. Managing to compose herself, she turned away, nearly colliding with another man. The scent of ale assaulted her. Auguste stared back, his dark-rimmed eyes glossy, shirt stained and hair in disarray.

"Who is that fool?" he slurred, glaring up at Christophe. "He thinks he can maul you like that and get away with it?"

Madeleine easily caught her brother around the waist before he could advance on the much larger and sober ship captain. "Leave him alone, Auguste. He's only the past." With that, she started for the door again, determined to put the idea of Christophe Roux behind her for good.

"Wait. I need to talk to you." Auguste tripped on his own feet in an attempt to follow her.

"Not tonight." Ignoring her brother's repeated protests, Madeleine pointed herself toward the tavern door and strode into the peaceful night. Whatever became of her, she had stopped taking orders, stopped living her life to appease someone else. She journeyed back to the château with head held high, preparing to have her heart ripped open.

Twenty Six

"It's sweet of you to try and cheer me up, Cecile, but this won't make me feel better." Madeleine looked across the bouncing carriage at her friend, barely visible in the shifting strands of moonlight pouring in through the window. "We might as well ask Serge to turn back around now."

Cecile relaxed into her velvet-upholstered bench. "And spoil my surprise? You wouldn't dare."

Sighing, Madeleine squinted through the passing trees, trying to determine which direction the speeding carriage traveled. A hand reached over her, untethering her curtain. "No peeking," Cecile said with a trite laugh. Soon, the entire cabin was immersed in black as she unleashed every curtain.

"Who even gave you permission to take this coach? Désirée?" Madeleine asked, bracing herself as the road turned rougher, shuddering the wheels beneath them. "It doesn't matter, anyway. I just want to go home."

"You want to work yourself until you can't move and then lay in your bed, wallowing in self-pity," Cecile said through the dark. "I won't let you grovel another minute."

Lulled by the steady clop of the horse's hooves, Madeleine let her head sink back and closed her eyes. "He hasn't spoken to me in nearly a week." Her voice strained, sounding hollow in the little space. "Six days, I've been left to go mad, prohibited from even seeing his face, unable to check if he's healing."

"He's recovering just fine. I've told you that."

A chill meandered up her arms, inciting Madeleine to hug herself. "I know, but I'd like to see it with my own eyes. I want to hear from his own lips that he hates me." As if she needed to. Since she'd emptied the contents of her heart at his feet, Madeleine had been restricted to the kitchen and servants' quarters. She'd spent the entire week scrubbing out dishes and pans, wondering what went on above her head. Any time she suggested she help with a matter upstairs, Georgette assured her that the master still forbade her presence in the main house.

Through her sorrow, she felt a hand squeeze hers on the bench. "You don't know that he hates you. That's only your imagination at work. Why do you always assume the worst for your life?"

"Do I have evidence to the contrary?" The agonizing days spent beneath the château had cemented her dismal reality. If she were allowed to stay at Avance, she would likely never see the baron again.

Soon, the Clements' coach trundled to a stop. Madeleine reached for the door handle, but Cecile's hand jetted out to detain her. "Here, put this on first." She extended an unseen garment at Madeleine, the feel of lace brushing beneath her fingertips.

"You can't be serious." Madeleine swept her hand over the fabric, determining a gown had settled into her grasp.

"I most certainly am serious," Cecile said. "Where we're going, you need to look your best. I won't have you ruining the night, looking drab in your soiled work dress."

With a huff, Madeleine began unbuttoning her tired cotton dress. It would do no good to argue with Cecile when she got an idea in her head. Nevermind her blossoming curiosity at whatever her friend had planned. Setting the new gown beside her, she struggled to pull the old one off, wrenching and pulling in the cramped space.

"Ow! You're kicking me!" Cecile yelped.

Madeleine growled from beneath the dress pulled around her head. "Pardon me for not having practiced disrobing in a pitch-black carriage before."

Cecile snickered. "You're forgiven." Leaning in, she tugged at Madeleine's dress until it released her.

A balmy breeze rustled her skirts as Madeleine stepped down from the coach, garbed in the gown Cecile had brought. In the tiny orb of lantern light, she couldn't see beyond a small circle in front of her. She glanced down to find herself encased in a stunning gown of silk and silver lamé, trimmed with lace at the neckline and hem.

"Where are we?" she asked Cecile, who descended behind her. "We didn't travel nearly far enough for Paris, and I don't hear a village nearby." In fact, she heard nothing but the distant warble of a woodthrush. The scent of pine whirled on the pleasant breeze.

"Patience, my love. You will see in just a moment." Cecile reached up to fix the errant strands of Madeleine's hair. Satisfied, she turned and pulled an item from the coach, concealing it behind her back. "Come this way." Seizing Madeleine's arm, she led her around the back of the coach.

The sight that lay beyond made Madeleine's breath catch. "St. Philemon," she whispered, watching the ancient church remains glowing with unearthly light. She turned a questioning frown on Cecile, just as the woman deposited a sweet-smelling bouquet of lilies into her hands.

"You make a stunning bride." Face full of mischief, Cecile leaned in and pecked her cheek. At Madeleine's bewildered stare, she laughed. "Go on, now. You've made him wait long enough."

Every step Madeleine made over the moist earth felt like walking through a dream. Passing through the veil of trees, she approached the hollow archway, peering through it. All around the abandoned church, candles had been lit, casting flickering shadows over the broken walls. At the end of the aisle of dirt and grass, Gabriel stood proudly, garbed in a silk waistcoat of sapphire blue and a long tailcoat, a cream-colored cravat knotted beneath his chin. Beside him, Père Andre held a large Bible open in his frail arms. They both grinned at the sight of her.

Madeleine sauntered through the candles, eyes locked with the man she had thought lost to her forever. The fingers clutching her bouquet quivered, her heart racing. Could he really want her after all she had plotted against him? It felt impossible.

"How can this be?" she asked, stopping beside Gabriel, looking from him to the elderly priest.

The baron shone with a smile that stretched to his ears. "Forgive me for not asking you first. I didn't want to wait another moment to call you my wife."

Her head wagged in disbelief. "I have so many questions."

"I will give you two a moment." Père Andre's eyes twinkled with mirth as he closed his Bible and shuffled out the back door, robes dragging behind him.

As she watched him go, Gabriel lifted Madeleine's bouquet from her hold and set it on a jagged wall of brick jutting up from the ground. His warm hands captured hers, compelling her to look up at him. Nothing but the deepest love dwelt there, his adoring eyes sweeping her face.

"You may believe that because you were born to peasants, you are somehow unworthy of me," he said, chest swelling. "But that's a lie. And you may think that what happened in your past dictates our future together, but I won't let it."

His fingers moved over hers, his shaven jaw working. "This week has taught me to seek what's truly important in life. For me that is you. I want all of you—your past, your present, who you will become. I *need* you."

Madeleine swallowed, his sincere declaration sinking into the parts of her she'd allowed to grow cold and cynical. As fiercely as she loved him, she couldn't let him proceed without knowing everything. "There are things I haven't told you. My brother, he—"

"Wants to kill me?" Gabriel laughed at her quizzical expression. "Désirée gave me the whole story. We will figure it out." His fingers constricted around hers. "I believe we are stronger together."

"And Pascal? What if he returns to cause more trouble for you?"

His head shook. "He won't come back if he wants to see anything but a prison cell for the rest of his life. I told the law what he did. I doubt he'll even return to his own estate for fear of being arrested."

"What about Caroline? The ring?" When last she'd seen them together, Madeleine had supposed the two of them in love.

"If only you had let me explain." Gabriel shook his curly head. "I never intended to ask her. My uncle fished that ring out from among my mother's old jewelry and was pressuring me to propose. It was only sitting on my desk because *he* put it there."

Gabriel cast her a sad smile. "She understands. She told me the minute Christophe Roux walked through those doors looking for you, she knew it was over between the two of us. She saw in me a love for you that would never be tamped down, no matter how close she and I grew." His hand lifted, his thumb moving down her cheek.

Madeleine looked past him at the lights gleaming off the crumbling stone walls. Poor Caroline. She didn't deserve more heartache. "I must go to her and apologize." It was the least she could offer the thwarted woman.

"She left the château days ago," Gabriel said, propelling her eyes back to him. "Just after the attack."

Her brows scrunched. "Is that why you kept me locked downstairs all week? I thought you were punishing me."

His broad shoulders raised. "I didn't want to ruin the surprise." His brow hooked above his sparkling eyes. "Nor could I have you snooping around my bedchamber with Cecile preparing it for my bride."

His words flooded Madeleine's skin in a rosy hue. Cheeks burning, she smiled sheepishly, hands instinctively flying up to shield her eyes.

"Don't hide your face." Gabriel covered her hands in his own again, pulling them down. When she managed to quell her embarrassment enough to look at him, his face glowed with surety. "I have wanted this since the second I first saw you in that parlor. I want to share with you my life, my home, my bed, my heart." He brought her hands to his chest, the steady rhythm of his heart thudding beneath her palms.

Gabriel cocked his head, tears sprouting in his eyes, mirroring her own. "Please say you'll have me, Madeleine. Please say you will marry me—here, tonight."

She laughed through her salty tears, head bobbing. "Of course. There's nothing I want more in the whole world."

Overcome, Gabriel caught her in a tight embrace. Madeleine breathed in his rich, woodsy scent, resting her head in the crook of his neck. He held her there for several minutes, a united pair beneath a canopy of leaves twisting in the nocturnal breeze. The trees around them creaked and shivered, the crickets striking up a strident song beneath the moon. Gabriel's strong arms encircled her, protecting her, promising never to let her go.

"Père Andre, we're ready for you now," he called through the empty arch the old man had disappeared behind. Gabriel pulled away enough to look at her, his blue eyes taking her in rapturously. "She said 'yes'."

The aged priest hobbled back within the church walls, eyes regarding them merrily as he took up his position again and propped his giant Bible open. "Oh God, who ordained and foreshadowed the sanctity of marriage by the outpouring of love for his church, grant to these your servants peace and everlasting communion through the holy bond to which they will heretofore abide within."

His words echoed over the shattered church, mingling with the baying wind. Madeleine kept her gaze fixed on Gabriel, their future stretching before her in the calm assurance of his eyes. Repeating the ancient vows of the catechism, she promised to walk with him always, to love and to cherish him. His mother's ring slipped over her finger, diamond and topaz winking atop a circle of white gold. As Madeleine gazed through the wavering candlelight at her new husband, her heart at last found true solace.

His bedchamber glowed in orange light when he led her into it. She had walked through that door a thousand times, but never like this. Never secure in the bond of matrimony, never knowing it was not only his, but hers now. With his palm pressed to hers, her gaze wandered from the marble hearth to the canopy bed. Rose petals peppered the downy, cream-colored bedspread. Near the window, a woman's vanity with a silver scrolled mirror had been constructed. The washstand had a second set of towels hanging from its wooden bar—terry cloth embroidered with rosebuds.

"Do you like it?" Gabriel had moved behind her, setting his hands on her shoulders. "Cecile put her all into making it comfortable for a woman. She wanted it to be perfect for you."

Madeleine blinked, noticing her friend's little touches here and there—the ivory hairbrush and perfume bottles lining the vanity table, the new gowns hanging in the open wardrobe. "It's more than I ever dreamed," she said. Truly, more than she had ever or would ever deserve.

"You're the Baroness d'Avance now." His fingers squeezed her shoulder blades. "Everything I have is yours—the house, the land, the carriages."

The reality of it all still hadn't hit her. Madeleine turned, meeting the expectant face staring back. "It's very surreal to me." Her head shook, her hands planting on his solid chest. "I will perform whatever duties the role calls for to my utmost. But you know all

I really cared about was you. I would have wanted you even if you were a penniless sheep farmer."

Gabriel's mouth twitched upward as he wrapped his arms around her. "I do." His hands anchored at the small of her back. "Though I would have been one terrible sheep farmer." He laughed, catching her up in his mirth, his joyful face infectious.

A carriage winding up the drive hooked Madeleine's attention. Through the polished window pane, she saw the Clement coach rumbling to a stop before the drawbridge. "That must be Désirée," she said distractedly, brows tapering. "Does she know about us? About tonight?"

"Only Cecile and Père Andre know. And I suppose Serge does now, as well." His arms tightened around her waist. "She will want to come in here and check on me, but the household is under strict orders not to let anyone in. Tonight is for me and my wife alone."

Madeleine blushed, her gaze refusing to meet his eyes. "I wonder what Georgette will think when I'm not in my bed at the allotted time. She will probably send out the hounds on me."

"Cecile already told her that you have a sick aunt who needs your help in the village."

Eyes climbing from her hands to his amused face, Madeleine released a disbelieving breath. "My, you two thought of everything, didn't you? You're a pair of regular schemers."

His hand raised, his thumb brushing her jawline. "I had planned to propose to you around the time of the Planters' Ball. Then Pascal trounced in here, Caroline in tow. Then he convinced you to suspend our romantic attachment." His thumb anchored at the divot in her chin, eyes mournful. "I spent the last few months laying in that bed over there, agonizing over you. I would look at the empty pillow beside my own and imagine you lying next to me."

Gabriel heaved a heavy sigh, his head shaking. "We were ripped from each other, forced to endure apart, even as our love still burgeoned." His adoring gaze meandered over her hair, her face, the curve of her neck. "But now that we're finally here together, man and wife, I'm not about to waste that time accepting congratulations."

Before she could manage another breath, his lips had found hers. Madeleine sank into the protective arms of her new husband, basking in the warmth of his sturdy form. His lips moved over hers, gentle at first, his passion growing every second they spent tangled in each other's arms. Soon, her every sense was lost in the haze of his masculine scent, in his deepening kisses, in the strong hands roaming her back, clutching the delicate fabric of her wedding gown.

Even before the heat of flames dancing in the hearth, her body trembled. With gentle, caressing hands, Gabriel stroked her face, his eyes aglow in the snapping firelight. He lifted her palm, kissing it before pressing it against his cheek. His eyes closed, one arm anchoring her to him in sweet affection. "Oh, Madeleine," he murmured against her neck. "How long I've waited for you. I feel like I am finally home."

Madeleine sighed against him as he released her dark hair over her shoulders and combed his fingers through it. His balmy lips found her neck, his legs propelling her backward. Warm and safe in each other's arms, the pain of their separation melted away as their spirits united, body and soul, fearless, unbreakable. They were one beneath the eyes of God. Secure in this knowledge, Madeleine held her husband close and promised herself she would never let him go again.

Twenty Seven

T he morning sun barely peeked through the fluttering leaves outside her window when Madeleine woke and peered across the bed at her slumbering husband. He still held her hand, even as his lips parted in soft puffs and quiet snorts issued from his nostrils. Madeleine smiled, slipping her fingers from his, watching him sleep a while longer before she rose and glanced around for something to clothe herself with. A feminine silk robe hung from a hook on the wardrobe side. Cecile really had thought of everything.

Careful not to disturb Gabriel, Madeleine eased herself off the mattress and tiptoed across the room. The cool silk slid over her skin with ease, encasing her in luxury she still couldn't quite fathom belonged to her. Out of habit, her eyes darted around the room, searching for something to clean or pick up.

With a shake of her entire body, Madeleine reminded herself of the new position she had stepped into. What would a gentlewoman do when she rose in the morning? Gingerly pulling out the cushioned stool, she sank down in front of her new vanity and tried to keep her back straight as she gazed at her reflection in the mirror. Her soft brown eyes stared back, exhausted but happier than they'd ever looked.

Reaching for her ivory hairbrush, she lifted it and swept it over the unruly mane curtaining her face. One by one, the knots released until the brush glided through her hair like a boat through calm waters. Exploring the glass bottles stationed before the mirror, Madeleine selected a jasmine-laced scent and dabbed it below her chin.

"Getting acquainted with your new things, I see." Gabriel's voice directed her eyes to the bed, where he had propped himself up on one arm. "You can sleep past dawn, you know."

Madeleine simpered, unable to keep her eyes from roaming the magnificent plains of his exposed shoulders and chest, where a cloth bandage was still wrapped around one side. "I am used to rising with the sun and immediately pulling on my boots to milk the cows. This is all going to take some getting used to." She laughed. "In fact, I can't help wondering if anyone has milked poor Patrice and Gizelle yet. They get impatient when their udders are full."

Chuckling, Gabriel relaxed against a pillow. "I am sure Cecile made the proper arrangements. I know this is new, but you will grow accustomed to it."

"Doing nothing while everyone around me is working?" Madeleine set her hairbrush on the vanity table, sick with the thought of it.

"Doing a different kind of work. There is still a lot of responsibility in running a household. I plan to share that with you."

Madeleine blinked, her face heating. "Forgive me, Gabriel. I didn't mean to sound so cruel." She rose and meandered to the bed, noting the way his eyes followed her every move. "I know you work very diligently to see that the barony flourishes. Of course I'll walk beside you in that endeavor. Whatever you need me to do, I will."

With an adoring smile, he brushed his palm down the side of her face. "Today, I just need you to be my wife. To bask with me in it. The work will wait for tomorrow."

Drawn to him like a bee to honey, Madeleine stretched herself out on the mattress and slipped beneath the covers. His strong form warmed her skin as she wrapped her arms around him, allowing him to capture her in a passionate kiss. When they pulled apart, she saw an eternity thriving before them in his vibrant eyes.

"And what, exactly, do you propose to do today, Baron Clement?" Her fingertips drummed a path on his bare chest.

"What? I don't get to stay here all day?" His shaven lips broke into a joyous smile as she nuzzled her head in the crook of his neck. "Forgive me for not whisking you straight off on a proper bridal tour. The wedding was hastily prepared as it was. Soon we will go somewhere, have all the time in the world just to ourselves."

Lifting her palm in the sunlit air, Madeleine pressed it to his and watched the way her fingers laced perfectly with his. "And today?"

Gabriel folded an arm beneath his head and stared at the intricate satin canopy over their heads. "Today, we can do whatever we like. We can go into Paris and lounge at a café or take a walk on the Seine. We could stay here and go horseback riding through the woods."

"The blackberries are ripe for picking on the other side of the hill," she said, relaxing against his chest. "I could make a pie."

His gaze shifted down to her, eyebrows tweaking. "I suppose we have a rather different view of this estate. You may do whatever you like, my dear."

A rumbling from within her disturbed the lovely silence between them. Madeleine popped up, her robe pooling around one shoulder. "First I want breakfast. I'm starving."

She rose and scampered barefoot to the wardrobe, where an assortment of taffeta and lace lined up for her amusement. Pawing through the colorful array, she found twice as many gowns as her once cherished collection from Christophe Roux. In fact, the captain's gifts were missing from among them. Selecting a lilac muslin from within, Madeleine yanked it into the sunlight and quickly got to work disrobing and pulling on clean undergarments.

"I'm sorry you have to prepare yourself alone today," Gabriel said, pushing off the bed. "I have commissioned Cecile to act as your lady's maid, but for today I requested that all servants leave us to enjoy the morning together."

After heaving a fresh chemise and her usual jumps over her head, Madeleine reached for the dress she had flung over a chair. "That's all right, I'm quite used to getting ready alone." The beautiful day dress she had picked fluttered over her body with ease. "I don't know that I'll need her to wait on me hand and foot. I'm quite capable, you know."

"Oh, I'm aware." Gabriel leaned on one of the hawks stationed around the bed. "But make no mistake, you will need her. You are a baroness now. People will expect you to wear corsets and have your hair perfectly styled. You can't manage that all on your own."

Expertly tying the strings at her back into a perfect bow, Madeleine sashayed toward him. "Ah, the price of aristocracy," she said, stopping before him. "I forgot about corsets. Is it too late to rescind my vows?" She grinned, mounting on her toes to kiss his cheek. "And as a baron, don't people expect you to wear—clothes?" she said into his ear.

"They *are* rather bothersome, but I suppose you're right." With one last rapturous kiss, Gabriel pointed himself toward the wardrobe and had soon donned a linen shirt and breeches.

The château's dining room had never felt so chipper as Madeleine waltzed into it, knowing she could enjoy partaking of the food rather than serving. Sunlight bounced off the crystal chandeliers, casting a rainbow of prisms over the oil portraits lining the wall. Madeleine glared playfully at them as she walked past, picturing the absolute uproar steaming on their painted faces to wake this morning and find her an equal.

Gabriel hauled a gilded chair from beneath the polished table, standing aside to let her sit. Sinking onto the cushioned chair, Madeleine drank in the scent of peonies adorning the table's centerpiece. Her fingers instinctively laced with her husband's as he took his usual chair at the end, his loving gaze tumbling over hers.

Within seconds, an out-of-breath Georgette flew through the doorway. "Baron, I just heard you ring. I would have sent one of the girls, but I—" She stopped short when she saw Madeleine, her eyes rounding. "There you are, girl. I thought you spent the night in the village. How dare you disturb the master in such a manner? What are you wearing? Of all the insolent—" Her scrutinous gaze plummeted to the couple's intertwined hands, to the ring glittering atop Madeleine's slim finger.

Jaw unhinging, Georgette visibly flinched. After a moment of shock, she managed to recover, her diminutive form straightening and mouth clamping shut. "Forgive me, if I'm not mistaken, Baroness?"

Gabriel couldn't squelch his beaming pride. "She is indeed your new baroness. Madeleine and I were married last night." His fingers tightened around Madeleine's, their warmth infusing her in a sense of belonging.

"Very well, then." Clasping her hands before her, Georgette nodded. "Baron and Baroness, your breakfast is but a few moments from being ready. Is there anything I may fetch for you before it is brought?"

At Gabriel's raised brow, Madeleine sprang to life. "Oh, no—no Georgette, thank you."

With one last disbelieving glance, Georgette spun on her heel and shuffled to the door. How bizarre she must have felt, shifting instantly from barking orders to becoming Madeleine's subordinate. Madeleine detached her hand from her groom's and raced after the retreating maid.

"Georgette, wait." She jogged down the hall toward the older woman, who had halted on her order. Madeleine slowed when she reached her, breathing heavily, wondering why Georgette still hadn't picked her gaze up off the floor. "You're not cross with me, are you? I should have told you, but there wasn't time—"

Without warning, the old housekeeper's arms flung around her, pinning her in a tight embrace. Surprised, Madeleine returned the hug, the scents of flour and fried oil besieging her. When Georgette finally pulled away, her gaze poured over Madeleine, softer than she'd ever seen it.

"You're a good girl," Georgette said, squeezing her forearm. "Don't let them ruin you. Don't let them break your spirit."

Touched, Madeleine gulped back her rising emotions and nodded. "Of course not."

An almost imperceptible smile twitched Georgette's lips. "You look better in lilac than you ever did in black." With that, she turned and continued down the hall, leaving Madeleine to trek back along the landscape-adorned wall to her waiting husband.

Only minutes later, another form burst through the door. This time, Cecile's shining face rushed toward her. "You did it? You actually did it?" Seizing Madeleine from behind, she crushed her neck and shoulders in a loving hug. "I can't believe you two are finally married."

"In no small part thanks to you," Gabriel said. "Thank you again for all you did to assist me."

Cecile stood and waved him off, flipping her long red braid over her shoulder. "Find me a handsome duke and we'll be even," she said with a wink.

"Why don't you join us, Cecile?" Madeleine indicated the chair beside her. "You can tell me all about your schemes this past week."

Cradling her freckled cheek in one hand, Cecile already backed away toward the door. "That sounds marvelous, but I just came up to congratulate you. Georgette will murder me if I stay too long. She's flying around the kitchen, traumatized over having to serve breakfast early."

As the sound of her running footsteps faded down the hall, Gabriel pivoted back to Madeleine with brows raised. "It seems we've caused a whirlwind amongst the staff. Perhaps we should get married every day."

Madeleine grinned, mind wandering over the beautiful candlelit ceremony and the night that had followed. "I wouldn't mind." Indeed, she couldn't remember a time when more happiness filled her weary soul.

Soon, the mahogany table before them had filled with platters of sliced bread and freshly-churned butter, of apples and pears cut into delectable squares. Madeleine partook of the food with hesitancy, having grown accustomed to waiting for whatever leftovers filtered down to the kitchen by midmorning. After she poured two steaming bowls of *café au lait*, Gabriel waved Cecile off in favor of their privacy.

"I like the way this feels," Madeleine said, watching him slather a slice of bread in butter. "No more secrets between us, no Guardians to put us in danger. Just the two of us having breakfast." Lifting her bowl to her lips, she savored the creamy hazelnut coffee as its warmth rushed down her throat.

"If only it would stay that way." Gabriel set his butter knife atop his plate with a clink. "Let's not forget your brother still lurks out there among the villagers, just waiting for his chance to strike at me."

Setting her coffee bowl in its saucer, Madeleine frowned. She still wanted to help Auguste, to support him while he healed from all that tormented his unwell mind. But would he let her? Could she get through to him before he put her new family in danger?

"I will go to him," she said. "He's bound to listen to me now that we're married. He has to realize you're not the evil person he's painted in his head."

"You certainly won't go alone," Gabriel said between bites of bread. "I won't put you at risk, even if he is your brother."

Madeleine sighed, toying with her silver fork. "I'm more concerned with that pirate roaming around, murdering people who stand in his way. He must know about Auguste. I doubt he'll show him mercy if their paths cross."

"All for some ridiculous treasure which may or may not exist." Gabriel stared back a quiet moment, jaw working. "They presumably have the key and the letter with the island's coordinates. You would think someone would have looked behind that waterfall by now."

She speared a piece of pear with her fork. "Perhaps there is more to the puzzle on the island." Madeleine stared at her dripping fruit, the possibilities frightening to contemplate. "Either way, I don't want to live in fear my whole life. Our family will be in danger as long as the possibility exists that treasure hunters might break in here looking for that map."

Gabriel's jaw tensed, eyes solemn. "I won't let that happen." He leaned back in his chair, fingers drumming the table's grainy surface. "If only there were a way to throw the scent off this house, away from us."

"You mean by creating a diversion?" Madeleine took a bite, the pear's sweet juices instantly delighting her tongue.

"Perhaps." His gaze roamed the ornate ceiling, his blue eyes shimmering in sunlight. "Désirée can draw. You know the island well enough to recreate it." His gaze drifted down until it fastened with hers, his lips tilting into a slanted smile. "What do you say we put a forged map out there, pointing to some obscure place they'll have to dig for years before they realize the treasure isn't there?"

A giggle bubbled up Madeleine's throat. "And what happens once they discover they've been tricked?"

"Hopefully they'll think someone got there before they did and give up." Gabriel reached for another slice of bread. "I don't have a care for Henri's treasure, but I'm not about to see it fall into the hands of murderers if I can help it."

Madeleine regarded him softly, leaning on her elbow. "You would really leave it there, alone on that island forever? It doesn't make you the least bit curious?"

"Of course it does, but it isn't worth my life, and certainly isn't worth yours." He gestured around him at the lavish dining room.

"I have already been blessed with more than most men ever dream of. There is no need to be greedy."

Inhaling the earthy scent of her steaming coffee, Madeleine considered his words. How enticing that treasure had seemed when she was fighting for every bit of money that came her way. She could see why men clamored over each other to obtain it. Something about leaving that great an amount of money to the earth while people starved to death felt just as greedy as taking it.

Before another thought could mull in her mind, a new form breached the doorway. Madeleine looked up to find Désirée, garbed in a yellow, high-waisted gown, arms braced on the doorjamb. Désirée regarded them both silently for a strained moment, her incredulous stare swinging from Gabriel to Madeleine. Then she marched forward, almost as if a cat stalking a bird.

"The house is abuzz with rumors about you two," she said. "Scandalous rumors of an elopement. I thought, *it can't be true. They would have told me before taking such extreme measures.*" She stopped short before the table, eyeing their gold wedding bands. "But it seems I was wrong." Her hands flew to her face, sheltering her glowing cheeks.

Madeleine started to rise. "Désirée, I'm so sorry—"

Before she could manage another word, Désirée's arms had entrapped her in the tightest hug she'd ever felt. "I can't believe you're my sister," she squealed in Madeleine's ear. "You're really my sister after all this time." When she pulled back, pride emanated off every plane of her pretty face.

"It's my fault," Gabriel said with a laugh. "I didn't want you telling her before the wedding."

Désirée shot her brother a playful look of annoyance. "Oh, I'll deal with you later." Letting Madeleine go, she flounced into the chair across from her. "I could have kept your secret if I set my mind to it."

Gabriel's head shook fervently. "You couldn't keep a secret if your life was at stake."

Sticking out her tongue, Désirée reached for the food and began daintily filling her plate. "I will forgive you this time because I know you will make me lots of nieces and nephews to spoil." She paused, concentrating on Gabriel's face, then Madeleine's. "I wonder if they will have blue eyes like yours or brown like yours. What color were your parents' eyes, Maddy?"

"My father's were dark like mine, but my mother's were blue." Her soul warmed just to picture the beautiful parents of her childhood memories.

"Then they will most likely have blue," Désirée said with an excited smile. "Perhaps one or two may have your eyes."

"Might we please be married longer than twelve hours before you start giving us children and naming them?" Gabriel laughed, reaching for Madeleine's hand. "Better yet, how about you get married yourself and have your own? You might meet someone at the ball tonight."

Désirée sank her teeth into her buttered bread, waving him off. She chewed and swallowed, dabbing at her mouth with her napkin before answering. "You know the men at your parties are never going to interest me. They're all too thin, too pale."

Smirking, Gabriel addressed Madeleine. "My sister is convinced she can't find a man of true strength among the nobility. She won't be happy until she marries a stone cutter."

Madeleine tossed him a smile but she couldn't shake his earlier words from her mind. "Did you say you were hosting a ball tonight?"

The two faces beaming back at her confirmed the answer. "Another surprise I tucked away for you," Gabriel said, fingers curling around hers. "A ball in honor of my stunning new bride."

The very thought of parading herself in front of Gabriel's wealthy friends so soon sprouted unexpected anxiety in Madeleine's middle. "You've barely had a week to prepare. How could you get guests to come on such short notice?"

Désirée snorted. "I believe you're underestimating the lure of alcohol among our friends and neighbors."

"It will give them a chance to get to know you, to begin to love you as I do." Gabriel's gentle gaze washed over her, every moment they'd spent apart shattering in the depths of his obvious affection. "It might attract uninvited visitors, as well."

Madeleine leaned in. "You mean the pirate?"

"I didn't attempt to make this ball a secret. If he's here, I'm sure it will entice him."

Despite her roiling stomach, her interest was piqued. "Do you really think we could fool him?"

A slow smile spread over Gabriel's face before he turned his attention to Désirée. "Madeleine and I may have formed a plan. With your help, I think it just might work."

Twenty Eight

Madeleine stood at the threshold of the ballroom, awed by the dazzling sight of it. Everywhere she looked, robust pink and cream roses peeped back at her—from vases on tables garbed in white linen, from garlands strewn over the windows and walls. The heavy cashmere drapery had been pulled aside to admit the moonlight, throwing an ethereal glow over the candlelit crystal winking on every surface.

Her breath hitched at the milling throng of people within the ballroom's gold-trimmed walls. Ladies in Grecian-like dresses trimmed in lace and intricate bows chattered and flicked their fans at men with high-collared jackets and frilly neckties. Many conversed behind glasses of champagne, while others engaged in the merry waltz singing from the quartet stationed in the corner.

"I'm not sure I can do this." Madeleine's hand rose to her stomach, where butterflies flitted around. "They're all so elegant, so rich. I will never fit in with them."

"Nonsense." From beside her, Gabriel touched a gloved hand to her elbow. "They are all just people. You might be surprised how easy it is to converse with them once you let down your guard."

Glancing up, Madeleine arched one brow at him that incited a grin to tickle his lips. "All right," he said, "I admit I'm not the authority on this subject. But I'm right—you'll see." Gently propelling her by the arm, he steered them both into the fray of laughter and dancing.

Soon, a champagne flute rested between her fingers, the bubbly liquid calming her agitated nerves. Madeleine caught sight of her reflection in a window, her slender form clad in white muslin with gloves that extended past her elbows and a glittering silver band in her curled hair. Thanks to Cecile, she looked the part to perfection, yet still she couldn't stop wiggling within the loose gown and low neckline. How much of their bosoms these women were expected to expose, she would never grow accustomed to.

With each new face that greeted her, Madeleine prayed none would recognize her as the servant girl who had waited on their every need only months before. The truth would emerge eventually, she knew, but tonight Gabriel deserved a wife at his side whom he could be proud to introduce to his circle of acquaintances.

"You're in good spirits, I see." A young man approached Gabriel, patting his back as the two embraced.

"Justin! Good of you to come on short notice." Pulling back, Gabriel pivoted toward Madeleine. "I'd like to introduce you to my—"

"Oh, I know quite well who you are." The man's eyes glittered mischievously as he bent low before her, clasping her extended hand.

Madeleine's brows tapered, her gaze searching the rising form before her. How could he know her already? Had he visited the château enough to recognize her face, even in such lavish attire? Suddenly she gasped, her eyes lifting from his knowing smile to the sandy blond hair stylishly slicked back. His hair had been loose that night, falling into his eyes as they breathlessly danced around in that moonlit parlor, swords entangled.

"Justin Aubert," she said, cheeks flushing. "Forgive me for not initially recognizing you."

"You're forgiven. I thank you for not trying to take my head off this time." He let go of her hand, glancing back at Gabriel. "You would not mind me taking your lovely new wife for a turn on the dancefloor later?"

Gabriel grinned, hauling her to his side with one hooked arm. "I do intend to monopolize her time most of the night, but I suppose I might part with her for one dance"—he turned to her with one raised brow—"assuming she is willing, of course."

"It would be my honor. As long as you don't plan to retaliate on my rude intrusion of your townhouse by punishing my feet."

Justin released a full laugh, tinkling the crystal chandelier over his head. "I will do my best to put the past behind us." Moving in, he slapped Gabriel on the upper arm. "You've done well, my friend. Not only is she lovely, but skilled with swordplay and a sense of humor? You won't find another like that."

"I agree." Her husband's adoring gaze took her in, pride emanating off every curve of his handsome face. "She is everything I could ever have dreamed of."

The crowd mingled around them, dropping in to say hello and make introductions. Madeleine's anxiety soon melted away, knowing she was safe at her husband's side, knowing he would love her even if his wealthy friends looked down on her. Despite Georgette's ominous warnings, she knew his approval was the only real thing that mattered to her.

"Well, I think that's just about all of them," Gabriel said with a sigh, turning to her. "Are you exhausted yet?"

"Surprisingly, no." Her gaze swept the sea of people—laughing, dancing, chattering in friendly circles. "You forget, I'm used to running back and forth from the kitchen at least twenty times at these social functions."

"Ah, that is true. Lucky for my staff, I don't have many of them." His hand brushed the skin from her bare elbow to her hand, gently seizing her fingers. "Would you care to join me for a waltz?"

Madeleine nodded, her breath high in her chest as she allowed Gabriel to lead her into the swirling mass of dancers. It still felt so surreal—warm in his strong arms as he expertly piloted her under the sparkling chandeliers and winking flames of candlelight. The warbling medley of violin and cello propelled them around in a three-step pattern, their music soaring over the crowd in rich, satisfying tones.

She could almost imagine herself in a garden—the perfumed ladies around her creating an aura of flowery scents. Madeleine inhaled rose, lavender, and gardenia as she locked eyes with the man above her. He looked so dapper in his snug silk waistcoat, his long cotton breeches and knotted cravat. His hair was styled for the occasion, but still it escaped whatever concoction his valet had attempted to tame it with, loose curls framing his forehead.

"You're staring at me awfully hard," he said, a grin tugging one corner of his mouth upward.

"I'm just admiring my magnificent new husband," she said, the words sweet on her lips. "It's been a long time."

"Far too long." His gaze seared through hers, burning with passion, love, an eternal promise to protect her.

In spite of the merry tune crooning from the violin's strings, she sank against him, her head cradled in the solid plane of his chest. The couples around them kept an arm's length away from each other, but Madeleine basked in his nearness, his arms enfolding her tightly. Closing her eyes, she breathed in his musky aftershave, listened to the rhythm of his beating heart. She had longed to be nestled within these arms too many times to waste another moment apart from him.

"How are you?" she finally asked, gaze climbing his neck. "All these people haven't driven you into your study yet."

Gabriel pulled in a deep breath through his nose, his chest ballooning. "It is not without effort. I've had to fight the urge to run more than once tonight." His hand stroked the back of her neck, his fingertips weaving with her hair. "But then I look at you and I feel strong again. As long as you are with me, I can face anything."

Pushing off his chest, she searched his gaze for a long moment, a smile spreading over her face. "As can I. There is nothing we can't do together." Ignoring the curious stares around her, she stretched on her toes and kissed him.

"Have you noticed anyone suspicious around here yet?" Gabriel asked, prompting the hairs on her neck to stand up.

Gaze darting covertly around them, Madeleine shook her head. "Nobody that I have seen, but I don't know these people well. Are they all your invited guests?"

Gabriel followed her eyes to the numerous number of friends filling his ballroom. "As far as I can tell, they are. But it's impossible to make sure of that."

"You have the map in case he does show his face?" she asked.

He patted the broad lapel of his jacket. "Right here. Do you really think it looks authentic enough?"

Madeleine tried not to burn a hole through his jacket, staring at the spot she knew housed the fabricated map Désirée had drawn that afternoon. "These treasure hunters are so desperate for any new clues, I'm sure this pirate won't notice if the details aren't perfect."

He nodded, throat visibly swallowing. "Now, all we have to do is find him, get him to talk about the treasure, and convince him we need his help to find it." The fingers holding her began to shake. "Suddenly, my study *does* sound like a welcoming escape." Whipping out a handkerchief from his pocket, Gabriel swept it over his perspiring brow.

"Don't worry. We can do this, remember?" She gripped his arm in her unwavering grip. "We fought off a whole band of murderous Guardians to be here. We can handle one pirate."

Gabriel's anxious stare met hers. "But what happens if our plan works, and he goes to the island to search the spot we told him the treasure would be? He'll kill us if he finds out we've hoodwinked him."

"He *won't* find out." Madeleine moved closer, casting a furtive glance around her. "This *must* seem genuine. If we convince him we're just as lost about the treasure's location as he is, he won't suspect us when it's not there. Then he'll leave us alone for good, since he'll think he already has every piece of information Henri left behind." Her fingers tautened. "But we *must* stay calm for this to work."

Drawing in another trembling breath, he nodded. "You're right. And we have faced far worse than this before." Gabriel raked a hand through his hair, undoing his valet's styling. "Let me just have a moment to collect myself in the bedroom. I won't be but a few minutes."

Madeleine watched him go, his fear echoing in her own thumping heart. Perhaps if this pirate were really here, he might be more inclined to approach her without Gabriel at her side. But the longer she stood alone, hopefully looking into the cavorting crowd, the lower her heart plunged. If only Christophe had known this man's identity, they might not be floundering around at his mercy.

Several guests greeted her as she stood alone, lending her a pleasantry or moment of conversation. Frowning, Madeleine glanced at the longcase clock near the refreshment table. Gabriel should have been back by now. Starting through the swarm of people, she wound her way toward the arched entrance. Even at a distance, the face she saw beneath it made her blood run cold.

Slippered feet jogging the swirled marble floor, Madeleine reached her brother in seconds. "Jean-Paul, what is it? Why are you here?" From the worried look in his eyes, one might have thought a tidal wave might sweep through the ballroom at any moment.

Jean-Paul clutched the back of his neck, frantic gaze darting around the party. "It's Auguste." His chest pitched with exhaustion. "I tried to beat him here, but he must have run his horse to death."

An icy chill trickled through her body. She reached out to grasp Jean-Paul's wrist. "Auguste is here?"

Eyes finally anchoring on hers, Jean-Paul swallowed before nodding gravely. "Someone sent him a correspondence. They told him the baron had bewitched you, that he planned to get you to believe he loved you, then make a laughing stock out of you in public. Auguste was so angry, he threw down the letter and raced out to the stables immediately."

Madeleine released a long-held breath. "It's that terrible pirate. J.C. I can feel it in my gut." She stepped back, the wicked pieces of his plan falling into place. "He never planned to just slip into this party without a distraction. He *knew* what would cause the biggest waves. He's been watching us."

"What do you want to do about it?" Jean-Paul asked, brows climbing his forehead.

"You survey the rest of the house. If he's gone through this much trouble to distract us, he's bound to be rooting around somewhere." Madeleine seized her brother's arm, dragging him toward the exit. His presence in this ballroom alone was enough to cause an unwelcome stirring among their guests.

Once they reached the hallway, Madeleine set her sights on the stairs. "I'm going to find Gabriel. Here's to praying Auguste hasn't found him first."

"Madeleine, wait." Jean-Paul's deep voice halted her. "I can't let you go alone. What if he hurts you?"

Mind wandering to the gleaming sword stand stationed upstairs, Madeleine lifted her chin. "I can handle myself. You worry about finding that blasted mercenary." Pushing past her whirling thoughts, she raced toward the stairs. If Auguste gave her no choice, she knew she must save her husband. But could she really harm her own flesh and blood?

Two steps up the staircase, a pleasant face rushed toward her. "Oh Madeleine, there you are. Don't you look lovely." Désirée fiddled with her bracelets, her face flushing beautifully. "I know I'm late, I just—" She paused before Madeleine, eyes rounding. "What's wrong? You look like you've just seen a ghost."

"I wish I had time to explain, but I don't." Madeleine continued up the stairs, pointing toward Jean-Paul. "Stay with my brother. He will protect you."

Désirée glanced at the retreating blond man. "Your—" Her skin blushed deeper. "Are we really in danger?"

"Please, Désirée," Madeleine called to her, nearly at the top of the stairs now. "Go with Jean-Paul. If you run into anyone, don't try to defend yourself. Just get behind him."

With that, Madeleine ascended the final few stairs and quickly found the sword stand beneath a window, brushed with moonlight. Gripping the hilt in one balled fist, she wandered down the darkened hallway, heart in her throat. Most of the bedroom doors were closed in this wing, not a soul moving within them. Madeleine crept past them, turning the corner toward the bedroom she now shared with Gabriel.

As she approached the wrought iron railing running up from the main pair of stairs, the sounds of their soirée touched her ears. The violins still chirped gaily, the chatter of conversation and tinkle of crystal masking the fact that any peril lurked within her home. Eyes trained on the opposing hall, Madeleine crouched low and snuck toward the door open to their chamber.

The closer she came, the more details emerged. Muddy bootprints dotted one side of the staircase, wandering aimlessly this way and that before disappearing into the open bedroom. A thin sliver of candlelight shone from inside, just enough space to give Madeleine a glimpse of the canopy bed. Gulping back her trepidation, she crept closer, craning her neck to hear anything beyond the din of revelry downstairs. A cold feeling engulfed her to hear nothing, sense nothing from the room her husband had chosen to collect himself in.

Without warning, the door flew open, a torrential wind of movement blasting through it. Madeleine leaped backward, narrowly escaping a mass of locked bodies, writhing with great effort against one another. In the dim light, she made out Auguste's maniacal face, teeth clenched and thin arms wrapped around the other man. Within his grips, Gabriel grunted and thrashed, trying with every fiber of his being to break free.

The pair tussled harder, slamming against a wall, shattering the vase of hydrangeas Georgette had meticulously placed there. A stray foot kicked from within the reeling brawl, dashing the window into a thousand shards. Gabriel bellowed, jamming his elbow into Auguste's ribcage. Swearing, Auguste produced a knife from his sheath, its short blade catching the candlelight in petrifying brilliance.

"No!" Madeleine lunged toward them, but neither seemed to hear her.

Auguste's knife flashed as he attempted to drive it into Gabriel's side. Avoiding his attack, Gabriel wrenched free enough to knee Auguste's groin, following up his assault with a jab to his face. Auguste released him, teetering backward, clutching his bleeding face. "You'll pay for that," he growled, his narrowed eyes spewing venom back at his opponent.

Gabriel rubbed his injured hand, but hadn't the time to recover before Auguste lurched at him again, blade aimed at his neck. Dodging his advance, Gabriel ducked and somersaulted away, springing up behind Auguste. The dance continued on, Auguste thrusting his knife through the air and Gabriel jumping back, the knife sometimes slicing through his clothes. At last, the baron grabbed Auguste's wrist, squeezing until the knife dropped from his hand. Auguste yelped in pain, glaring as his weapon skittered into the shadows.

Not missing a beat, Gabriel landed a punch to Auguste's cheekbone, then another under his jaw. Auguste emitted a tormented howl and reeled backward, the rage in his dark eyes merely kindling. Setting his enraged glower on Gabriel, his rapid breath hissed through his gritted teeth before he charged him at full force. The pair smashed into the wall again, dangerously close to the broken window. A side table toppled as they wrestled on, muscles swollen and faces determined.

Just when Madeleine thought Gabriel had subdued her brother with superior strength, Auguste's shoulder slammed into Gabriel's with an audible crunch. Yelling out, the baron let him go, instinctively clutching the spot where Pascal had stabbed him. Auguste seized his advantage, hitting him in the injured shoulder again and again, producing bone-chilling wails of pain. Unsteady on his feet, Gabriel slid down the wall until he was nothing but a crumpled, defeated form on the floor.

Madeleine gulped back the painful lump in her throat, horrified as Auguste ducked into the bedroom and emerged with Gabriel's sword. Standing over the defenseless man, he smiled as he slowly examined the gleaming blade. Through her pulsing heartbeat, Madeleine's inner voice screamed at her frozen feet to move. Yet when she imagined spilling her brother's blood, an unseen force anchored her in place.

"I have imagined this moment for many years," Auguste said, his haunting voice rising between gasps for air. "For my father, for my mother, for my brother and sister—I dispatch the Clement family to hell." Holding the blade high over his head, he aimed it straight down at Gabriel's reeling chest.

"You will not." Madeleine heard her own voice, clear and authoritative. She pressed the tip of her sword into Auguste's back. "If that blade goes anywhere near him, I promise I will drive this straight through you."

Auguste flinched, eyes narrowed as he turned slightly her way. Below him, Gabriel barely clung to consciousness, eyelids fluttering. "Step away, sister." Auguste's nostrils ballooned, his lips curling. "This isn't your fight."

"You're wrong, Auguste. This is everything." Madeleine pushed her sword harder, the tip breaching his clothing and inciting a frustrated grunt from his snarled mouth. "I will kill you before I let you harm a single hair on his head." Taking in Gabriel's broken body, the blood seeping through his jacket, she finally knew it was true.

"Have you forgotten what Raphaël Clement did to our father?" Auguste fumed. "You would let yet another liar from this family manipulate you into taking your own brother's life?"

Madeleine's sweaty hand tightened around the pommel of her sword. "This man was but a child when his father had our father killed. Let Raphaël's sins stay in the past. Do not add to them this night."

"Somebody must pay!" Auguste stomped his ire into the floorboards.

Holding her blade high, Madeleine begged her hand to remain steady. "It will not be him." Resolution fortified her voice despite the fear budding within.

With an exasperated grumble, Auguste leaped forward and spun, locking his sword with hers. "Then you will have to fight me for it, sister." He bared his teeth. "You will have to kill me before I kill you." Lunging forward, he propelled her several steps back, his sword clanking with hers.

Madeleine caught her breath, instincts kicking in as steel clashed with steel, the once quiet hallway alight with the thrashings of combat. The motions came almost instinctively, her arm darting out to block his advances, her body twisting away from his polished sword. All that lived within her screamed that she could not harm her brother, yet to refuse to fight meant certain peril.

The clash continued for several minutes, nothing but the smell and scrape of metal crowding her senses. Each time Auguste's blade thrust dangerously close to her, she maneuvered away, avoiding him on nimble feet. Sweat seeped through her pristine gown. The glittering band Cecile had placed on her head tumbled out, chunks of moistened hair cascading around her face. Madeleine's weapon swung this way and that, bashing with Auguste's, defending her life against her own flesh and blood.

Soon, exhaustion crept over her body. The hand gripping her sword felt heavy, her entire arm pleading for rest. Swaying on her feet, Madeleine retreated backward, into the corridor overlooking the stairs. Auguste followed her with a hunter's prowess, his eyes burning with delirious violence. She stared at him a quiet moment, her chest pitching and sword steady before her despite her aching extremities. Nothing of her little brother remained in him. Only a cold, empty stranger looked back at her.

Without warning, he ran at her, blade posed over his head. Madeleine tried to dart away from him, but her gown snagged beneath her slippered feet. At once, he rushed her, forcing her backward, smashing her against the rail. Sword crossed over her chest, she could barely summon the strength to prevent his weapon from piercing her. Auguste pushed harder, propelling her off her feet, her body edging closer to toppling over the rail with every second.

From somewhere below, Madeleine heard the rise of concerned voices, of feet rushing up the stairs. Focusing on the foe before her, she clenched her teeth together and pushed back at him. The higher he managed to get her off her feet, the less resistance she could muster. His crazed, perspiring face loomed over hers, murderous rage hazing any humanity still left in him. One more second, one more shove of his quaking arms, and she would fall to her death.

Madeleine glanced past Auguste to Gabriel, his unconscious form still rumpled against the wall. She couldn't let this horrifying moment be their last together. She couldn't let this be the final time she ever beheld his face. Yet the harder Auguste pressed her, the more power drained from her weary body. Forcing her fatigued legs to fold, Madeleine braced her feet against Auguste's thighs.

She funneled all her remaining energy into one movement, thrusting her legs out, breaking Auguste's hold on her.

Clattering to the floor with a thud, she barely perceived that Auguste had flown backward and crashed into a wall. Already, his bleary form scrambled around the floor, searching for his weapon. Seizing her own, Madeleine sprang to her feet and marched toward him. His eyes clamped on his discarded sword, but in a flash, she had kicked it away and shoved hers beneath his chin before he could make another move.

Auguste's disgusted expression traveled the length of her sword, up her extended arm and into her eyes. A mingling of hatred and shame curdled there, the love he had once harbored for her cluttered with a million contrary emotions. He didn't even blink as her blade pushed harder against his neck, threatening to end the torment he had put her through for so long.

Behind her, two figures rushed in from the stairwell, one bending to retrieve Auguste's fallen sword. At the sight of Gabriel lying unconscious by the shattered window, Désirée gasped and ran to him.

"We saw you two from the atrium," Jean-Paul said, stepping forward with the blade aimed at their brother. "Are you hurt, Maddy?"

Madeleine wagged her head. "Nothing but my heart." How it ached to comprehend she had almost met her death at the hands of her beloved brother.

Jean-Paul's skin flooded in color, his nostrils widening as he swung his gaze on Auguste. "You deserve to die for what you did. I wouldn't blame her for killing you on the spot."

With a gentle hand to his chest, Madeleine held him back. "No more blood needs to be shed tonight." Turning her disillusioned gaze back to the man at her mercy, she pulled back her sword. "You will leave this place at once, and you will never return. If you come near us again, I will show no mercy." She swallowed, her final words sticking in her throat. "You are not my brother. You forfeited that right when you barged in here trying to kill the man I love."

He regarded her for a long, painful moment. "All I ever did was try to protect you." His lips twisted. "You still have this delusional fantasy that a man like that could love you, that he could—" He stopped short at the sight of Madeleine's raised hand, the diamond and topaz ring glittering on her finger.

"We are *married*, Auguste. He promised to love me eternally in the sight of God." Arm weary, she pitched her sword to the floor, steel clashing with marble. "I'm so very tired of taking orders from men who underestimate me in every way. Gabriel never treated me thus. He is my new family. You are the past."

Sighing, Madeleine pivoted toward Jean-Paul. "Did you find the pirate?"

"I believe we did." Jean-Paul looked to Désirée, who blushed under his gaze. "We discovered a man rooting around in the library, but he escaped out an open window before we could get a good look at him. All I saw was a brown hooded cloak."

Her mind flew back to the man who had thrown her in a storage cell the day the key was stolen. "It's just as well." Forcing her weighted legs over the littered floor, Madeleine knelt before her husband's unconscious form and dug beneath his jacket until she found a folded slip of parchment. "Here." She tossed it on Auguste's chest. "Take this and leave."

Examining the forged map, Auguste's eyes exploded. "But why would you give this to me?"

"Because I'm done with it. I'm done looking for the Moon King's treasure." Swiveling back on her heel, she entangled her fingers with Gabriel's wild hair. "Everything I care about is here. Go find your riches and leave us be." Let the pirate and Auguste chase each other until one of them killed the other.

Lost in the sight of her injured husband, Madeleine hardly heard Auguste's footsteps as he rose and retreated from her life. Unexpected peace descended over her, the knowledge that she would no longer allow a bully to dictate her life. That the man she had chosen to walk beside would never exploit her for his own gain.

He stirred beneath her gentle touch, his eyelids fluttering open. Blinking, he glanced confusedly around the wrecked hallway before noticing her staring back. "I—" He winced, clutching his bleeding shoulder. "I couldn't defend you."

Madeleine cupped his shaven face. "You did more for me than you'll ever know. You changed me." Because of him, she would never doubt her own strength again.

Mouth inching upward, his thumb found her chin. "No." His loving gaze hunted every curve of her face. "You were already perfect when I found you."

Folding herself into his side, Madeleine rested her head atop his chest and drank in his luxurious scent. His heartbeat thudded beneath her palm, strong and unstoppable. No matter what life threw at them, she knew they would weather it together. So she sank against Gabriel's warm frame and thanked God for him once again.

Twenty Nine

In the quiet of the deep night, Madeleine followed her husband into the depths of their ancient home. Together they passed through the grotto-like room once employed as a mill and climbed over its mysterious waterwheel. Gabriel worked at the spot they'd discovered on the wall, rearranging the wooden puzzle pieces until they broke from their bed within the stone.

Their lantern flung spidery shadows over the walls as the couple approached the still waters of the moat. Madeleine yanked the pack off her shoulders and reached inside for the wood and kindling they'd brought. After they'd built a small pile on the stone, Gabriel touched a single stick to the flame in their lantern and laid it gently among the kindling.

The fire burst to light, blazing away the chill skittering up Madeleine's arms. She glanced up at her husband, his thoughtful face illuminated by the rising inferno. "Are you sure you want to do this?" she asked. The treasure was his birthright, his heritage. Who could blame a man for cherishing the idea of finding it?

Without hesitation, Gabriel tossed the pieces of Henri's puzzle he'd collected into the snapping fire. "The pursuit of this treasure, whatever or wherever it may be, only brings about evil." His hand dipped into her pack, emerging with Henri's copy of Arcadia, his letter from Colbert, the clue he'd left them to find in the library. With a flick of his wrist, Gabriel tossed them into the fire, watching the flames leaping to collect them.

Moving closer, Madeleine wound her arm around his trim waist and stared into the fire's licking tongues as they devoured their offerings. Smoke drifted through the diminutive space, singeing her nostrils. Soon, the pages of Henri's book had blackened and curled into soot. No evidence remained of his treasure's existence save for the stolen letter and key, and an invisible map with no way to find.

"Does it make you sad?" she asked, her fingertips tracing his shaven jawline. "You must have spent a good portion of your childhood dreaming of finding it."

"I did." Gabriel's lips curved poignantly. "But those dreams died a long time ago. Now I have new ones." Wrapping his arm around her, he pulled her closer and let her head sink against his solid chest. "All I want is to start a family with you, to grow old within these walls together. I have everything I need right here."

Relaxing against him, Madeleine savored the feel of his fingers in her hair, the way she fit perfectly into the bend of his arm. Somewhere in the far reaches of the world, Pascal probably still roamed about like the Devil, and Auguste hunted riches that would never fulfill him. But here, in the silence of their country home, she had found peace. Let the world chase after its ghosts. Let it torment itself seeking gratification in earthly possessions. She would fall into her husband's arms day after day, knowing no treasure in the world could come close to his love.

As the last of the flames disintegrated Henri's clues to ash, Gabriel stomped out the fire and kicked the soot into the moat. "Now if they want to find it, they'll just have to use their own minds." Stretching out his hand, he lent her a placid smile. "Come along, Baroness Clement. What do you say about a walk around the moat before bed?"

Madeleine returned his tender smile, eyes twinkling. "I would like nothing more." She laced her fingers with his, her heart impossibly full.

Books by Laurie Sanford

The Winds of Freedom

November Rain
Moon Over Blazing Star Field
Midnight Road to Heaven

The Memory Chase

The Guardians' Plot
The Moon King's Bounty
Traitor Isle

For exclusive scenes you can't get anywhere else, head to
www.lauriesanford.com/signup.

Acknowledgments

First, thank you, reader. Without you, my words would stay with me. I would have a million stories in my head, never finding breath and life. Every time you read one of my books, it pushes me to write more and to pursue the dream of my childhood with renewed vigor. I hope to always bring you stories that touch your heart and make you think, while having a little fun along the way.

Special thanks to my ARC team for devoting your time to reading and reviewing this book. Thanks also to my editor Jacelyn Schley for your thoughtful words and valuable input, as well as Evelyne Labelle for another beautiful cover. I would be remiss not to mention the tireless work of fellow authors who share their knowledge and gifts, many of whom I've learned so much from. Thank you for your invaluable wisdom.

My books would never get written if not for my amazing family. To my husband, who watches our son in the mornings so I can write, then puts up with me talking about writing the rest of the time, I love you. Your constant support upholds me on the days I can't believe in myself. To my children, you are my light and my joy. My world did not truly exist before you came into it.

About the Author

Laurie Sanford is a writer of historical Christian adventure and romance. Her first series, the *Winds of Freedom* trilogy, tells the story of a young woman whose experiences on an antebellum cotton plantation lead her on a journey of self-discovery and ultimate freedom. Her new series, entitled *The Memory Chase,* is an adventure through Napoleonic France and beyond, through the eyes of a woman devoid of memory.

Laurie attended Pacific Union College in Napa Valley, where she earned her Bachelor's Degree. She studied to become a teacher, but wound up as a dispatcher, a job she loves and finds fulfillment doing. Laurie is happily married with two small children.

When she's not at work or wrangling little ones, Laurie enjoys writing (her first love that now comes in fourth in line), reading or watching anything historical, traveling (32 states and counting), exploring nature, playing guitar, and studying genealogy. Having a family is the greatest blessing she has ever been bestowed, and everything she has she owes to Jesus Christ.